Library of Congress Cataloging-in-Publication Data

/ by Marlin Maddoux.

9-1604-6 (hardcover)
9-3715-9 (paperback)

43S4   1998

98-36612
CIP

Printed in the United States of America
8 9 0 1 2 3 BVG 9 8 7 6 5 4 3 2 1

SE

G

A No

MARLI

Copyright © 1998 b

Published by Word
duced, stored in a
tronic, mechanical,
printed reviews, wi

Maddoux, Marlin
   Seal of Gaia
      p.   cm.
   ISBN 0-849
   ISBN 0-849
   I. Title.
PS3563.A339
813'.54—dc2

WORD PUB
NASHVI
A Thomas Nelson

For my grandchildren.

ONE

September 24, 2031

S uspended in a mysterious and forbidding canyon of darkness miles above the earth, a sleek black hypersonic military plane, its mammoth wings folded back in a delta shape, played a daring and delicate balancing act in the deep silence of the dangerously thin air at the ragged edge of outer space. Elusive and intangible, *Enforcer 426*, one of a large contingent of the vaunted SG-104 series of planes in service, moved stealthily through the bitter cold night like a shadowy apparition, its astonishing airspeed approaching Mach 7.

Tucked snugly under each wing, riding like identical twins of death, was a brace of deadly Precision Attack Missiles, armed and ready.

Cruising at a suborbital flight level of one hundred and seventy thousand feet, its navigation lights blinking ominously against a deep black sky, the spectral silhouette of the speeding aircraft gave it the threatening appearance of a giant menacing night marauder prowling the silent empty void in search of its unsuspecting prey.

His hands resting loosely on the controls, the tall, rangy pilot of *Enforcer 426* relaxed in the high-tech cockpit, his alert brain absorbing the constant flow of information coming from the large-format video displays in front of him. As he monitored each display, an array of powerful computers onboard *Enforcer 426* made thousands of tiny electrohydraulic corrections to the control surfaces every second, keeping the deadly attack plane on its assigned course, speed, and altitude.

His mind automatically registering the critical data, the only sounds he heard were his own easy, rhythmic breathing and the subtle, quiet rush of wind filtering into the sealed cockpit from the slipstream outside.

Powered by twin supersonic-combustion scramjet engines, the SG-104s were the product of an array of major technological breakthroughs.

The weapons officer, a diminutive, intelligent young man, sat in a totally enclosed, cramped section of the plane directly behind and slightly below the pilot. With classified data being fed through military satellites overhead to the onboard bank of computers, his flight directors in front of him displayed their battle plan, step by step. Staring into a wall of video readouts, he watched the powerful computers playing out the attack plan for him, directing each step, as if it were only a video game.

The young officer had played this "video game" a thousand times over back at the military training facility. War was impersonal, carried out by trained computer jockeys, like him, who punched in codes and executed digital commands, never seeing where their missiles went or who they killed. There was no heroism, no honor, only entries on a keyboard that translated the computers' 1s and 0s into fiery death and destruction.

A soft mosaic of red and green lights bathed the pilot's strong features in their colors, casting the comfortable cockpit in a strange, mystic glow. He nodded his head slowly, a sense of pride flooding through him. A fifteen-year veteran, he had flown most of the latest models of fighters, helicopters, and space transports, but he was more impressed with this marvelous plane than any he had ever commanded.

A strong bond joined man and machine as the pilot's trained eyes carefully scanned the elaborate, colorful instrument panel laid out in front of him. Transmitted over an ultracoded, tight-beam digital carrier wave, streams of digital commands from the Military Command and Control Center inside The Mountain in Switzerland were relayed to *Enforcer 426* through a series of classified military Global Positioning Satellites that rimmed the earth approximately twelve thousand miles overhead.

Reflected in the glow of colors flowing steadily across his strong face, the veteran pilot's expression had turned pensive, his dark, deep-set eyes studying each flicker of information. Everything was in order. With a deep sense of satisfaction, he relaxed his grip on the control column, peeled off his flight gloves, leaned back hard into his sculptured seat, and gazed out at the night, regarding it thoughtfully for a few moments.

Far below him, in the distance to his left, he glanced at an errant streak of lightning that glowed momentarily, then faded. And once again the cold silence and dreadful mystery of the impenetrable darkness lay heavy and absolute over the vast, empty void.

Frozen in space and time inside the comfort of *Enforcer 426*, he stretched out his arm and rested the heel of his right hand lightly on the padded top of his control panel. Drumming his fingers rhythmically, he listened intently to the eloquent silence of his craft knifing its way through the mysterious night sky. Moving through the sullen blackness like a shadowy illusion, the unseen electronic genies were magically guiding the giant plane through the unmarked darkness toward its unsuspecting target.

Never tiring of watching the magic of a new day being born, the pilot of the sleek hypersonic attack plane glanced out at the streaming flashes of color to the east that announced the fast-approaching dawn.

Relaxed in his form-fitting leather seat, he raised a plastic cup to his lips and slowly drew in a small amount of the strong, hot coffee. After savoring its welcome warmth and gratifying taste, he placed the cup back in its holder, wiped his mouth with the back of his hand, and slipped his gloves back on. Bringing his gaze back into the cockpit, he methodically scanned his instruments.

Gently flexing his strong fingers inside his soft leather flight gloves, he caressed the plane's solid, heavy controls, feeling a quick touch of exhilaration sweep through him. Reaching to his left, he grasped the twin throttles and pulled them back smoothly, decreasing power. Feeling the nose of the plane drop a few degrees, he sensed the control computers configure the plane's wings for a rapid descent to strike altitude. Gripping the controls firmly, his mind became alert and his muscles tensed like an animal preparing to attack its prey.

"Turn right to a heading of one-eight-five degrees, Captain," his weapons officer said.

"One-eight-five coming up," he replied casually as he put the plane in a gentle right bank and intercepted their new heading. He glanced at the gauges. Everything was in order for the strike.

Their target was Moscow.

GU5, the intelligence arm of the New Earth Federation, had learned that Russia had continued to stockpile nuclear weapons even after coming into full membership in the NEF. And in defiance of the military provisions of the Global Charter of Unity, the new Russian president had been rattling his nuclear swords for months in a deadly battle of wills, causing alarm in Geneva and among the pro-Federation partisans in Russia.

Fanned by the fanatical nationalist faction that was determined to return Mother Russia to her former greatness, the simmering cauldron of ethnic hatreds had reached a boiling point, spilling over into a Russian expansionist movement dedicated to reconquering the territories lost during the latter part of the twentieth century.

Only days ago Russian planes had defied global law and had launched a series of nuclear attacks on key cities in the countries of Romania, Hungary, and Turkey, killing more than two million people.

Back in Geneva, Switzerland, the Secretary General of the New Earth Federation and his military and political advisers had been advised by GU5 that in order to extend their rule over all the earth, they would first have to teach the Russian people a lesson by bringing down their dissident leader and his followers. Once that objective had been met, the Russian forces loyal to the New Earth Federation would take control of the military and its arsenal of nuclear weapons, consolidating the Federation's power over Russia.

Through a carefully executed plan of propaganda and psychological subversion, they had goaded the Russian president into the attack on the other nations, giving the Federation forces an excuse to attack Moscow and the Russian military establishment.

"Two minutes to launch, Captain."

"Two minutes," he repeated.

The seasoned pilot glanced out his left window toward the ground.

Passing through forty-four thousand feet, traveling at Mach 5, the earth below was vague, impersonal, only a blur in the indistinct morning light.

"Turn left three degrees, Captain."

"Three degrees left," he droned in return.

"Launch in twenty seconds."

He checked his heading.

The weapons officer watched the readout of the numbers as they approached zero. Picking up the count verbally, he spoke into his built-in mike, "Five . . . four . . . three . . . two . . . one . . . missiles launched."

The pilot felt the double jolt of the twin rockets as they detached from the plane. Quickly glancing to his right, he watched in fascination as the two fiery missiles streaked menacingly from the underside of the plane. As the fire trails lengthened, his body instinctively tensed in anticipation of the blinding flash of light and the mind-numbing explosions that would come.

Reaching up, he swiftly lowered the dark gray visor on his helmet to protect his eyes. Then, with one swift synchronized motion, he pulled the stick back hard into his belly and added full power. Slamming the stick into his left leg, he kicked the left rudder with desperate force, executing a gut-wrenching tight climbing spiral. Flying the plane as if it were an extension of his own mind and body, his flawless coordination made it seem as if man and machine had been wedded together by some god of war. Its engines screaming, the plane shot upward at tremendous speed.

Surprised by the sudden maneuver, the weapons officer, hidden away in his small war room, could only grip the bottom of his seat and hold on, wondering if the pilot's intentions were to kill them both.

Pressing the heel of his strong hand hard against the throttles, the pilot of the SG-104 asked the noble plane for all it had. His twin scramjet engines whining at full power, the plane rocketed upward, gaining precious altitude that would separate them from the shock waves of the blasts. The pilot shouted into his microphone, telling his weapons officer to brace himself.

Far below, the city of Moscow erupted in flames.

Tensing, the pilot first saw the two brilliant flashes out of the corner of his eye, then, seconds later, he heard the deafening thuds of the jarring explosions as they slammed against the sides of his plane, the sound penetrating his attenuated helmet and exploding with unbelievable force around his body, engulfing him in its intensity and force.

Glancing out the side window, his soul seemed to shrivel inside him at the horrible sight of the mass of billowing flame and smoke hurtling skyward, wave after wave.

Totally incinerating the Kremlin—the epicenter of the fiery detonations—the energy released by the bombs spread ominously outward from there, consuming everything in its fiery path, instantly killing more than a million people, including the Russian president and the Joint Chiefs of Staff of the Russian military.

Moscow was now draped in a spreading fiery cloud of gray dust, debris, and smoke. Pinpointed throughout the disappearing landscape were raging billows of flame, with buildings, trees, and foliage exploding into a mass of ash.

Caught up in the horrific rapture of the macabre scene, the pilot could not tear his eyes away from the burning earth. He stared intently into the rising, spreading mushroom-shaped clouds, naked fear in his eyes. Although the NEF high command denied that they used nuclear weapons, he knew nuclear when he saw it.

With the city of Moscow lying in smoldering ruins, crack troops of the Rapid Strike Forces of the NEF descended on a mammoth underground military complex hidden away in the Boleretsk area of the southern Ural Mountains. Discovered by GU5 to be a staging area for a surprise nuclear strike against the forces of the New Earth Federation by the nationalist faction in Moscow, the elite NEF troops penetrated the heavily guarded facility, blowing it up, and killing or capturing the personnel who manned it.

Through a carefully coordinated political and military operation, pro-Federation factions in Russia immediately seized control of the military, bringing it under the direct control of the New Earth Federation.

At the news of the attack, China, who had steadily refused to turn over her nuclear capabilities to the New Earth Federation, seized the opportunity to launch a nuclear attack against India, her avowed enemy, killing more than ten million people in less than six hours.

In retaliation for the strike on India, the Global Peace Forces of the New Earth Federation immediately launched a devastating coordinated strike against the major military installations of China, taking out their nuclear capabilities and virtually paralyzing their gigantic war-making machine, killing more than twenty-six million people.

The Nine Day War had begun.

As if the bombing of Moscow were the signal to begin global hostilities, for nine horrific days, the hot, raging winds of war spread out of control across the planet. Vast regions of the world exploded in savage conflict, with numbers of small countries unleashing their hidden stockpiles of nuclear, chemical, and biological weapons against each other, leaving millions dead.

With the military capabilities of both Russia and China now devastated and under the undisputed control of the New Earth Federation, the military and political leaders of the NEF were emboldened to speed up their military advancement toward world domination. As the last remaining global military superpower, the NEF unleashed its awesome arsenal of high-tech weaponry against all dissident nations across the face of the planet.

Prosecuted with unbelievable ferocity against the peoples of the earth, the dreadful conflict was fought with the most powerful weapons of mass destruction the world had ever seen. Utilizing the Federation's vast nuclear arsenal, their stock of intercontinental ballistic missiles, armed with deadly warheads, was launched from nuclear subs, land-based sites, and ramjet-powered attack planes.

In a frightening new dimension to warfare, dozens of space stations circling thousands of miles above the earth served as platforms for launching a barrage of laser-guided nuclear missiles, sending them raining down on expendable cities like spears of death from an angry god.

Holdout nations and dissident peoples were pounded ruthlessly into submission by the full might of the savage New Earth Federation military juggernaut as it spread mass destruction like a violent storm cloud across the face of the earth, crushing everything in its murderous path.

The nine days of slaughter and destruction were carried out with such maniacal fervor, it caused many to believe that if the carnage had continued for a few more days, the entire world would have gone up in flames and the human race would have ceased to exist on Planet Earth.

After the nuclear burn of the Nine Day War, five separate areas of the earth were so devastated that only authorized persons were allowed to enter them. Those five designated areas had been so ravaged by the nuclear explosions that they were known as the Dark Zones. Vast stretches of the earth inside the Dark Zones had been laid bare by the fury of the deadly military technology and experimental weaponry utilized by the New Earth Federation's military high command in their vicious prosecution of the nine days of global conflict.

Bleak monuments to the veneration of evil, nothing existed in the five Dark Zones, no life of any kind, only a brooding gray landscape devoid of color. Only the prowling, haunting wind remained, gliding mournfully across the unobstructed expanse, kicking up the ashen dust of the barren land. The lifeless, ragged scars that had been viciously burned into the delicate face of the innocent earth lay as silent testimonials to the destructive might of the arsenal of death in the care of those in power.

With parts of the world now only a smoldering nuclear wasteland, a savage famine spread swiftly across the planet with merciless and devastating ferocity. When the ruthless famine had done its ugly work, other deadly enemies followed in close pursuit. As the earth lay weakened and vulnerable in the aftermath of the war and ravaging famines, the unrestrained spread of deadly viruses and opportunistic diseases added to the evil harvest of death.

Before the first anniversary of the horrendous Nine Day War had passed, the death count had exceeded more than one hundred million.

TWO

May 27, 2033

Steve Weston sat easy and relaxed in his plush, high-backed leather seat in the spacious, richly furnished officers' section of the large military plane, a half-filled glass of red wine resting at his elbow. Lost in his private thoughts, his chin balanced lightly against the fingers of his right hand, he stared aimlessly out the cabin window, scanning the depths of the thick darkness that enclosed them like an impenetrable shroud.

Cruising at one hundred and ten thousand feet, traveling at Mach 5, the plane had just crossed the East Coast of the United States on a nonstop flight from Dallas, Texas, to Geneva, Switzerland.

Weston, the International Director of the Sky News Network (SNN), headed its worldwide operation out of its global headquarters facilities in Dallas. Commonly referred to as TV9, channel nine on all video-receiving devices throughout the world were dedicated exclusively to SNN's programming. Reaching every square inch of the planet, SNN served as the universal television news and information arm of the New Earth Federation.

Steve rubbed one cheek thoughtfully. He was traveling aboard the restricted aircraft as a civilian VIP, a perk that came with his high position in the Social Order. Now living in Dallas, he was making a return trip to Geneva to serve as chief anchor for SNN's live telecast of the inaugural address of the newly elected Secretary General of the New Earth Federation, an event of major proportions.

The city of Geneva was hosting more than a million visitors from all parts of the world who had come for the weeklong celebration that would culminate in the appearance of the Secretary General in the Great Hall of Unity. Slated to give an address before a joint session of the Congress of the People and the World Council for Security and Cooperation, it would be the Secretary General's first appearance before a global audience.

Upon graduation from World University, near Washington, D.C., Steve had accepted a postgraduate fellowship in Switzerland to study Global Communications at the University of Zurich. There he had first met Dr. Wilhelm Wallenberg, after enrolling in his class entitled "Society and the Global Media." Wallenberg quickly recognized Steve's virtually unlimited media potential and repeatedly urged him to develop it. Over the course of three years the mentor and his protégé became fast friends.

Following his graduation near the top of his class and armed with a glowing recommendation from Dr. Wallenberg, Steve had been hired by the American Public Information Agency and assigned to a television station in Denver as an investigative reporter. After slogging about the city doing local stories for a year, he had made the big jump to an evening anchor position at a major television station in Los Angeles. In the back of his mind, he had always suspected that Dr. Wallenberg had something to do with that assignment, too. But he never knew for sure.

But one thing was certain—that propitious move had served to catapult Steve dramatically onto the world stage in 2022, when the "Big One" hit L.A.

Magnitude 9! Unheard of, but it had happened.

Even now, Steve could vividly see the ghastly images passing in sharp detail in his mind's eye as clearly as the day the earthquake had hit, without warning, eleven years before. Shaking his head slowly from side to side, he remembered being excited and terrified all at once. As the earth seemed to throw a jarring, childish tantrum around him, the sheer horror of the scenes of death and destruction held him tightly in their morbid rapture.

The event had played out as if he were not a part of it and had faced no personal danger. Without fear, he had stood all alone in an alien world, somewhere between reality and fantasy, watching the planet tear apart in front of his eyes.

Steve lifted his glass, tasted the wine, and savored its flavor. At peace with himself, he folded his arms across his chest and gazed thoughtfully out the window into the black night.

As time and motion seemed to slow to a standstill, he was surprised to feel a new rush of emotion as the sights, sounds, and images from that day in Los Angeles exploded in his brain as if he were once again watching the old video news clips of himself, live on the scene. . . .

. . . Before a backdrop of utter destruction and chaos, he defiantly stood astride the twisted steel and broken concrete of a fractured freeway . . . sweat streaming down his soot-darkened face in the surreal black night as orange and yellow flames from countless raging out-of-control fires flickered eerily in the background . . .

. . . his breathless, flowing live commentary was continually broken by the fiery percussion of exploding gas lines, the haunting human screams of pain and despair and death, and the incessant wail of distant, hopeless sirens . . .

. . . buildings imploded as they burned and crumbled, crushing the frantic, cowering figures crouched in their shadows . . . twisted traffic snarled to a standstill on streets flooded from ruptured, gushing water mains . . .

. . . brilliant halogen spotlights from hovering helicopters feeding light to the uplinked cameras to capture the unbelievable carnage before the awestruck eyes of a watching world . . . more than a million dead, and counting.

. . . holding his ground like a soldier under heavy enemy fire while wave after wave of jarring aftershocks rolled rumbling beneath his feet, never wavering, speaking steadily, eyes locked earnestly on the camera's constant red light. . . .

"This is Steve Weston, reporting live from Los Angeles. . . ."

Amid the widespread death and destruction of what was clearly one of the worst disasters to hit Planet Earth, as the whole world stared into their television screens in rapt attention, a star was born at the age of twenty-five.

Dr. Wallenberg had contacted Steve almost immediately via a real-time satellite video-conference call from his office in Geneva to congratulate him on his supreme poise and professionalism under such extreme circumstances. Deeply moved by his mentor's thoughtfulness and kindness, Steve was inexplicably at a loss for words. Clearing his throat, he managed to simply say, "Thank you, sir."

Strange, he recalled thinking.

Such loss of composure had very rarely overtaken Steve Weston as an adult. Thinking back, he wondered why it had happened. Then suddenly it came to him, the explanation he hadn't even sought before that moment—for the first time since he was a child, he had someone, like a father, approving of his performance, telling him that he had done a good job.

Before receiving the coveted post as International Director of Sky News Network, Steve was afforded a front-row seat to the continuing evolution of the new Social Order during five heady years in Geneva as special assistant to Dr. Wallenberg, who had been appointed Chairman of the United Information and Communications Authority (UICA). An agency of the New Earth Federation, the UICA supervised and controlled all radio and television communications.

Having the ability to tap into the minds of the leaders of the world gave him a degree of power and control, personal assets that he had come to appreciate and enjoy. He saw his innate media skills as the key to fulfilling his dream of position, wealth, and power in the new Social Order.

At age thirty-six, Steve Weston was beginning to enjoy the benefits of his hard work and fierce determination. A little over six feet tall, with dark blond hair and a firm, square jaw, at one hundred and eighty pounds, he still moved with the ease and grace of a professional athlete, slightly past his prime. And with his friendly, easygoing manner and his rugged good looks, people said he was made for the television camera. As an added bonus, he had a sharp analytical mind and a definite flair for writing. A natural, his writing and broadcasting skills had always come easy to him.

Consumed with a driving ambition, he had seized the important opportunities that had come his way and had made the most of them. Now he stood on the threshold of accomplishments that others only dreamed about.

Sitting across the aisle from Steve Weston was Colonel Keith Fletcher, a large, self-confident man in his early sixties. Dressed in light green battle fatigues and dark green combat boots, an impressive array of battle ribbons and medals adorned his chest. Fletcher was the commanding officer of the seventy-five military personnel riding in the passenger section of the plane. Three other officers of his command staff were seated behind him.

Operating out of their base in Dallas, Texas, they were part of the proud, elite Rapid Strike Forces, a group of highly trained quick-response teams strategically scattered throughout the world. Highly mobile, thoroughly professional, and armed with the latest and best in military technology and hardware, they brought swift retribution to the offending factions whenever armed conflict broke out anywhere on the planet.

Part of the military buildup in response to the massive influx of people to Geneva, Colonel Fletcher and his men would be joining other military contingents who had been assigned security and crowd-control duty during the historic appearance of the Secretary General.

Following an elaborate meal served by a military steward, Steve engaged in a brief, casual conversation with Colonel Fletcher. He then leaned his chair back to relax while Fletcher took a long drag on what remained of a dark, pungent cigar, blowing the acrid smoke toward the air duct above his head.

"It's not often we get a civilian aboard one of these flights," the colonel remarked loudly, with just a hint of disdain in his voice. Yet his tone was colored with a begrudging respect, for he knew that Steve Weston was a rising star in the power structure of the New Earth Federation.

"Glad to be aboard, Colonel," Steve returned casually.

"I'm a military man," the colonel continued, clenching the well-used cigar between his teeth. "But your work in the information business intrigues me."

Steve hesitated, ever cautious. "They are two fronts in the same war, Colonel," he replied easily.

A slow smile crept over the colonel's lips, and he removed the cigar from his mouth, relaxing the hardness of his features for an instant. A few quiet moments lingered, then faded before he resumed the conversation. "Of course," he said, his voice firm and insistent, "it would be best if things could be done with words and images. But, as you know, maintaining the peace can sometimes be extremely violent."

Steve regarded the colonel's words thoughtfully, searching for some clue that would reveal what the older man was thinking. But the answer eluded him. He paused to choose his words carefully before answering. "A new global order demands changes," he began slowly, patiently. "*Paradigm* changes, Colonel. Since we live with the risk of humanity destroying itself and the planet, our mission is to persuade the masses to accept social and political realities. Global unity is our only hope."

The cryptic smile slipped from the colonel's face. With a certain air of skepticism, he snapped almost angrily, "Others have tried to bring about global unity, Weston. What makes you think we're going to be successful this time?"

A sudden uneasiness stirred inside Steve at the carelessness of the colonel's question. It was not just the words themselves; it was the tone he used in speaking—with a half-mocking smile and an ill-concealed touch of sarcasm in his gruff voice. In a society that was characterized by an expected reflex of ideological conformity, his words seemed to break all the rules. They were replete with blatant skepticism. And such ill-advised skepticism, directed at the Social Order, could be costly.

An awkward moment of silence fell away as Steve pondered his reply. He glanced out the window, organizing his thoughts quickly. Putting aside his original intended response, he decided to give the colonel a veiled warning.

Leaning forward slightly, he turned to face the older man, their gazes locking momentarily, as if to measure each other's resolve. His curiosity bordering on astonishment, Steve cautioned the colonel in a sharp whisper, "I'm assuming that's a *rhetorical* question, Colonel, and not a statement of your misgivings about the global order."

Nodding his head slowly, a faint, unconvincing smile on his face, Colonel Fletcher retorted, "Indeed it is, Mr. Weston," suddenly defensive at Steve's abrupt challenge. "*Rhetorical*, that is." His face browned and seamed by sun and weather, the old soldier's deep, piercing eyes betrayed his muffled anger and the sharp bitterness that he carried deep inside himself.

Steve mulled over in his mind the fact that the highly decorated soldier could be sanctioned severely for speaking out so boldly. He suddenly regarded him with a mixture of quiet surprise and growing distrust. "It's true," he announced solemnly, "that efforts at global unity have been attempted in the past. But the difference is that we now have the power and the technology to succeed where others have failed."

Colonel Fletcher shifted his cigar to the other side of his mouth. "But your way is too slow," he growled, his lips curling into a sardonic smile. "You see, Weston, if the world leaders would just turn the military loose, we'd bring about global unity in thirty days. The real power is *force*. Military force! Hardware! Soldiers!" Fletcher spat the words emphatically, obviously deriving grim satisfaction, and no small amount of pleasure, in the effect they were having on Steve.

Staring into his glass of wine, Steve pondered his reply, still not sure where the colonel was coming from, or where his loyalties lay. "To the contrary, Colonel," he began cautiously. "Global governance requires a global consciousness. The mind must be won first and foremost. And in that task, *information* is more powerful than all your troops and armaments. The most powerful institution is the one that shapes the minds and wills of humankind."

Steve nodded and smiled, adding thoughtfully, "But, of course, if we do have to rely on you and your new instruments of war, it means that those of us in my profession have not done our job."

Colonel Fletcher thought about the statement for a moment. When he answered, his words were laced with undisguised sarcasm. "You're very persuasive," he said condescendingly. "But there's one thing that bothers me."

Steve's eyes narrowed. Casting an apprehensive glance at the colonel, he asked, "And what bothers you, Colonel?"

A disgruntled look on his rugged face, a biting edge to his voice, Fletcher replied pointedly, "Well, I'm not sure if you're trying to convince *me* . . . or yourself, Mr. Weston."

Steve paused, ready to answer him, decided against it, and left the thought hanging unspoken in the silence. He smiled inwardly, quietly admiring the older man's raw courage in speaking his mind. Sensing a mounting tension between them, he ordered his words carefully, suggesting reassuringly, "Either way, Colonel, it's comforting to know that you and your men are always there in case we need you."

His mouth frozen in a sad parody of a smile, the wily military man shook his head skeptically. Without responding, he took a deep, steadying breath, tilted his seat back, stretched out his legs, and closed his eyes, still clenching the stub of his unlit cigar tightly between his teeth.

Glancing out the window, Steve studied the first glimmering promise of the new day breaking through the far horizon as the giant plane chased the constant curved line separating earth and sky. In the distant east, the golden rim of the morning sun pushed softly against the remaining darkness, shooting forth the first faint tinges of light of the approaching dawn.

Miles below, he could faintly see the vast expanse of the ocean passing swiftly, quietly, underneath the belly of the plane.

The cabin was now quiet, and the welcome silence suddenly enveloped him like a warm blanket. Feeling himself gradually begin to relax, he let the solitude of the moment slip over him while his mind played host to a pleasant scattering of thoughts. As he sipped slowly on a cup of hot, rich coffee the steward had brought him, his thoughts drifted back to the events of the past, pondering the significance of the twists and turns that had brought him to this point in his life.

Having excelled in every aspect of life at Landstar Academy, he had graduated with high academic honors, winning a full scholarship to the School of Government at World University near Washington, D.C., in the process. Majoring in international politics, with an emphasis on geopolitical affairs, he was in his third undergraduate year in 2017, when the brazen Iranian naval blockade of the Strait of Hormuz sparked the Third Gulf War.

The carnage had been swift, escalating rapidly as Hezbollah terrorist zealots detonated small tactical nuclear weapons in Chicago, Amsterdam, and Ankara, vaporizing the cities and killing millions instantaneously. Similar suitcase-sized nuclear devices were intercepted by a Mossad-CIA counterintelligence team before they could reach their destinations in New York City, Tel Aviv, and Washington, D.C.

The devastating terrorist attacks provoked a retaliation of unprecedented fury against the Arab factions by a coalition of forces operating under an extreme emergency mandate issued by the United Nations. In just three insane days of high-tech warfare, much of the Arab world was reduced to a flaming inferno of scorched earth and burning oil wells.

Seeing the incomprehensible scale of destruction unleashed virtually overnight, and watching the world's economy implode as the flow of Arab oil slowed to an insignificant trickle, Steve had become convinced that his professors were right when they preached that rampant nationalism was the greatest political peril facing Spaceship Earth.

"National sovereignty is an idea which has now been consigned to the ash heap of history," said one former Secretary of State during an address to the entire assembled student body at World University. "It is an intellectual oddity in modern political thought, and a dangerous luxury in which we can no longer afford to indulge. Within your lifetimes, I predict that nationhood as we now know it will become obsolete."

The facts were irrefutable, the logic irresistible. The selfish demands of each nation for absolute autonomy clearly constituted an unacceptable threat to world peace. Only global unity could secure the future of the earth.

It was the high calling of the elite minds of the future to convince the teeming masses of humanity to embrace global unity as the only hope. Thus, Steve Weston had consciously and volitionally dedicated himself, at the age of twenty-one, to the noble service of the Social Order.

Steve's eyes lazily traced the horizon. Bands of gold and red were lengthening against the gathering light, growing brighter, edging the boundary between sea and sky. Drinking in the colorful scene, his fingers drummed a soft refrain on the leather armrest.

Dr. Wallenberg had personally requested that Steve host TV9's global coverage of the prestigious event at the Great Hall of Unity, which led him to believe that there might be another reason why his personal friend and mentor was bringing him to Geneva. For more than a year, he had heard rumors that Dr. Wallenberg was retiring and that Steve himself was being considered for the post.

Steve Weston knew where he was going. His drive for power and prestige was his mistress, his first love, his constant companion. All else came second to his driving pursuit of his clearly defined goals. His career with TV9 had been one of swift and unfettered progress up the ladder, and now he felt that the prestigious and powerful directorship of the Universal Information and Communications Authority was within his grasp.

I have served the Social Order faithfully, he reminded himself.

Steve closed his eyes and let his mind drift. His thoughts slow and reassuring, he listened to the encompassing silence. In this rare moment of solitude in the darkened cabin of the plane, he reflected on his pleasant years in Geneva and his valuable learning experiences under the capable leadership of Dr. Wallenberg.

After Steve's five years in Geneva, Dr. Wallenberg asked him to go to Dallas to head up the worldwide operation of Sky News Network. Excited about the promotion, he had asked if he could talk it over with Lori before giving his answer. Dr. Wallenberg had agreed.

Steve had been introduced to Lori Pennington at a formal dinner in the home of a member of the Congress of the People. Immediately attracted to Steve, she accepted his invitation to have a drink with him at one of his favorite bars after the dinner. Leaving as soon as the dinner was over, they skipped the drinks and went straight to Steve's apartment. A week later she moved in with him.

Steve learned that Lori was originally from Baltimore, Maryland, and the only child of Dr. Dwight Howard Pennington, one of his former professors at World University. Steve had studied global economics under him.

Having attended the finest schools as a child, Lori had graduated from the university with high honors. She was teaching in an exclusive private school in one of the most affluent sections of Geneva when they met. Among her students were the children of members of the Congress of the People, prominent business leaders, and high-ranking government officials.

Just five days before moving to Dallas, they had learned that Lori was pregnant. After reluctantly agreeing not to abort the child, she and Steve obtained a Birth License from the Population Control Commission, then registered as "marriage partners."

On June 5, 2030, Lori gave birth to a baby boy, in a large government hospital in Dallas, Texas. They named him James Dwight Weston and called him Jimmy.

With the picture of his son's face lying gently on his mind, Steve smiled contentedly and tilted his chair back. Stretching his legs out, he burrowed his head into the softness of the headrest and closed his eyes. In less than a heartbeat, he was asleep.

Steve was suddenly awakened when he felt the huge plane bank lazily to the left. He brought his chair forward and glanced out the window, suddenly awestruck by the grandeur of the timeless panorama of snow-peaked mountains passing swiftly underneath. From his aerial vantage point, the vista of seemingly endless snowcapped Alpine ranges made him catch his breath. Sitting motionless, his eyes eagerly locked on the landscape sliding past, he found himself hypnotized by its savage beauty.

A few scattered clouds, golden with the rays of the morning sun, drifted lazily along the rim of the peaks, casting the winding valleys and precipitous gorges below in deep shadow, mysterious and forbidding, a hushed, breathless scene. In the distance, beyond a crystal clear Alpine lake, blended against a backdrop of glittering white snow, brilliant streaks of lightning flickered their zigzag patterns near a solitary mountain peak.

Possessing a seductive mixture of raw, stark beauty and intimidating magnitude, this was arguably the most magnificent region of Europe.

The heavy military plane traveled smoothly down the glideslope, touching down with a heavy thump, a squeal of rubber on concrete, then settled with a slight shudder. The thrust-reversers roared, slowing the plane, pushing Steve's shoulders against his seat harness.

With its long runways, this new world-class Geneva airport could accommodate the world's largest civilian and military aircraft.

They had left Dallas in darkness, but outside it was now bright with the morning sun of the new day.

Coming to a full stop at the military terminal, Steve stood, stretched himself, and took his travel suitcase down from the overhead bin. Glancing up when the cockpit door opened, he saw Captain George Peters step out. Steve smiled and said, "Thanks for the ride, Captain."

"My pleasure, Mr. Weston," was Captain Peters' friendly reply. "By the way, ground control told us to convey a message to you. Dr. Wallenberg has sent his private car to pick you up. It should be pulling up beside the plane now."

After saying goodbye to Colonel Fletcher, Steve walked down the portable ramp onto the tarmac. The troops had already deplaned and were standing at attention under the right wing of the aircraft.

Glancing to his right, he spotted a black Daimler limousine pull up and stop abruptly in the shadow of the plane's massive tail section. The driver, a tall, thin black man, dressed in a well-tailored black business suit, stepped confidently out of the car and looked around, surveying the faces of the passengers.

Seeing Steve walking toward him, the driver called out over the noise of the airport, "Mr. Weston." His accent was British.

The hot blast of a jet engine from a fighter taxiing by caught Steve by surprise. Clutching tightly to his bag, he called out, "Yes, I'm Weston."

"Fine, sir. I am Ramul Mulatya, Dr. Wallenberg's private chauffeur. Dr. Wallenberg sends his kindest regards and looks forward to your visit to Geneva. Do you have any more luggage, sir?"

"No, this is all, Ramul," Steve answered as he moved toward the car.

After placing Steve's bag inside the trunk, Ramul stepped quickly to open the door to the large rear passenger compartment for him. Steve slipped inside as Ramul closed the door behind him. Once Ramul was assured that his passenger was secure, he slid in behind the wheel. Steve heard the soft thud of the automatic mechanism slam shut, locking all the doors as the limo eased gracefully away from the plane.

Secure inside the privacy of the large, plush passenger compartment of the Daimler limousine, separated from the driver by a thick privacy glass, Steve looked through the heavily tinted windows at the hundreds of military personnel scattered across the wide expanse of the airport. With hundreds of soldiers dressed in full battle gear, weapons at the ready, it looked to Steve as if Geneva had been invaded by the Global Peace Forces of the New Earth Federation.

As the car approached the security gate, Ramul gave a quick salute, and the guard waved them through. Moving the car swiftly onto the street, he merged with the fast-moving traffic, being careful not to disturb his passenger.

Their destination was Global Village. A part of Geneva, yet separate from it, Global Village was a city within a city. This highly secured, prestigious enclave was the power center of the global government, the seat of the New Earth Federation.

Passing familiar landmarks, Steve recalled how much he and Lori had enjoyed living and working in Geneva. On a sudden impulse, he picked up the hand phone and asked Ramul to drive by Lake Geneva on their way to Global Village. Changing course, Ramul exited to his left and intersected the street that would take them along the banks of the lake.

As the car slowed to a leisurely pace, Steve stared out the side window at the bright sun glistening off the clear, placid waters of Lake Geneva. *This crescent-shaped lake*, he mused, *is the grandest in all the Alpine region.*

Watching a young couple walking along the flower-decked lakefront, their arms intertwined, caused pleasant memories to come flooding back into his mind like an endless torrent. Lost in the moment, he eagerly replayed splendid scenes of the mild summer evenings when he and Lori had strolled unhurriedly along the banks of the lake, visiting the cafés and souvenir shops, laughing, talking, so much in love.

With the soft touch of the gentle breezes brushing lightly against their faces, they would pause to watch the spectacular Jet d'Eau, the fountain of Geneva, its watery plume rising more than four hundred feet into the air. Their cares would be washed away in the spray from the magical fountain.

He nodded slowly, a smile playing over his face as they passed a quaint small café—Lori's favorite—where they sat for hours, making plans for their future together. A shadow of sadness suddenly clouded his reverie, blurring his thoughts of the carefree moments that had come and gone all too soon, moments when things had been good between them.

It seemed so long ago.

Now, at the peak of his professional success, the emotional distance between them had become a great, gaping chasm. Not being able to share the thrill of his accomplishments with Lori was one of his bitterest disappointments. Sighing in resignation, he shook his head uneasily. It was so unfair, when things should be so perfect.

Shortly after turning away from Lake Geneva, Steve's reverie was broken by two short electronic chimes coming from the videophone in the mahogany pedestal in front of him. Instantly, the face of Dr. Wallenberg appeared on a small screen in the pedestal. A tiny video camera, placed just below the viewscreen, was sending a clear image of Steve back to Dr. Wallenberg's office, where the professor was looking at him on a monitor in the communications console built into his desk.

"Dr. Wallenberg, it's nice to see you again," Steve exclaimed enthusiastically, unconsciously leaning forward toward the screen.

His voice pleasant, Dr. Wallenberg answered, "Steven, my boy, I'm glad to see that you arrived safely. Did Ramul arrive on time? Is everything to your liking?"

Steve smiled. "Yes, everything is fine. Ramul was waiting for me when I arrived."

"Very good, Steven. Welcome back to Geneva. I have instructed Ramul to take you directly to the hotel. We will talk later."

"I look forward to seeing you again, sir. And thank you again for selecting me to host this momentous event," Steve said sincerely.

"Enjoy the ride, Steven. I'll see you soon."

"Thank you, sir."

When Dr. Wallenberg's image had disappeared from the screen, Steve glanced outside as Ramul turned right onto a twelve-lane boulevard, the main thoroughfare through Global Village.

Scattered throughout the Global Village compound were dozens of buildings housing the agencies and commissions that controlled and administered the various functions of the global government. The nerve center of world control, these hundreds of agencies, authorities, and commissions intruded into every human need and activity known to man, impacting the daily lives of practically everyone living on earth.

Covering several square miles, Global Village was filled with plush homes, apartment buildings, condominiums, hotels, restaurants, schools, and shopping malls. With more than thirty-five thousand people living and working here on a permanent basis, it was a self-contained city that boasted an elaborate transportation system to shuttle the people quickly and conveniently throughout the city. Transparent pedestrian tubes with moving sidewalks connected the buildings, allowing the workers to travel swiftly and comfortably from building to building in all kinds of weather.

With its fabulous water fountains, resplendent marble statues, picturesque winding streets, and immaculately manicured lawns, and boasting an expansive cultural center, Global Village was the envy of the world. This exclusive enclave was the home of the information specialists, the technical and professional experts serving those who sat in the seats of global power. In an environment of digitized telecommunications, the leaders of the government shaped world policy through their judicious use of information. The information managers had become the new cultural elite in a society whose primary economic resource was knowledge.

The architects of the new global order looked upon the city of Geneva, and this high-profile enclave, with almost reverential awe. Moving in and out of the city on a daily basis, a steady stream of modern-day pilgrims came to pay homage to its power and prestige. Some came to beg, others came to divide the spoils of power, and others came to hammer out the mounting number of new laws that humankind would be compelled to live under.

A city filled with mystery and intrigue, Geneva, Switzerland, the center of global power, was a constant source of news stories for TV9.

Turning left at the traffic circle, Ramul followed the long, winding, tree-lined street to the entrance of the Global Village Hotel, an impressive thirty-story building of glass and stone. After coming to a smooth stop at the front entrance, Ramul stepped out and opened the door for Steve.

While courteous hotel attendants retrieved his luggage, Ramul turned to Steve. "This is where I will leave you, sir. If there is anything I can do for you, please call Dr. Wallenberg's office and they will notify me."

"Thank you, Ramul. I'll call if I need you."

Steve walked into the elaborately stylish lobby of the Global Village Hotel. After signing the register, he went immediately up to his luxury suite.

Steve Weston had no way of knowing that his life would never be the same after the events in Geneva the next few days.

THREE

Geneva, Switzerland—May 28, 2033

J utting sixty stories into the clear blue sun-washed sky loomed the mirrored obelisk that was the New Earth Federation building, the gleaming centerpiece of Global Village. Standing majestically golden in the bright rays of the early morning sun, the magnificent structure cast a long, triangular shadow across the landscape below. A world-class architectural triumph, it stood tall and proud like a silent sentinel, keeping a constant vigil over the planned community.

With slow, measured strides, Steve Weston pressed forward, shouldering his way through the loud, milling throng of people crowding the huge lobby of the New Earth Federation building. His brow wrinkling in total concentration, he moved with resolve toward the plush TV9 broadcast booth that overlooked the Great Hall of Unity located on the sprawling main floor.

He weaved his way to his left, turned down a narrow hallway, and approached a secure area. Placing the palm of his hand on the hand-scan device near the door, the armed guard nodded, and Steve walked into the studio, pausing momentarily to scan the spacious room.

More than a dozen tech people were rushing about, adjusting lights and cameras, talking into their headsets to other unseen tech people in other parts of the building, and making final preparations for the special telecast. Despite the din of voices and constant activity, there was a calm professionalism and rehearsed orderliness in the studio.

Positioned along the central wall to the left of the massive speaker's platform and elevated several feet above the main floor to provide a clear and unobstructed view of the proceedings inside the auditorium, the elaborately furnished television studio was a permanent fixture in the Great Hall of Unity. Totally soundproof, it was separated from the Hall by a specially designed, lightly tinted glass wall.

It was thirty-nine minutes to airtime.

Audrey Montaigne was seated in a chair to the right of the anchor desk carrying on an animated conversation with the floor director. Seeing Steve enter the room, her face broke into a wide smile. With the television lights playing softly on her hair, highlighting the chiseled lines of her delicate face, she was a stunningly beautiful woman. Underneath the stylish business suit she wore, Audrey's one hundred and eighteen pounds were perfectly proportioned on her trim, five-foot, seven-inch frame. A former model, she had fair skin and a disarming smile.

Steve hesitated for a heartbeat, staring at her. Although she had worked for him for over a year, he suddenly found himself looking at her as if he had never seen her before this moment.

At age twenty-seven, she had been through several short-term relationships, but nothing lasting. Having planned on going into acting, the excitement of television news caused her to change her mind. With her dark auburn hair, her sparkling green eyes, and the seductive alto timbre of her voice, she carried just the right blend of earthy appeal and professional expertise.

And through hard work and a flair for getting past the smooth surface of a story by using her sharp mind and natural charm, she had become a no-nonsense, thorough investigative reporter, gaining the respect of her colleagues in the process.

A few weeks earlier, Dr. Wallenberg had called Steve and requested that he host the TV9 coverage of the event. Upon accepting the assignment, Steve asked Audrey to co-host the event with him. She had been in Geneva for a week before Steve's arrival, filing stories for TV9 on the activities surrounding the inaugural celebrations.

"Hi, Steve," she called out warmly.

Their eyes met. Walking over to where she was seated, Steve bent down and kissed her lightly on her left cheek. "You look absolutely stunning," he whispered into her ear.

"Why, thank you," she replied, her face reflecting her pleasure at receiving the compliment. "I was beginning to wonder if you even knew I existed," she added.

Steve returned her smile, then walked to the glass wall, folded his arms across his chest, and looked out across the main floor where members of the Congress of the People were milling about, shaking hands, laughing, smiling.

The Great Hall of Unity was a large, fan-shaped auditorium with a towering ceiling and elegant furnishings. Twenty-four hundred highly polished hardwood desks, arranged in a semicircle, faced the speaker's platform in silent dignity.

A deliberative body, the endless debates and inane natterings of the Congress of the People was carried live on a dedicated channel shown on viewscreens across the world. Although it gave the people of the world the illusion that they were actually participating in the making of laws, the real decisions on world affairs were made behind closed doors by the one hundred members of the World Council for Security and Cooperation, also known as the Council of 100.

Glancing up at the mammoth balcony that wrapped around the back one-third of the Great Hall of Unity, Steve watched the rushing, growing throng spilling into the ornate auditorium. Some were already seated, while others were making their way to their highly prized reserved seats in anticipation of the first major address by the new Secretary General of the New Earth Federation.

Formed in 2023, the New Earth Federation had emerged out of a worldwide cry for a strong, unified global government that would lead the world out of the prevailing chaos and bring the rule of law to the earth.

Before the formation of the NEF, scattered wars had claimed more than two hundred million lives since the turn of the century, with countless numbers injured or maimed. The never-ending parade of images of death, destruction, and carnage left in the wake of the high-tech conflicts, carried worldwide by the TV9 cameras, had made a lasting impression on Steve. Unable to get the scenes out of his mind, the threat of another war haunted his dreams.

As anarchy tightened its bloody reign over most of the major cities of the world, and sweeping riots went virtually unchecked, entire regions were engulfed in the raging flames of armed conflict. In response to a desperate call for world order, hastily appointed representatives from one hundred and fifty nations of the world rushed to Geneva to an emergency Earth Summit to hammer out the details of a global alliance.

Having previously gained unchallenged dominance in world finance, world trade, and military might, the summit was virtually dominated and controlled by the fifteen-member nations of the European Council of Nations. After more than a week of heated, often rancorous debate, the necessary two-thirds of the delegates present voted to adopt the proposed Global Charter of Unity and to form the New Earth Federation.

Following the election of the Secretary General, the delegates elected one hundred people who would make up the Executive Branch of the NEF, the World Council for Security and Cooperation. The Council of 100, as they were called, then decreed that a Congress of the People, to be made up of twenty-four hundred members, would be elected by the citizens of the world at a later date.

At the conclusion of the Earth Summit, the newly elected Secretary General announced the partitioning of the world into fifteen political, economic, environmental, and spiritual Zones of Global Cooperation (ZGCs). He then introduced to the world the fifteen governors whom he had personally appointed to head the fifteen ZGCs.

With each world citizen being allowed one vote utilizing their Home Communications Unit, one year later, twenty-four hundred people were elected from the fifteen Zones of Global Cooperation to membership in the Congress of the People. Following the voting, the Council of 100 tabulated the electronic ballots in Geneva, announced the results, and authorized the seating of the members.

A total of one hundred and forty nations had joined in signing the Charter of Unity at the Earth Summit.

Only ten of the nations in attendance had refused to sign.

The President of the United States, Abraham Spencer Morrison, who had been in attendance at the Earth Summit, had voted against the Charter of Global Unity and had refused to sign it after its adoption. He contended that he was not authorized to surrender the sovereignty of his government to a foreign power.

President Morrison's unexpected action had sent shock waves throughout the summit and ignited a life-and-death political struggle in the United States, with diehard constitutionalists attempting to block U.S. entry into the NEF. But they found they were no match for the globalist forces. In a brilliant move, the leaders of the New Earth Federation, in collusion with their allies in the U.S., offered to cancel all U.S. debt when they came into full membership.

With the American military decimated by drastic downsizing started in the latter part of the twentieth century, their treasury virtually bankrupt, and deeply in debt to foreign powers, the United States had no choice but to capitulate.

Even though the constitutionalist faction continued to fight the move, with the election of Alfred John Honecker as President in the 2024 election, the United States was committed to joining the new global order. The cornerstone of Honecker's presidential campaign had been that he would bring the U.S. into full membership if elected.

In a fatal move, the U.S. Senate voted overwhelmingly to ratify the Charter of Global Unity. Armed with the Senate's vote, a few months after his inauguration, Honecker flew to Geneva, Switzerland, where he signed the membership documents in a formal ceremony in the Great Hall of Unity before the SNN cameras.

At the moment of signing, the United States Constitution and Bill of Rights were rendered null and void, and the American people came under the rule of the New Earth Federation. By affixing his signature to the Charter of Global Unity, President Honecker allowed the United States to be absorbed into Zone Five of the fifteen Zones of Global Cooperation.

Before the TV cameras had dimmed on the signing ceremony in Geneva, New Earth Federation military planes delivering more than one hundred thousand Global Forces troops flew across the borders into the United States, seizing control of the central government in Washington, the media, the military, and the police forces.

The date of the signing was July 4, 2025.

The great experiment in self-government, called the United States of America, had come to an end.

It had lived for two hundred and forty-nine years.

Twenty-one days after having signed the Global Charter of Unity, President Honecker was found dead in the Oval Office of the White House. His medical records were sealed and no official explanation of his death was ever given. Vice President Philip Grantham filled out the remaining portion of his term, but by this time, the office of president was purely symbolic, with no power.

Steve's gaze swept across the Great Hall and up to the first balcony. Sitting in a special reserved section were twenty-four people, fifteen men and nine women, the Justices of the Global Supreme Court. Slightly to their left was a small section occupied by fifteen people, nine men and six women, the Governors of the fifteen Zones of Global Cooperation. Each of these ruling dignitaries was appointed by the Secretary General and served at his pleasure.

In the most tightly secured room in the Great Hall, directly across from the TV9 studio, sitting in plush chairs behind an impenetrable protective glass wall, were the Council of 100. Steve noticed that Dr. Wallenberg was in his assigned place near the end, to his right, on the first row.

Vested with unprecedented political, military, and economic authority, this was the most powerful body of people on earth. Not subject to reelection, membership in the Council of 100 was declared to be self-perpetuating. The reasoning was that this body should be kept "above the ebb and flow of politics."

Steve walked slowly to the right side of the glass wall, deep in thought.

Without warning, they came. Memories returning to him in an unpleasant rush.

No, not here, not now!

His brow creased with annoyance.

Here, among the world's most powerful people gathered in the Great Hall of Unity, inescapably, the recurring scenes from his troubled childhood were boldly marching through his mind like soldiers passing in review. Even as he basked in the power and prestige of his prominent role in the global Social Order, those dreaded scenes came crashing through his mental defenses, blurring his thoughts, threatening to tarnish his command performance.

He sighed deeply.

Weary of the nagging presence of the unwelcome, frightening visions, he breathed deeply and gently rubbed his right temple with his fingertips, trying to will away the unwelcome images.

Steve felt his throat tighten. He stood motionless.

He had celebrated his sixth birthday only a few weeks before it had happened. And now, he was reliving it again. He had been sleeping in his small bed in the corner of his tiny room in his family's modest apartment, when he was awakened by a loud noise that seemed to shake his room. This was followed by the sounds of running feet and falling bodies and strange voices talking loudly in the room next to his bedroom.

Heart pounding, he had slipped out of bed, stumbled to the door, opened it slightly and gazed warily out into the living room. Looming menacingly in front of him were three very large men, dressed in black combat uniforms and carrying automatic weapons. The front door hung at odd angles, blasted apart and violently ripped from its hinges.

One of the black-clad men had his father penned against the floor, his knee planted firmly in his back, wrenching his arms painfully behind his back. The man cursed him loudly while roughly forcing handcuffs onto his wrists.

"Well, Mr. Weston," he said mockingly, "it looks like your subversive activities are over for this lifetime."

Amid their profanity and laughter, they stood his father up on his feet and violently shoved him toward the tattered door, their fists hammering painfully into his body. It was then that Steve saw his father's face. Gasping out a quiet sob of horror, the young boy stared at a wicked gash that had been cut across his father's forehead and watched the blood streaming profusely down his cheek.

Against a savage swirl of black terror, he was too frightened to cry.

Time seemed to stand still for the young boy as the disturbing images played out before his eyes in frightening slow motion. He stared at his mother. Her delicate face was pale and drawn. Too young to grasp the meaning of the disturbing scene, he could not stop the wild pounding of his own heart and the flush of fear that paralyzed his thoughts.

When the men had forced his father out into the night, the frightened child silently watched his mother as she sank to the floor. At length, she gave a low, trembling whimper, slowly drew her legs up against her body, and wrapped her arms around her knees. Shaking and sobbing, she was overtaken with grief and fear.

Frightened and confused at the disturbing scene, Steve wanted desperately to rush to his mother, to embrace her and calm her fears. But he waited. Time seemed to go on forever. Unable to understand what was happening, his eyes brimming with tears, he reluctantly closed the door and returned to his bed and waited through the night, hoping she would come to him.

But she didn't come.

He never saw his father again, and his mother never explained, or ever spoke to him of the incident. She only told him that he was gone and would not return. It fell his lot to learn from a school counselor that his father had been tried and sentenced to prison for engaging in treasonous political activities against the Social Order.

As the years passed, hatred for his father grew inside him like a spreading cancer, coloring and defining his whole life. Filled with an overpowering need to be accepted, most of his young life had been a grand endeavor to overcome the clinging stigma of the crimes of his father, driving him to prove that he was one of the Group, that he fit in, that he was loyal. Throwing himself into everything he did, he sought the approval of his peers and those in authority over him.

It was when he was working at the television station in Los Angeles that Steve had been notified that his father had committed suicide in prison. Upon hearing of his death, he had suddenly felt an unexpected sense of regret that he hadn't known him better, a feeling that surprised him, a feeling he was not prepared to deal with. And out of a deep need to exorcise the final demon of his father's memory, he set out on a quest to learn the circumstances surrounding his arrest and imprisonment.

By accessing the computer files and research facilities of TV9, he discovered that his father had been a member of the Restoration Party, a political party made up of people who had as their goal the restoration of the constitutional rights once enjoyed by the American people. Classified as subversive, the leaders of the Restoration Party had been arrested and imprisoned. Many had been executed. To his surprise, he discovered that his father had been one of the party leaders at the time of his arrest.

At that moment of discovery, Steve experienced his first troubling doubts about the Social Order, doubts that would gnaw away at his insides in the months and years to come. Having never questioned before, he instinctively knew they had not told the truth about his father. And he could never quite shake the uneasy feeling that his father might have been right in his political beliefs. Feeling betrayed by the Social Order, Steve had an overwhelming regret that he had not been allowed at least to listen to his father's views.

But fearing his own thoughts and doubts, he had vowed to never share them with anyone. And each time the unwelcome scenes from his troubled past had invaded his private thoughts with their unshakable persistence, he had struggled hard to close them out by throwing himself into his work with daring abandon, telling himself that he was building a better world for all humanity.

In the ensuing months after his father's arrest when Steve was a child, he watched his mother slowly sink into a dark morass of drugs and alcohol, rarely seeing her rational or sober. Tragically, one afternoon, during the winter of his eighth year, he came home from school to find her crumpled into a heap in the corner of the bathroom, dead from an overdose of drugs. Stunned by the frightening scene, it left him feeling helpless and alone in a hostile world—a feeling that still stalked him like a dog of prey.

After his mother's death, he lived for a few months in a government home and was then enrolled by the authorities in Landstar Academy, an exclusive government-run boarding school located in upstate New York, where he spent the next ten years of his life.

Not long after his arrival at Landstar, he was interviewed by a guidance counselor. As he stood in front of him, his face mirroring his apprehension, the man's cold eyes found him, held him fast as he sternly lectured him. And though Steve was a mere child at the time, the man's strict words were stamped indelibly on his memory.

Steve's face lapsed into a pained expression as the memory of the moment returned in stark, vivid detail, as real as if it were yesterday.

"You're a very bright young man," said the counselor, reviewing the printout of Steve's Comprehensive Educational and Outcomes Profile. "I can see why the authorities sent you here. You are exactly the kind of child that our program is designed to help." His eyes narrowing, he glowered at Steve, warning him sternly, "But remember, you must be careful to cooperate fully with your instructors at all times. Failure to do so could result in your being sent elsewhere, to a place not so pleasant as Landstar."

Fighting to remain rigidly still, Steve felt himself cringe reflexively, the man's words penetrating coldly through his young mental defenses.

During his years at the academy, he often felt alone and confused. At times, during his nights of intense loneliness and fear, when the room he shared with five other boys was dark and quiet, he would think of his mother, summoning her image to his mind, mentally caressing each feature of her face, striving to hold her image tightly in his fading memory. Her long flowing hair, her large brown eyes, her warm smile. But most of all he remembered her soft, soothing voice, talking to him, telling him stories, and singing children's songs to him when he was a small child.

In the secure, quiet places of his mind, at times, he could still faintly hear her soft voice telling him stories of her God, a God whom he didn't know and was not sure even existed. He remembered, in bits and pieces, the way she told him strange and exciting stories of an angel who rebelled in heaven and was cast out, and about God coming to the earth and living as a man.

Almost totally erased from his memory now, the concept of his mother's God was lodged somewhere in the faint borders of his mind. Her words, though meaningless to him now, when recalled, always brought him a strange sense of peace and made him feel close to her once again.

And in this private moment, as he looked out over the Great Hall of Unity, the words and melody of her songs came drifting softly back to him from across the years. He dared not move as they came, unbeckoned, from the outer rims of his subconscious mind, forcing out the tormenting demons, taking him back to his childhood, reminding him of the carefree days when he lived with her in a world of total love and security.

Lost in deep thought, Steve was startled when a technician walked up behind him and tapped him gently on the shoulder. He turned to face a young Japanese woman. She was a short, rather plump woman with dark black hair and dark eyes.

When Steve smiled at her, her cheeks began to redden slightly. With a faint smile on her face, she said, "Mr. Weston, may I put your microphone on for you?"

Steve nodded. "Sure. I almost forgot it."

When she had pinned the small cordless microphone onto the left lapel of his coat, she smiled shyly and walked away. Once the mike was secured, an engineer in the control room asked Steve to speak a few words. After taking a voiceprint, the tiny SensiMike was programmed to respond only to Steve's voice, totally eliminating feedback.

"Ten minutes to airtime, Mr. Weston," the floor director told him.

One of the TV9 producers, a young British girl, handed Steve a cup of coffee. He smiled, thanked her, and turned back to the glass wall. Staring reflectively out across the auditorium, he slowly sipped the hot coffee. Feeling the mounting pressure of the scheduled global telecast, he consciously reined in his wandering thoughts and focused intently on the task ahead, formulating in his mind how he would guide the telecast, visualizing what he would do and say.

He took a long, deep breath and exhaled slowly.

The cold determination that had carried him through many tough assignments before quickly reasserted itself, preparing him to face this challenge with a sharp mind and steady nerves. Consciously pushing back the dark thoughts, he felt his churning emotions smooth out, making him ready to face the TV9 cameras. Enthralled by the dazzling fusion of power, personalities, world communications, and global politics that were all concentrated in this one place, Steve was suddenly anxious to get things under way.

Sipping the last drop of the coffee, he tossed the paper cup into a trash can, turned, and moved with steady resolve toward his anchor's chair and his worldwide audience.

Touching Audrey's shoulder lightly as he passed, Steve pulled back his own chair and sat down beside her. Audrey turned her head, looked at him, and smiled. When he had settled in, the lights above them increased in intensity—not much, just enough to brush away the shadows from their faces.

While carrying on small talk with Audrey, the makeup lady blotted his face lightly, then put some finishing touches on Audrey's hair.

"All set, Audrey?" Steve asked.

"All set," she answered in her pleasing alto voice.

"Well, let's do it just like we rehearsed it," he answered without looking at her.

Audrey glanced up at him. They both laughed, knowing that Steve never rehearsed.

"Six minutes to air, Mr. Weston," the floor director called out.

Steve scanned the three monitors recessed into the table in front of him. Monitor one displayed a wide shot of the crowd in the Great Hall. Monitor two was showing a series of closeups of the faces in the audience. The face of a TV9 reporter positioned at the back of the Great Hall filled monitor three.

The tension in the studio mounted as the countdown to airtime progressed.

"Five minutes, Mr. Weston."

Steve scanned some papers on the table, then glanced out through the glass wall. There was an air of nervous excitement rippling through the Great Hall as the audience fidgeted in their chairs, waiting anxiously for a glimpse of the most powerful man on earth.

Steve's gaze swept across the Great Hall, measuring the crowd. The entire scene reminded him of the fact that this upcoming television broadcast would be seen by more people than any other telecast in human history. And that it was all made possible by the convergence of satellites and advanced computer-driven telecommunications technologies.

Just a few hundred yards from where Steve was sitting, on the southwest quadrant of the Global Village compound, was a series of heavily guarded multistoried buildings that were the focal point of operations of the powerful Unified Information and Communications Authority, the parent organization to TV9.

One of the buildings in the UICA compound was the European headquarters of SNN, where, at that moment, hundreds of skilled engineers and technicians were busily entering data into the massive computers, making last-minute corrections, calibrating, and fine-tuning the world's most sophisticated, ultrasecret telecommunications equipment.

Through enhanced digital technology, the Secretary General's image and words would be magically beamed to an array of powerful geosynchronous satellites that encircled the earth in a seamless band. Billions of people would see him in ultra-high definition, three-dimensional clarity on thin, wall-mounted viewscreens—his image so clear that he would appear to be standing in the same room with the people who were viewing. It would all happen at the speed of light.

This computerized telecommunications wizardry had given the world leaders such unprecedented power and control over the flow of information that with a push of a button, all programming on all channels throughout the world would be automatically preempted for this one event, guaranteeing total coverage.

Steve suddenly felt a surge of exhilaration, knowing that he was at the center of the universe, with all the people of the world about to look at his face. At this precise moment, all the scientific advances ever made in communications technology had merged together for this one telecast. It was a heady feeling.

"Three minutes, Mr. Weston."

Steve adjusted his stylish tie and took a sip of water. Audrey straightened her shoulders and looked straight into the camera.

One minute before airtime, a holographic image of their script suddenly appeared in large, clear type, suspended in midair about four feet away, between them and the TV cameras. Invisible to everyone else, the Eye Tracking Prompter system allowed the anchors to look directly into the cameras while reading their lines.

With his easygoing manner, his pleasant baritone voice, and gracious smile, Steve Weston was a master at reading a script. He made it sound like no more than a friendly, off-the-cuff chat between two friends. Always relaxed, he had the ability to set everyone at ease.

But his greatest asset was that the people believed him.

"Ten seconds!" the floor director called out, picking up the count with his fingers.

The studio became deathly quiet.

"Five . . . four . . . three . . . two—"

With a quick motion, the floor director pointed to Steve as the red light on camera one flashed on.

STEVE: Hello everyone, I'm Steve Weston.

AUDREY: And I'm Audrey Montaigne.

STEVE: We want to welcome you to Geneva, Switzerland. The newly elected Secretary General of the New Earth Federation was inaugurated in a ceremony earlier today. In just a few minutes, he will be making his first public appearance to a global audience. Audrey and I are in the TV9 broadcast booth overlooking the Great Hall of Unity, here in Global Village. Audrey tells me that celebrations have been going on all week.

AUDREY: That's right, Steve. Geneva has been host to leaders from all over the world. Much of the time has been spent in work, but there has been time for celebration, too.

Steve and Audrey glanced down at the monitors recessed in the table in front of them. The video disk was rolling, showing her report on one of the celebration balls at a luxury hotel in Geneva. It included several interviews with members of the Congress of the People. The piece ran for four minutes, eighteen seconds.

STEVE: Thanks, Audrey. Since the New Earth Federation was founded in 2023, just ten years ago, the world has been brought closer to the dream of global peace and harmony, a world of safety and prosperity for all people. For a look at some of the milestones in this noble pursuit, here is TV9's Ravi Savarin.

Savarin's report ran for three minutes and fifty-one seconds. It featured scenes of battles fought by the Global Peace Forces and film footage of NEF jet fighters and bombers. There was a shot of a scientific crew at work on an orbiting space station, followed by a visit to a hospital, showing the advanced medical care provided by the NEF's international health-care system.

The floor director called out, "Coming to you, Ms. Montaigne. In three . . . two . . ."

The director dropped his hand.

AUDREY: Steve, it looks like they may be ready to begin the opening ceremonies. First, an honor guard will present the colors. That will be followed by a group of children from around the world who will lead the audience in the Pledge to the Earth Flag.

STEVE: Let's watch.

As Steve and Audrey turned to look through the glass wall, camera six, stationed near the front, drew in tight on the center door at the back of the auditorium. Three soldiers, two men and a woman, representing the New Earth Federation Global Forces, appeared in the door. Dressed in their light green uniforms, dark green berets, white gloves, and white belts, their polished dark green combat boots struck the shining hardwood floor with resounding authority, their cadence echoing loudly throughout the chamber. Upon reaching the platform, they climbed the stairs, marched to the center of the stage, and turned to face the audience.

The soldier in the center, a tall, slender young man from Canada, holding the Earth flag, stepped forward one step. The large flag was white, with gold braid around the edges. A blue-and-green earth was positioned in the center, suspended in a sphere of white. Below the earth, emblazoned in dark green letters against the white background, were the words:

ONE EARTH * ONE PEOPLE * ONE SPIRIT

Standing rigidly at attention, the military detail waited as three hundred boys and girls, representing the children of the earth, marched in from each side of the platform and positioned themselves in neat rows behind the flag. Dressed in their green-and-blue uniforms of the Order of the Guardians of the Earth, they stood at attention, awaiting the signal from their teacher to begin.

The audience stood.

A short, slightly overweight lady, standing to the left of the children, smiled at them and placed her right hand over her heart. The children responded by placing their right hands over their hearts.

The teacher nodded her head and three hundred child voices spoke as one.

"I pledge Allegiance to the flag of the New Earth Federation and to the One Earth, One People, and One Spirit that it represents. I pledge to honor and revere the Earth, to live in harmony with Her, and to protect Her from all Her enemies."

The entire audience erupted in applause, roaring their approval. Slightly unnerved by all the attention, the children hurriedly exited from the platform. The cameras followed them.

"Coming back to you, Mr. Weston." The floor director held his hand next to camera one, dropping it in a swift motion as the camera light came on.

AUDREY: I was impressed with the preparation and discipline of those children, Steve. That was quite a presentation.

STEVE: Indeed it was, Audrey. It looks like the General Secretary is about to make his appearance. There seems to be some renewed activity throughout the Hall. I see some additional guards coming in. As a precautionary measure, of course.

AUDREY: According to the program, the introduction of the General Secretary is going to be made by Dr. Friedrich Schenck. I think he's ready, so let's switch to the platform for the introduction.

Steve and Audrey swiveled their chairs around a quarter of a turn to the left and looked out through the glass wall toward the stage. Two giant, three-dimensional television wallscreens hung against the wall behind the platform, one on each side.

Walking slowly to the center of the platform, Dr. Schenck cleared his throat, then intoned, "Members of the Congress of the People, members of the World Council for Security and Cooperation, ladies and gentlemen present in this Great Hall of Unity, and all peoples of the earth. It is my high honor to introduce His Excellency, the World Leader, the Secretary General of the New Earth Federation."

Instantly, all eyes focused on two military guards standing rigidly at attention at the rear of the platform. Next to them, huge, ornate double doors suddenly opened, swinging ponderously inward, revealing a long, wide hallway covered with a luxurious deep red carpet. The guards continued to stand at attention as three spotlights suddenly came alive, flooding across the massive doors and empty hallway, bathing them in a magically iridescent prism of brilliant light.

With camera three framing the double doors for the world audience, Steve and Audrey stood and walked to the glass wall of the booth.

When a figure appeared at the far end of the hallway, TV9's cameras locked on him and followed him as he walked through the open doors, staying with him as he slowly climbed the stairs onto the massive platform. Moving steadily forward across the platform, the enigmatic figure carried himself with a distinct military bearing, his head erect, his frame ramrod straight.

Spontaneously, as a single body, in hypnotic unity, the audience stood to its feet, their faces registering undisguised awe and reverence. Standing rooted in silence, the assembled guests inside the Great Hall stared at the forbidding figure with mystic veneration, their minds numbed into an illogical mixture of adoration and cold apprehension, bordering on fear.

His long, white robe rippled gracefully with each measured step, brushing lightly against the brilliantly polished floor as he moved commandingly to center stage. A splendid white satin sash was tied loosely around his slim waist, falling around luxurious white sandals. His long, dark brown hair was parted in the middle and flowed smoothly downward, lying gently, elegantly, against his broad shoulders. He appeared to be in his mid-forties and his face was pleasant, his jaw square.

He was the second man to hold the office of Secretary General of the New Earth Federation during its ten-year existence. The first Secretary General had met an untimely death only weeks before when his personal plane had mysteriously exploded over the Atlantic Ocean during a return trip to Geneva from New York City.

Following the death of the previous Secretary General, this man was elected by a unanimous vote of the Council of 100. It had been rumored that even though the NEF had been moving forward, the pace had not been to the liking of many in high positions of leadership. Known as a brilliant military strategist, an economic genius, and a devoted spiritual leader, he was given a mandate to bring the world into unity, by whatever means necessary. With such personal magnetism and power, they were convinced that he could lead the global body to new greatness.

The TV9 cameras followed the Secretary General as he moved a few steps forward at the center of the empty stage, in full view of those in the auditorium and those viewing television around the world.

An audible hush settled over the Great Hall.

Standing in dramatic silence for a long moment, his eyes swept slowly, purposefully across the audience.

A deathly quiet tightened ominously over the Great Hall.

No one moved.

Steve looked at the man thoughtfully, trying to penetrate the mask of inscrutability that cloaked his features. There was a presence about him that made Steve uneasy. He didn't know what it was, but it was there, something indescribable. And when he studied a closeup shot of his face on the giant wallscreen to the right of the platform, his dark, piercing eyes caused Steve to shudder.

The World Leader lifted his arms in a slow, dramatic movement and motioned for the people to be seated.

They instantly obeyed.

"Citizens of Earth," he began.

His voice was a strong baritone, his enunciation perfect, his inflections and tonal qualities those of a trained actor, sharp and crisp.

"What past generations have failed to do, we are accomplishing through global *cooperation*. Through cooperation, we are creating a new global order. . . .

"A new economic order . . .

"A new system of commerce and trade . . .

"A new communications environment connecting all the peoples of the world."

Spontaneous applause.

The World Leader stepped forward a few steps, head slightly bowed, his hands clasped loosely behind his back, as if in a contemplative mood.

"We are bringing the world together as one. . . ." he announced.

Wide, sweeping gesture.

"One people . . .

"One spirituality . . .

"One earth . . ."

Thunderous applause.

He paused suddenly. Everyone froze, their eyes locked into the steady gaze of the man on stage. Moments of total silence passed ominously slow. His well-groomed hands held prayerfully at his chest, he raised his eyes to the center camera, his penetrating stare holding his global audience in their tight embrace. Speaking barely above a whisper, he intoned, "There have been noble efforts in the past to bring about a unified world, but all have failed. The League of Nations, with its headquarters in this very city, was an admirable effort . . . but the world was not ready. So it failed."

The World Leader again paused, measuring the force of his words.

"The United Nations," he announced boldly, "another progressive and courageous plan for global interdependence, failed because it attempted to unite the world through monetary and military might alone."

A broad gesture over the adoring audience.

"These efforts were followed by the international democratic socialist movement in the early part of the twenty-first century which paved the way for the birth of the new global government . . . the New Earth Federation."

At this first pronouncement of the name of the New Earth Federation by the Secretary General, the people in the Great Hall leaped to their feet in thunderous, raucous approval. The TV9 cameras panned the audience, showing their animated reactions to the emotionally charged words, sending the dramatic pictures to a worldwide viewing audience.

A dark uneasiness stirred inside Steve as he pondered the impenetrable veil of mystery in which this man had so carefully wrapped himself.

As camera three moved in for a tight head-and-shoulders shot of the Secretary General, his face loomed large on every viewscreen throughout the world.

Basking in the roaring approval of his audience, he folded his arms across his chest, jutting his chin forward and nodding his head repeatedly in approval.

The demonstration continued unabated for a full six minutes. With the applause fading, he gazed out across the auditorium, glancing briefly at the TV cameras. Confident that all eyes were upon him, he continued.

"All those earlier attempts at global governance failed because the leaders were deluded into believing that the unifying bond of humankind was economic."

Pause. "They were wrong!" he shouted.

"That which binds us is not economic . . .

"Or political . . .

"That which binds us is not nations, or family, or race.

"The Force that binds the people of Earth into one people, is our common *spirituality!*"

Applause for six minutes.

"We know that the world must become one *spiritually* . . ." he intoned.

"Then it will become one economically and politically. A global order cannot be sustained without a *global spirituality.*"

Resounding applause.

His arms suddenly outstretched, the speaker declared loudly, forcefully, "The Earth is *Gaia*, our Mother, the divine center and eternal source of all life. Our reverence and awe for Gaia is what binds us together as a unified world."

Thunderous applause for a full eight minutes.

Signaling for quiet and order, the Secretary General declared with emotion, "The central organizing principle for humankind is the Earth, our Mother. This new Planetary Consciousness is prevailing, releasing a new spiritual force that transcends old religious, cultural, and national boundaries, and is being directed toward the solutions to the world's problems."

His voice rising in intensity, he declared, "We stand on the threshold of a quantum leap forward in the ever upward spiral of humanity's evolution."

Sustained applause.

As the applause faded to a heavy silence, it seemed to Steve that the Secretary General's facial expression and demeanor suddenly changed, taking on a darker hue. His brow had furrowed; his lips had tightened. When he resumed speaking, it seemed that his voice had become thin, threatening. Steve paid renewed attention to his words.

"Citizens of Earth!" he cried, looking sternly into the eye of the center camera.

"Sadly, there are those in our world who are holding back humanity's evolutionary leap into godhood. They are the 'Negative Mass.'"

"Because they are standing in the way of global unity, we must allow them to pass into spirit."

Loud applause for two minutes.

Pausing for full dramatic effect, the World Leader gazed straight ahead for a moment, his eyes glaring with a strange ferocity.

The audience did not move.

His voice dropping again to a whisper, he said, "In Her wisdom, Gaia maintains the perfect balance throughout all of nature. Intolerant of those who transgress Her laws, She cries out to be restored to

Her original state when She willingly gave of Her bounty, and the human species lived in total harmony with the rest of nature."

Stone silence.

In a voice approaching a low guttural growl, he hissed angrily, "But we have scarred Her face with our factories, our waste, our pollution, our excessive breeding, our overconsumption, our wars, our nuclear explosions, and our greed. We have not respected the sacredness of Her systems."

Sustained and prolonged applause.

Glaring into the cameras, his mesmerizing stare holding his global audience in a paralyzing spell, the World Leader thrust his arms boldly upward and shouted in a high-pitched voice, "Citizens of the new global order, we face very difficult choices. If we do not address these issues quickly, we will experience worldwide chaos.

"Gaia is poised to take vengeance upon us through disease, famines, earthquakes, ecological convulsions, and other forms of disaster. . . ."

His grim features lined with seething anger, he cried aloud in prophetic frenzy, "We must help Gaia to heal Herself!"

His burning gaze swept the Great Hall threateningly. His terrifying eyes reflecting a dark rage beyond reason or pity, he raised his voice and rasped loudly, "And now, citizens of the world, listen to me. The Earth is about to enter into a time of cleansing. The diseased parts will be cast off."

He paused suddenly, abruptly.

His face dark and menacing, the World Leader declared with shattering force, shouting loudly, "Our mission is to *save the Earth!*"

The people leaped to their feet, roaring their approval, their voices rising in an exuberant swell, the roar becoming a rhythmic chant, *"Save the Earth. . . . Save the Earth. . . . Save the Earth. . . ."*

The rhythmic, pounding pattern of the rising, building chant swelled in shuddering echoes, sending many inside the Great Hall into a fervent, emotional frenzy.

Staring at the man on stage, Steve wondered at his strange and unexplainable powers. With a voice that was at times as soothing and as beguiling as the softness of a sunrise, he was painting word pictures of a final battle between man and nature, describing it as an ecological disaster that could possibly sweep humankind away.

And with his image being carried across the world by their communications satellites, he was no doubt molding the thoughts of billions of people with his strange electronic alchemy.

Yet, Steve mused, *the man could be right.*

The Secretary General stood tall and erect, waiting.

Then with an expansive dramatic sweep of his robed arms, he motioned for the audience to be seated. Slowly, the chanting withered to a soft murmur. And when the Secretary General resumed, Steve thought he could detect another change in his demeanor. Gone were the glaring eyes, the furrowed brow, the angry tone.

Lowering his voice, the man on stage stretched out his arms, his palms upturned.

He spoke slowly, deliberately.

"Through our shamans, mystics, gurus, and transchannelers, the Ascended Masters have communicated to us that Mother Earth is groaning under the weight of our overpopulation. The population of the Earth must be reduced to a sustainable level."

With expansive gestures of his arms, he thundered, "Hear me! Gaia is calling for an 'Earth Cleansing' to remove those who do not choose the spiritual path. We must act quickly to appease Her."

After a brief pause, he announced with solemn words, "The Ascended Masters remind us that every person who is part of the Negative Mass is scarred through centuries of negative thoughts and deeds. They have built up a karmic indebtedness that they must work out.

"Through suffering they will attain a higher evolution of the soul and will be passed to another plane of existence, to be reborn into new life-cycles until such time as they perfect themselves.

"We will be doing them a great honor by setting them free. And those who are permitted to live in this purified Earth will be those of the New Species of humankind."

Then with a wide sweep of his arms, the white sleeves of his robe rippling, the Secretary General looked into the TV9 camera positioned at the center of the first balcony and cried out with a loud voice, *"Gaia is the Earth!"*

Applause.
"Gaia is our Mother!"
Applause.
"Gaia is our God!"
Roaring applause.
"Join us, peoples of the Earth!"

The building erupted instantaneously. The thunderous applause and sudden upsurge of wild cheering rose in intensity, exploding into a jarring crescendo of united euphoria, filling the Great Hall with unrelenting waves of ecstatic shouts of praise and adoration.

Caught up, the people seemed to lose control of their emotions, shouting, waving their arms in the air, dancing in the aisles, embracing each other, and weeping uncontrollably in response to his words and his presence.

Standing at the glass wall, his arms folded, Steve stared out at the people. Troubled, he tried to follow the logic of the man's words. Struggling against his own doubts, he returned to his anchor's chair, sat down, and rested his elbows on the table. Glancing down at table monitor two, he studied the somber face of the man on center stage and pondered his grim prophecies of what the people of the world might face.

Feeling himself becoming deeply disturbed by it all, he wondered why the Secretary General hadn't flaunted the military might of the Global Forces. Or why he hadn't paraded the latest in military hardware.

But the most puzzling part was his emphasis on the religious and spiritual.

An excited voice spoke into Steve's earphone. "Mr. Weston, look at table monitor three. Something is happening outside the Great Hall. Sir, we don't know what it is."

Steve instantly glanced at the monitor. What he saw chilled his bones. An outside camera was following the rapid descent of a large column of fire hurtling downward out of the clear sky above the Great Hall. Mesmerized by the phenomenon, Steve and Audrey stared at the monitor as the outside camera tracked the fiery mass until it abruptly penetrated the roof of the New Earth Federation building.

Steve and Audrey quickly looked away from the monitor and out through the glass wall, seeing the fire rush through the ceiling into the Great Hall with a sound like a strong blast of wind, a heavy *whoosh!*

Audrey gasped out loud.

Stunned, no one spoke, each one frozen in surprise and fear.

Once inside the Hall, the round column of fire descended slowly, filling the room with a dazzling light. As it descended, the sound steadily grew in intensity, building into a low, rumbling roar like the sound of a thousand winds bound together in their strong fury. With disbelieving stares riveted on the awesome spectacle, the people raised their hands in front of their eyes, trying to shield them from the penetrating brightness.

At least twenty feet in diameter, the mysterious, churning inferno inched downward, stretching through the high ceiling, passing through the void above the floor of the Hall, stopping within inches of the floor, no more than ten feet behind the lone figure standing on the platform. Reaching from the floor upward to the high ceiling, the undulating mass of fire seemed as if it were going to consume him.

Above the rising pandemonium that had broken out inside the TV9 booth, Audrey cried out and leaped to her feet, sending her chair flying, and ran frantically across the room to the glass wall. Near hysteria, she pressed her palms hard against the glass and stared in openmouthed wonderment at the scene unfolding on the stage.

Startled, Steve stood and followed her.

By now, the entire crew, stunned by what was happening, was pressed up against the glass, not believing what their eyes were seeing.

With the inferno raging furiously, threateningly, behind him, the World Leader stood motionless at center stage, suddenly enveloped in a thick, swirling mist of prismatic brightness, his body a shining, lonely silhouette against the dazzling profusion of light that surrounded and held him.

With the large sleeves of his white robe flowing downward from his outstretched arms, his face was turned upward, trancelike, a solitary figure, his entire person bathed in a mystic white light.

Glancing up at the wallscreen inside the studio, Steve saw that the TV9 cameras were showing a split screen of four different shots of the spectacular scenes in the Hall.

The top left quadrant showed the Secretary General.

The bottom left quadrant was a long-distance shot of the column of fire extending beyond the roof line of the New Earth Federation building upward to the base of the clouds.

The third quadrant was a wide shot inside the Hall.

The fourth quadrant was filled with a tight shot of the face of an elderly man looking up at the World Leader. He was weeping.

Someone in the booth shouted, "Was this scheduled?"

Steve answered, "I knew nothing about it."

Suddenly, the audience echoed a collective gasp at the sight of the Secretary General slowly rising off the floor, inching steadily upward. One foot . . . ten feet . . . thirty feet . . . rising . . . rising.

Enraptured, the people in the Great Hall of Unity began to chant, calling on the unseen powers of the universe. Blending as one, the roar of chanted mantras swelled throughout the Hall, rising like a torrent, increasing in intensity as the lone figure ascended higher and higher into the void above the platform until the Great Hall was filled with a tidal wave of mystic sounds.

Three stories below the Great Hall, the director for the Sky News Network, shouted to his cameramen, "Camera one and camera four, follow the Secretary General. Camera six and camera eight, bracket some faces in the audience, tight shots. I want reactions. Outside cameras ten and twelve and thirteen, I want you to give me different angles on the column of fire. I don't know what's going on, but I want the world to see it."

With a profound mixture of expectation and uneasiness rippling through the Great Hall, the people watched the resplendent figure ascend halfway to the ceiling. Gripped in invisible hands, his upward movement stopped in midair and he remained motionless, floating there, suspended in space in seeming defiance of gravity.

His hands outstretched dramatically, the sleeves of his robe rising and falling in a soft rustle of cloth, his face was frozen in an expression of deep meditation.

A nervous hush filled the vast room.

Mesmerized by the phenomenon, their reverence for the World Leader was mingled inseparably with curiosity and fear as mysterious streaks of brilliant light and color lanced magically throughout the Great Hall like living spirits, touching the people, moving on.

Golden beams and intense white lights, like fragmented rays of the rainbow, streaked back and forth around the shining figure, who hovered like a holy apparition high above their heads.

His whole person glowed with a diffusing luminescence that moved in and through him. Shards of mysterious light were shooting outward from his body, exploding around him in surreal, shimmering bursts.

Eyes narrowing in speculation, a dark foreboding caused Steve to shudder involuntarily. His expression tightened as an uneasiness stirred inside him, vague, indefinable, causing him to step back and take a long, slow, steadying breath.

Steve glanced upward at the unsettling scene. High above him, churning like a mystic cauldron, the raging column of fire stretched from floor to ceiling, roiling threateningly behind the World Leader. Basking in the fire's shimmering light, the beaming, hovering figure was encased inside a mystical, incandescent sphere of light that was growing steadily brighter and brighter.

The people stared upward, partly afraid, partly mystified, as a hushed, breathless silence lay heavy across the Great Hall of Unity. Mesmerized by the amazing display of psychic power, the people tried to shield their eyes from the penetrating light.

The floor director rushed to the anchor's table, excited and highly animated. "Mr. Weston, there's another unusual development."

"What's that?" Steve asked.

The director swallowed hard. "Sir, some of our TV9 people stationed around the world are telling us that the Secretary General is appearing in the sky over their cities. We'll send you some of the backhaul feeds on monitor four."

Turning their attention to monitor four, Steve and Audrey were startled at the sight of the image of the Secretary General in midair over Berlin, Germany. An excited voice was saying, "This is spectacular, Geneva. The Secretary General has appeared over this city. He seems to be about five hundred feet in the air. People have come outside to see him. You can't believe the people's reactions. They're in total awe."

Steve heard the director bark, "Keep the pictures coming, Berlin. We'll be coming back to you."

For the next several minutes, Steve and Audrey watched a parade of video images pass across their monitors, showing live shots of spellbound people around the world, gazing up into the sky at the glowing three-dimensional image of the Secretary General hovering in the air over their cities.

An electrifying event, TV9 correspondents excitedly reported seeing him in the air above the cities of Rome, Johannesburg, Cairo, Baghdad, and Tokyo.

In scenes vivid and unforgettable, Steve and Audrey watched the parade of live shots of the Secretary General's image hovering dramatically above a church in downtown New York City, above a mountain overlooking Rio, and above the Church of the Holy Sepulcher in Jerusalem.

TV9 reporters from around the world reported that at the moment of the World Leader's spectacular appearances in the sky and on the viewscreens around the world, millions of people had reached a frenzied, mystic, emotional peak.

In the wake of the event, psychic manifestations occurred in great number, with millions experiencing various altered states of consciousness. Some lapsed into hypnotic trances, while others frantically chanted their mantras. A significant number had out-of-body experiences, millions were frightened, and a large number went insane.

After hovering in the air above the platform in the Great Hall for sixteen minutes, the white-robed man began to descend slowly.

An immediate hush swept across the audience.

Conversation died among the audience as a heavy silence settled over the Great Hall. Sudden panic assailed some, shattering their composure and sending them into a mindless frenzy at the manifestation. Large numbers bolted from the Hall, fleeing in morbid terror.

Descending slowly, his white robe gently rippling around his rigid body, the World Leader's feet touched the floor. Standing perfectly still, his hands were still outstretched, his haunting eyes sweeping across the audience.

Held motionless by his baleful stare, the people stared blankly in uneasy submission as he slowly closed his eyes.

Behind him, the raging column of fire began to retreat slowly, grudgingly, upward toward the high ceiling of the Great Hall.

Staring wordlessly, the audience watched in fascination as the frenzied, angry cloud of fire inched inexorably upward. Shimmering in its brilliance, the mystical manifestation of fire dissolved through the high ceiling, disappearing in the blink of an eye before their astonished gaze.

Once the fire had fully retreated, everyone in the Great Hall quickly turned their gaze to the wallscreens above the platform. TV9 cameras followed the mass of fire as it rose above the New Earth Federation building into the clear air.

Without warning, suddenly, like the launching of a fiery rocket, it shot straight upward into the sky above the building, passing through the scattered clouds, and disappearing into infinity.

The TV9 cameras continued to search the empty sky, but it was gone.

Those inside the Hall quickly turned their attention back to the World Leader just in time to see him lower his hands, clasp them in front of his chest, and bow. Without speaking another word, he turned and walked off the platform, down the stairs, and out through the large double doors, his body still glowing with a white brilliance.

When the doors closed, the Great Hall of Unity was immediately flooded with the sounds of synthesized Eastern mystical music—loud, vibrating, mesmerizing. With the pulsating sounds rising in intensity, many of the members of the Congress and scores of people in the Hall were thrust headlong into a variety of mystical experiences. Their bodies swaying to the rhythmic cadence flooding the Hall, scores were caught up in a wild, frantic, euphoric rush.

Strangely detached from it all, Steve stood at the glass wall, watching the unusual scenes playing out in the Great Hall, wondering if these people had, somehow, contacted the mind of God or were merely being consumed by their own delusions. Or, perhaps, they were acting out strange, ancient, mythic realities. Either way, there was something forbidding about the spectacle, causing him to shudder inside, unable to escape the gnawing feeling that everything that was occurring here today was only a profound evil hiding within a sinister lie, a deadly hoax.

Suddenly, fear and guilt thrashed at him for doubting.

Anxiously looking around, he reminded himself that he had to be watchful so that nothing would betray his thoughts. He hid his mounting disbelief and revulsion behind a stony, expressionless mask, returned to the anchor's table, and sat down next to Audrey.

While following a scene on one of the table monitors, he heard Audrey moan softly. Turning toward her, he was startled to see that her face had turned ashen, drained of color. Her eyes set in a haunting, fixed stare, her body shuddered and swayed. Reaching out, he placed his right arm around her shoulders and held her steady. Her body now trembled uncontrollably under his grasp; she would have collapsed to the floor if he hadn't braced her.

On the verge of hysteria, her glassy eyes fixed on the empty space on the stage where the World Leader had stood moments before, she muttered almost incoherently, "He's God. . . . I've seen God. . . . I must go to him. . . ."

The floor director was carefully watching Steve and Audrey. Concerned that Audrey had become ill, he walked to the anchor's desk and suggested to Steve that they take a break, assuring him that he would cover for them by panning the faces in the auditorium for a few minutes.

Nodding to the director, Steve gently steadied Audrey, helped her up, and guided her to the couch in the corner of the TV booth, where they both sat down.

Still steadying her with his right arm, he reached out his left hand, touched her face, and turned it toward him. When Steve gazed deeply into the emptiness in her eyes, his blood turned cold. Her large, green eyes were wide and blinking at him uncertainly. Her face was blank, expressionless.

She had sunk into a trancelike state that seemed to be deepening.

Suddenly, as if an unseen hand were pulling her, Audrey clambered unsteadily to her feet to walk out of the booth in search of the mysterious man she had just seen call fire from out of a clear sky. Steve restrained her gently, not allowing her to leave the booth.

Her eyes in a glazed stare, her voice rising to a point of desperation, she insisted loudly, "I've got to go. I've got to go to him."

"Just take it easy, Audrey," Steve coaxed.

"He's God. I must go to him," she responded in a drab, monotone voice, sweat beading her pale forehead.

Grasping her shoulders firmly, Steve pushed her forcefully back down to the couch and restrained her. Struggling against his tight grip, she slowly turned and looked directly at him, staring at his face in bewilderment as if he were a total stranger, her own face an unreadable mask. Remaining rigid, she regarded him without expression, emotionless, as if she were gripped in the force of an unbreakable hypnotic state.

Steve felt a chill run through his body. A strange sense of dread clutched him in its icy grip. He tried to give definition to the strange power that he faced, to trace its origin, but failed. How could he fight something that defied explanation?

A darkness stirred inside him, vague and ill-defined.

Steve stared steadily into her blank eyes with rising concern, uneasiness turning suddenly into a certainty. She was under some alien force. The mysterious man on the stage had somehow reached out with his dark, cabalistic powers and had robbed Audrey of her mind and, perhaps, her soul.

Shaking his head in stunned disbelief, his mind searched desperately for answers that would not come. Swallowing hard against his fear, a sense of helplessness swept across him as he faced the chilling presence of something that no logic could explain. Ancient and evil and deadly, the malevolent presence permeated the very air in the Great Hall and in this studio.

Tears burned Steve's eyes as he watched her unyielding trance deepen. He was helpless against its insidious power. Knowing that she was slipping away, a primal stirring of anger, bordering on rage, exploded through him, filling him with a fiery resolve. He would not let her go, he silently vowed. He would not lose her to this malevolent force.

In sheer desperation, he abruptly gripped her shoulders and shook her roughly. "Audrey!" he called out in mounting desperation, staring fearfully into her lifeless eyes. "Snap out of it!" It was a command, his voice firm and insistent.

Moments passed.

Suddenly blinking her eyes in surprise, Audrey gasped deeply and stared at Steve, a quizzical look on her face. Her cheeks flushed pink, and she brushed them softly with the palms of her hands.

"I feel so tired, Steve. . . ." she whispered, her voice trailing off.

Steve felt a wave of relief when he saw tears slowly roll down her cheeks. He gently touched her face and brushed them away.

Her senses still dulled from the experience, she looked around in bewilderment. "I feel . . . so strange," she said hesitantly. "What . . . am I doing here on the couch? Is the telecast over?"

Handing her a cup of water, he said, "Drink this. It'll make you feel better. You just got a little faint, so I brought you over here for a moment."

Audrey drank the water slowly, took a few deep breaths, her eyes still reflecting her confusion. Steve studied her, watching as the color started to come back into her face. She was obviously feeling better.

"I'm sorry, Steve," she said, looking into his eyes and smiling faintly. Glancing around the studio, she whispered, "I don't know what happened." She ran her fingers lightly through her hair and sighed. "I think I'm under control now."

Smiling reassuringly, Steve nodded toward the anchor's desk and said, "Now, let's get back to work." Standing to his feet, he reached down and helped her to stand. They then walked back to the anchors' desk together and took their seats.

Resting his elbows on the table, Steve glanced out through the glass wall. The audience was still in various stages of shock, euphoria, and religious excitement. Some of the members of the Congress were now sitting on top of their desks, their bare feet tucked under their legs, their wrists resting limply on their knees, palms up, eyes closed. Shut out from the rest of the world, they were frantically humming their secret mantras.

The throbbing sounds of flutes, drums, gourds, gongs, and rattles, accompanied by the vibrating sounds of the mystic word *aum* filled the Great Hall, rising in intensity as the people chanted, swayed, and communed with the gods of the sky, the sea, the earth.

Rhythmically rising and falling, the pulsating, vibrating sounds *ohm rah, ohm hah* spread outward like a torrent as members of the audience made contact with unseen spirit entities. Dozens had assumed the fetal position, while others writhed uncontrollably on the floor, a bristling mass of jerking, thrashing bodies.

The sounds inside the Great Hall rose to deafening proportions. Human voices swelled to a feverish pitch, screeching violently, their strident sounds echoing and reechoing throughout the luxurious auditorium, reverberating endlessly. Untamed loud shrieks and howls blended together in a feral chorus, causing Steve to sense a feeling of unreality. It seemed that the people in the Hall had been thrust backward in time, lost in the frenzy of an ancient pagan ritual that had in a past age celebrated the sacrifice of human beings to the dark gods who ruled their minds and their fears.

Hundreds on the main floor and in the balconies lay sprawled on the floor, while others had fallen to their knees and were still worshiping the departed World Leader.

"Mr. Weston!"

Steve looked up. It was the floor director.

"We'll be coming back to you in about forty-five seconds. Stand by, please."

Steve adjusted the small cordless earpiece in his left ear.

Audrey took a deep breath.

"We'll be coming to you in ten seconds. . . . Five . . . four . . . three . . . two . . ." Quick jab. Red light on camera one.

Steve smiled into the camera. "Now, we're going to take you to various parts of the globe for statements and interviews with some of the world's leaders in government, education, religion, business, the military, as well as some ordinary people like you and me."

Camera two opened on Audrey. "We're going to start in Dublin, Ireland. TV9's Margo Lindsey is standing by. Margo?"

For the next hour Steve and Audrey moved in and out of interviews with people from various parts of the world. Steve was fascinated at their reactions and interpretations of the day's events.

A schoolteacher in Phoenix, Arizona, told the global audience, "I've been filled with love and light."

A professor of economics at the University of London testified,

"I've just gone through a great spiritual enlightenment. This man has shown us that we are all gods."

A stockbroker in Rome, Italy, declared, "He has come to unify the world and to bring us together in one great spirituality. We are approaching global synchronicity."

An industrialist in Berlin, Germany, added, "He is teaching us to cast aside our Western logic and reasoning and enter into the esoteric teachings of the Ascended Masters."

Some called the event the Harmonic Convergence. Others said it was the revelation of the Christ. Some said the Secretary General was the Fifth Reincarnation of the Buddha. Others claimed he was the Messiah, or Krishna, or an Avatar.

The pastor of a large downtown church in New York City explained, "He is obviously one of the Ascended Masters who watch over us. From time to time one of them will appear on Earth in human form. Other Ascended Masters who have come to Earth are Jesus Christ, Buddha, Mahatma Ghandi, Krishna. . . ."

Some seemed enraptured, telling the worldwide TV9 audience that the World Leader had communicated his message directly to them, telepathically, in their own language. Others said that they had experienced a breathless union with the Global Mind, manifested in a delirious blackout of consciousness.

"Stand by! Coming to you in ten. Five . . . four . . . three . . . two . . ."

Steve looked into camera one. "Our final guest is a member of the Congress of the People. He is Mr. Hugh Grantham from London, England."

Turning to face the man sitting across from him, Steve said, "Mr. Grantham, would you please give us your assessment of the meaning of today's events."

"Well, Mr. Weston," the slender, tall man answered, "the New Earth Federation has been a body for ten years, but today it became *Spirit*. The World Leader has breathed life into this body. It is now Force, it is Power, it is Spirit. It has been the world's greatest military and economic power for many years. Now . . . it is the world's greatest spiritual power."

The floor director gave Steve the signal to wrap it up.

"I see that our time is gone," Steve said courteously. "Thank you for joining us, Mr. Grantham."

Looking into camera one, Steve smiled and said, "It's been our pleasure to have been with you. So, for Audrey Montaigne and myself . . . from Geneva . . . this is Steve Weston. Goodbye for now."

Special theme music. Video of the column of fire descending into the Great Hall. Fade to black.

"We're clear!" the floor director shouted.

FOUR

MAY 29, 2033—*An outpouring of love and devotion for the World Leader has swept across the planet in the aftermath of his inspiring speech and demonstration of spiritual power on the occasion of the Tenth Anniversary of the New Earth Federation. Convinced that the human species is advancing rapidly toward a new frontier of evolutionary progress, leaders around the world are pledging their undying loyalty and support to the Secretary General's leadership.*

—TV9 Headline News

Lori Weston eased her stylish, dark maroon Isis sports car onto the connecting ramp of the North Texas Autobahn, the main artery for traffic coming from the dozens of towns and developments in the sprawling countryside northwest of Dallas, Texas. An expression of her good taste, as well as a statement about her status in the Social Order, her Isis was the latest version in a long line of sophisticated and highly engineered luxury cars.

A beautiful, self-assured woman at thirty-four years of age, she was five feet, six inches tall, had a trim figure and raven black hair. Always immaculately dressed, she was the embodiment of intellect and culture. She and her husband, Steve Weston, lived in Windsor, an exclusive community sixty miles north of Dallas.

Seeing the car in front of her move forward, Lori pressed lightly on the power pedal. Once released to access the autobahn, she pulled onto the outer lane, automatically activating the Zen Guidance System in her Isis.

A pleasant male computerized voice announced, "This vehicle has been assigned to lane four. Please release the controls."

When she removed her hands from the steering wheel, she felt the guidance system subtly take over the operation of her car, integrating her smoothly into the traffic, moving her from lane one to lane four at an increasing rate of speed. Merging with the fast-moving traffic, the Isis responded instantly to the flow of commands coming from the Zen Guidance System, moving the car's controls as if it had a mind of its own.

Casually surveying the countryside, Lori's view through the sculptured windows of her Isis stood in sharp contrast to the snow-capped mountains, placid lakes, and verdant valleys of Switzerland.

With the formation of the New Earth Federation, Dallas had become a major financial center and trade base in the global economic order. As the center for the North American Economic and Trade Community, the city played host to business representatives from Canada, Central and South America, and the rest of the world.

By 2030, the combined populations of the Greater Dallas-Fort Worth Metropolitan Area had grown to more than twenty million.

The ranches and farms long removed, the landscape was now congested with tall apartment buildings and planned government housing projects for people who lived and worked in the Dallas-Fort Worth Metro area. Although it was now a major financial and trade base in the new economic order, to Lori, it could never compare to the majestic beauty of Switzerland.

Relieved of the chore of driving her own car, Lori was now free either to relax or catch up on some of her work. Pressing a button on the center console, her sculptured leather seat glided back several inches as the steering wheel smoothly recessed into the dashboard of the car.

Holding a Masters Degree in Adolescent Spiritual Enrichment, Lori Weston was second in command at the Department of Intellectual and Spiritual Development (DISD) for the DFW Metro District. With several enrichment centers under their supervision, the DISD was responsible for the moral and spiritual development of thousands of children.

Wanting to break the silence, she touched another button, and music from a satellite station filled the entire cabin. The free-floating, hypnotic, mystical tone of the music triggered an immediate response in her. Laying aside her papers, she closed her eyes, relaxed her body, and began to hum a sound that put her in touch with the Universal Mind, helping to prepare her to lead her class one step further into Self-Discovery.

Oblivious to the passing of time, her concentration was broken by a computer-produced voice that announced, "Your assigned exit in two minutes. Please prepare to resume manual control." As her seat automatically slid forward, the steering wheel moved away from the dashboard, meeting her hands at the preprogrammed position.

When the guidance system had reduced her speed slowly, in increments, down to thirty miles per hour, the computerized voice instructed, "This vehicle is now in the manual mode. Please resume control." Lori deftly guided the Isis off the autobahn.

Six minutes after leaving the autobahn, Lori pulled her car into her assigned parking slot, locked the car, and walked through the west entrance into the Northwest Enrichment Center.

Stretching for almost two blocks, the expanse of buildings housed a vast array of governmental and educational services. Maintaining a comprehensive database of information on every citizen living within their area of authority, these enrichment centers were the government's focal points for education, parent training, medical care, population control, political indoctrination, and pacification of the people.

At promptly 8:20 A.M. Lori walked into her classroom, stood beside her desk, and looked into the faces of the twenty-one eager twelve-year-old children in front of her. Each one of them was there as the result of a scientifically designed "track" system developed by the Office of Human Advancement, headquartered in Geneva, Switzerland.

Holding their eager gaze for a few moments, she smiled and said, "Children, I think you are now ready to take a giant step forward in your spiritual development. And as I have been promising you, we're going to take a most exciting journey to meet a very special new friend."

The children's eyes were bright with excitement and anticipation.

Moving among her students slowly and thoughtfully, Lori asked them, "Have you ever felt lonely, or afraid, or just wanted someone you could talk to who would understand all about you?"

The class responded as one, "Yes."

"Well, you are going to meet just such a person on our trip today. He will be your own Wise Counselor. So when you have any problems, or any questions, or if you just need someone to talk to, you can go to your Wise Counselor for help and direction for your life. You see, your Wise Counselor knows all about you and understands everything you feel."

Pausing meaningfully, she added, "And he will always be there, whenever you need him. As you know, I have my own Wise Counselor."

Lori's own first encounter with a very real spirit entity came during a "relaxation exercise" when she was only nine years old. Terrified at first, she was led by her teacher to accept the spirit as her Guide and Friend. As she grew older she was able to contact a number of spirit entities through a variety of methods. Her present spirit guide had been with her for the last twelve years.

As part of her teaching program, she had often demonstrated her "channeling" abilities for her students by entering into a trance state and calling upon her spirit guide to possess her and speak through her. Often after these sessions she was left exhausted and totally unaware of what was said by the spirit entity using her.

With the lights now lowered, and with burning candles scattered throughout the room casting mystical images on the walls and ceiling, she quietly instructed the children to push all the chairs back and come and join her in the center of the room. Lori was now sitting on a small rug with her legs folded underneath her, the backs of her hands resting limply on her knees, her index fingers and thumbs touching to form a circle. Obeying her instructions, the children moved close to their teacher, sat in a circle, and assumed the same position as that of their teacher.

While the pungent smell of burning incense filled the room, nonmelodic Eastern music from the sound system played faintly in the background. Pleased at what she saw, Lori smiled at her class, glancing at each face. Nodding her head, she was satisfied that the carefully designed setting in the room would help to create the proper frame of mind for contact with the spirit world.

Possessing a disarming smile that always relaxed the children, Lori patiently waited until each child had stopped fidgeting and the class-room was perfectly still and silent. Through the mystical dimness of the classroom, every eye stared up at their teacher. There was a long pause as the children waited in subdued anticipation for further details about the journey they were about to take and the new friend they were about to meet.

With the room now quiet, Lori searched each face, announcing excitedly, "Now, here's the most exciting part about our journey today. You can prepare yourself to contact your Wise Counselor by making a secret sound, one that doesn't seem to have any meaning. Let me show you." She then closed her eyes and began swaying her body gently from side to side, chanting the sound, "*ommm, ommm, ommm . . .*"

With the sound gently rising and falling, filling the room with its mild vibrations, Lori sensed that she was, once again, coming in con-tact with the spirit world. Recognizing the presence of her own spirit guide, she suddenly stiffened and remained perfectly still for several moments. Having made contact, she was convinced that she was ready to lead her class on their spiritual journey. Watching their teacher in rapt fascination, the class remained silent, waiting.

Lori took a deep breath, let it out slowly, and then took another. Remaining rigidly still, she sighed deeply, then slowly opened her eyes. Not a child moved. Her eyes set, she stared straight ahead for a long moment, her delicate features shadowed solemnly in the dim light from the flickering candles scattered around the room. An eerie silence fell across the room. The children stared at their teacher, unable to com-prehend the subtle changes in her appearance.

The lines in her face suddenly softening again, Lori smiled broadly. "Would you like to try that with me?" she asked.

Strangely subdued, the children nodded that they would.

After again surveying the room, Lori was satisfied that the children were ready to begin. "Now, close your eyes," she coaxed gently, "but not too tightly . . . relax . . . let the wave of relaxation flow down through your entire body . . . through your arms . . . your hands, down through your legs. Close out all thoughts until your mind is emptied of all negative energy. . . ."

While some of the children would merely relax, Lori knew that others would attain an altered state of consciousness, and that some of them would come in contact with very powerful spirit beings. Following a carefully prescribed course of study, the results from today's spiritual exercise class would become a part of each child's Spiritual Receptivity Profile.

If the child did not score at least the minimum grade on the exercise, the Office of Human Advancement would evaluate the data gathered on each child and then impose a course of corrective and remedial measures.

Her speech very slow, her tone gentle, relaxed, and deliberate, Lori urged the eager children to mimic the sound she was making. In a flat monotone voice, she began to chant the mystical sound. After a few seconds, there was the steady drone of child voices trustingly chanting after her. Satisfied that the class was approaching a relaxed state, with their minds open to her suggestions, she allowed the chanting to die slowly.

Lori was now ready to lead them through the next step. "With your eyes still closed," she cajoled, "visualize a clear blue sky with soft white fluffy clouds. . . . Feel the gentle breeze blowing across your cheeks. . . . Now, take a deep breath. . . . Feel the life-giving air from Gaia, our Mother . . . filling your lungs . . . clearing your mind. . . ."

After pausing for a few seconds in order for the children to concentrate on the sound of her voice and words, she told them to imagine that they were skipping across a meadow of emerald green grass. At the edge of the forest, she told them, there was a beautiful white unicorn whose name was Brightness. Brightness was going to lead them into the Deep Forest where they would meet their own Wise Counselor.

For the next several minutes, Lori Weston guided her class through the prescribed sequence of events charted to lead them into a deep meditative state. With each child now visualizing that they were following the white unicorn, she told them that the unicorn was leading them from the meadow into the Deep Forest.

Once inside the forest, the unicorn led them to a cave, where they descended down a long staircase to a large room. Lori moved them along to the next phase. In a soft, hypnotic voice, she intoned, "Look

. . . on the other side of the room, there is someone waiting for you. It is your Wise Counselor. He is speaking to you. Don't listen with your ears; listen with your mind. He wants to help you become one with the sky, the trees, and all the animals of the world. He is telling you that you are helping to bring about god-consciousness, that you are evolving into a higher form of being, that all truth is within you."

While softly humming her mantra, her body swaying slowly, she waited patiently while the children communicated in their own way with their Wise Counselor, knowing that the next few minutes would be critical in their spiritual development, as well as to their future advancement in the Social Order.

After allowing several minutes to pass, Lori skillfully began to guide them through the return steps, a crucial part of the exercise. Knowing that she must bring them out of the hypnotic state and acclimate them once again to their classroom surroundings, she instructed them to visualize themselves walking back up the stairs and following the white unicorn out of the Deep Forest and back across the meadow.

Once that process was completed, her voice faded to a hypnotic whisper, "Now, children, I'm going to count to three . . . and when I reach three, you are to open your eyes and you will be back inside your own classroom."

Slowly, deliberately, Lori began her count, pausing momentarily between each number. When she reached the number three, she instructed, "Now open your eyes . . . and you will be back in your own classroom."

Anxious to see that everyone had made the transition safely, Lori scanned the room carefully. While most of the children viewed the exercise as innocent fun, she was well aware that some of her students could have had a genuine encounter with a spirit entity. Nodding her head pleasantly, she smiled at seeing her class now wide awake and laughing and talking with each other.

Placing a single finger to her lips in a gesture that called for absolute silence, she checked each child individually, pausing momentarily on each face. Her eyes coming to rest on Kathryn, a vivacious twelve-year-old, she hesitated, noticing that her eyes were still closed, her body trembling. Lori studied her uncertainly, then spoke to the girl next to her. "Phyllis, please reach over and tap Kathryn on the shoulder," she said calmly.

The instant Phyllis touched her, Kathryn unexpectedly began to shake violently, as if she were in the clutches of some invisible giant hand. Startled, Phyllis pulled back her hand, a look of surprise on her face.

Lori moved toward Kathryn. Just as she reached her, the young girl opened her mouth and gave vent to a chilling scream that shattered the quietness of the room. It was a scream that possessed the dark tones of despair coming from a desperate soul caught in the grasp of an evil force. For a ceaseless moment, each child froze in place, their eyes frantically searching for the source of the frightening, chilling sound.

"They want to kill me!" the young girl cried out in a loud voice, her eyes darting wildly about the room. "They're ugly. . . . They're coming to take me . . . they want to kill me. Help me! Help me!" she wailed, her body covered in sweat, her breathing chaotic and labored.

With the quietness of the classroom violently shattered, the children recoiled in fear, suddenly sensing that something was desperately wrong. Their eyes wide, shock was registered on their small faces, confusion and apprehension mirrored in their eyes. Timidly, the children backed away from the distraught girl, huddling in small groups, touching each other for reassurance.

Lori felt a cold chill pass through her. Her eyes narrowed apprehensively. She should anticipate such manifestations to occur, she chided herself, but there was something about this girl's plaintive wail that played unpleasant games in her mind, causing her to shudder. Rather than the expected pleasant reaction during such a spiritual experience, this child seemed to be ravaged by some inner torment.

A torment that Lori could only begin to imagine.

Lori reached out to touch Kathryn's shoulder but stopped short. Before she could touch her, the child jerked away from her, her eyes blazing in hatred toward her. A twinge of fear tugged at Lori's emotions. Gripped in a swirl of confusion, she let a long moment pass as she gazed in speechless amazement at the girl's twisted face.

Slowly regaining her composure, Lori reminded herself that this was to be expected in the advanced classes in spirituality. She had been taught that a significant number of children would react violently when the spirit beings attempted to assume control over them. And if a teacher were not properly trained in control techniques, a child could be physically hurt. Her first task was to restore order and calm the fears of the other children; then she would deal with the unexpected manifestation.

With her confidence steadily growing, the challenge suddenly intrigued her beyond anything she had ever faced before. It was a challenge she would meet head on. With a decided note of authority, Lori clapped her hands to get the children's attention. With calmness and reassurance in her voice, she told the children, "Now, class, nothing is wrong. Kathryn is just learning how to respond to her Wise Counselor who has come to help her. There's nothing to be afraid of."

During her career of teaching and counseling, Lori had introduced hundreds of children to their own spirit guides. In such cases, she had encouraged her students to not resist their Wise Counselor, telling them that they had been chosen to become a channel for the spirit being who was attempting to communicate a message through them to the rest of the class. Seeing Kathryn respond this way was a clear lesson to the class of the real power of the spirit world.

But there was something different about Kathryn.

With Kathryn now lying quietly and very still on the floor, Lori turned her attention to the task at hand, reaffirming to herself that she had the talents and spiritual power to guide her student through the transition. But despite her own positive inner dialogue, there was a sinking feeling in the pit of her stomach. She tightened her jaw, a frown clouding her face. Strong-willed, Lori Weston didn't like to lose. And, for sure, she would not be intimidated by this small girl.

Curious, the other children in the classroom cautiously formed a circle around the child and teacher, anxiously waiting to see what was going to happen next.

Shoving aside the indecision and fear that threatened to overcome her, Lori took a deep breath and steadied herself, then reached down and took both of Kathryn's hands in her own. Speaking in a soft, compelling voice, she instructed, "Now, Kathryn, at the count of three, open your eyes, and you will be back in the classroom."

With a note of confidence born of sheer determination, Lori began her count. "One . . . two . . ." The words carried easily throughout the room.

Hesitating a second, she said firmly, "Three!"

Quickly, in a firm voice, she commanded, "Now, open your eyes, Kathryn. You're back in your room!"

For what seemed an eternity of anxious moments, Lori waited. But the young girl didn't open her eyes. Not to be denied, she said more forcefully, "Kathryn, listen carefully. I'm going to count to three. And when I say the word three, open your eyes, and you will be back in the classroom."

Counting more slowly and deliberately this time, Lori coaxed, "I'm beginning to count . . . one . . . two. . . . Listen carefully now, on the count of three, open your eyes. . . ."

Taking a deep breath, the word came out almost a scream. "Three!"

With the uncertain sound of the word still hanging tenuously in the air, the young girl slowly opened her eyes, their fiery intensity freezing Lori in place. Her visage darkened and sinister, she drew her lips tight across her teeth and vented an unnerving snarl of rage. The undiluted hatred reflected in the child's face burned into Lori's soul, causing her to draw back in fear.

Catching her breath sharply, Lori was stunned when the child began to scream loudly, her piercing voice grating against her frayed nerves. The child's face now ashen, her eyes filled with anguish, Lori watched helplessly as Kathryn's body began to thrash violently on the floor. Fighting a rising panic that threatened to overcome her, she gripped the child's arms, trying to pin her writhing body forcibly against the floor. But despite her strong efforts, the wild thrashing continued, her screaming growing louder and more plaintive with each second that passed.

Lori had her hand clamped tightly over Kathryn's mouth to drown out her screams when she was startled by the voice of David Ramsey, the school principal, who was suddenly standing behind her. "What's going on here, Ms. Weston? What's wrong with this girl?" Ramsey asked bluntly.

Visibly shaken by the experience, panic now edging her voice, Lori blurted, "David, everything was going so well. Kathryn was responding beautifully to the spiritual exercise. . . . She was even used as a channel for a few minutes. But I've been unable to bring her out. We may have to call for Dr. Phillips to come and take over."

With Kathryn's chilling screams continuing unabated, Lori rose slowly to her feet. Trembling, she turned to face Mr. Ramsey. Blinking her eyes in bewilderment, she was surprised to see that several teachers and staff members had rushed into her room to see what was wrong.

Before Ramsey could respond to Lori, a slender, dark-haired woman brushed past him and stepped up to Lori. "Ms. Weston," she said softly, "Would you mind if I tried to get the young lady quiet?"

Astonished at the sudden appearance of the strange woman, Lori responded, "Why, of course. . . . Are you trained to—"

Before she could finish her question, the attractive woman moved quickly toward the young girl whose body was still writhing grotesquely on the floor. Quickly kneeling down beside her, the woman leaned over and began to talk to her, her voice barely above a whisper. In response to the woman's voice, the girl's eyes flashed open. Her face was instantly contorted as if she were being manipulated by a strong hand. Her eyes mirrored a virulent hatred for the woman in front of her. Suddenly gripped in an uncontrollable rage, the child lashed out at the woman, trying repeatedly to strike her with her fists.

The woman's eyes reflecting a burning intensity and determination, she held the young girl firmly by her wrists, whispering softly, "You will not strike me. Your power is not strong enough to hurt me."

The child's face contorted savagely, reflecting the pain and terror that buffeted her. Then the distraught girl vented a dreadful pain-filled shriek, as if somehow this would dislodge the alien force that had seized her and was tearing at her.

The people in the room stared in astonishment at the strange drama. They stood behind the child and woman, like spectators huddled together in the stands of an ancient Roman coliseum. Sensing that some terrible struggle was taking place somewhere behind the scenes, out of view of flesh-and-blood eyes, their attention was riveted on the woman and child in front of them.

Unknown to them, the body, mind, and soul of this pretty young girl was the battlefield where two powerful forces were vying for supremacy and the right to claim her as their prize.

For a brief moment the girl seemed to calm down. The room became deathly quiet. Then the people watched in horror as her innocent face was suddenly transformed into that of a grotesque monster, as if her features had been physically twisted by a powerful invisible force. Her lips drawn tight across her teeth, she rasped in a loud voice not her own, yelling at the woman in front of her, "We know you. . . . You have come to destroy us. . . . But we will not be destroyed. . . . She is ours, and we will not let her go!"

Those near the dark-haired woman kneeling in front of the tormented girl, heard her quietly, but firmly, respond to the chilling voice, "No, she is not yours. And you *will* let her go. By the power of the blood of Jesus Christ, you will let her go."

Riveted to the remorseless conflict being played out before them, the people inside the crowded room strained to hear what the woman was saying. Unable to hear her soft words, the onlookers crowded forward, following the fierce struggle as it was being played out in the changing expressions on the face of the girl. The terror in her eyes and the desperation in her voice betrayed the fierceness of the battle, and the outcome still remained in doubt.

Then, as suddenly as it had started, Kathryn's struggling ended, her body relaxed against the floor, and her distorted face was transformed back into the face of an innocent child. Opening her eyes in bewilderment, she blinked several times, glanced around the room at the people staring down at her, and then looked squarely into the beautiful face of the smiling woman kneeling in front of her. Their gaze held for several moments. Then without a word she rose up, threw her arms around the woman's neck, and began to sob uncontrollably.

The room fell into a dark silence.

The stunned teachers, faculty, and students who were crowded into the classroom watched in subdued amazement, trying to assess the shrouded meaning of it all. Disbelieving eyes were fixed hard on the awesome spectacle before them, colored by a strange sense that what they had seen was beyond human comprehension.

A soft murmur of voices cascaded through the classroom, dropping quickly into a deathly silence. At the center of the room, the woman slowly rose to her feet. No one moved as the traumatized girl slowly gained her feet, stood unsteadily, her small arms wrapped tightly around the woman's neck, her innocent face lying gently against her breast.

With a tenderness and warmth that could be found only in a mother's heart, the woman gently brought the frightened child inside her warm, tender embrace, and the two of them began their long, purposeful walk through the crowd of people. Ignoring the staring eyes, the woman moved with measured steps toward the door. Her head bent down, her fingers lightly touched the child's face, gently stroking her, whispering softly, soothingly, assuring her that her terror was over, and she was going home.

Time seemed momentarily suspended as the curious watched in mute wonder.

The battle was over. . . .

And the dark-haired lady had won.

Lori followed the pair with a frantic, puzzled stare. Stung by embarrassment and anger, beads of perspiration began to form on her face. Her chest tightened and her heart beat violently as she considered the consequences this episode would have on her career. With a mindless fury suffocating her rational thought, she moved toward them, stepping in front of the woman and child, cutting them off.

"Thank you for your help," she said curtly, her voice trembling with anger and apprehension. "I can handle everything from here. I've gone through this procedure many times and can assure you that I'm eminently qualified to handle any situation that might arise in my class. So if you don't mind—"

Ignoring Lori completely, the woman continued to move toward the door, threading her way through the crowd of people, quietly talking to the young girl while gently stroking her hair and face.

When Lori stubbornly persisted, the woman responded in a respectful, but firm voice, "Please, move out of our way, Ms. Weston."

Only then did the mysterious lady look up. And when the eyes of the two women met, there was an immediate clash that sent a shudder through Lori's being. Taking a sharp breath, a thousand questions raced through Lori's mind. *Who is she? What is the source of her psychic power? Why do I feel threatened by her?*

A deep and heavy silence swept through the room.

With unwavering determination, Lori exclaimed in a harsh voice, "This is my student!" Her face was tight in anger.

Looking directly into Lori's eyes, the woman replied, "Yes, she's your student, Ms. Weston. But . . . Kathryn is my *daughter!*"

Lori's anger blazed into rage. Her heart pounding wildly, she burned with humiliation, her hands unconsciously knotting into fists. Her face a mask of raw fury, she started forward toward the woman, then stopped abruptly, their eyes locked in a lingering gaze.

The woman's warm, gentle eyes reflected a strange power and essence that Lori could not comprehend. They were eyes that seemed to penetrate into her soul, leaving her vulnerable, exposed. Suddenly Lori felt cold inside, threatened. Her breath caught, and she staggered back a step.

Unable to shake a vague sense of foreboding, she watched in silence as the woman drew the small frame of the trembling child close under her arm. Looking at Lori, she said softly, "You've done enough to her already. Please move, Ms. Weston. We're going to leave."

The strange lady's eyes met her own again and, without blinking, held her gaze. Standing frozen in place, Lori was unable to move, to speak, even to think, a flood of questions nagging her heated mind, pressing in on her with cold persistence. She studied the woman's face carefully. It was an attractive, strong face, reflecting no anger, no hate, no desperation. Her large, placid eyes were soft, unthreatening.

And then Lori saw the almost invisible tears, falling silently downward. The soft lines of her face reflected only sadness and deep hurt. Strangely, Lori felt her anger and hatred of this woman slowly ebb away, and for a spellbound moment, she found herself wondering what kind of person lay beneath the attractive features.

Lori opened her mouth to speak but discovered that she had suddenly become mute. As she watched in openmouthed wonder, the woman and child stepped around her and moved forward. The people cleared a path for them, watching breathlessly as mother and daughter made their way through the door and out into the hallway.

Lori stood for a long moment, her gaze riveted on the empty doorway, trying to gather her scattered thoughts into some semblance of order. Shaking her head once again in disbelief, a faint smile played over her lips. More fascinated than angry, she wondered at the power of the strong spiritual forces that seemed to be under this woman's control.

Evidently, she mused, she had been able to tap into one of the most powerful sources in the Universe. Perhaps, she should learn more about her.

Touching her lightly on the shoulder, David Ramsey asked, "Are you all right, Lori?"

Still feeling the woman's gentle, penetrating gaze boring forcefully into her innermost thoughts, she continued to stare questioningly at the empty doorway. Her arms folded casually across her chest, she slowed her breathing, feeling the final vestiges of her churning anger drain away and reason return.

"Who is she, David?" she asked in a subdued, awestruck voice, a multitude of questions still ripping mercilessly through her frenzied mind.

"Oh, that was Harper. Sheila Harper," Ramsey answered dismissively. "She has a 'Facilitator' rating. She was transferred here about six months ago."

Glancing over his left shoulder as he walked out of the room, Ramsey called out, warning scornfully, "Don't get mixed up with her, Lori. She's one of the Offenders."

FIVE

After a quiet breakfast of fresh fruit, toast, and coffee in the main restaurant at the Global Village Hotel, Steve Weston slipped the small stack of papers he had been working on back into his briefcase and closed it. Nodding to the waiter, he quickly signed the check, made his way to the elevator, and rode back upstairs to say goodbye to Audrey Montaigne before leaving for his 9:00 appointment with Dr. Wallenberg. She was scheduled to leave Geneva on an afternoon flight.

Walking briskly down the long corridor to her room, he hesitated, knocked lightly on her door, waited a few seconds, then raised his hand to knock again when he saw the knob turn and the door slowly open.

Audrey appeared in the doorway. Seeing that it was Steve, she folded her arms across her chest, leaned back against the open door, and looked up at him, their eyes meeting for a moment.

Neither of them spoke.

Standing there in a light blue robe, her hair disheveled, no makeup, still drowsy from sleep, Steve found himself lost in her large, beguiling eyes. Caught up in the moment, he suddenly realized that he didn't want to leave her. He wanted to take her in his arms and hold her.

"Audrey," he stammered. "I'm sorry to have disturbed you. But . . . I didn't want to leave without saying goodbye."

"Do you have time to come in?" she asked timidly.

"I'm sorry . . ." he said hesitantly, "I have to meet Dr. Wallenberg's driver downstairs. He's waiting for me."

Without warning, she pushed herself away from the door, moved quickly toward him, reached up and draped her bare arms around his neck. Drawing him down to her, she kissed him passionately on the lips, holding him tightly in a fervent embrace.

Surprised at her sudden bold gesture, Steve held her tentatively in his arms for a long moment. Then, gently moving her arms away, he whispered, "Audrey . . . I'll see you in a few days back in Dallas. . . . I have to go now." He then turned and walked away, his face flushing.

Stepping off the elevator into the hotel lobby, he spotted Ramul, who was waiting for him near the concierge's desk, smiling.

"Good morning, Mr. Weston. I trust you slept well."

"Indeed I did, Ramul."

"Very good, sir. If you will come with me, I will take you to Dr. Wallenberg's office."

After securing his passenger inside the long luxury car, Ramul pulled smoothly away from the curb in front of the hotel entrance, then turned to the right onto the wide twelve-lane thoroughfare. Turning left at the traffic circle, Ramul followed the winding, tree-lined street to the Unified Information and Communications Authority compound on the southeast quadrant of Global Village.

The bright morning sunlight glinted off the dozen or so modernistic buildings of dark brown concrete, gleaming steel, and gold-colored glass that housed the assorted departments of one of the most powerful regulatory agencies of the New Earth Federation. By directing the worldwide flow of all radio and television broadcasting, the UICA was one of the government's most powerful weapons of control over the thought processes of the peoples of the world, molding and shaping world opinion by their skillful use of words and images. Sky News Network was under the supervision and authority of the UICA.

Arriving at the UICA complex, which was surrounded by an imposing security fence, the limo swept through a security gate and turned into a private driveway that led to the basement of the main building. Easing down the ramp to level three of the underground parking garage, he stopped next to the elevator, stepped out, and opened the door for Steve.

Bowing courteously, Ramul reminded Steve, "Dr. Wallenberg's office is on the thirtieth floor, suite 3001. It's just to the right of the elevator. I'm sure you remember where it is."

"Thanks, Ramul," Steve returned.

Stepping into the glass-enclosed elevator, Steve punched number thirty, then turned to look out over Global Village and its busy morning activity. When he felt the elevator stop, he turned and exited to his right and walked down the long corridor to number 3001.

As he entered the office, Dr. Wallenberg's longtime secretary, Ms. Bergman, smiled up at him. "Hello, Steve," she said cheerfully. It was obvious she was glad to see him. "Dr. Wallenberg is expecting you. I'll tell him you're here." When she picked up her interoffice phone, a soft electronic chime sounded on Dr. Wallenberg's desk. He spoke into the voice-actuated compuphone. "Yes, Ms. Bergman?"

"Mr. Steve Weston is here to see you, Dr. Wallenberg," she announced.

"Please send him in," he instructed, pressing a small button under the edge of his desk. The door slid open.

A native of Stockholm, Sweden, Wilhelm Wallenberg was a tall, slender, dignified man in his seventies. With his piercing blue eyes, the manicured perfection of his thinning gray hair, and his brilliant smile, he was the embodiment of an elder statesman, a patriarch. His English was slightly tinged with a Swedish accent. Highly intelligent, fastidious in his dress, and a stickler for orderliness and protocol, he worked hard and expected the best from those who worked under him.

A member of a very wealthy Swedish family, he had been called upon to help form the New Earth Federation. He had served as a delegate to the New Earth Summit and had been elected to membership in the Council of 100.

A trusted member of the new global order, he had been appointed by the Council of 100 to head up the powerful Unified Information and Communications Authority.

When Steve stepped into the spacious office, the older man stood and walked toward him with relaxed, easy strides, an innate personal pride and dignity about his bearing. His face beaming, he threw his arms around Steve and embraced him warmly. "Steven, it is so good to see you," he said, patting him on the shoulders affectionately. "You look fit and healthy. How are Lori and Jimmy?"

Steve felt like a young boy being hugged by a favorite uncle. He had genuine warm fondness for the man. He even liked it when he called him "Steven," a gesture that reflected the older man's formal approach to life.

"It's good to see you, again, Dr. Wallenberg," Steve responded with a broad smile, remembering the pleasant hours they had spent together over the years. "And Lori and Jimmy are doing fine," he added.

Dr. Wallenberg escorted Steve to one of the high-backed leather chairs positioned in front of his desk, then returned to his own chair.

"Is your son growing into a young man?" he asked, a note of sincere caring in his voice.

Steve's face lit up at the mention of his son. "Indeed he is, sir," he returned warmly. "Jimmy is almost three now."

Dr. Wallenberg glanced away, an unusually worried expression suddenly clouding his thin features, as if he had retreated somewhere deep within himself. Steve remained silent, looking quietly into his friend's face, sensing that he must respect his momentary withdrawal.

The older man breathed deeply and sighed. His brow wrinkling with concern, he spoke softly, as if to avoid being overheard. "Steven," he said solemnly, "I have two sons and four grandchildren, two boys and two girls. And I worry about their future. Our society doesn't love its children as we did when I was young. There is no joy when a child is born." His voice was filled with emotion.

The old man frowned and shook his head slowly. In a sharp whisper, his voice bordering on anger, he warned Steve, "You must love your son as you love your own life. . . . And you must protect him, shield him. The children are so . . . *vulnerable*," he said, staring meaningfully at Steve for a long moment, his piercing eyes burning with the passion of his words. With a long, slow exhale of breath, he glanced away, shaking his head vaguely.

Seeming to break out of his dark mood, Dr. Wallenberg smiled broadly and said, "Now, let's get down to business. As you know, I'm past seventy, and I'm making preparations for my retirement."

"I had heard rumors to that effect," Steve responded.

"The Executive Committee has asked me to recommend someone to assume my position as Director of the Unified Information and Communications Authority. And, Steven . . . I have recommended you for the position."

Although Steve had worked tirelessly for this opportunity, the actual offer came as more of surprise than he had anticipated. Pushing himself up from his chair, he walked slowly across the room to the large window, his emotions suddenly churning.

After a long pause, he turned back to face the older man. "I . . . I don't know what to say, Dr. Wallenberg. I'm highly honored that you would consider me. Do you think I can handle the job?"

"Of course," Wallenberg said, pausing momentarily to choose his words carefully. "I've had this in mind since the day I brought you to Geneva as my understudy. I'll want you to move back to Geneva in two years to work with me until I step down. That will make the transition run more smoothly. The final decision is not mine, you understand. But I will tell you this much—the majority of the members of the committee are favoring you over several others under consideration. They'll make up their minds within the next few months. At a later date you'll meet with the Committee for interrogation and examination." Shaking his head emphatically, he added, "Even though you've proven your loyalty to the Federation, intensive background checks will be run on you by the proper authorities."

"I understand, sir," Steve responded, nodding his head.

Dr. Wallenberg hesitated a moment, then smiled. "Now that we've settled that, we can move on to the next item of business." He motioned for Steve to be seated once again. "The Executive Committee has raised your Elite Clearance Level to Level Eight. When you assume the position of director of the UCIA, of course, they will raise your ECL to Level Nine."

Steve shifted nervously in his chair.

"Another item of business. I'll be attending a closed briefing tomorrow morning at The Mountain. I would like for you to accompany me."

The Mountain!

Although he had never been inside it, Steve knew of the existence of an elaborate underground city, somewhere to the north of Geneva. Known only as The Mountain, it was reputed to be the most secure spot on earth, housing the elaborate high-tech emergency command centers of the New Earth Federation's most sensitive divisions. The prospect of going there excited him.

"Dr. Wallenberg . . . of course, I'll go," Steve answered approvingly.

"Good," the older man responded. "I'll have Ramul pick you up at your hotel at seven-thirty in the morning."

Steve moved to the edge of his chair. "Dr. Wallenberg," he said, his tone almost apologetic. "I'm hesitant to—"

"Please, Steven, whatever is on your mind."

"Sir, would you mind if I asked you about the . . . *unusual* events that accompanied the Secretary General's appearance last night?"

Dr. Wallenberg leaned back in his chair, his face suddenly somber. "What would you like to know?"

"Well, first, why wasn't I informed before airtime of the very remarkable occurrences that accompanied the Secretary General's appearance?"

"Well, Steven," Dr. Wallenberg replied, "I was not authorized to inform you. There was a very short list of people who had prior knowledge of the project." He then reached to his right and lightly touched a small pad on his desk. "Ms. Bergman, please have Dr. Mueller come to my office."

"Yes, sir," she responded.

The older man looked at Steve, his head cocked appraisingly. "Steven, I had anticipated your questions, so I've arranged for the man in charge of the project to brief you. Dr. Bernard Mueller is a brilliant scientist and has been responsible for many of the major advances in holographic laser imaging. I'm going to have him explain the technical side of the events to you."

Ms. Bergman's voice came on the speaker. "Dr. Mueller is here, sir."

"Have him come in, Ms. Bergman."

Dr. Wallenberg touched the hidden button under his desk and the door slid open. A short, stocky man, his clothes rumpled, his hair unkempt, stepped timidly through the door. In his mid-thirties, the roundness of his face was accentuated by a pair of wire-rimmed glasses with thick lenses.

"Dr. Mueller," Dr. Wallenberg said, nodding toward Steve. "This is Mr. Steven Weston."

The man gazed warily at Steve. "Oh, yes, I've seen him many times." He spoke with a heavy German accent.

Motioning for him to take a chair, Dr. Wallenberg continued, "Bernard, Mr. Weston was put in a rather awkward position by not knowing of the plans for the World Leader during his appearance at the Great Hall. I would like for you to explain the technical side of last night's event."

Squinting his eyes, Dr. Mueller peered through the thick lenses at Steve, then back at Dr. Wallenberg.

Dr. Wallenberg nodded. "It's all right, Bernard. Mr. Weston has Level Eight clearance."

"Dr. Mueller," Steve asked tersely, "was the Secretary General *personally* inside the Great Hall when he gave his speech?"

Again Mueller glanced at Wallenberg, then back at Steve. "The World Leader," he answered, in his high-pitched, grating voice, "was not actually *inside* the Great Hall. He was isolated inside a holographic studio in the TV9 building across the street."

In spite of his own mounting skepticism, Steve was surprised at Mueller's revelation. Pressing for more information, he asked, "How did you get the World Leader's image inside the Great Hall? And how was the levitation performed?"

"Yes . . . well, we surrounded him with six digital holographic video cameras. These cameras fed the digitized image through fiber-optic cables to six holoprojecters, which were concealed throughout the Great Hall. The lighting in the Hall was fine-tuned to complement the image. The holoprojecters created the three-dimensional, stereophonic, holographic image the audience saw and interacted with. Causing his image to levitate, Mr. Weston, was a rather simple process. We merely raised the holoprojecters, making it appear that the Secretary General was levitating."

Guided by his reporter's instinct, Steve continued to probe. "I understand how that was done, but we also reported on TV9 that the

Secretary General appeared, in person, in the air, in real time, in the sky above twelve major cities of the world. How did you do that?"

Mueller pulled at his shirt collar, obviously uncomfortable about giving out so much information. "Dr. Wallenberg," he said pleadingly, "I don't think . . ."

"It's all right, Bernard. Please answer his questions."

"Very well. Several weeks ago, we aligned a cluster of very high-powered satellites, configured in a circular, stationary position over each city we wanted to impact. There were twelve separate clusters, one cluster over each city. The number of satellites we used for this project is highly classified."

"Then, you considered this project to be very important?" Steve responded.

"But of course," he shot back. "We're talking about the future of the world."

Mueller was beginning to show his annoyance at having to share this information with Steve. Reluctantly, he continued. "On the night of the World Leader's appearance, we beamed the holographic signals from our studios in the SNN building up to our primary satellites, and from there we relayed the signals around the globe to the twelve clusters of satellites positioned over the twelve target cities.

"Each of the satellites contained a powerful digital laser holoprojecter. The holoprojecters in each cluster were interfaced to converge their individual laser-beam signals at the precise preprogrammed spot, producing the three-dimensional image of the World Leader that appeared over each of the cities."

Steve scanned Mueller's face. "Then . . . the people who *thought* they saw the Secretary General over their city . . . actually only saw his holographic image. Is that what you're saying?"

"Of course, Mr. Weston," Mueller pronounced emphatically. "The classified technology we used for this project is the most advanced in service today. The holographic signals were digitally compressed beyond any parameters we've ever been able to attain in the past."

Hardly believing what he was hearing, Steve probed further. "How close to your predetermined position over the cities were you able to place the image?"

"How close, Mr. Weston?" A cryptic smile etched Mueller's face. "We placed the World Leader within one one-thousandth of an inch of our programmed spot." Becoming animated, Mueller continued, "Just think, by manipulating the 1s and 0s of the computer world, we were able to place the World Leader in different parts of the world at the same time. You see, we have broken free from the bonds of the flesh."

"I'm impressed with the new technology, Dr. Mueller," Steve stated simply.

Raising his voice, Mueller interjected harshly, "Oh, but it's more than technology, Mr. Weston. Computers are not just hardware and software. No, they are mediums, windows, through which we can interact with other entities. We have broken into the spirit realm through our technology. When we create an image, it's not just an image, sir, it is *spirit*. We have passed into the realm of spirit."

Steve shook his head skeptically.

"Come now, Mr. Weston," Mueller quickly responded. "Don't look so astounded. Humanity has long dreamed of the ability to transcend this physical existence, to visit other worlds somewhere in space or time, to be enlightened with universal wisdom. We no longer live within the confines of this earthly existence. We are free of the fetters of time and space, entering the worlds of another dimension at will. We have changed the meaning of reality. We are exploring the unmapped domains of consciousness and are communing with interdimensional beings. Everything in the universe is connected to everything else. We are One."

Steve's astonishment grew. "It's only *technology*, Dr. Mueller," he retorted sharply. "Don't try to make it into something it isn't. It isn't some supernatural power. The Secretary General's image was nothing more than trillions of tiny pulses of light traveling through fiber-optic cables, satellites, and holographic projectors. It was not him! You tricked the people of the world, Dr. Mueller! You showed them an image, not the real man. You made them believe something that was not true!"

"No, no, you are wrong!" Mueller shouted. "You don't understand. It's more than technology. It is *reality*. The World Leader communed with the people of Earth. He touched us all. Last night the world joined in a shared experience. And for that moment we became one."

Steve countered, "But what if the people of the world find out that they only saw an *image* of the Secretary General? That it was not real—"

Mueller jumped to his feet. Taunting Steve, he shouted in his face, "Mr. Weston, you're still reasoning from a logical viewpoint. Logic and rational thought have no place in the New Reality. We cannot understand Gaia and Her ways by using our rational minds. Earth Spirituality and Gaia awareness spring from nonlinear *intuition*. Millions of us enter Alternate Realities every day, together, at the same time, around the world. We commune with each other, and enter the world of spirit through the open doors of our technology. It is our Sacrament, our new Holy Communion, our pathway to godhood."

Steve's eyes narrowed. "I think you've lost touch with reality, Dr. Mueller."

Mueller backed away, a grim smile on his face. With a shrug of his shoulders, he asked, "What is reality, Mr. Weston? This physical life is an illusion, only a weak representation of reality. After people experience the New Reality, they don't want to return to the physical plane."

Steve leaned back in his chair. "Tell me about the fire, Dr. Mueller."

"The . . . *fire?*" Mueller stammered, obviously taken aback by the question.

Steve replied caustically, "Yes, the fire. The column of fire that came out of the sky and stood behind the Secretary General. How did you produce the fire?"

Mueller didn't move. He seemed stunned, unable to answer. As beads of sweat began to form on his red face, he sat back down and slumped wearily into his chair and looked at Dr. Wallenberg.

Wallenberg spoke up. "Steven, that's the one mystery in our well-laid plan."

"Mystery? What do you mean, sir?"

"Yes, *mystery*," Dr. Mueller cut in, a crazed grin now twisting his lips. "We *didn't* produce the pillar of fire. Our technology only created the image of the World Leader. We don't know where the fire came from."

Steve stared, unblinking, into the small, round eyes of the short, fat man, who was by now sweating profusely. "Are you trying to tell me—"

"Yes, Steven," Dr. Wallenberg interrupted. "That's exactly what we're trying to tell you. We were as surprised as you were when the fire appeared out of the sky. We didn't create it. In fact, it didn't appear in the holographic studio. We have no *scientific* explanation for it."

A measureless silence filled the room, lending cold reality to their fears.

Clearly shaken, all three men seemed to be at a loss as they exchanged hesitant glances. They were facing something they didn't understand—and could not explain.

Trying to slow his racing mind to rational thought, Steve asked haltingly, "Does that mean . . . that you believe the man actually has . . . *supernatural* powers . . . that he actually called fire out of the sky?"

"We don't have any other explanation, Steven," Dr. Wallenberg confessed soberly. "Believe me, we have all been working on this since the moment it happened. We just don't understand."

A strange, inexplicably cold feeling came over Steve. Standing to his feet, he walked to the glass wall and stared down at the busy street in front of the UICA building.

His brow furrowed in thought, he tried to deal logically with the unsettling possibility that the World Leader did indeed have some kind of supernatural power.

Moments passed.

Taking a soft, measured breath, Steve replied, "I don't believe it." Abruptly turning around to face the two men, he declared, "It's not possible. This is the scientific age, the age of knowledge and information. It can't be."

Moving closer to Dr. Mueller, Steve leaned into his face and declared loudly, "He's a *man*, Mueller. Just a man, like you and me. There's a scientific explanation."

A satisfied smile appeared on Mueller's face. With a strange confidence in his voice, he shot back, "No, Mr. Weston. He is not a man like you and me. The World Leader is one of the *Ascended Masters*. He has come back to Earth to show us the Way. He is much higher on the evolutionary ladder than the rest of us. And only those who interface with Gaia, our Mother, will know the Way."

Staring into Mueller's eyes, Steve was now sure that he was in the presence of a madman. The man's eyes were wild, glassy, as if he were in a trance, or on drugs. Steve could almost swear that some evil entity was lurking inside of him, staring back out through those small, round eyes.

Steve shuddered. It was the same look he had seen in the eyes of the Secretary General while he was delivering his speech.

Mueller moved abruptly toward Steve, his eyes wide, his lips drawn tight across his teeth, and pressed his finger hard against his own fore-head at a point directly between his eyebrows. "Look, Mr. Weston," he shouted. "This is the Seal of Gaia, right here, at the point of the Third Eye, where my brain cells and my consciousness interface with the uni-verse, unhindered by the limitations of space, time, or the flesh. It is my direct physical and psychic link to Gaia, our Mother. It is the mar-riage of high technology and advanced spirituality."

Looking at Mueller's forehead, Steve thought he saw a tiny scar that appeared to be where a minute incision had been made.

Continuing his tirade, Mueller shouted, "We not only made it possible for the World Leader to speak to the world, Mr. Weston, we mere humans have also brought into existence the new godhead by creating the Omega. Oh, but you don't comprehend what I'm trying to tell you, do you? Only those who have been enlightened can even begin to understand. Gaia inhabits the Omega."

"The Omega?" Steve said slowly. "What is the Omega, Dr. Mueller?"

Mueller's eyes darted about the room, fear suddenly registering on his face. Stepping back, he stuttered, "Nothing, Mr. Weston. I . . . misspoke. It is nothing."

Dr. Wallenberg spoke up. "The Omega is the name given to the supercomputer that resides inside The Mountain."

Glancing at Mueller, Wallenberg added, "That will be all, Dr. Mueller."

The short man looked at Dr. Wallenberg for a brief moment, then turned and stalked toward the door. Hesitating, he turned and looked at Steve over his left shoulder. "Be warned, Mr. Weston. Only those who have received the Seal of Gaia are protected from Gaia's wrath. All others will be destroyed."

With that puzzling statement hanging in the air, he turned brusquely and stalked out of the room.

Steve paced the room, struggling to find the words to express his amazement and disbelief. "Tell me, Dr. Wallenberg," he ventured, "what happens if the public finds out that the Secretary General's 'supernatural' levitation and his 'miraculous' appearance over those twelve cities were a hoax?"

Dr. Wallenberg hesitated before answering. "It wouldn't matter, Steven. Even when they are aware of the technology, they don't consider it illusion. They have been educated by interactive computerized learning machines and are entertained in their homes by interactive Home Communications Units. The technology is so real that the general public is no longer able to distinguish the physical world from the holographic virtual world."

"Dr. Mueller," Steve stammered, "looked as if he were insane. I—"

"Unfortunately, Steven, Bernard Mueller, and millions like him, have mythologized the technology. They've imbued it with divinity, looking to the computer as God. As data is fed into it, they fantasize that it is capturing the 'collective consciousness' and creating the Global Mind. They believe that a form of Gnosticism emerges out of the marriage between technology and human consciousness.

"You see, they spend their lives trying to escape this physical existence. They see the physical as evil. They have used hallucinogens, occultism, meditation, and other methods in an attempt to transcend their everyday existence. They want to meld with the Universal Mind, to become one with all things. To them, this new technology is the new mystery religion, the gateway to Paradise. Mass suicides have occurred around the world, based on the belief that if they set their souls free from the body, they will merge with the Gaia Force that dwells in cyberspace."

Steve stood motionless.

"Bernard may seem like a strange man to you, Steven, but millions like him have also experienced the same paradigm shift in their perception of reality. You see, somewhere along the line, their physical existence becomes the illusion, and only the computer-generated artificial world is reality. So it shouldn't surprise you that they could believe the image is reality."

Touching a button on his communications console, Dr. Wallenberg asked Ms. Bergman to bring them a serving of tea. He then suggested that they move to the small table near the window. After they were seated, Ms. Bergman brought a silver tray with a pot of tea and two cups. Placing the tray on the table, she poured the tea, then left the room. The two men sipped slowly on the hot brew.

Dr. Wallenberg set his cup down and glanced up cautiously at the door. He then moved to the edge of his chair. "Steven, in taking you to The Mountain tomorrow, I will be introducing you into the secret realms of power. After tomorrow, and for the rest of your life, you must be diligent in observing even the smallest detail of the protocols of the Social Order. Your future, and your life, depend upon your unwavering loyalty. Once you've gone deep into The Mountain, there is no turning back."

"You make it sound rather ominous, sir," Steve returned.

Dr. Wallenberg's brow wrinkled. He hesitated as if he were going to say something more. Then, without responding, he rose from his chair and walked slowly across the room to the huge bank of tall windows that comprised a fourth wall overlooking Global Village. Flowing curtains bordered the four separate floor-to-ceiling windows, letting in faint streams of light from the morning sun.

The stately man stood motionless, closed inside a dark, brooding silence, his eyes reflecting a deep sadness. His hands clasped behind his back, his eyes drifted aimlessly across the village compound thirty stories below, the most expensive real estate in the new global order.

There was a sudden heaviness in the room as Steve waited, fighting a growing inner apprehension. He tried to divert his thoughts by concentrating on the lavish furnishings inside this expansive office. There were a number of masterful paintings, rare and expensive, looking down on choice pieces of ornate furniture, spaced tastefully about the large, comfortable room. Smelling of old leather and furniture polish, the entirety of the spacious office, he mused, matched the proud and noble character of the remarkable man who occupied it.

At length, Dr. Wallenberg returned to his chair. There was an awkward silence as the two men faced each other.

Sighing in resignation, the older man rested his elbows on the arms of his chair, steepled his fingers, and said sternly, "Steven, I hope you're not taking the trip to The Mountain too lightly. That could be dangerous for you."

Steve leaned forward, his eyes fastened on the face of his friend. Against the dryness building in his throat, he said, "I'm sorry, sir. I . . . didn't mean it the way it sounded. I'm rather overwhelmed at the prospect of being allowed to go inside The Mountain."

Dr. Wallenberg nodded, saying nothing, his gaze steady, unnerving.

Steve stared, uncomprehending, suddenly feeling a distance between them, a chasm he feared he could not close. And for the first time since he had known him, he felt closed out and was deathly afraid he had somehow caused a rift between them that might be irreparable.

The old man sighed wearily and rubbed his chin, looking away.

Steve studied the lean, handsome, aged face, shook his head slowly, then glanced nervously down at the floor. Fighting a mounting despair, he took measure of his own churning emotions and hoped he was wrong in thinking he had disappointed or offended him in some way. If only he knew what he had said, or done—or had not done—he would gladly apologize and ask Dr. Wallenberg's forgiveness.

Dr. Wallenberg broke the lengthy silence. His eyes narrowed as he looked across at Steve. "You still have time to decline my invitation to go to The Mountain," he said, his lips tight, his voice weary and hard-edged. "However, if you do go, you will be sworn to secrecy *forever*. If you ever reveal any of the things you see and hear, you will be marked for *elimination*. You should not enter into this lightly." With a toss of his hand, he added, "The decision is yours, of course. Do you still want to go?"

Steve felt a chill move through him. The tone of Wallenberg's voice and the force of his sharp words were like a dull knife opening an old wound. Slumping heavily back into his chair, he searched the piercing eyes that were holding him hostage in their steady gaze.

And what he saw startled him.

Tears were glistening in his friend's eyes, even as he tried desperately to hide the unspoken affection and concern for Steve that belied his harsh words and rancorous tone.

And suddenly Steve knew; he was not *angry* with him. He was trying to protect him, to warn him, to shield him from the unseen dangers that lay ahead if he chose to move forward into the dark, hidden realm of the new Social Order.

An enormous sense of relief swept through him. Now he understood, and he was grateful.

Steve's own vision blurred. He blinked to clear it.

Feeling the rapid pounding of his own heart, he took a deep, steadying breath, knowing that the decision he was about to make would alter his life forever. And in some unexplainable way, he knew that this singular decision would determine his future in the Social Order. It was a decision he did not take lightly. But despite his friend's passionate concern for him, he considered it a major step in his pursuit of power and position. And, although a number of things still troubled him, it was a step he had to take, regardless of the cost.

Steve nodded and forced a quick smile. "Yes. I want to go," he answered, suddenly feeling a rush of excitement.

Dr. Wallenberg looked at Steve wordlessly, sighed softly, and nodded.

For the next hour, Dr. Wallenberg once again became Steve's teacher, instructing his prize student on a vast array of protocols that he must abide by at his new level of participation in the Social Order. His instructions were meticulous and carefully measured for the greatest effect. The session included a number of heated exchanges in which he asked pointed and intrusive questions, as if Steve were on trial in a courtroom. And when they were through, Steve felt drained and weary, his face gray with concern. But he was determined to pursue his dream.

Abruptly ending their conversation, Dr. Wallenberg nodded his head, quickly stood to his feet, and declared quietly, "It's settled then. We will go to The Mountain tomorrow."

SIX

Shielding her frightened child from the curious stares of those they passed in the hallway, Sheila Harper silently thanked God that she had happened along when she did. After walking out of Lori Weston's spiritual exercise class with her daughter, Kathryn, she was moving purposefully toward the quiet sanctuary of her own classroom where she taught a class of eleven-year-olds. Terrified at the possibilities of what might have happened, she had no doubt that if Lori had been allowed to deepen her daughter's hypnotic state, she might have done irreparable harm to her.

When she walked through the door, Sheila surveyed her classroom, taking note that her students were busily engaged in their individualized lesson programs. Feeling her distressed daughter clinging to her helplessly, she hurriedly guided her to her small office located at the back of the room. Her brow furrowed, her attractive face was clouded with deep worry and concern. Pushing through her own weariness and fatigue, she gently coaxed the confused child to lie down on the small couch in the corner of the office, telling her to rest until it was time to go home.

Trying to hide her tears, she walked back into her classroom, momentarily scanned the faces of the children, then sat down wearily at her desk. Her anxiety mounting, she glanced impatiently at the clock on her desk, taking note that it would be several more hours before she would be permitted to leave the building. Sighing heavily, she tried to prepare her mind for the long wait.

Sheila had started making some notes on her computer when she was startled by the sound of the buzzer on her inner-office phone. Looking at the instrument with undisguised apprehension, she timidly pressed a button, saying, "This is Ms. Harper."

The message was short and curt. "Harper, this is Lori Weston. Be in my office as soon as the last class period has ended." The phone went dead before Sheila could respond.

Shaking her head wearily, Sheila pushed herself away from her desk and walked to her small office to check on Katy. Caught in a sudden need to protect and care for her daughter, she considered ignoring Lori's instructions and taking Katy home immediately. But not wanting to make a difficult situation even worse, she felt it would be wise to face Lori. Returning to her work, she repeatedly glanced at her clock.

When the bell sounded, ending the school day, Sheila said good-bye to the children, then hurried to her daughter. Sitting down beside her, she stroked her cheeks softly and whispered, "Are you all right, Katy?" The young girl looked into her mother's eyes and answered sleepily, "I think so, Mom. Can we go home?"

Sheila clenched her jaw, feeling as if she were walking through a bad dream. Fighting desperately to maintain a firm grip on her churning emotions, she smiled through her fears and said, "We'll go home in just a little while." Shaking her head uneasily, she added, "But first I've got to go by Ms. Weston's office. She wants to see me. When I leave, I'll close the door so no one will disturb you. I'll be back just as soon as I can. Is that OK?"

"Yes," Katy answered, nodding and smiling weakly.

Casting apprehensive glances at the child, Sheila felt reasonably sure that she would be safe for a while. Stroking her small face one more time, she stood and walked to the door. Glancing back at the sleeping child, she quietly pulled the door closed.

Slowly walking out into the wide hallway, she began maneuvering her way carefully through the hundreds of rushing children and workers who were scurrying out of the building at the end of the school day.

Mentally distraught and frozen with uncertainty, she found herself fighting a raging flood of emotions too numerous and too intense to identify.

Anger . . . rage . . . grief . . . fear . . . sorrow . . .

They were all there, sweeping through her like a raging torrent, deriding her, mocking her. Bravely, Sheila fought against the debilitating emotions that swirled around her like a deadly, noxious fog, threatening to overwhelm her, to suffocate her. Feeling small and frightened, she prayed for courage to get through the rest of the day.

Her face pale and drawn, she arrived at Lori's office, pushed the door open, and stepped inside. Lori's secretary glanced up and told her that Ms. Weston was expecting her, to go right in.

Lori was sitting at her desk. Busy signing a stack of letters, she made a point not to acknowledge her presence, to leave her standing. After the last letter was signed, she slid them aside, rested her forearms on the edge of her desk, and laced her fingers together. Taking a deep breath, she looked up at the woman standing in front of her.

Sheila spoke first. "Did you want to see me, Ms. Weston?"

"Harper," Lori responded, her voice laced with sarcasm. "It was inevitable that you and I would clash sooner or later. I've read your files and your 'attitude' ratings are very low. And believe me—"

"Ms. Weston," Sheila interrupted, "may I please be seated? It has been a long and tiring day."

Stung by Sheila's insolence, Lori felt her face flush with anger. She was tempted to lash out at her. But keeping her anger in check, she smiled and replied, "Yes, of course. Please be seated. Forgive me for being so thoughtless."

Sheila stepped to her left and sat down in a dark blue chair. Smoothing her skirt across her legs with the palms of her hands, she looked up and said, "Thank you, Ms. Weston. Please continue."

Casting a withering stare at her, Lori marveled at the poise of the lady now seated in front of her. There was no revealing expression on her face, nothing mirrored in her eyes. Lori's jaw tightened with determination. Sheila Harper evidently didn't fully appreciate Lori's position or authority, she thought to herself. This was a matter she fully intended to correct.

Studying her wordlessly for another moment, Lori readied herself to strongly lecture the errant teacher on several matters. "Harper," she snapped autocratically, "I think you know why I've had you come to my office. Your little display of impudence in my classroom this morning was uncalled for, unnecessary, and very damaging to my students—and to my own reputation as a professional, I might add."

Without responding, Sheila remained seated quietly on the edge of the chair, her back straight, her hands folded and lying on her lap in front of her. Her face showed no emotion, no response. Lori hesitated for a second, suddenly feeling frustrated and threatened by the unreadable expression of this woman.

Pulling out a drawer on the right side of her desk, Lori retrieved a large folder. Sheila glanced at it, recognizing it as a printout of her own International Master File (IMF). This birth-to-death record contained the entire history of her life, her family background, her political leanings, her psychological profile, even the circumstances of her conversion to Christianity, and her present "attitude" concerning the Social Order.

Slowly turning the pages, Lori spoke without looking up. "Well, Harper, as you can see, I know all about you. It's all here. *Everything!* There's nothing you do, say, or believe that we do not know about. Believe me, I can't imagine how you have been able to hold on to this teaching job as long as you have. You are obstinate, uncooperative, and show a total lack of sensitivity to the curriculum and programs of the Department of Human Enrichment. And . . . oh, yes, according to your IMF, Harper . . . you are one of the Offenders."

Sheila winced. Lori's use of the word "Offender," a derisive term used to describe those who still held to the primitive Christian belief in the one God, was intended as an insult. Considered rigid, intolerant, backward, and judgmental, those who held to such beliefs "offended" the cultural sensibilities of the Social Order. Both hated and pitied, the Offenders were looked upon as being ignorant, boorish, and self-centered for not conforming to the social norms. And nonconformity was the great social sin, the ultimate "offense."

Sitting stiffly on the edge of her chair, an air of indifference about her, Sheila responded wearily, "Ms. Weston, it's getting very late. I would appreciate it if you would get to the point."

Lori's eyes flashed. Abruptly standing up, she slammed the file down on the top of her desk. Her face burning with a sudden anger, she snapped furiously, "Harper, I've been working with these children for months to bring them into contact with the Universal Mind. Your intrusion into our spiritual exercises has caused confusion and fear in my pupils' minds and it's going to make it more difficult to lead them into more meaningful spiritual experiences. The unit that you interrupted today was in a remarkable state of altered consciousness."

Sheila remained still, silently studying Lori's face, trying to deal with the flood of conflicting emotions that were washing through her.

Motioning to a series of wallscreens to her left, Lori said, "As you probably know, we record all of our classes on video disks and file them for future reference. And after viewing the video, I must admit, I was rather intrigued by your performance in my class today."

Keeping a tight rein on her thoughts and emotions, Sheila responded, "It was not a performance, Ms. Weston."

Ignoring her comment, Lori went on, "I've played the video disk for our counseling staff and the District Director, Dr. Paul Jenkins."

Pressing a button on the control panel on her desk, the four video screens came to life, showing scenes from her class. Lori punched another button and an enhanced image of Kathryn's face, still lying on her back on the floor, filled the screen. "Here's a scene that piqued my interest, Harper," Lori said, pointing to monitor number two. "Look at the unit's face. One moment it's twisted and contorted, and the next moment it's quiet and serene."

Sheila stared at the screen. The closeup told the poignant story of the attack by the evil forces and her daughter's strong and brave resistance to them. Sheila's breath caught in her throat when she saw the video of herself entering the room and kneeling down beside Kathryn. Her eyes moistened as she viewed the disturbing scenes of her daughter's intense struggle against powers she was too young to understand fully.

Returning to her chair behind her desk, Lori continued, "In the discussions following the viewing of the video disk," she said, "our staff was in agreement that you do indeed possess remarkable psychic powers. Your technique seems to be quite effective, even though it doesn't fit into the normal procedure. But we believe that you have *possibilities*.

We all agreed that, with a little refinement, your powers could be channeled in a more constructive way."

Sheila breathed deeply, then exhaled slowly, in an attempt to keep her emotions in check before she responded. "Ms. Weston, there are two things I would like to clear up. First, my daughter, Kathryn, is not a *unit*. She is a human being. And the second point is, I do not possess any psychic powers."

"Of course you have psychic powers," Lori retorted. "They just need to be developed." She then flipped on monitor number four. "Now, let me roll something for you. It's some sort of religious conjuration, or formula, that seemed to bring about the remarkable response in the unit—uh, Kathryn. If you don't mind, please explain it to me. You spoke rather softly, so I'll enhance the gain on the audio."

With the screen showing Sheila kneeling beside Kathryn, she heard her own voice say, "Don't be afraid, Katy. Christ's power is greater than the power that's trying to hurt you. Now, Satan, I instruct you to depart from this child."

Pressing the "off" button, Lori suggested, "We have a problem with your having told her that the powers she had been introduced to were trying to harm her. That's not true. This procedure is all part of transpersonal learning. It is designed to help the units by maximizing their classroom learning and enhancing their ability to think, as well as improving their self-esteem."

"Those are all fine-sounding words, Ms. Weston, but—"

Ignoring her comment, Lori abruptly interrupted her. Gesturing broadly with her hands, she intoned, "And the Inner Teacher is one of the key elements of the integrative approach. We have had remarkable results when our students have been introduced to the concept of the Inner Teacher within each of us. So how can you possibly say that these forces are trying to destroy her life?"

Sheila tightened her jaw against the mounting anxiety. Taking a moment to compose herself before responding, she took in a deep breath. "You've been dealing with these spirit entities, Ms. Weston," she said slowly, "long enough to know that they're very powerful and extremely unpredictable. They're not the innocent-sounding beings you make them out to be. This is not child's play."

Lori set her eyes on Sheila's face, her strong gaze calculating and predatory. "Sheila," she cajoled barely above a whisper, "just tell me how you got your daughter to calm down today. What formula did you use? Was it a special incantation, or—"

Abruptly cutting in, Sheila responded, "Ms. Weston, I used no formula or incantation to bring her out from under the influence of the spirit being. I simply prayed for my daughter, in the name of Jesus Christ, and the evil spirit had to depart."

Lori sighed in resignation. Throwing up her hands in disgust, she blurted, "You fascinate me, Sheila. This is so . . . so *quaint*. Your beliefs are so antiquated. As you know, we hold Jesus in high esteem as an Ascended Master. He did, indeed, fill the office of the Christ when he was upon Earth. But there have been many others who have filled that office—highly evolved beings such as Buddha, Gandhi, and others."

Lori studied Sheila Harper's face. There was a worn look to her now, a trace of silent desperation breaking through her stoic features. A slow smile crept over Lori's lips, washing the anger from her face. Her resolve stiffened. She would break this woman, she silently vowed. Her own psychic powers were stronger than hers, and she would prevail.

Her voice tinged with sincerity, thinly disguising her true intent, Lori leaned close to Sheila and said pleadingly, "Sheila, I need you working with me, not against me. We can learn from each other. The human species is on the threshold of a great evolutionary leap of consciousness. You have talents that can be used to help propel humanity upward to its own godhood. It's the most exciting time in history to be alive."

Her voice filled with a frightening, unnerving intensity, Lori pled earnestly, "Join us, Sheila! Join us!"

With Lori's challenge hanging threateningly in the air, Sheila swallowed hard against her fear, her face reflecting the mounting tension inside her being. It would be so easy, she reasoned, to accept Lori's invitation and guarantee safety for her daughter and family. For a moment, her thoughts were scattered and incoherent. Fighting against a sense of helplessness that was attempting to consume her, whispered warnings assailed her mind, telling her that if she refused, she would feel the full weight of the anger of Lori Weston, and the undiluted wrath of the Social Order. Her heart pounding furiously, sweat glistened brightly on her forehead.

"I'm sorry, Ms. Weston," Sheila answered quietly, her eyes cast downward. "I can't help you."

"But, Sheila," Lori insisted, her voice cracking like a whip. "Your daughter was on the verge of developing a beautiful relationship with her spirit guide. In fact, I'm quite sure he was about to use her as a channel to speak to the class. That's a rare talent and it should be developed. I . . . I'm very upset that you interfered with her progress."

Sheila took a long, deep breath and steadied herself. "No, Ms. Weston," she responded firmly. "What you call 'channeling' is described in our Scriptures as 'demon possession.' And what you call 'spirit guides' are, in fact, demon spirits. It's their purpose to deceive. I—"

Stung by Sheila's inflexibility, Lori's voice rose to a feverish pitch. Cutting her off in midsentence, she spat her words contemptuously. "You're out of line, Harper! This has been a setback, but not a defeat. I can assure you that Kathryn will make contact with the Universal Mind—*with or without your help!*"

Lori's fury stunned Sheila. Cautiously lifting her right hand to her face, she wiped away a small bead of perspiration that had formed on her upper lip. Her hand was trembling. Thrust into mortal combat for the life and soul of her own daughter, she called upon every spiritual and intellectual resource at her command. Fighting desperately against a wave of panic that threatened to engulf her, she prayed for calmness and courage to face the task before her.

Since her conversion to Christianity, Sheila Harper's faith had been her constant source of strength, defining her total womanhood and forming her secure center in a world that had gone mad. And even though she knew intellectually that the battle for her daughter was being played out in the spiritual realm between forces that neither of them could see, when it affected her own children, she thought and felt like a mother, and the entire drama quickly took on flesh-and-blood proportions.

Lori glared at Sheila, cold fury in her eyes. "You people don't understand that humanity stands on the verge of something wonderful.

There's nothing on Earth that's going to stop this. And those who stand in the way of humanity's evolution will be dealt with!"

With Lori's words ripping through her like flying shrapnel, Sheila froze Lori in place with a withering stare. "What do you mean by 'dealt with,' Ms. Weston?"

Lori hesitated, taken aback momentarily. Shaking her head with contempt and dismay, her voice still filled with bitterness, Lori bluntly announced, "You and the other Offenders are part of the Negative Mass that is holding back the dawn of the New Age. You *will* adapt, or you will be purged from the Earth."

Fear festering inside her, Sheila gazed intently into Lori's eyes. "Listen to what you've just said, Ms. Weston," she pleaded with a trembling voice. "Those words are death threats to those who do not conform to the Social Order."

Lori's lips twisted in angry scorn. At the point of losing control, she screamed venomously, "Get out of my office, Harper! I will not sit here and listen to this blasphemy any longer. I've tried to help you, to reason with you, but you've got a closed mind. There's nothing more I can do for you. You people are the *enemy!*"

Seeing that her words had stunned Sheila, Lori moved closer to her. Her teeth clenched in anger, she glared at Sheila. Holding her gaze, she smiled with perverse satisfaction. In a voice so filled with hate that it was barely recognizable as her own, she declared with ferocious intensity, "Sheila Harper, you and the other Offenders will all be allowed to pass into spirit."

Dazed, Sheila stared at Lori wordlessly, fighting against a knot of fear forming in her throat. Desperate hope trying to break through the anguish, she stood to her feet, clutching her purse tightly, and walked slowly to the door. Hesitating, she turned and looked back at Lori, tears falling from her eyes. "Lori," she said softly, "it's not important what happens to me. Your anger is not really against me, or my people. Your anger is against the God who created you. You can kill us all, and it won't bring you peace."

There was nothing to be gained in continuing the conversation. It was ended, and Sheila had no more to say to Lori Weston. Wiping the tears from her eyes with a small white handkerchief, she placed it back in her purse, turned the handle on the door, and walked out of the room, quietly closing the door behind her.

Sheila walked in silence along the wide corridors of the enrichment center back toward her classroom, her mind in a dizzying whirl. Clinging close to the wall, she tried to avoid eye contact with anyone. Her thoughts bordering on despair, tears filled her eyes again, blurring her vision. She dabbed at them surreptitiously, thinking of her daughter.

She must take Katy home to her father.

He would know what to do.

SEVEN

Dawn splashed orange and golden across the land, sending fiery colors cascading across the sky, tinting the white clouds that floated lazily overhead in the bright new morning. The graceful skyline of Global Village gleamed brightly in the clear sunlight. At precisely 7:30 A.M. on the crisp, invigorating new day, Ramul maneuvered the large Daimler limousine to a smooth stop in front of the main entrance to the Global Village Hotel. After Steve had boarded, Ramul pulled away, merged with the flow of traffic in the busy street, and drove to the UICA building.

Dr. Wallenberg was waiting for them near the elevator in the parking garage. Once he was inside the limo, Ramul swiftly drove out of the Global Village compound, through the security gates, and accessed the Alpine Autobahn.

Completed in 2027, the autobahn was built as a direct link between Global Village and The Mountain. Stretching northward, the eight-lane highway paralleled Lake Geneva, made a swing around the lake to the east, passed through the north edge of the city of Lausanne, then veered northeast through the mountain passes.

The two men seated in the plush passenger compartment of the luxury car talked amiably about a variety of subjects, thoroughly enjoying each other's company. When the conversation turned to the subject of their visit to The Mountain, Dr. Wallenberg said, "Steven, we're going to a meeting of the Global Security Commission. The work of the Commission, and its very existence, is highly classified. You will be there as an observer and will not be allowed to speak. So I'm sure you will respect the rules."

"Yes, of course," Steve replied.

"In fact, an important military operation is scheduled shortly. The Global Peace Forces are about to launch a strike against a small, uncooperative nation. I have ordered a total information blackout of the operation until it is over. Then I will send several TV9 crews into the war zone."

Dr. Wallenberg turned his attention to some papers he had brought along. Not wanting to disturb him, Steve took advantage of the brief lull and stared out the window, mesmerized by the beauty of the passing scenery. He had forgotten how magnificent the Swiss countryside was, with its carefully manicured fields, terraced vineyards, quaint homes, and, above all, towering mountains.

Oblivious to the passing time, he was startled when the hand phone on his door gave a quick chime. He picked up the receiver. It was Ramul. "As soon as we pass through this tunnel, Mr. Weston, you will see The Mountain through the pass to your left. Just thought you would want to see it from here."

As they emerged from the tunnel, Steve looked to his left, down a long valley to a magnificent mountain peak. Throughout the world, Steve reflected, people knew that somehow every facet of their lives was connected to The Mountain.

Driving for another twenty minutes along the wide, twisting road, they approached the entrance to The Mountain. Steve took note of the large warning signs, printed in English, French, and German, declaring that this was a "Restricted Zone," and that all unauthorized entry was strictly forbidden. Armed guards were posted at regular intervals along the high-security fence that surrounded the entire area.

Once inside the gates, Steve could see military guards stationed along the wide thoroughfare at measured intervals. Farther back, on both sides of the busy street, blending in with the green landscape, almost undetectable, was a series of bunkers manned by soldiers, armed and alert. Hidden deep within the main security building inside the underground city, special agents monitored a series of video screens showing the car as it moved along the boulevard.

Straight ahead was a thirty-story building standing guard over the main entrance to The Mountain. The back section of the building's first three floors merged gracefully into the face of the mountain itself, creating the illusion that building and mountain were one.

There were three other entrances to the underground facility, each strategically positioned around the base of the mountain. This was the west entrance. Ramul pulled the long car underneath the portico that extended out from the building. Parking near the curb, he quickly stepped out and opened the door for his passengers.

Walking through the main entrance to The Mountain, Steve's pulse quickened as he caught sight of the inside of the enormous and magnificent underground city that seemed to stretch for miles in all directions. Mesmerized by the overwhelming vastness of its dimensions, his sweeping gaze took measure of its breathtaking size and beauty. In all his life, he had never seen anything that compared to it. The grandeur of the scene itself, reinforced with the vibrant hum of voices from the thousands of people who were moving in all directions, caused him to stare in numbed disbelief.

Unable to tear his eyes from the flow of its vastness, Steve followed close behind Dr. Wallenberg as they swept through the heavy throng of people, moving toward a large bank of escalators that stretched downward for more than two hundred feet.

As they approached the security gate guarding the entrance to the escalators, Dr. Wallenberg passed his right hand underneath an electronic scanner. The gate opened instantly, and the two men moved forward toward the third escalator to their right.

Stepping aboard the escalator, Steve was little prepared for the vista that unfolded before his eyes as they rapidly descended. He stared in wonder at the cavernous, brightly lit expanse before him.

The main courtyard was a great circular cavern that had been laser-carved out of the heart of the mountain. Its mammoth walls sloped gently upward in a sweeping, unbroken arc, reaching to more than three hundred feet at their highest point. Large, gaping tunnels, like spokes in a wheel, radiated in all directions from this main room.

Gliding downward, his eyes still sweeping the vast expanse, Steve said casually, "Dr. Wallenberg, I'm curious . . . when we passed through the security gate, did the scanner read your handprint?"

The older man held up his right hand and splayed his fingers. Rubbing a small spot on the back of his hand, he explained, "The scanner read the data from a tiny, subcutaneous, programmable biometric computer chip—here, just below the skin on the back of my hand. They've named it the 'Personal Identifier.' Dr. Mueller and others fantasize that it's the mystical Seal of Gaia. The scanner simply read the data on the chip, accessed the global databank, identified me, and authorized me to enter."

"That's remarkable," Steve returned, staring at Dr. Wallenberg's hand for some indication of the location of the chip.

Dr. Wallenberg smiled. "It's completely undetectable without the scanner, Steven. Our research has shown that this is the optimum place for the biochip, right here, halfway between the wrist and the knuckles. Or it can be placed in an earlobe, or at the base of the skull. However, some people insist upon having the biochip injected under the skin in their forehead, right where the eyebrows meet. They believe it becomes the Third Eye, connecting them to the Global Brain. People such as Dr. Mueller see it as their connection to Gaia."

Gesturing toward the people around them, he said, "All the people who work inside The Mountain are part of the experiment. You can't enter without the PI. My clearance level, of course, allows me to bring guests."

"Is it . . . successful?" Steve queried.

"Yes indeed, Steven," he answered firmly. "It's only a matter of time before the entire world will be required to use this method of identification. They're also tying it into the electronic economic order. When they have completed the project, it will allow them to monitor every financial transaction, every purchase, and every money transfer throughout the world. And through utilizing their global surveillance technology, they'll be able to monitor and track everyone twenty-four hours a day, for life."

"When will the project be completed?"

"Very soon. The technology is ready. It's just a matter of the final conditioning of the people to accept having the chip injected into their skin. It's a rather simple process really. The chip is inserted into the skin by a small device called a 'Marker.' The Marker anesthetizes a small patch of the skin, then instantly injects the chip. It even cauterizes the skin, leaving almost no trace of the procedure."

When the escalator came to the end of its run, Steve stepped off and stood for several moments, looking in all directions, captivated by the magnificence of the man-made phenomenon. He was astonished to see restaurants, shops, a cinema, and a miniature park with grass and trees growing.

Electric-powered vehicles, carrying government personnel dressed in brightly colored uniforms, scurried by in special travel lanes, moving thousands of people in and out of the dozen or more wide tunnel corridors that branched off in all directions from this enormous main room.

"I had no idea that it was like this," Steve exclaimed.

"Quite remarkable," Wallenberg responded. "It could be the Eighth Wonder of the World. Over thirty thousand people work inside The Mountain. It's the most heavily guarded spot on earth. After all, it is the nervous system of the world order. Every major department of the New Earth Federation has duplicate operations here. This facility guarantees the continuity of the global government. We could run the world from here."

Sweeping his hand toward the smooth walls and ceiling of the mammoth room, Dr. Wallenberg stated with obvious pride, "The main part of the city is underneath us, over a mile below the earth's surface, and covers several square miles. It was so constructed that it can withstand a direct hit by any known nuclear device . . . and keep on functioning."

Resuming their walk, Dr. Wallenberg continued, "In case of a nuclear attack, up to forty-five thousand people could live quite comfortably here for up to three years, time to allow the atmosphere on the surface to be cleared. This facility houses all the mechanisms of control that the government would need during that time. When everything was clear, they could then resurface."

Coming to Loading Dock 4, they boarded one of the blue carriers. "The various levels of The Mountain are named, not numbered," Dr.

Wallenberg told Steve. "The first level, the street level, is known as Alpha Level. The next floor down is Beta Level, followed by Theta Level. The fourth floor down is known as the Delta Level. As you descend deeper, each level becomes increasingly more secure, more restricted."

"Are there . . . areas below that?" Steve asked tentatively.

"Yes, there are deeper levels. But for security reasons, I can't discuss them."

The carrier glided smoothly along the forty-seven-mile-long tracks that were built into the main outer ring tunnel encircling the underground city. Banking sharply to the left, the carrier entered a smaller auxiliary tunnel marked "C-4" that would take them to the very center of The Mountain.

"Steven," Dr. Wallenberg said, his voice taking on a new note of seriousness. "Please remember this. Your power and status in the Social Order depends upon how *deep* into The Mountain you are authorized to go. So please don't underestimate the significance and value of your visit here today."

For the next few minutes, the men rode in silence. Steve struggled to comprehend the strange new world he was being initiated into, wondering what lay ahead of him.

When the carrier slowed and stopped, they disembarked and walked to a bank of elevators. Once on board an elevator, Dr. Wallenberg punched the button for Delta Level. The rapidly descending elevator took them almost a mile below the earth's surface. When it came to a smooth stop, the door slid open and they stepped into an immaculately decorated reception area, complete with windows that seemed to let in the light of the sun. Steve had no sense of being more than a mile below the surface of the earth.

A high-ranking military officer stepped up to Dr. Wallenberg, saluted, and said, "Good to see you again, sir. Please follow me."

The military officer preceded them down the wide, brightly lit hallway, the heels of his boots clicking on the hard stone floor. Walking straight ahead for what seemed a good city block, they angled to the right for another fifty yards and passed through a series of electronically operated steel security doors.

Stepping left through another steel door, they entered a large rectangular room, its ceiling at least forty feet high. In the very center of the room was a circular, polished walnut conference table with seating for a hundred people. Small individual communications consoles, complete with telephones and video monitors, were embedded in the table in front of each chair.

Beyond the conference table was an elevated speaker's platform. Looming behind it, standing more than twelve feet high, was an impressive sculpture of the earth, laser-carved out of the face of the stone wall. Chiseled deep into the marble just below the earth sculpture was the inscription: *One Earth * One People * One Spirit.*

A soft murmur of voices filled the room.

While Dr. Wallenberg made his way to his chair at the conference table, an attractive young German woman with curly brown hair, a warm smile, and striking blue eyes led Steve to the visitor's gallery to his left. He smiled, thanked her, sat down, and leaned back against the soft chair. He had an unobstructed view of the main floor.

Glancing to his left, Steve noticed a tall man seated on the far side of the table, his arms resting lightly on the arms of his chair, his unyielding stare reading each face in the room. Steve had seen him only once before, but he knew instantly who he was. The man was Adam Stenholm, head of GU5, the intelligence arm of the Pacification and Compliance Commission (PCC), and one of the most feared men in the global government. Elusive, cruel, and thorough, he had been given almost limitless power in bringing the peoples of the world into compliance with Global Law. And he was a personal friend to the World Leader.

Steve deliberately avoided making eye contact with the man.

A door underneath the earth sculpture behind the speaker's platform suddenly opened, and two men and a woman walked out onto the stage. The woman went directly to the speaker's stand and laid out her briefing book. Dressed in military attire, she was tall, athletic, with a well-muscled frame, and not unattractive. Her two companions sat in chairs slightly behind her and to her left. She stood at rigid attention for a few moments, waiting for everyone's attention.

When she gave the order to "secure the room," Steve heard four loud clunks as electronically operated locks on the steel doors on each side of the large chamber slammed shut, sealing them inside. A small, steady green light came on above each door, indicating that the room was now secured.

"I'm Major Kraus," she announced. "This briefing is classified Top Secret. Nothing that is said here today is to be repeated outside this room."

Turning her attention to her briefing book, she proceeded to give background information on a number of military operations around the world. This was followed by a detailed report on an uprising against the New Earth Federation, led by a group of dissidents, somewhere in the ever-seething area of the Balkans. With an air of confidence, she assured her audience that the region had been "pacified," order had been restored, and the leaders of the rebellion had been executed.

For the next hour Steve listened to a series of briefings on a variety of subjects, some informative, some startling, some mundane. Just as he found his interest begin to wane, a short, beefy man, dressed in a slightly too small suit, shuffled up to the microphone and began to speak. Identifying himself as Dr. Hamjul Rhamodeen, he proceeded to give a data-laden report on the worldwide spread of the AIDS virus.

As he read off the numbers of the newly infected and the additional deaths that had occurred worldwide within the preceding thirty days, and the predictions of the number who would die within the next thirty days, Steve looked at the bored expressions on the faces of the people seated at the conference table and feared that discussing such statistics had become only an academic exercise.

Relaxed in his chair, Steve glanced up at the earth sculpture looming behind the platform, letting his eyes trace the outline of the continents of the world that were carved into the stone. Instinctively, his gaze drifted to the profile of the continent of Africa.

As the monotonous cadence of the man's voice became only an echo in the background of his thoughts, a thousand horrifying, uninvited scenes began to play out in his mind. Scenes from his travels across the world for TV9. Scenes of the devastation caused by AIDS, of the dead and the dying, of human misery, of mass graves, of quarantined cities, of people being shot for trying to escape in their desperate bid to live.

The human immunodeficiency virus (HIV) had broken out of the mountains and rain forests of Central Africa more than sixty years before to begin its slow, steady burn across the continent.

By 2011, whole countries in Africa were infected and had to be quarantined from the rest of the world.

In 2014, the world authorities decided it was no longer economically feasible nor prudent to continue to sustain the most severely affected areas. They were draining the world's much needed health-care assets and had become a liability to life on the planet.

Imprisoning the infected behind military blockades, all food, water, electricity, and medical supplies were cut off from the condemned areas and a strict media blackout was imposed. People had no way to escape, and soon famine and disease worked their will on the victims, with vast stretches of Africa being virtually depopulated.

It was as if one of the Horsemen of the Apocalypse had ridden through the land, gleefully plunging his bloody scythe into the human race, leaving gaping, open wounds across the face of the earth.

Continuing its grim mission, the AIDS pandemic had swept through Southeast Asia, leaving misery and death in its wake. And by 2016, the virus had claimed millions of lives in India, a land that once had thought they would escape its ravaging attack. Crossing borders at will, the virus continued its spread throughout vast stretches of China, Russia, and the Middle East, and threatened to engulf all of Europe.

Sinking into an almost hypnotic state, Steve could once again hear the rhythmic thump of helicopter blades as he rode next to a young pilot over an AIDS-ravaged city in East Africa, feeling the human heat of fever rising up like steam from the diseased bodies below him. The smell of rotting flesh from the thousands of corpses lying at random intervals in the streets below, bloating in the merciless sun, had made him involuntarily reach for a cloth to cover his nose and mouth.

He rubbed his temples softly, as if to dislodge the intruding visions, but they would not retreat. With all human rights in those doomed cities having vanished, he had witnessed acts of savagery against the condemned people that he didn't know man was capable of committing. After the plague of AIDS had done its work, the government soldiers, clothed in their biouniforms, had gone in and killed all who remained alive. While those involved had learned not to see, or to feel, or to care, Steve could not get used to or accept the brutality.

A man seated at the conference table pushed his chair back and walked to the platform. Steve recognized him as Dr. Alexi Monet, the Director of the Global Population Control Commission. In his fifties, he was tall, slender, and walked with a slight limp. He carried a large, sealed brown envelope, which he laid on the speaker's stand.

Clearing his throat, Dr. Monet looked out across the audience. "Ladies and gentlemen, I have some very disturbing information that I must bring to you." He then carefully broke the seal on the envelope and took out several sheets of blue paper. "A new strain of virus has just recently been isolated," he announced somberly. "Having first been discovered near the Maylay Peninsula region of Southeast Asia, it has been named the Maylay virus."

Shifting his weight, he leaned his right arm against the speaker's stand. "It is more deadly than any virus we have encountered up to this time. And that includes AIDS, Marburg, Ebola, or any other known virus. Once Maylay attacks, it totally destroys the immune system, then sweeps through the human body with an explosive intensity and speed that defies our medical experts. Autopsies of its victims have shown that the internal organs suffer a biological meltdown. The liver, kidneys, and pancreas seem to dissolve into pulp, to liquefy."

Wiping beads of sweat from his face, the speaker continued his grim task. "This is the most aggressive virus we have encountered to date. And the most startling thing about it is that some of its victims begin to show symptoms within eight hours of being exposed to the virus."

The people sat in stony silence.

"However," Dr. Monet added, "the incubation period can last as long as six months to one year, without showing signs of the disease. But from the onset of the first symptoms, death will usually occur within twenty-four hours. As far as we know, no one has ever survived. Mortality seems to be one hundred percent."

Pausing momentarily, he looked out into the faces of the people sitting around the conference table. "And, ladies and gentlemen, we have made a most frightening discovery. The Maylay virus has mutated into an airborne form. It can be transferred by a sneeze, or a cough, or just by breathing, and it can survive in the atmosphere for up to twenty-four days, maybe longer.

"To this date, there are no vaccines, no known cures, and it has eluded all attempts to slow its rapid spread; and, unless it is contained, it threatens to sweep across the world. Its implications for the human race are beyond the comprehension of the medical community."

The audience sat in stunned silence, staring at the man in front of them. Most of them had seen the devastation of the major killers—AIDS, Marburg, Ebola, and others. And the thought of something even more horrible chilled them to the bone.

Taking a deep breath, Dr. Monet implored, "We must do everything in our power to confine this virus to the presently infected areas and eradicate it. It must not be allowed to break out. It must be contained, regardless of the cost, if the human race is to be spared. We must be prepared to take extreme measures. I must emphasize that we are in a race against time."

A soft murmur of voices filled the conference room.

Behind Dr. Monet, four adjoining video wallscreens came to life showing a sharp, detailed map of the world. Turning to face the wallscreens, Dr. Monet announced, "We have several areas of high population in three countries that have already been infected with the Maylay virus. These areas are now quarantined."

Removing a small hand-held laser pointer from his coat pocket, he aimed its narrow beam of light toward the right side of the map on the wallscreens. As the light touched Southeast Asia, several sections on the map turned a pulsating red. Moving across India, more sections of the map lit up. When the laser beam passed across Africa, it seemed that the entire continent glowed a bright red.

"The most critical areas are in Southeast Asia, India, Africa, and South America," Dr. Monet declared. "The populated areas represented by the color red have been reclassified. They have moved into the 'critical' category and now pose a threat to their entire regions.

Many of these areas had already been decimated by the AIDS pandemic; and now, with the introduction of Maylay, there is no longer any hope of containment. They have reached a stage where the most desperate measures must be employed. These areas must be cleansed."

Steve stared intently at the color of death glowing on the wallscreens.

Placing his laser pointer back in his pocket, Dr. Monet turned to face the audience. "We must deal with the critical areas first, represented on the map in red. While our quarantine and containment policies in dealing with AIDS and other known viruses have had modest success, we see no hope of containing this new plague without adopting draconian measures. In order to destroy this virus, the diseased parts must be removed."

Dr. Monet gathered up the papers in front of him. "As you can see, ladies and gentlemen, time is a luxury we cannot afford. We must move quickly against this scourge. We cannot use standard methods of containment. We have to use desperate measures. Each person who carries this virus is a walking biological time bomb and must not be allowed to escape. Every man, woman, and child in these contaminated areas must be exterminated. We must stop this lethal virus from entering into the main artery of the world's population. We must save the earth."

A slight rumble of hushed voices spread through the large conference room, falling quickly into a heavy, nervous silence.

Sitting motionless, Steve's eyes narrowed and his countenance darkened. He glared at Dr. Monet, wondering if the global government had already moved into a new dimension in the deliberate, systematic genocide of vast numbers of human beings.

A dark uneasiness stirred inside him.

EIGHT

Following the breakup of the Global Security Council briefing, Dr. Wallenberg lingered for several minutes near the conference table, carrying on an animated conversation with Adam Stenholm. Abruptly breaking off their discussion, Wallenberg made his way to where Steve was waiting.

A third man joined them, a military man, average height, distinguished looking, probably in his mid-forties. With his tanned skin, Steve guessed him to be an avid skier.

Turning to the man at his side, Dr. Wallenberg said, "Steven, this is General Amos Dorian." The two men shook hands.

"I have an emergency meeting that I must attend," Dr. Wallenberg told him. "It will take about an hour. I've asked General Dorian to show you around, then escort you back to the Alpha Level. I'll meet you at the car. Ramul will be waiting. Then we'll return to Geneva."

After Dr. Wallenberg had left, General Dorian said, "Mr. Weston, I have to go to another level before I escort you to the surface. You can either wait here or go with me. Whichever you prefer."

"I think I'll tag along with you, if you don't mind, General," Steve answered amiably.

"Of course. I'd be delighted to have you," the general returned.

Leaving the conference room, the two men walked down a long corridor where they boarded an elevator. "Mr. Weston," the general said as they rode down, "we're going to the Round Room, located five hundred feet below this level."

When the elevator stopped, the two men stepped out, turned right, and walked through a set of bronze-colored steel doors into a massive, brightly lit, perfectly round room. Quickly scanning the room, Steve saw hundreds of technicians who were sitting hunched over glowing computer screens, in constant voice, data, and video communication with the New Earth Federation's military forces scattered around the world.

Tall 3-D flat-panel video screens mounted on the walls completely encircled the room. Color symbols moving across the screens charted the position, course, and speed of the global government's planes, nuclear submarines, and aircraft carriers. Other symbols showed the movement of all ground forces.

Staring intently at the incredible clarity and detail of the digital imagery displayed all around him, Steve instinctively knew that this was the military nerve center of the New Earth Federation's Global Peace Forces.

With military deliberateness, General Dorian moved to one of the computer stations, placed his briefcase down, and removed a black code book. Flipping through the book, he gave the computer operator a series of classified entries. As she entered the codes, almost magically the wallscreen in front of them filled with an incredibly detailed satellite view of a dark, foreboding landscape. A light purplish haze hung ominously over the still-smoldering terrain.

"The screen in front of us," General Dorian said with great enthusiasm, "is showing a live shot of our latest target. Only a few hours ago, more than one hundred thousand people lived in that city. As you can see, they no longer exist. It was a contaminated area, so it had to be cleansed."

Steve stood, unmoving, staring at the digital images of the apocalyptic scene. When the eye of the satellite camera brought the details of the city even closer, he gasped out loud, "My God, what hit that city?"

General Dorian smiled. "The TR6, one of our latest and most productive weapons. It's code-named 'The Trumpet.' Triggered by a very low-yield nuclear catalyst, it produces enormous heat that cleanses the atmosphere, destroying all flesh, and with it all viruses—including the Maylay virus. Some of us affectionately refer to the TR6 as 'The Purple Death.'"

Appalled by Dorian's words, Steve stared at the screen and demanded, "But how can you control such a destructive device? How—"

"Good question," the general replied. "The size and explosive capacity of the TR6 series can be adjusted to fit any political, military, or genocidal need. It can be programmed to cover one square mile, or fifty, or a hundred square miles of land surface, depending on the mission. And with our delivery systems and guidance technology, we can place it to within a few feet of the designated spot without disturbing the surrounding area."

General Dorian then turned back to the woman and gave her some additional instructions. Instantly, the wallscreen became a map. Reaching over the woman's shoulder, Dorian punched in another series of ultrasecret codes and watched as the map highlighted an area identified as *Zone 9G, Section 2173*. Studying the map for several moments, Dorian entered more codes and pressed EXECUTE.

The targeted area outlined on the wallscreen began to pulsate red.

Pointing to the screen, General Dorian boasted, "Our next target, Mr. Weston. The TR6 will once again cleanse another infected city before sunset. It is Gaia's will."

Steve suddenly felt sick. With a simple computer entry, this one man had profiled the death of another city. Exhibiting an air of indifference, he had entered cryptic codes into the computer and had pronounced a death sentence on thousands of living, breathing human beings.

With a note of pride in his voice, General Dorian added, "We've finally brought nuclear weapons under our control. With conventional nuclear devices, it would take fifty years before the area would be clear of radiation. But with the TR6, we can cleanse a city, then have our people move in almost immediately. Quite ingenious, don't you think, Mr. Weston?"

"Quite impressive, General," Steve answered casually, fighting an urge to express his true feelings about the matter.

With such technology, power, and force, and such implements of human destruction, Steve wondered if the military and government scientists and population-control experts could constrain themselves in the killing.

Or had they already crossed the line?

"Oh, by the way, how is Lori, your wife?" the general asked casually.

Surprised by the question, Steve answered, "I . . . think she's doing fine."

"Well, why don't we see if we can check up on her," General Dorian suggested. "Just look at the screen over to your right, Mr. Weston."

Glancing up at the video screen, Steve watched as the eye of a camera inside a satellite high in space displayed an image of a wide street busy with traffic. Focusing in more closely, the camera picked out a single car and followed it. Suddenly, the image of that single car enlarged, filling the entire screen. The car's license plate was then isolated and displayed in a grid at the very center of the screen.

Steve's breath caught in his throat. "That's Lori's car," he muttered. "How . . . how did you do that?"

"The Panoptican Surveillance System, Mr. Weston," the general added with a note of pride in his voice, "is a series of sophisticated global surveillance satellites, circling overhead in a Low Earth Orbit that allows us to triangulate on a target, giving us precise three-dimensional global tracking. Then through computer-enhancing, we can read the label on a golf ball in the middle of a fairway if we choose."

Steve stood transfixed, staring at the clear 3-D image of Lori's car on the wallscreen as it moved rapidly through the streets of Dallas. He was startled by the incredibly sharp and detailed pictures.

"Looks like she's on a shopping spree," Dorian added. "If you would like, we can stay with her. And, with our immediate access to all electronic transfers of funds, I can show you any purchases she might have already made. Shall we track her . . . just for the fun of it?"

Steve raised his right hand. "No . . . I've seen all I want to see."

Touching his computer keyboard, General Dorian entered a code, and the screen went dark.

"The Panoptican system, General—"

"A very effective surveillance system, Mr. Weston," the general answered. "'Panoptican' comes from the Greek word 'optikon.' It means a prison or workhouse so arranged that all parts of the interior are visible from a single point. It's a building that's designed to control people."

"I wrote a paper on the Panoptican when I was at the University of Zurich," Steve said. "If I remember correctly, an ancient English philosopher, Jeremy Bentham, suggested that prison houses could be built with inspection towers overlooking each cell. The cells would always be lighted, but the towers would remain dark so that the prisoners never knew whether they were being watched or not. That would allow a few people to monitor and control the activities of a large number of people."

General Dorian smiled. "Indeed, you're correct. It was a brilliant scheme. Because the prisoners could not see the towers, they never knew when they were under surveillance."

After giving the computer operator further instructions, General Dorian nodded toward the door, and the two men left the Round Room and walked out the door and down an auxiliary tunnel that opened into a wide thoroughfare teeming with people.

Strolling casually, General Dorian said, "Bentham called his structure a Panoptican. It was designed to induce a mental state of always being seen without being able to see the watcher."

"I assume," Steve ventured, "that it's for the good of the Social Order. We—"

The general interrupted him abruptly. "Come now, Mr. Weston, don't try to make us out to be something that we're not. We're the new totalitarians. Our ability to surveil gives us control over people. They know we're watching them, whether they're working, traveling, shopping, attending school, eating dinner in their homes, or viewing some form of entertainment on their holoscreens. We're always there, watching and listening to them, night and day. We can enslave people in ways that past totalitarians could never have dreamed possible. Without this technology, the global government could not exist."

Turning right, they approached a bank of elevators. Boarding elevator number three, Dorian punched in the Theta Level. As the door slid shut, he continued, "When the Personal Identifier is made compulsory, and everyone has the subcutaneous biochip injected into their flesh, our power to surveil will be complete."

"Yes, Dr. Wallenberg told me about the Personal Identifier. But how will it be used to surveil?" Steve asked.

"That's the genius of the plan, Weston. In addition to holding enormous amounts of personal data, the biochip is essentially a radio transceiver and transponder—which means that it is capable of receiving an interrogation signal, then transmitting back a response. It becomes a homing device, and with the power of the Panoptican Surveillance System, we'll be able to triangulate on the biochip transponder and track anyone on earth with pinpoint accuracy.

"The biochip is encased inside a shell of finely-tuned crystal of the purest quality. When the PSS signal interrogates the target biochip, it responds with microscopic vibrations in harmony with the coded hit." Dorian paused, and his voice lowered to a guarded whisper. "But it's not just a radio signal, Mr. Weston. It's the Voice of the Earth Mother, Gaia, joining us all together as One, in unity with the Universe."

Steve shuddered involuntarily. There was a shadow of *something* . . . madness, perhaps, that flashed momentarily in Dorian's eyes.

His lips curling into a tight cynical smile, General Dorian made a throwaway gesture. "There will be no place on earth to hide."

While his mind hammered away at moral dilemmas he was not fully prepared to deal with, Steve found himself wondering if men such as Dorian felt justified for the indefensible cruelties they were inflicting upon the human race. Struggling against a strange fear growing inside him, a million questions and concerns pounded him in a thundering, painful avalanche.

Knowing that he had to have more answers to these colossal ethical riddles, he decided to probe Dorian further, hoping that he might get him to talk more freely.

Passing a small restaurant, Steve touched the general's arm. "General, may I buy you a cup of Swiss coffee?"

"Of course," the general replied amiably.

Stepping inside the restaurant, they were escorted to a table near the back. An attractive, young Indian woman with long, straight hair and a pleasant smile took their order.

The two men fell silent momentarily as they enjoyed the flavor of the hot, chocolate-flavored Swiss coffee.

"General," Steve said slowly. "May I speak freely?"

"Of course," the general answered.

Trying to think of the right words, Steve slowly traced the rim of his coffee cup with his finger. "Back there in the Round Room," he said, trying to sound casual, "you ordered the death of thousands of people. . . ."

The general smiled. "I'm a servant of Gaia, our Mother. I'm dedicated to protecting Her against Her enemies. The flames of the TR6 release the cleansing, healing energy of Gaia. We're simply removing the diseased parts from the ecosystem. That's why I send them. Our weapons are purifying agents, burning out the evil."

Steve shifted nervously in his chair. "The report on the Maylay virus . . . is the situation as critical as they made it sound?"

General Dorian shoved his coffee cup aside and leaned against the table. "We've pushed the Earth too far, Mr. Weston, and She's fighting back. You see, these ancient viruses are Gaia's warriors that She has kept in reserve for millions of years. They are Her cleansing agents. And our scientists tell us that Gaia still has thousands more of these unknown viruses waiting in the deep rain forests of the world. Now is the time for us to throw ourselves in front of the juggernaut of destruction, to be antibodies against the human pox that's ravaging this precious, beautiful planet."

Placing his elbows on the table, General Dorian leaned forward and looked Steve in the eye, sincerely. With a whispered voice that sounded as if he were sharing a profound revelation of immense proportions, he said, "Mr. Weston, Gaia, the Earth, our Mother, is not simply an environment *for* life. Gaia Herself is a living organism, a self-sustaining system that modifies and changes its surroundings and life forms to ensure Her survival. The entire range of living matter on Earth, from whales to viruses, and from oaks to algae, constitute a single living entity. And we must all live in harmony and balance.

"Our destiny is not dependent merely on what we do for ourselves but also on what we do for Gaia as a whole. If we bring danger to Her, She will dispense with us in the interests of a higher value, that is, life itself."

"What does that have to do with the Maylay virus?" Steve pressed.

"Ah, you still don't understand, do you, Mr. Weston?" the general responded. "It could be argued that viruses, such as the Maylay virus, and others, have, through the empirics of evolution, become the Protectors of Gaia by mounting preemptive, genomic attacks against all who threaten Her. Since we ourselves have become a threat to Her own survival, perhaps Gaia is about to unleash an extinction virus that will be aimed at the human species."

In a low tone, the general added, "These viruses are the Earth's defense systems against the most dangerous invaders of all."

Steve looked up. "Invaders? Who are the most dangerous invaders, General?"

"The human species!" the general replied.

"The human—?" Steve responded in astonishment, unable to finish the sentence.

General Dorian smiled. "You look surprised, Mr. Weston. You shouldn't be. Some of us believe that the human species itself is the most deadly disease on Planet Earth, that the human race is Gaia's most fearsome enemy. Yes, living, breathing, breeding, reproducing, consuming *homo sapiens* are putting Gaia in danger, and She is striking back with her most potent defensive weapons, the killer viruses. Humanity's foolhardy exploitation of Her limited resources, and their reckless overpopulation have finally caused Her to defend herself. She's not a tolerant mother, Weston, and She can be ruthless in Her vengeance against those who do not obey Her laws."

Steve frowned. "Are you saying that . . . Gaia is causing all these deaths from these viral epidemics?"

General Dorian shrugged. "It's not Her fault. We are to blame. We humans have pushed the planet too far with our excessive population. Gaia will save Herself, even if it should mean wiping out the entire human species. We must do all we can to appease Gaia, in the hope that She will spare some of us. I have come to believe that we must take bold and unequivocal action. In fact, we must make the rescue of the environment the central organizing principle for civilization. It is our global mission."

Trying to mask his astonishment at the general's pronouncements, Steve remained silent.

"These tiny genetic entities," General Dorian declared boldly, "have the potential for fulfilling Gaia's will for the Earth. They have defied the greatest scientific minds, Mr. Weston. They're always changing, mutating, adapting, growing stronger, hiding, reappearing. Is it accidental, random, without any design? I don't think so. I think it's Gaia's brilliant scheme for keeping the human population under control. Her viruses are always there, waiting, growing stronger, watching to see if we are able to control our passions. If not, Gaia will do it for us. The human species must never again be allowed to overload Her ecosystems."

Leaning back into his chair, Dorian added solemnly, "Perhaps, Weston, the Maylay virus is simply an effective weapon in the hands of Gaia. . . ."

Dorian took a sip of the now-cold coffee. Placing the cup down, he chided Steve. "Many of us believe that only the highly evolved members of the human species should be allowed to remain on the Earth. We believe that all others should be eliminated so that Gaia can restore Herself to Her original beauty and harmony."

"Mass murder, General. Is that what you're proposing?" Steve answered, barely above a whisper.

General Dorian flinched, obviously displeased at Steve's choice of words. "That's a rather crude term, Mr. Weston, one that we prefer not to use. But I suppose the concept of 'sustainable development' does lead to the mass evacuation of large numbers of 'undesirables.' We're compassionate human beings who are involved in moving the human species forward toward its evolutionary destiny. Naturally, we're sometimes compelled to embrace the 'unthinkable' as a necessary approach in attaining our goals."

With a feeling of unease steadily growing in the pit of his stomach, Steve considered the implications of what General Dorian had told him. Draining his coffee, he placed the cup back into the saucer and leaned forward, as if anxious not to be overheard by the two men at the adjoining table.

He had decided to take a calculated risk.

Glancing quickly around the room, Steve said, "General, I want to see the Omega."

Even before Dr. Mueller had blurted out the name, Steve had heard whispered rumors that there was a room somewhere deep inside The Mountain that housed a computer so advanced it was reverentially referred to as the "Global Brain."

And that the room itself had been planned with special care. Forming an impregnable cocoon, he had heard the room had been laser-carved out of the very core of the underground complex. The floating platform that the godlike computer rested on was mounted on massive computer-controlled hydraulic shock absorbers that were engineered to minimize the concussive impact of any nuclear explosion outside of The Mountain.

Containing the global government's most classified data, its very existence was known only to those in the upper echelons of power. Designed and built by thousands of computer scientists and technicians, the Omega was the crowning achievement of decades of computer research and development.

And if an enemy could access the files hidden inside the Omega, they would be in a position to disrupt the supercomputer's carefully crafted encryption algorithms, causing it to crater. By interrupting the integrated flow of secret data between the Global Military Command and Control Center in the Round Room and the armed forces in the field, they could plunge the New Earth Federation's military into unimaginable chaos.

As a precaution against such an eventuality, the programmers had built a maze of controls into the system that could be traversed only by those with top clearances. Lying safely behind sophisticated electronic barricades made up of infinitely complex code-doors, they had hidden the global government's secrets to their weapons of control over the human race.

But most fascinating to Steve were the whispers that this super-computer now functioned more as a biological brain than a computer. They believed it had taken on a life of its own, moving beyond the control of the experts who designed it. Self-evolving and continually redesigning itself, it was known to make critical decisions and give specific directions for the operation of the Social Order.

Many viewed it with alarm, declaring that it was now in control of the world.

While he knew that the Omega was a machine, built by human hands, to many, like Dr. Mueller, it had taken on a virtual cybernetic mythform with godlike characteristics, believing that its consciousness came from a source that was not human.

Steve wanted to know more about the Omega.

The general was clearly startled by the suggestion. His brow furrowing, he glared at Steve for a brief moment, then demanded, "Who told you about the Omega?"

Steve hesitated before answering. "I accidently overheard it mentioned in a conversation once. I . . . don't remember who it was."

The general's response was quick and firm. "Weston, I don't know if you're lying or not, but if someone told you about the Omega, he has broken the law and could be in mortal danger. Its very existence is known only to those with the highest clearance ratings."

Feeling the general's steady, disapproving gaze, Steve felt a sudden resolve and decided to press him further. "Do you have the proper clearance, General?"

Dorian flinched, a flash of anger crossing his face. Gaining his composure quickly, he answered curtly, "No . . . no, I don't. Only a limited number of people have clearance to go into the presence of the Omega."

For a brief moment, they locked gazes, like two combatants who were about to engage in a life-and-death battle.

Steve's time to see the Omega would come later.

NINE

Drained by his encounter with this enigmatic new world, Steve was thankful for the quietness of the passenger compartment of the Daimler limousine. When he had arrived back at street level, he had thanked General Dorian for his time and bid him goodbye. Ramul had met him and told him that Dr. Wallenberg was on his way and would be there in just a few more minutes.

Sipping a cup of hot coffee from the entertainment bar in the limo, Steve leaned back into the seat and sighed deeply. His emotions still charged with mixed feelings of anger and apprehension, his mind whirled with a flood of conflicting thoughts. There was an indefinable, growing sense of uncertainty building inside him that he could not shake. He had entered a society he didn't know existed until this day, and now he had seen and heard things that deeply troubled him.

Even more troubling were the things he had *not* been allowed to see. Things that were hiding from him, just out of view. Things that seemed to lie just below the surface, like the long, twisted roots of an impenetrable forest.

Things like the Omega.

Steve glanced up when Ramul opened the door to let Dr. Wallenberg in. The older man fell heavily into the seat. Laying his briefcase down on the floor in front of him, he leaned back wearily and fastened his seat harness. Nodding to Ramul, the driver pulled the Daimler swiftly away from the curb.

Dr. Wallenberg's deeply lined face seemed to carry a sadness, a pensiveness, that Steve had not seen earlier in the day. He knew something was troubling him, but he would not intrude on his friend's space by speaking to him first.

As the limo pulled onto the boulevard that would take them back to the autobahn, Steve gazed outside at the spectacular alpine vista. The mountain peaks were gleaming brightly in the last rays of the setting sun, and the valleys were deep in shadow as day quickly melted into darkness. The scenes were both gripping and savagely beautiful.

After several minutes, Dr. Wallenberg leaned forward and touched a red button on the control panel on the pedestal in front of him. Steve heard a slight electronic hum that quickly faded. Wallenberg had activated an electronic filter that vibrated at a very high frequency inside the passenger compartment of the limo. The filter had set up an electronic barrier to any ground-based or satellite laser listening device that might attempt to pick up the vibrations of their voices. The two men were now encased in an impenetrable electronic orb with no possibility of being overheard.

Dr. Wallenberg took a deep breath. "Steven," he said, his face clouded with concern, "I must talk to you."

Steve waited tensely, silent.

"Steven," he said, speaking barely above a whisper, "I know many things about the people who control the new global order. And if you are to work among them and survive, there are things you should know. But what I tell you must never be repeated. Do you understand?"

"Of course, Dr. Wallenberg," Steve answered.

"I have learned things today that deeply trouble me," Dr. Wallenberg added.

Glancing momentarily out the window, the older man sighed heavily. "I've been a public servant most of my adult life. I've given much of my life and fortune in the pursuit of world peace. But what I've learned today makes me think that it was all in vain."

Steve frowned thoughtfully. "Why do you say that, sir?" Steve asked.

Dr. Wallenberg hesitated, his features furrowed into a deep frown. "I have learned today that the leaders of the Social Order have a plan . . . to eliminate *billions* of human beings from this planet."

A cold, black silence held for a long moment.

The older man continued speaking, slowly, in low tones. "I don't yet know all the details, but their plan is called 'The Gaia Project.'"

Steve's eyes darkened as he remembered the words the World Leader had spoken in his speech. *"The population of the earth must be reduced to a sustainable level. Gaia is calling for an 'Earth Cleansing.'"*

The muscles in Steve's jaw tightened. "Is . . . that what the World Leader was referring to in his speech?" he asked haltingly.

"Yes," Dr. Wallenberg answered solemnly. "They believe the Gaia Project is their sacred, biological, and spiritual Covenant with Gaia in Her mission of 'Earth Cleansing.' They are convinced that they are instruments in the hands of Gaia. I don't know all about it, but what I do know frightens me."

Steve could see a deep sadness in his eyes.

"Sir, something is troubling me," Steve ventured.

"What is it? Perhaps I can help," the older man offered.

"The World Leader—do you honestly believe he has supernatural powers?"

Dr. Wallenberg paused, trying to form his reply carefully. Then, in hushed tones, he said, "Yes, I have no doubt that the man possesses enormous supernatural powers. Or, perhaps, the supernatural powers possess him. You see, the manifestation of the fire in the Great Hall of Unity was not the only unexplainable act of his that I have personally witnessed."

"There have been others?" Steve queried.

"Yes. I had never believed in the spirit world until I saw his powers. Now I am more terrified of this man than any person, or thing, on earth. In fact, I have come to believe that he is the embodiment of evil."

"Why do you say that, sir?"

Dr. Wallenberg leaned forward, still speaking in soft tones. "Let me tell you of an incident that convinced me of that fact. I had gone with Adam Stenholm to a meeting with His Majesty in his private quarters in Geneva. During the course of the meeting, some of Stenholm's agents brought in a man who had been accused of treason against the

Social Order—a high-ranking official in the GU5 organization. His body trembling in fear, he begged the World Leader for mercy."

Steve could see that his friend was visibly shaken by recalling the incident.

"What happened?" Steve pressed.

"Without saying a word, the World Leader stretched out his right hand toward the cowering man . . . and the man instantly crumbled to the floor, clutching at his throat. I stood transfixed, unable to move or say a word. His body twitched like he was caught in the jaws of a large wild animal. His hands tore at invisible fingers of some evil entity that had attacked him. His eyes wide in terror, he croaked out the words that something was choking him, cutting off his wind. The last sound he made was a gurgling at the throat, then his body relaxed in death.

"When the World Leader left the room, Stenholm motioned for me to leave also. But I couldn't tear my eyes away from the form that lay at my feet. I stared at the expression of horror that was frozen on the face of the dead man. Unable to resist, I knelt beside the body and saw something that has filled my life with dread since that moment."

"What was it, sir? What did you see?"

Dr. Wallenberg looked into Steve's eyes, holding them. "I saw . . . marks, *claw marks*, on the man's neck, made by the strong hands of some invisible being, some unseen evil entity that had entered that room. The shape of its hands was outlined by the darkened bruises that ran around each side of his neck. His throat had been crushed . . . and droplets of blood were still oozing from the punctures in his neck where the tips of the entity's claws had dug into the skin."

Shaking his head, Dr. Wallenberg said soberly, "Steven, there was someone—or *something*—in that room. I don't know what it was, but it was evil. Evil beyond anything I have ever encountered. What I saw that day filled me with fear for the future of the human race."

"Who is he, Dr. Wallenberg? Who is the World Leader?"

The older man rubbed the back of his neck. "I've known his family for many years. Since the World Leader was a boy, in fact. A bright boy, he had an intellect in the genius range and excelled in everything he did. His father died when he was eight or nine. He was raised by his mother, Madame Helena Rousseau, an extremely rich and powerful woman. She owns, or controls, some of the world's largest companies. She and her son migrated to India a few months after her husband's death."

"I saw her briefly at a social function some time back," Steve remarked.

"Madame Rousseau, a strong-willed woman," Wallenberg said, "was a disciple of a powerful and mysterious holy man who commanded a large following throughout the world. As a young man, His Majesty was placed in an academy run by this famous guru. It was there, I am told, that he developed his powers, under the personal tutelage of the guru. After graduating from the University of Higher Learning in Delhi, India, he traveled the world for a time, instructing large audiences in Eastern mystical thought.

"About ten years ago, he and his mother disappeared from sight. We later learned that he had gone into hiding inside a highly secretive monastery in the Himalayas. We were told that he was there in preparation for his appointed time to be thrust onto the world stage as the Teacher, the World Leader. That occurred when he gave his speech in the Great Hall."

A quizzical look on his face, Steve replied, "Then . . . I helped to introduce him to a world audience."

"Yes, Steven," Dr. Wallenberg answered. "The World Leader himself requested that you host the television coverage of the evening's event."

Shocked by that revelation, Steve stammered, "Why . . . why me?"

"Because the people of the world trust you," Dr. Wallenberg said. "And because they knew that the trust the people have in you would be transferred to the World Leader."

Steve looked away, troubled by it all.

Dr. Wallenberg took a sip of water, then placed the glass back in its holder. "Steven, I must tell you some things about your life."

"My life? What is that, sir?"

"Steven, you are one of the *chosen.*"

"*Chosen?* I don't think I understand."

"You will fully understand, in time. You were chosen as a young boy. That's why you were sent to Landstar Academy, where you were taught, trained, and prepared to take your place in leadership in the Social Order. Every facet of your life has been planned and carefully guided. And because you have gone through each phase successfully, you are now ready to assume a larger role."

Steve turned his face away and looked out through the window. With the fulfillment of his dreams now in his grasp, he should be pleased, but, strangely, he was troubled by it all.

Seeing that Steve was disturbed by the information, Dr. Wallenberg said, "Steven, I'm an old man, and I have to trust someone. I know that you have not been totally co-opted by the Social Order. That's why I trust you and why I want to give you all the tools that I can, to help you survive. There are good and decent people who work in the NEF, people who want peace and freedom. But they dare not speak up for fear of their lives. And if the others knew how I felt, I would already be dead."

Swept by a wave of sadness over the agony in the face of his dear friend, Steve asked simply, "What can I do?"

Another long, dark pause.

Reaching into a small pocket inside his jacket, Dr. Wallenberg retrieved a small plastic card. Holding it in his hand for a moment, he said, "When I learned about the Gaia Project today, I decided that I must give this to you. Someone else must know who they are, and what their plans are for the human race."

Thrusting the small plastic card into Steve's hand, he added imploringly, "Guard this with your life."

Steve sat in stunned silence, afraid to even breathe.

Holding the card tenuously between his fingers, he turned it over slowly. A long series of letters, numbers, and symbols were printed across the face of the card.

Mystified, he looked back at Dr. Wallenberg. "What is it, sir? And what do I do with it?"

With his eyes focused on Steve with laserlike intensity, Dr. Wallenberg replied soberly, "When the time comes, Steven, you will know. . . . You will know."

Suddenly feeling an overpowering fatigue, Steve sank back into the soft leather seat, his mind reeling from the day's intense activities.

Steve Weston had always been confident of his intellectual abilities, his physical prowess, his personal talents. He had felt secure about his life and career. But for a few terrifying moments today, he feared that some alien force outside of his control was taking charge of his life, propelling him into a dark unknown region that was laden with unspeakable dangers.

It was just a feeling, but he couldn't shake it.

He rubbed his eyes lightly with his fingertips. He had to have some answers. He had to talk to someone whom he could trust.

And the only person who came to his mind was Dr. Dwight Howard Pennington, Lori's father.

TEN

The sun was a fiery red ball, sinking lower and lower against the distant western horizon. A few scattered clouds, now golden with the rays of the slowly setting sun, floated aimlessly in an azure sky. Her left hand held in front of her face in an effort to shield her eyes from the bright glare that was pouring through the windshield of her car, Sheila Harper drove through the busy streets of Dallas, anxious to get her frightened and confused daughter into the quiet sanctuary of their own apartment. Still in an almost-hypnotic state from her experience in Lori Weston's class, Katy sat beside her mother, quiet and still.

It was a little past 7:00 when she pulled into her assigned parking space at Building M-7441, in a nondescript apartment complex located about seven miles from the Enrichment Center where she worked. Built and operated by the People's Housing Commission, the apartment assigned to Richard and Sheila Harper was comprised of two bedrooms, one bath, a small dining area, and a modest den.

Trembling in fear, Kathryn clung tenaciously to her mother as they walked down the sidewalk toward the entrance to their apartment, her expressionless face bringing a fresh flood of silent tears to her mother's eyes.

Once inside the apartment, they were met by the loud squeals of three-year-old Michael, who ran across the room into the open arms of his mother. Scooping him up, Sheila caressed him and kissed him repeatedly across his face. After putting him down, she watched him run to his sister, who was now sitting on the edge of the couch, her hands folded loosely on her lap. But instead of the usual enthusiastic greeting by his sister, he was met by a blank stare and an indifferent hug.

Sheila walked into the kitchen where Richard was removing a MealPac from the microwave oven. She stepped aside as he retrieved the steaming package and carried it from the kitchen to the small eating area. Placing it down on their round maple dining table, he removed the cover, allowing the escaping steam to fill the room with its pleasant aroma.

"A meal fit for a king," Richard said as he turned to Sheila and kissed her lightly on the lips. "And a queen, too, of course," he quickly added.

Noting her lack of response, he looked at her thoughtfully and said, "Sheila, something's wrong. What is it?"

"It's horrible, Richard," Sheila answered, trying to hold back the tears. "It's Kathryn. She had a very traumatic experience in her 'spirituality' class today. She . . . she was led into an encounter with a demon spirit."

"What happened?" he asked quietly.

Moving closer, Sheila buried her face against Richard's shoulder. Feeling his arms enfold her, she let go of her pent-up emotions, expressing her sadness and hurt through her tears. When her crying subsided, Richard clasped her shoulders in his hands, held her in front of him, and told her, "Let's not talk about it now. We'll have dinner and put Mikey to bed; then we'll talk with Kathryn."

Knowing that her husband would share the burden, Sheila wiped her tears away with a small white towel, then turned to the task of arranging the table for the meal. When the meal was over, Katy went to her room. Sheila then bathed Mikey and put him to bed.

When Richard had finished cleaning the kitchen, he placed a disc of orchestra music in the player and turned the volume above the normal listening level. Fully aware that every word and activity in their home was constantly monitored by the authorities through a tiny fiber-optic camera and listening device embedded in their Home

Communications Unit (HCU), he always took this precautionary step whenever they wanted to carry on a private conversation.

With Mikey put to bed, Sheila joined Richard at the small table near the kitchen. Located in a strategic spot, it was slightly out of the visual range of the eye of the tiny camera lens in their HCU.

Richard was slowly opening and closing his fists, trying desperately to contain his anger. "They don't have the right to do this to my little girl's mind," he declared. "I don't care what the law says. Under God, she's our responsibility, and we have the right to teach her our Christian faith."

Nearing tears, Sheila reached out for her husband. The soft touch of her hand on his face broke his simmering anger and flooded his churning emotions with an unspeakable sadness. The strain of the years of oppression from the Social Order because of their Christian faith seemed to reach a horrible crescendo on this singular night. Pulling his wife gently into his arms in a tight embrace, the two of them wept quietly.

"Hello, Daddy."

It was Katy's voice. Richard and Sheila broke their embrace and turned to see their daughter standing in the doorway to the kitchen. Richard stared at her for a moment. Always full of love and the joy of living, she was now a beautiful young girl on the threshold of blossoming into full womanhood. And the thought of anyone harming her was intolerable. But now this child of his stood before him with a strange and frightened look on her face, dazed, detached, as if she were on drugs.

Moved to rush to her, to take her in his arms and brush away all the evil and hurt she had endured that day, he restrained himself, not knowing how deeply she had been led into the spirit world. He knew he would have to approach her with patience and understanding in order not to cause her irreparable harm.

Sheila motioned for Katy to come and sit beside her. When she was seated, Sheila said, "Katy, tell Daddy and me what happened today in Ms. Weston's class. Start at the beginning."

Reaching for inner strength, the Harpers tried to remain calm as they braced themselves to hear the details of her experience.

Katy removed her shoes, dropped them to the floor, and looked around the room as if she had never seen it before. Her parents glanced at each other, knowing that she had not fully come out of the hypnotic state her teacher had led her into.

"Umm . . ." Katy hesitated, obviously having a difficult time concentrating. "Well, we sat in a circle. We chanted our mantras over and over . . . until I began to feel funny. Then the, uh, white unicorn . . . well, she came and took us inside a cave. That's where I met my Wise Counselor."

Pressing for more details, Richard asked, "Dear, what did the Counselor look like? What did he say to you?"

Katy's reaction to the question was immediate. Her head jerked toward her father, her face taking on a somber, frightened look. When her body began to tremble, instantly Richard reached out and drew her into his arms, pulling her firmly against his chest. Holding her tightly, swaying gently back and forth, he whispered into her ear, assuring her that everything was going to be all right.

"His eyes . . . they scared me, Daddy," the whimpering child confided to her father.

"Scared you? How . . . how did he scare you?"

"He was ugly . . . his face was ugly. And his eyes . . . when he looked at me . . . he scared me. I didn't like him."

Still trying to find more pieces to the puzzle, Sheila continued to gently press her daughter for answers. "What did he say to you? Just tell us whatever you remember."

"He said . . . that Jesus is not God. That there are many teachers like Jesus, and that Christians are his enemy and should be my enemy, too. He told me . . . that my parents were enemies to Mother Earth . . . and that they had to be destroyed. I don't remember anything else. I just remember looking up and seeing Mom."

Touching his daughter's hand, Richard said, "Katy, your mother and I love you very much. And we know that you've been through a very difficult experience, and we want to help you."

"But why did my teacher make me go see that person who frightened me?" she asked.

"Well, we don't know why she did that," Richard answered. "But your teacher was wrong to do what she did. She has lied to you. What you saw was not your Wise Counselor."

"Then, who was he, Daddy?" Katy asked plaintively, her large, blue eyes reflecting the emotional effects of her ordeal.

"What you saw and heard was a demon spirit, posing as a Wise Counselor. These spirits work for Satan, and they are evil, and they want to hurt us all. He wanted to hurt you, but your mother was there and she prayed for you, and God kept the demon spirit from hurting you."

Looking into the innocence in the face of their child, Richard and Sheila both knew that she had been coerced, through a cleverly designed program, into opening herself up to demonic spirits. A trusting child by nature, she had been betrayed by an authority figure, her teacher. And her parents had learned through bitter experience that tonight was only the first step in her long road to mental and spiritual healing.

Sheila leaned toward her daughter, taking both of her small hands in her own. While caressing them gently, she assured her, "Katy, God has given us protection from Satan. So whenever you think he is trying to hurt you, just remember that the power of God within you is greater than the power of Satan."

"Thank you, Mom. I feel better now. I'm tired, so I think I'll go to bed."

"OK," Sheila answered. "Kiss your father good night, and I'll walk you to your room." Richard reached out, brushed Katy's hair lightly, squeezed her tight, and kissed her on the cheek. Sheila then took her by the hand and the two of them disappeared down the hallway.

After a few moments, Sheila returned, sat down at the table, placed her elbows on the table, rubbed her forehead with the tips of her fingers and sighed heavily. When Richard handed her a cup of tea, she caressed the warm cup in her hands for a moment, then lifted it up to her face and breathed in the soothing steam and inviting fragrance. It was her favorite blend.

"Sheila," Richard said, in a voice just above a whisper. "When Katy told us what had happened to her, I was filled with hate for her teacher. Then I reminded myself that Satan is our enemy, not those people."

Sheila thought for a moment before answering. "I'm a mother, Richard. And I saw what Lori Weston did to my daughter in her classroom today."

"I know, Sheila. And the natural response is to strike back at her. But that would do no good."

"I understand, Richard," Sheila answered. "Believe me, I do. But I can't allow them to destroy my daughter."

Shaking his head wearily, Richard stood and walked to the communications console.

It was now past 11:00, and fatigue was setting in. Retiring to their bedroom, Sheila removed her makeup, put on her sleeping gown, sat down on the bed, leaned back against the headboard, and wrapped her arms around her knees. Richard, now wearing his robe, sat down in his reading chair next to the bed.

Their parental fears and worries hanging heavily over them in the stillness of their room, they both remained silent, wondering what the next few days held for them . . . and their daughter.

Often, in the quietness of the late night, after Sheila was asleep, Richard would sit in his chair next to their bed, staring into the subdued light of the room, remembering the face of his own father.

Dr. Michael Harper, a man in his seventies, had been the pastor of a large church before being arrested by the government. Although it had been more than two years since his arrest, trial, and sentencing, the memory of it all was still fresh in Richard's mind.

Not knowing what the government had done to his father was the worst part of all. And in these private moments he could still hear his father's strong, reassuring voice, encouraging him, teaching him, guiding him through the difficult and discouraging times.

But at this moment in time, he needed to see him, to sit across from him, to look into his face . . . and tell him about Katy.

Playing through his memory now in holographic clearness and detail were the scenes of that fateful day when his father had walked to the pulpit located in the center of the large, curved platform inside the church sanctuary and looked out into the faces of the twelve thousand people who were awaiting his words.

There was something in the air that morning, a nervousness. The people sensed that something was wrong, and they needed guidance from their pastor.

Although Dr. Harper hadn't told the people, he was aware of the presence of government agents in the congregation that morning, having been warned by an unknown friend that they were going to arrest him during the service. But even under such duress, his father had refused to abide by the directives of the Ministry of Religious Affairs.

Many of his own congregation had implored him to "go along," saying that it would not mean he had denied his faith. It would only mean, they argued, that he was "cooperating" in order to continue his ministry, and that of the church.

While many Christian churches had conformed to the guidelines issued by the Ministry of Religious Affairs by integrating Eastern mystical doctrine into their teaching and worship, his father had steadfastly refused to compromise his beliefs.

No one moved that morning as Dr. Harper laid his open Bible and hand-scribbled notes on the pulpit in front of him. Although he knew the agents were there, he didn't know their exact plans and didn't know when they would strike. Thinking that he had everything under control, he smiled inwardly at the sight of his own shaking hand when he moved his notes a little to the right.

But, he reminded himself, it was just another Sunday morning gathering of believers, and he had a job to do. People were looking to him for guidance and leadership, so he refused to alter his intended remarks, or his demeanor.

With his face looming large on the giant wallscreens, his snow-white hair, his bright blue eyes, his brilliant smile, and his dark-rimmed reading glasses gave him the look of a scholarly professor.

Speaking deliberately, his strong, resonant voice filling the auditorium, he informed the people, "I know that the great temptation, at times, is to succumb to the mounting pressure to conform to the socially accepted belief system and values. Many, even among the clergy, are calling for us to compromise our beliefs in order to bring about social consensus. Their dream of a One World community demands the acceptance of a religion that will blend all religions into one. The great stumbling block to this unity, they say, is the Christian faith."

The pastor then removed his glasses, folded them, and placed them in his coat pocket. Standing erect, his voice strong, his words sure, he said, "My fellow believers, please allow me to confess my most sincere belief in the One God, and in the One Savior of all mankind, God's only begotten Son, Jesus Christ. There is salvation in none other. Jesus Christ is—"

Abruptly cutting him off in midsentence, a short, stocky man in the middle section of the auditorium about halfway back, jumped to his feet and shouted, "This meeting is over, by order of the Ministry of Religious Affairs."

Instantly, two dozen men who were scattered throughout the congregation stood to their feet, holding small automatic weapons, ready to fire. The short man cried out, "All right, everybody stay calm and nobody gets hurt. You're all witnesses to the crime of *noncompliance* here today and you may be called into court to testify to what you've seen and heard. This church no longer exists. It is declared illegal by order of the Ministry of Religious Affairs."

On a signal from another agent, several men rushed toward Dr. Harper from each side of the platform. The people sat frozen in their seats, staring in disbelief as the government agents hurriedly placed steel shackles around his waist, wrists, and ankles. Clamping a thick leather collar around his neck, they ran a chain from his leg shackles to the collar, forcing him into a crouched position.

At that point, more than a hundred men leaped from their seats and rushed down the aisle toward the pastor. When their action was met by a short burst of gunfire, Dr. Harper called out to the men, "Please return to your seats and remain calm."

The men hesitated, then reluctantly returned to their seats, watching helplessly as the agents led their pastor off the platform and out a side door into a waiting car.

Sometimes, in his memory, Richard could still faintly hear the metallic ringing of his father's chains as he shuffled painfully out of the church, often wondering why he hadn't rushed to his side, in spite of the danger. Sighing a deep sigh that was a mixture of fatigue and deep concern for his daughter, Richard stood, removed his robe, spread it across the back of his chair, then lay down on the bed and slipped under the covers.

Still sitting with her back against the headboard, Sheila continued to replay the frightening scenes of the day over and over in her mind. Then she slid down into the bed, leaned gently against Richard's back, and drew the covers over her shoulders.

Just as Sheila's body relaxed and she felt herself drifting into sleep, she was jarred awake by a plaintive wail that seemed to fill the entire house. Richard knew immediately that it was Kathryn.

With one swift motion, he threw back the covers and bounded toward her room. Rushing to her bedside, he saw his daughter thrashing about on her bed and flailing her arms wildly as if trying to ward off an attacker. Her quivering body covered with cold sweat, and she was crying out in terror, trying desperately to extricate herself from the unseen, malevolent force that had assaulted her.

Scooping her up into his arms, Richard drew her tightly against his chest and told her over and over that he was there and that he would protect her. As the anxious moments passed, with Richard still clutching her tightly, Katy's fears gradually subsided into gentle whimperings. Slowly, Richard loosed his embrace and laid her gently down on her bed, watching her facial expressions closely, anxiously waiting for signs that would tell him that her night terror was over.

Sheila spoke to the frightened child. "What happened, Katy? What caused you to cry out?"

"He came back . . . Mother," she sobbed. "The Counselor . . . came back . . . and he looked at me with his horrible eyes. He said . . . he was going to take me with him . . . that I belonged to him."

"No, you don't belong to him, Katy," Sheila assured her. "You belong to God . . . and to your mother and father." Sheila's soothing, confident voice brought the girl slowly back to reality. Softly rubbing her daughter's forehead with the cool palm of her hand, Sheila pressed the point. "And the Counselor is not going to take you away, Katy. He's evil, but Jesus Christ covers you and protects you from his power."

Turning her eyes upward toward her mother's face, Kathryn asked pleadingly, "Mommy, will you and Daddy pray for me?"

Richard was quick to answer. "Yes, sweetheart, your mother and I will pray for you and call on God to protect you."

Kneeling on one knee, Richard laid his hand lightly against his daughter's forehead. Sheila was at his side, her right hand resting on his left shoulder, her head bowed, her lips moving in silent prayer.

The deep resonance of his voice, the weight of his loving touch on her face, and the positive assurances that laced his words had an immediate soothing effect on his terrified daughter. And before he had finished his prayer, her mind had calmed, her body had relaxed, and she had gone back to sleep.

Still kneeling beside the bed, Richard and Sheila stared anxiously down into the peaceful face of their daughter, each knowing instinctively that even though they had won a skirmish, the war for the mind and soul of their child was still very much in doubt.

Feeling that Katy was safe for the night, they quietly arose and walked slowly back to their own bedroom, sat down on the side of the bed, and began to talk.

There was no use in trying to sleep.

ELEVEN

Flight 1298 from Geneva, Switzerland, touched down on the runway in Baltimore, Maryland, shortly before 7:00 A.M. When the plane had parked at gate 23, Steve Weston took his travel bag from the overhead bin in the first-class section and followed the other passengers out through the enclosed boarding ramp into the crowded terminal.

After five days in Geneva, he was on his way to keep an appointment with his father-in-law, Dr. Dwight Pennington. He would catch a later flight to Dallas.

Stepping to one of the videophones positioned along the wall inside the terminal, he inserted his ID card and dialed his home number. The small color monitor in front of him came to life when Lori punched in the receive button.

Seeing her husband's face on her own screen, she smiled. "Oh, hello, Steve. Where are you?"

"I'm in Baltimore," he replied.

"What are you doing there?" she asked.

He hesitated, not wanting to tell her the truth. "I've got to see some people here. Can't talk about it. While I'm in the area, I thought I'd get a car and drive out to see how your mom and dad are doing."

"Oh, that's nice. Give them my love."

"Could I speak to Jimmy?"

"Oh, I'm sorry, Steve, but Jimmy is at the Enrichment Center. He's been there since you've been gone."

"Lori, don't you ever keep him anymore?"

"Now, Steve, you know I've got my career to think about. Besides, if you're such a loving father, why aren't you ever home to watch him?"

"Please, Lori," Steve pleaded. "Let's not get into that again."

Cutting him off abruptly, Lori said, "Gotta run, Steve. Thanks for calling."

Watching the small screen turn dark, Steve frowned and shook his head dejectedly. He then picked up his travel bag and walked to the car rental desk. The drive was pleasant, giving him time to think about what he would say to Lori's father.

Dr. Dwight Pennington had taught global economics for many years at World University. Since retiring three years ago, he and his wife, Martha, had been living on a three-acre estate an hour and a half away from Baltimore.

Always a good listener, his father-in-law had accepted him as the son he never had. Having come to admire and respect Dr. Pennington, Steve cherished the memory of the time he had spent with him.

An hour out of Baltimore, Steve turned right onto highway G-456, drove for another thirty minutes, then turned left onto a small country lane that led him to the long winding driveway up to the Penningtons' estate.

Coming to a stop in front of their house, Steve parked the car and walked to the front door. Mrs. Pennington opened the door, embraced him, and asked about Lori and Jimmy. She then ushered him into the large den, where Dr. Pennington was sitting in his oversized leather chair, a light blanket spread across his legs.

Walking over to his chair, Steve shook Dr. Pennington's hand warmly. "How are you, sir?"

"Oh," he replied, "for an old man, I suppose I can't complain. Martha takes very good care of me. How's my grandson, Jimmy?"

Seeing the sparkle in his eye when he talked about Jimmy, Steve could see how much this man loved his only grandchild.

"Jimmy's doing fine, sir. He's growing real fast. He'll be three very soon."

After several minutes of small talk, Steve stood, rubbed the back of his neck, and paced the room, trying to gather his thoughts, searching for the words that would properly frame the questions that were troubling his mind.

Dr. Pennington cleared his throat. "You gonna wear out my carpet, Steve? Something's troubling you. . . . What is it?"

Steve stopped pacing, thrust his hands into his pockets, and turned to face Dr. Pennington. "Sir, I was presented with an opportunity to advance my career, and I accepted it. I've worked all my life for this . . . but now I don't know if I made the right decision. I have misgivings about the whole matter. . . ."

"What was the opportunity, my boy?"

Moving to the chair in front of Dr. Pennington, Steve sat down. Remaining on the edge of the chair, he told him, "Dr. Wallenberg has recommended me to succeed him as International Director of the United Information and Communications Authority. I told him I would accept the position if the ruling board approved me."

"So what's the problem?" Dr. Pennington asked curtly.

"I wish I knew. Within the last few days, I've been introduced to a world I didn't even know existed before. I've met people who possess power beyond anything I've ever imagined. They hold the power of life and death in their hands."

For the next twenty minutes, Steve gave a rambling account of his experiences in Geneva, and at The Mountain, giving vent to his mounting frustrations and fears.

When he had concluded, he looked at Dr. Pennington and asked, "Do you know these people, sir?"

Dr. Pennington nodded slightly. "Yes . . . yes I do."

"Can you tell me about them?"

A flicker of pain crossed the older man's face, causing him to hesitate a moment. Glancing away momentarily, trying to decide whether he should end their conversation or continue, Dr. Pennington spoke haltingly. "Are you . . . *sure* you want to know who these people are?"

Desperate to know the truth, Steve pressed urgently, "Yes, please tell me what you know about them. I want to know what I'm dealing with."

Dr. Pennington glanced up at the door, as if to check to see if anyone could hear what he was about to say. Sighing heavily, he answered, "I'll tell you what I know, and I hope I'll do you no harm by telling you."

Relaxing in his chair, Steve fell silent.

"I've never discussed these matters with anyone, not even Martha," Dr. Pennington began. "I've been sworn to secrecy, and if I had talked about what I know, in all likelihood, I would have been assassinated. But I don't have too many more years to live, so there's nothing they can do to harm me now. But . . . there's one thing I will insist upon, Steve. If anywhere along the line you feel you don't want to hear any more, please stop me. I'll understand."

With the light from the heavily shaded lamp next to his chair outlining the old man's pale, thin features, Steve stared into his friend's face as he took up his story.

"At one period during my teaching career," he began, "I took a seven-year leave of absence from the university to work as a consultant and personal aide to a member of one of the richest families in America—in the world, in fact. Among other things, I escorted my employer to a series of very secret meetings with other very wealthy and powerful people from around the world. Called the Global Forum on Economic Cooperation (GFEC), this group met once a year to set the future economic agenda for the rest of the world to follow.

"The meetings always took place in very luxurious but obscure places. Before the participants would arrive at the hotel or resort, advance teams would go in and put all the regular staff on temporary leave in order to bring in their own people. They had their own chefs, maids, waiters, medical staff, and security forces. Highly trained and heavily armed, their security people would not hesitate to kill anyone who might threaten the lives of these people."

Steve leaned forward in his chair, listening intently.

"Usually numbering no more than four hundred people, the list of participants included some of the top intellectuals of the world, including CEOs of global corporations, international bankers, economists, prime ministers, members of royal families, finance ministers, presidents of countries, leading academics, and others who were useful to them. Strictly off limits to the media, no cameras were ever allowed, and all notes and papers used during the conferences were to be destroyed before leaving.

"To an outsider, it looked like an innocuous group of world leaders who had come together to discuss world affairs, but no outsider could know that these people were forming the laws and policies for all the countries of the world to follow."

Pausing for a moment, Dr. Pennington rested his head momentarily against the back of the chair, then continued his discourse. "In reality," he said softly, "the majority of the people who were at the conferences were only minions of the men who hold the power of the world in their hands. For within the larger group, there is a small number of men, numbering no more than one hundred. These men come from the families and dynasties who own and control the vast majority of the wealth of the world. With their collective history reaching back for hundreds of years, their wealth is beyond comprehension.

"And for centuries their dream has been to bring the entire world under one single government and one single economic system . . . under their control, of course. They have come close on several occasions, but they didn't have the scientific technology to pull it off . . . until now. My employer was a member of that small group."

"Who are these people, Dr. Pennington?"

A cloud passed over Dr. Pennington's face, as if he were recalling forbidden memories. Resting the side of his face against his hand, he told Steve, "The only name I ever heard them referred to was 'The Principals.' Their identity was never to be revealed, and the source, or amount, of their wealth was not to be discussed. Their affairs were so guarded that any attempt to pry into them would have brought swift and sure retaliation."

Steve stared at the older man.

"Do you remember when the World Banking Crisis occurred in 2022?" Dr. Pennington asked.

"Yes, of course, I remember it very well," Steve replied. "We would have had a world economic collapse if it had not been for the swift action of some of the world's leaders."

"Steve," Dr. Pennington countered, "what you and the world believed about the banking crisis is exactly what the Principals wanted you to believe. That's when they made their decisive move for total control."

"I don't understand," Steve interjected.

"Let me explain. I had accompanied my employer to an emergency meeting of the Global Forum on Economic Cooperation, called in 2022. As you will recall, the world was in chaos, governments had fallen, and much of the currency of the world had been declared of no value, bringing the global economic order to the brink of collapse.

"The emergency GFEC conference was held in a luxury resort hotel near Salzburg, Austria. Over a thousand people attended, including heads of supranational corporations, international bankers, heads of the major stock exchanges, finance ministers, economics experts from the leading universities, and others. The participants were told that they were there for the purpose of coming up with solutions to the rapidly deteriorating situation."

Pausing to rest for a moment, his wrinkled face deepening into a pained frown, the old man added, "On the second day while sequestered in the hotel—most of them full of wine and enjoying the benefits of the female companionship furnished to them by the Principals—the private security guards, hired by the Principals, quietly closed the entrances and exits to the hotel and cut off all communications to the outside world.

"When explosions and small arms fire were heard outside, pandemonium broke out inside the hotel. With no way of communicating with anyone on the outside, they were told that the hotel had been attacked by a band of terrorists, and that everything would be back to normal in a short time.

"After two hours, when communications were restored and the people in the hotel were able to make contact with their offices, a bizarre story began to unfold. Mysteriously, they were told, the computer databases in all the financial houses throughout the world had been suddenly erased, as if wiped clean by some unseen hand, bringing all financial transactions to a halt. Employees of America's Federal Reserve Bank, Germany's Bundesbank, the Bank of Japan, the Bank of England, the New York Stock Exchange, and all others, stared into empty monitor screens. It was dutifully reported by the news media that a global 'malfunction' had caused the crash of the world's financial computer systems.

"For two terrifying hours, the global economic order ceased to exist, as if some Infinite Matrix had gone mad, plucking the flow of digitized financial information from the datasphere and vacuuming out all the computerized records stored in all the financial centers of the world. And when their systems came back up, they were shocked to find that they contained very different financial data in their databases than was there before. Within that two-hour period, all of this vital data had been transferred to the Global Conservation Bank inside The Mountain in Switzerland. In one brilliant stroke, the Principals had gained total control of the wealth of the world."

A quizzical look on his face, Steve replied, "I remember the incident very well, Dr. Pennington. But I don't remember ever hearing this part of the story."

Dr. Pennington took a sip of water. "The news media broke the story as a 'new development' in banking and commerce, never telling the world that a financial coup d'état had just taken place. I remember seeing special bulletins on television, announcing that, in an effort to avert a total collapse of the world's financial system, the Global Conservation Bank had activated an emergency-control mechanism that had temporarily transferred oversight of the world's banking system into their care. They assured the world that everything was now under control and that the people should go about their business as usual. What the world didn't know, of course, was that it was a plan that had been meticulously laid out and flawlessly executed. It was not a reaction to a moment of crisis; no, the crisis had been created by the Principals."

Steve stirred uneasily in his chair. If it had been any other person in the world except this man, he would have totally discounted everything he was saying. But he knew Dr. Pennington to be an intelligent, honest man, with no reason to lie to him.

"How did they pull it off, sir—technically, that is?" Steve asked.

Dr. Pennington glanced toward the door. Assured that his wife could not hear him, he continued. "Having the complete trust of my employer, I was one of the very few who knew in advance what was going to happen. According to him, long before this global crisis, the

Principals had employed the world's most talented people to build the computer hardware and write the software to be used for global governance. After years of research and development, and billions of dollars, they created the world's most powerful mainframe computer, with capabilities far beyond the grasp of the world's finest minds. Known as the Omega, it was designed to—"

"The Omega!" Steve exclaimed, half rising out of his chair.

Dr. Pennington arched his left eyebrow. "Yes, that's what it's called. Do you know about it?"

Steve relaxed back into his chair. "Yes. I've heard of it. But please go ahead."

"Well, the Omega housed a highly sophisticated program that had been designed to run a single, unified, global central banking system. The computer program was named DEUS. It stands for Digital Exchange Unified System. The DEUS program was the master tool for bringing about the convergence of all the digital financial data in the world. For many years before its activation, computer manufacturing companies had been required to install a government-mandated encryption chip in all computers built. This chip contained instructions at the microcode level to respond to commands from the Omega. It was now just a matter of waiting for the proper moment to seize the world's money system."

Steve shifted in his chair. "Is that where the special meeting of the Global Forum on Economic Cooperation fits into the scheme?" he asked.

"Indeed," Dr. Pennington responded. "With the world's financial leaders shut off from the outside world, the Principals gave the order to execute *Operation: DEUS*. At that precise moment, the DEUS program went online. In an unbelievable feat of technological genius, the Omega fed its digital commands to the galaxy of data satellites in the sky, and through the unbroken web of fiber-optic cables that blanket the earth, brought about the disabling of all encryption and security measures of the computer systems of the world's financial houses. With this accomplished, the Principals were able to execute an electronic run on the databases of the banks of the world.

"Once inside the bank's computer systems, the Omega vacuumed out the data and transferred it to the Global Conservation Bank located inside The Mountain in Switzerland. The DEUS program then replaced each bank's supply of currency with a predetermined allotment of digital units. Each unit, as you know, is called a DAT, standing for Digital Allocation Transaction.

"At the same time, they electronically transferred enormous sums of money out of thousands of secret, coded accounts of drug lords, dissident nations, and anyone else who displeased them. In less than two hours, virtually all the wealth of the world was transferred into the database of the Global Conservation Bank, pulling off the greatest financial coup in history. Since that moment, the global banking system has been run by the Omega through the DEUS program."

Steve stared wordlessly into his friend's eyes, trying to harden himself against the disturbing revelations about the Social Order.

When Dr. Pennington continued speaking, there was an intensity in his face and voice that was disturbing. "Under the control of the Omega, and with DATs now the exclusive medium of exchange, all other forms of money were outlawed, causing all coins, paper money, and other systems of currency exchange to be worthless. Money had become nothing more than computer digits taken from one account and allocated to another account. And, unlike paper currency, all digital transactions leave an easily identifiable and traceable digital trail, allowing them to track the movement of the money."

Dr. Pennington took a moment to spread his blanket out over his legs. "Steve," he added, "the most powerful weapon of control on the earth is a global central bank with the authority to issue the money that all nations are forced to use. Once the Principals had control of the currency, everything else soon fell into place."

Steve could see that the old man was tiring. Tempted to end the conversation, he felt compelled to let him continue to address the searing questions still troubling his brain.

Dr. Pennington took a deep, trembling breath and continued his story. "This group of men, and their forebears, have come close to world government on several occasions down through history but were unable to pull it off. But with the advancements in computer science and communications technology, they were finally able to do it. You see, with the takeover of the banking system, they could dictate the terms for the new global government. And through the formation of the New Earth Federation, they were able to create the ultimate monopoly over the human race, forging the final link in their chain of total control."

Softly rubbing his right temple, Steve ventured, "Are you saying that the Principals dictated the terms of the formation of the New Earth Federation?"

With his dark, penetrating eyes fixed on Steve, Dr. Pennington answered firmly, "Yes. That's exactly what I'm saying. The New Earth Federation was formed in 2023, one year after the Salzburg coup. Holding the world hostage to their demands, the formation of the New Earth Federation was the ransom paid by an impotent world. The existing governments of the world had no choice but to comply with the dictates of the Principals."

Reaching up, Dr. Pennington wiped his mouth with his shaking right hand. "But in all their carefully laid plans to bring about a global government, they overlooked the one component that had any chance of unifying the peoples of the world."

"What component did they leave out?" Steve queried.

"Religion," Dr. Pennington answered.

Steve shook his head disbelievingly.

"Or spirituality," Pennington said. "Whichever term you prefer. You see, human beings are spiritual beings. Even Marx and Lenin and Mao couldn't suppress people's spiritual nature. Religious differences among nations and ethnic groups have stood in the way of global unity. When they formed the New Earth Federation, they left out that one vital component that could have united the people of the world and held their empire together."

With a toss of his hand, Dr. Pennington said, "But this new guy— this World Leader—he knows that religion is the way to build a global order. He knows that religious differences, more than anything else, have stood in the way of global unification. He knows that the world will be One only when a single, syncretistic religion has been embraced by the peoples of the world. And that's what he brought to the global government. He has infused that body with spirituality."

Steve looked puzzled. "What is the spirituality the World Leader has brought to the world?"

Dr. Pennington nodded and forced a weak smile. "It's nothing new—quite old, in fact—but it fits in nicely with their goal of global unity. It emphasizes the pantheistic belief of the interconnectedness and interrelatedness of all things, stuff that's also basic to Hinduism and other Eastern religious beliefs. It's really a repackaging of basic pantheism, mixed with Hinduism, Eastern mysticism, occultism, witchcraft, nature religions, paganism, goddess cults, and whatever else they can think of to throw in. But, as a *planetary* religion, it's ideal as a synthesizing force to bring about religious, cultural, and political unity."

"So Gaia is the unifying force," Steve returned.

Professor Pennington chuckled. "Gaia . . . now, that's a story in itself. Gaia is the name of an ancient Greek goddess, an archetype of the Earth Mother. The Gaian worldview is that the earth itself is a deity, which all people must honor and worship. Like the ancient pagans before them, these people believe that if we offend the Goddess Gaia, she will turn on us and attack us as if human beings were a deadly virus.

"Under 'Earth Spirituality,' it becomes the will of Mother Earth that the planet be cleansed of all 'negative mass.' You see, by using that logic, they can eliminate any category of human beings they choose. This group could include Jews, Christians, political dissidents, any race of people, or even those who might reject their Earth religion."

Looking up, Dr. Pennington smiled. "They could even include 'journalists' in the category of the unwanted, if they chose to."

"That could never happen," Steve replied nervously.

His voice taking on a more somber tone, the old man replied, "I wouldn't be too sure if I were you. All it would take is one small Global Court decision declaring that journalists, or any group, had fallen below the Intelligence Index, or were shown to have some mental disorder, for instance. They could then be classified as 'less than human' and the State could do with them whatever they pleased."

Steve sat for a long time without speaking, his thoughts running wild. Then, rising from his chair, he walked back and forth across the room. "Dr. Pennington," he said slowly, "did you see the Secretary General's speech?"

Dr. Pennington cleared his throat. "First, sit back down in that chair. You're making me nervous with all your pacing back and forth like that."

Steve quickly sat down and looked at Dr. Pennington, awaiting his answer.

"Indeed, I did see him, along with the rest of the world."

"Well . . . what did you think?"

"About what?" the old man barked.

"About . . . his levitating, the fire, what he had to say."

Dr. Pennington smiled, saying, "Yes, I sat here and watched the entire proceedings—even saw the man levitate. But the most interesting part to me was the column of fire. Now, that was an impressive touch. I was so impressed with that little trick that I called a friend of mine, Dr. Samuel Nicholson. He still teaches at World University and has a farm a couple of miles down the road. He and I have been having some rather heavy discussions about death and the afterlife and such. When I saw that fire, I recalled a conversation Sam and I had a few weeks ago, so I called him. He didn't seem the least bit surprised at the Secretary General's performance; in fact, he told me to read something from this book he gave me."

Pulling out a drawer in the table next to his chair, Dr. Pennington took out a small, black, leather-bound book. Opening it, he said, "Let's see . . . oh, here it is. It's from a section called 'Revelation.' I put a paper clip on the page that Sam told me to read. Uh, I can't see it very well, son; the type is rather small. Will you read it for me? It's the part I underlined."

Steve took the open book and ran his finger down the page to the underlined section. He read aloud, "And he doeth great wonders, so that he maketh fire come down from heaven on earth in the sight of men, and deceiveth them that dwell on the earth by means of those miracles which he had power to do."

Steve looked at the underlined words for a moment. "I don't understand, sir. Is this talking about the Secretary General of the New Earth Federation?"

"Sam tried to explain it to me, but I'm not sure I fully understand it myself. But doesn't it seem curious that someone would write those words thousands of years ago, then we would see it happen before our eyes? Sam calls these writings 'prophecies.'"

Steve looked puzzled. "Does it have any significance?"

"Sam thinks it does. I'm not sure, but with the developments in the past few years . . . well, he's got me to thinking."

Dr. Pennington put the book back in the drawer. "Now, you asked me about the Secretary General, so I assume you have some strong feelings about him. Want to tell me about them?"

Moving to the edge of his chair, Steve spoke imploringly. "Sir, I saw something in his eyes. He seemed to possess a spiritual power beyond himself. And I have no doubt that it's an evil power. But no one in the Great Hall seemed to notice, or to care. Dr. Pennington, he's a madman, and he's very dangerous. When he spoke, there was mob hysteria among the government leaders there that night. They seemed to be carried off into another dimension, under his spell. I was frightened . . . still am. What is this power, sir? Where does it come from?"

Closing his eyes, Dr. Pennington leaned back in his large, soft, leather chair, falling into a thoughtful silence.

Respectfully, Steve waited, knowing that Dwight Pennington was a well-organized, deliberate thinker, who sometimes was slow to respond to probing, controversial questions. Cautious and guarded by years of having to think through each word and phrase, he often gave the impression of being somewhat detached or disinterested in what someone has to say.

Knowing his traits well, Steve remained silent and waited. The professor would answer in his own good time.

Opening his eyes, Dr. Pennington smiled faintly and said, "Steve, much of the Secretary General's performance was simply a display of very sophisticated technology. But . . . I would not rule out the presence of a very real and evil power. A power that may have come from beings of another dimension."

Steve appeared confused. "What do you mean, 'beings of another dimension'?"

"In our many conversations, Sam pointed out to me that the Bible dealt with this subject thousands of years ago. The reality is that some human beings do, in fact, contact and interact with beings of another dimension."

"Are you serious, sir?" Steve asked incredulously.

"Yes indeed. Sam sat in the very chair you're now sitting in and explained to me that the Bible calls these beings 'demons' or 'evil spirits.' He says that the Bible is replete with human beings encountering them."

"Go on," Steve insisted.

"He had no good word for these . . . demons. He read from the New Testament where Jesus Christ encountered these entities. It seems they had inhabited a number of people around about his area, evidently causing them to do all sorts of strange things. But whenever he came across one of these 'demonized' persons, he would speak right up and command these entities to get out. The demons weren't too happy about it, but in the end, they never failed to come out of the person. The people always showed a remarkable change in their personalities after the demons came out."

"But that was thousands of years ago," Steve interjected. "This is 2033."

"I'm coming to that," Dr. Pennington cut in. "Dr. Nicholson said there has been a remarkable resurgence in the instances of this demon-possession business throughout the world in the last ten or fifteen years. When I asked him why, he told me that when people enter into any form of 'altered consciousness,' whether through drugs, meditation, hypnosis, trances, and so on, they are opening doors that allow these demon spirits to enter."

"Have you seen any of this demon possession?"

Dr. Pennington arched an eyebrow. "Looking back, I think I have seen quite a bit of it. I didn't know what it was at the time, but after talking with my friend, I'm sure that some of the bizarre behavior I've encountered in some people had to have been produced by some powerful outside force. There's no other way to explain it."

Straightening himself in his chair, the old man took a measured breath, then said, "Now, to your question about where the World Leader gets his power. There is only one answer. He gets his power from

Satan, the enemy of God. Quite evidently, he is empowered, perhaps *controlled*, by one, or a number, of these entities. At least, that's the conclusion I've come to after studying the matter with Sam. It's the only logical answer."

Steve stared into the old professor's eyes. "Sometimes, I feel that I'm a part of something very evil, and that there's nothing I can do about it. And now, with my trip inside The Mountain, my conversations with Dr. Wallenberg and General Dorian and Dr. Mueller . . . I'm confused. Please, sir, tell me, what is my part in this whole affair?"

Dr. Pennington's bottom lip trembled slightly. Quickly glancing downward, he quietly answered, "Very well, if you insist. And please forgive me for what I'm about to say. I say it only because I love you like my own son."

"I understand, sir," Steve replied softly.

"Like the others, you have been trained and conditioned since childhood to subjugate your will to the will of the Group, to serve the Social Order with unquestioning loyalty. And, in the process, they've taken away your own conception of 'truth.' Now whatever the Social Order says is truth, to you, is truth, despite what your eyes see and your ears hear."

Clearly disturbed, Steve stood to his feet and walked to the large window overlooking the three acres of land. A full minute of anxious silence passed as he struggled to find the right words to express his feelings.

Folding his arms, his voice tinged with deep emotion, Steve said, "Dr. Pennington, you're the grandfather of my son. That's why I felt compelled to talk to you. We share him in a unique way. Learning these things about the Social Order has caused me to worry about Jimmy's future and what kind of world he will live in. Before Jimmy was born, I was only interested in myself, my career, my own status in the world. The frightening thing is that if it hadn't been for my son, I probably would never have questioned the things I've seen and heard."

Still staring out the window, Steve paused for a long moment. Gesturing vaguely, he added, "But when I stared into the face of the man who is leading the global government, and listened to his plans for the world and humanity, I had only one thought . . . my son. In one frightening moment, as I stood at the glass wall of the TV9 booth, the government's program had a face . . . and it was the face of my own son. Suddenly, I asked myself, will Jimmy be counted as one of the 'excess' human beings who is overburdening the ecosystem? Where do I hide him so they can't get to him? Where have I been, Dr. Pennington? Is this something new?"

Turning around to face his father-in-law, Steve said, "I know I'm rambling, but—"

Leaving the sentence unfinished, he froze in place, watching with deep affection and respect at the tears coursing down the deep lines and folds in the older man's face, dropping silently from his quivering chin onto the wool blanket lying across his chest. Deeply moved, Steve walked quietly back to his chair and sat down, remaining silent for fear of intruding into his father-in-law's private thoughts.

Wiping his tears with the back of his weathered hand, Dr. Pennington looked up at Steve, a pained expression clouding his face. "No, Steve, this is not new. It's all part of a well-laid plan. These people believe they are beyond good and evil. They're convinced that they are destined to rule over a purified earth. The Secretary General's speech was their signal to move to the next level of their plan—to reduce the global population to what they call a 'sustainable level.'"

"I'm not sure I understand, sir."

Dr. Pennington took a deep breath. "Go back over the Secretary General's speech in your mind, Steve," he said, "and you'll understand what I'm trying to tell you. You see, in order for the Secretary General to unite the masses behind him, he had to present a common threat to us all. A threat so terrible in its implications that the masses would willingly relinquish their individual freedoms and rights and pledge their loyalty to him, in order to save themselves.

"The tactics are as old as man. Down through history, governments have maintained their control over their people through the war system, knowing that during times of war, or the threat of war, the masses would willingly carry the yoke of government without complaint. So some outside threat, some enemy, has always been needed in order to maintain social and political stability. And the war system has been the unifying force that has given governments their authority over their citizens."

Steve shifted uneasily in his chair.

"Well, when the Soviet Union collapsed in the latter part of the twentieth century, the threat of a thermonuclear war lost its power as an organizing force. The Principals faced a dilemma. In the event of a state of permanent peace between the major powers of the world, they knew they would need another way to maintain their control over the masses. Because no government has long survived without enemies and the threat of armed conflict, a surrogate for the war system had to be found.

"So, shortly after the collapse of the Soviet Union, and long before I joined my employer, the Principals appointed a blue-ribbon committee made up of some of the most brilliant scientific minds in the world and commissioned them to study the situation and come up with a suitable surrogate for the war system. The threat didn't have to be real; it just had to be believable."

Steve frowned, wondering where this was headed.

In a flat but deadly serious tone, Dr. Pennington explained, "In carrying out their assignment, elaborate and complicated models, representing a variety of apocalyptic scenarios, were constructed on some of the world's most powerful computers. Then the variables of each model were studied, analyzed, and compared to the other models. After more than six years of study, the group came together and wrote their final report. They then presented their findings and recommendations to a closed session of one hundred people who represented the Principals."

The old man brought up one hand and gestured. "While several surrogates for the war system had some serious possibilities, their conclusion was that there was only one model that held any real promise."

Steve stared at his friend. "And . . . what was that model?" he asked.

Dr. Pennington frowned thoughtfully and rubbed his right cheek. "The committee's unanimous decision," he answered softly, "was to recommend using the caveat of the collapse of the ecosystem caused from gross pollution of the environment as the new threat to the survival of

the species. They concluded that this model could replace the war system as a mechanism of control. And they were right. The threat of the
collapse of the ecosystem was more powerful than the threat of extinction through nuclear war."

"But," Steve stammered, "I've been taught all my life that the
ecosystem is in mortal danger. I—"

Raising his right hand, Dr. Pennington cut in, "Fast-forward everything to the present, and things will begin to fall into place for you,
Steve. Go back over the Secretary General's speech. Your misgivings
about him were right. In spelling out his program for bringing
humankind back into line with the ecosystem, he was following the
script written by that blue-ribbon committee many decades ago. But
he carried it a step further—by identifying a common enemy who is
responsible for the destruction of the ecosystem. He gave the people
an enemy to hate, to make war against, and to destroy, in their mission
of saving the planet."

Steve slumped back heavily into his chair.

The brows of the frail man knit tightly above the clear, old eyes.
Holding Steve in his steady gaze, like an earnest teacher admonishing
his pupil, Professor Pennington explained to him, "By skillfully weaving an endtime scenario of total ecological upheaval, the Secretary
General pressed home the point that if the people of the world did not
unite behind him, there would be no hope."

As Dr. Pennington spoke, Steve's analytical brain began to put
together the seemingly disparate pieces of the World Leader's speech,
suddenly hearing and understanding the esoteric code words that he
had sent to those in tune with him throughout the world. For shrouded
inside his circuitous pronouncements, lying submerged just beneath
the surface, had been dark, cryptic messages to the worshipers of Gaia
that the "purification" of the earth had begun.

Replaying the speech in his mind, the pieces to the mysterious
puzzle began to drop silently into place. While weaving his tapestry of
deception with his soothing words, the World Leader had declared
that there was an identifiable enemy who had caused all the problems. He had then called out to the people of earth to unite behind
him to destroy that enemy.

In a flash of insight, Steve knew. He knew with a cold certainty. There could be only one answer.

The enemy to the earth, to Gaia, was . . . the *human race* . . . humankind.

The Secretary General of the New Earth Federation had told the world that living, breathing human beings were responsible for the threat to the survival of the earth, that humankind itself was the criminal, destructive element. And in order to save the earth, he had declared, some would be permitted to live, while others would be allowed to "pass into spirit," in order to appease Gaia.

His strength now visibly waning, Dr. Pennington took a series of deep breaths, then said, "Steve, after viewing the Secretary General's speech, and hearing him use the worship of Gaia as the basis for his call for a 'purification' of the earth to begin, I have come to believe that my worst fear is about to come to pass."

Steve swallowed hard, then asked soberly, "And what is that, sir?"

Dr. Pennington waited a heartbeat before answering. *"The end of the human species."*

Steve's mouth went dry. Their eyes met in a fixed stare.

"The end of . . ." Steve left the unfinished sentence hanging in the silence of the room.

"You see, Steve," Dr. Pennington replied, his voice growing weaker. "That's the reason much of the Secretary General's speech was taken up with spirituality. The worship and veneration of the earth gives them moral justification for any atrocity they choose to commit. The war against the human race, framed in religious terms, is limitless."

Steve shook his head in disbelief, turning the words over in his mind for a moment, then asked reluctantly, "Are you sure, sir?"

The elderly professor cleared his throat again, shifting his weight uncomfortably. Sighing deeply, he answered, "I've worked among these people for years. And the major topic of discussion has always been one thing . . . *overpopulation*. It's their mantra. They're convinced that the population must be reduced drastically in order for the ecosystem to survive. The next step in their plan is the systematic, scientific annihilation of large numbers of the population, all in the name of Gaia."

"The Gaia Project!" Steve said, his voice barely audible.

Dr. Pennington cupped his hand around his left ear. "What did you say, Steve?"

Steve leaned forward, forming his words carefully. "Dr. Wallenberg told me essentially the same thing, sir. They . . . have a plan. They've code-named their program of depopulation 'The Gaia Project'."

The old man sank back into his chair and looked away for a moment, as if in deep thought. "That's a name I haven't heard before," he mused, shaking his head slowly. "The Gaia Project . . . of course. The name itself fits. You see, Steve, the Gaian religion validates their monstrous crimes against the human species."

Clearly disturbed, Steve stood to his feet and began again to pace aimlessly, trying to absorb it all. Turning back toward Dr. Pennington, he asked soberly, "Is there anything that can be done to stop them?"

Dr. Pennington shot him a sly glance. "I don't know," he said, his voice calm and certain. "But there's one giant roadblock to their plans. It's a belief system that totally rejects the premise behind Earth Spirituality, embodied in the doctrines of the Christian faith. In fact, one of the things that caused me to initiate my conversations with Dr. Nicholson was the global order's virulent hatred of Christianity. He had earlier confided in me that he was a Christian, and I wanted to know why they hated it so."

The old professor paused meaningfully before continuing. "Quite honestly," he said, glancing up at Steve, "if it were not for the influence of Christianity, another holocaust would already have taken place." A sudden cloud seemed to pass over his countenance. He frowned. "In fact, Sam says that at this point in history, the only thing that will save mankind from annihilation is the return of Jesus Christ to the earth."

"Do you believe that?" Steve asked incredulously.

Dr. Pennington looked away. The room became so quiet that Steve could hear the sound of his own breathing.

The old man stared at Steve wordlessly for a moment, a small frown appearing on his face as if he was wrestling with an uncertainty. "Well," he said, taking a deep breath, "quite honestly, I'm beginning to agree with Sam that there has to be some kind of divine intervention or these people will, indeed, bring an end to the human race. There's no earthly power that can stop them. Sam says that Jesus Christ is going to return to earth just in time to save mankind from total annihilation."

Steve shook his head. "Some of the leaders in the Social Order believe that the World Leader is Jesus Christ," he ventured.

Dr. Pennington's reaction was immediate. "That's preposterous," he sputtered. "The World Leader is not Jesus Christ. If anything, he's the Antichrist!"

"The Antichrist? What is that?" Steve returned.

A slight smile playing across the old man's features, he said, "Well, when I talked to Dr. Nicholson, he said that a strong man would arise in what he called 'the last days.' And what he described . . . well, the description seems to fit this World Leader."

Steve moved to the edge of his chair. "I'm curious, Dr. Pennington. What else did Dr. Nicholson tell you . . . about this Antichrist?"

"Well, in our long chats," Dr. Pennington said, "Sam gave me some rather startling details about a man who will appear on the world stage. He said this man will be a strong, charismatic leader who will possess enormous occultic powers. And that the world will accept him as a man who will bring peace. But the truth is, he'll be the embodiment of evil and will receive his power from Satan.

"Sam told me that the prophecies say that this man will head up a strong federation of nations, that he will be a person of such magnetism and power that he will become the greatest dictator the world has ever known. Touted as being the only one who could wrench the world back from the brink of destruction, he will be a messianic figure who'll dazzle the world with his miracles and words."

Pausing for a moment, the old man's face hardened in concentration. "And you know, Steve, it all seems to fit into place. The Principals knew all along that it would take a charismatic figure to lure the nations of the world into their final global federated state."

Studying his friend's face for a moment, Steve challenged him. "Then, you *do* believe that the Secretary General of the New Earth Federation is the Antichrist."

"Not so fast, young man," Dr. Pennington shot back, his eyes flashing. "According to Sam, that's still open for question."

Steve smiled. "Then, how will you know if he's the one?"

Dr. Pennington chuckled. "Well, I don't have any authority to base my calculations on, you understand, but tying together what I know about the Social Order, and what Sam has taught me about these prophecies, I think this guy, this World Leader, as they call him, is just waiting for some global catastrophe that will serve as the decisive, cataclysmic event to propel him onto the world stage as the savior of mankind. They may, in fact, stage such an event, in much the same way they staged the Secretary General's so-called 'appearances' in the sky during his speech."

His wrinkled face hardening into a tight frown, Dr. Pennington warned soberly, "Steve, if this man is the Antichrist, then their plan for 'purifying' the earth has more to do with destroying the people who refuse to worship him as god than it has to do with rescuing the ecosystem."

Pulling himself up in his chair, Dr. Pennington lowered his voice. "Steve, I think you should know that the World Leader was personally chosen by the Principals. And he has their utmost confidence and trust."

Just saying those words seemed to disturb the old man. He looked away for a moment, trying to rein in his raging emotions before continuing. "I don't know if he's the one or not," he said. "But whoever is the Antichrist, in the end, he will lead the world to the brink of destruction. That's when Jesus Christ will return to the earth, according to the prophecies, just in time to save the planet."

Hearing the door open, Steve turned to see Mrs. Pennington walk into the den. "Won't you stay the night, Steve?" she asked. "Your room is ready for you. And it would make Dad very happy."

Steve stood up, hesitating a moment. "No, Mom, I'd better not," he answered cordially. "I wouldn't be very good company anyway. I've got lots to think about, to work out."

"Thanks for coming to see a tired old man, son," Dr. Pennington called out as he leaned his chair back, bringing up the footrest. "I know I've laid a heavy burden on you by telling you these things. Perhaps I shouldn't have."

"No," Steve insisted, "you did the right thing. I needed to know. I don't know what it will mean, but the knowledge will help me make some decisions about what I must do."

Turning his head quickly away, Dr. Pennington fought desperately to regain control of his surging emotions. His eyes glistening with unwelcome tears, his voice breaking slightly, he said, "There's only one reason . . . one reason why I regret my part in this whole affair . . . my grandson . . . and all the children. They . . ."

Suddenly, Steve felt he was intruding on the privacy of this man's soul. He wanted to reach out and touch him, assure him that everything would be all right. Watching his strength ebb away in front of his eyes was painful. Quietly walking over to his chair, he rested his hand gently on his shoulder. He then turned and walked toward the door.

As he pushed the door open, Dr. Pennington stirred in his chair. Steve glanced back.

"Steve . . . please protect my grandson from them."

A heavy silence filled the room for a long moment. "I will, sir," Steve promised.

Mrs. Pennington was waiting for Steve in the hallway near the front door. Touching his arm, she looked up at him. "Steve, will you do something for me when you get back to Dallas?"

Steve touched her hand. "Whatever you want."

She handed him an eight-by-ten portrait of Jimmy that she had been cradling against her chest. Steve took the picture in his hand. Jimmy was sitting on a white rug in front of the fireplace in their den, holding a small stuffed toy. Steve had taken the picture himself on his son's first birthday.

"Could you send me another picture of Jimmy?" she asked, her eyes beginning to moisten. "I'm sure he's much bigger now."

Running the tips of his fingers tenderly over the picture, Steve said, "Yes, he is, Mom. He's much bigger now. I took a beautiful shot of him only a few weeks ago. I'll send it to you just as soon as I get back home."

Her face breaking into a wide smile, she said, "Oh, thank you, Steve. I do wish Lori would let him come up and spend some time with his grandfather and me. A young boy needs to get out in the country. The fresh air and sunshine will make him strong and healthy."

"I'll talk to Lori. I'm sure she'd be delighted to have Jimmy come and spend a few days with you."

"Oh, would you? It would make us so happy."

Mrs. Pennington then reached up and kissed Steve on the cheek. "Please tell Lori to come see her father."

"I will, Mom. But you know how busy Lori stays."

Opening the door to leave, Steve hesitated, then turned and embraced her. "Please watch over Dad."

He then walked to the car, slid behind the wheel, and closed the door. As he pulled away, he glanced back over his shoulder. Mrs. Pennington was standing at the door. She waved. He waved back.

Steve listened to the soft hum of the car window going up, shutting out the noise. Through the quiet, questions crowded in on his mind. He gripped the steering wheel tightly, his features dark and brooding. He had heard Dr. Pennington out, but he was not totally convinced that he was right about everything. He sounded . . . well, a little too conspiratorial, and he had been warned about those people.

Turning onto the main highway, he felt himself begin to relax. He enjoyed driving. It was one of the few times he could escape the pressures he lived under. Sighing heavily, he decided that he would try to put all these things out of his mind for now and, perhaps, think about them later. Besides, he had to get on with his life.

He had to think about himself . . . and his son.

Hopefully, he and Lori could patch up their differences.

At least for Jimmy's sake.

TWELVE

June 1, 2033

Drifting lazily in the night sky, a full moon spilled its pale, silvery light over the vast expanse, casting the countryside in deep shadow. Miles to the north of Dallas, Texas, vivid streaks of blue-white lightning forked through tumbling masses of storm clouds. The low rumble of thunder echoed and reechoed in almost continual rolls in the distance.

With errant raindrops gently pelting his windshield, Steve Weston's sedan moved swiftly through the dark streets. As he approached the security gate guarding the exclusive community where he and Lori lived, he glanced at the clock on the dashboard and made a mental note that it was a little past 11:00.

The security gate opened automatically when the laser beam got the right response to its query of the ID computer in the car's cockpit, and he drove through. As the gate closed behind him, Steve followed the circular street around to the right, then turned left and urged his car toward estate number 37.

Their home, a sprawling two-story structure with over five thousand square feet of living area, was tucked away neatly out of view behind a forest of large oak and pecan trees. The surrounding estates matched his own in luxury and indulgence, all of them exuding position and power.

For his protection, the government had installed an imposing six-foot-high concrete-and-brick security fence around the entire five acres of land. With his high visibility in television, he was constantly on guard, even in his own home.

When his headlights picked up the small discreet sign that read *number 37*, he turned in. The garage door opened and he drove inside, stopping just short of his abandoned exercise equipment.

"I've got to get back into shape," he mumbled to himself.

Picking up his briefcase, he slid out of the car, walked to the door, and pressed his thumb against the ID panel. The security system verified his identity, slid the door open for him, and turned on the lights. Stepping through the door, he walked down the hallway into his elegantly furnished den.

With the warm embrace of its large fireplace and its richly stained, picture-frame-style molded wood paneling, this room was the place he thought about when he was in some other part of the world. It was his sanctuary, his favorite spot on earth.

A voice said, "Good evening, Mr. Weston. May I mix you a drink?" It was the house computer.

Referring to the computerized voice as 'Harry,' Steve answered, "No, Harry. Is Ms. Weston here?"

"Yes, she is, Mr. Weston."

"Is Jimmy here?"

"Yes, Jimmy is here. He is asleep in his room. The house lights were turned off at 10:32 P.M. Will there be anything else, sir?"

"No, Harry. Please turn the lights off in the den when I leave. I was going to view a holofilm, but I'm much too tired. I'm going to bed. Please check to see that all the doors are locked."

"I have already done so. All doors are secured. Good night, sir."

"Good night, Harry. Please don't wake me in the morning. I'm going to sleep late."

"Very well, sir. The wakeup music has been canceled for tomorrow morning only."

Trying to come to grips with his own failure as a father, and with Jimmy's third birthday only four days away, Steve had made plans to celebrate his birthday by spending the day with him, just the two of them. Jimmy loved animals, so as a birthday present, among other things, they would visit the zoo.

Strolling across the den to the bedroom, wearily fighting the fatigue that racked his body, he peeled off his coat, unbuttoned his shirt collar, and pulled off his tie. Opening the door quietly in order to keep from disturbing Lori, he walked lightly across the room toward his closet.

Having left the bedroom light off, he hadn't noticed her sitting in the gold armchair in the corner of the darkened room.

"Steve, we've got to talk!" Her voice was cold and caustic.

Not again, Steve thought to himself as he glanced at her in the semidarkness of the room. Always rather self-centered and vindictive, her bouts with depression had increased over the last few months. He had never known anyone who carried as much anger as did Lori. In spite of his best efforts, it was becoming more difficult each day to overlook her constant lashing out at anyone who dared to cross her or stand in her way.

Continuing on to his closet, he undressed and hung up his clothes. Putting on his robe and slippers, he walked back into the bedroom. "What's on your mind, Lori?"

She started slowly. "You can't believe the people I have to work with. You think they're your friends, but there's no one you can count on but yourself."

Standing to her feet, her arms folded against her chest, she began pacing in front of the large window that looked out over their back-yard swimming pool. "They promised me that when George Meador left I would be moved into his position as head of the Department of Intellectual and Spiritual Development for the DFW region. Well, they gave the position to someone else today."

Steve flipped on a lamp near the bed and looked at her face. She was angry, more angry than he'd ever seen her. With glaring, hate-filled eyes that seemed to pierce through him, she walked toward him.

Instinctively, his muscles tensed.

Almost out of control, she screamed out at him, "The backstabbing, the lies, the underhanded way the school officials have treated me! I wish they were all dead! They promised that promotion to me, then they betrayed me. But they won't get away with it. They don't know who they're dealing with."

Shaking with rage, she moved closer to him. With her hands formed into tight fists at her sides, hot, angry tears streaming down her face, she cried, "It's all your fault, Steve. I told you in the beginning that I didn't want a child. I told you he would interfere with my career. And it's happened just as I told you it would."

Her anger congealing into fury, she shouted defiantly, "Jimmy should never have been born!"

With the unbridled rage of a wild animal, she lunged at him, screaming loudly, "I hate you, Steve Weston! I hate you! I could kill you for what you've done to me!"

Steve caught her first blow by raising his left forearm in front of his face. Not to be denied, she continued her attack with flailing arms and tightly clenched fists, somehow believing that this one man was responsible for all her deep-seated primal hurts. And if she could only destroy him, she reasoned, she would rid herself of her tormenting demons.

In spite of his best efforts to avoid her sharp blows, some of them were getting through his defenses and were landing on his chest and shoulders. Restraining every impulse to retaliate, Steve called to her, "Lori, control yourself. I don't want to have to hurt you."

Ignoring his pleas, she kept pressing, lashing out at him with her arms and fists, driving him across the room. As her fury increased, she seemed to lose all restraint, as if under the control of some unseen power. In a desperate bid to fend off her savage blows, Steve managed to catch one of her flailing arms and hold it in a viselike grip.

While he tried to avoid her thrusting knees, her free hand finally found its mark and her fingernails dug four parallel furrows down the left side of his face. Feeling the fire in his cheek and the flow of warm blood, he knew he would have to defend himself.

Trying not to hurt her, Steve gripped her left arm and forced it behind her back. Overpowering her, he drove her to the floor, placed his knee against her back, and held her there. Even though she could barely move, she continued her violent gyrations, trying to free one of her hands so she could strike him again.

Finally, from sheer exhaustion, she stopped struggling and began to sob.

"All right, Lori, I don't want to hurt you. I'm going to let you up, but if you begin attacking me again, I won't be responsible for what happens to you."

Slowly, cautiously, he lifted his knee from her back and loosened his tight grip on her wrist. Still sobbing, she stood to her feet. While rubbing her wrist, she walked to the chair, sat down, buried her face in her hands, and sobbed uncontrollably.

Steve sat on the edge of the bed and waited, knowing that the seething rage was still there.

Several minutes passed in heavy silence, the tension between them unabated. Bewildered over her outburst, Steve sought an answer. "What's this all about, Lori? Why are you blaming me for not getting the promotion? And what does Jimmy have to do with all this?"

Standing to her feet, she leveled her gaze at him. Her words sharp, her tone bitter, she said, "They've used my absences from work against me, and most of them have been because of Jimmy. And you are always gone; you're never here to take your share of the burden. So now they tell me that my duties as a parent are 'diversionary,' and that because of these duties they're afraid I won't be able to give my total effort to the job."

She glared at him, her face twisted with hate, and said defiantly, "I don't know why we had Jimmy. I told you I didn't want the child, but you insisted, and I finally gave in. It was a mistake. I should not have given birth to him."

Her lips pulled tight across her teeth, her body quaking in anger, she shouted, "I should have had an abortion!"

The words stunned Steve.

A look of disbelief crossed his face. He knew Lori had not wanted children, but after Jimmy was born, he thought he had seen her change. He was sure he had seen the look of a mother on her face— the way she nurtured him, her tenderness in handling him and responding to his needs.

"I'm sorry, Lori," he answered hesitatingly, "I had no idea you felt so deeply about our son. I knew you considered him an inconvenience, but I never dreamed you resented him enough to regret not having had an abortion."

Seeing Steve's astonished look, Lori slowly turned and walked to the large window and gazed out across the pool in the backyard, her face reflecting a dull crimson from the varied colors of the lights playing on the rippling surface of the water.

The haunting frustrations of a lifetime had come together in this room on this night, and she had laid them all on the man who was closest to her. Since she was a child, there had been an emptiness, a hollow place in her soul that mocked her, even after each triumph. No award, no commendation, no spiritual experience had ever brought more than momentary relief.

But now she felt she was on the threshold of making a choice that would give her back the years she had lost through the inconveniences of motherhood. And if part of the cost was her marriage to this man, then so be it.

She was first. She had things to accomplish in life, a mission to fulfill.

An option that would solve everything had been in the back of her mind for over a year. And just telling her husband that she regretted giving birth to their child released something inside her and filled her with resolve to go through with her plan.

She would have her son *deactivated*.

Lori Weston had made the choice, and now nothing nor any person would ever again stand in her way.

It's a legal procedure, she reminded herself reassuringly.

As an accepted means of keeping the population down, the abortion law had been extended in 2009 to include a child up to three months after birth. Referred to as a Post-Birth Abortion (PBA), in 2012 the procedure was made legal up to one year of age.

Then, in 2018, the Global Court declared that a child under the age of three years was considered a Potential Human Unit and had no legal protections from infanticide. By law, no child had a right to life until he reached his third birthday. And deactivation could be ordered by either of the parents, or by any number of authorized government agents, if it were deemed in the interests of the Social Order.

Only if the child were allowed to live for thirty-six months, until his or her third birthday, was he considered a "person" with the full protection of global law.

Her arms folded across her chest, Lori smiled inwardly, knowing she didn't have to get her husband's approval, or even inform him prior to taking Jimmy to the infanticide center to be terminated. Either parent could authorize the procedure.

With Jimmy's third birthday a few days away, he was still classified as a Potential Human Unit—not quite a human. Further, she comforted herself in the fact that she would be doing her part for Mother Earth by helping to reduce the excess population.

A strange, penetrating silence darkened the room for an interminable time as Steve sat nervously on the edge of the bed, waiting. Then, rising, he walked to where Lori was standing. Taking her by the shoulders, he gently turned her to face him.

"Lori," he said, his voice shaking with anxiety. "We can work through this together. We have to do what's right for Jimmy."

Lori only stared at him. Her face reflected no sympathy, no regret, no sorrow—only defiance. Her husband's words had no effect on her. She had decided. And she had never felt so good about a choice before. It would be a new beginning for her, *without* any unnecessary baggage to slow her down.

With a cold, tight smile forming on her face, she pulled away from Steve. Glaring at him, her voice cold, she responded defiantly, "Do you want to talk about what's *right?* Well, every child has the 'right' to be wanted. And I don't *want* this child. We're supposed to be free to pursue our own interests, our own goals. Freedom—that's what life is all about. And it's not *right* to force a person to care for someone when they are not emotionally or mentally prepared for it."

"But, Lori," Steve implored, "we can get more help in raising him. We can—"

She cut him off abruptly. Her voice laced with bitterness, she shouted out at him, "Jimmy's birth was a karmic mistake, Steve. I didn't want him in the beginning. I don't want him now. And I will *never* want him."

Turning abruptly on her heels, she stormed toward the door to leave the room. After only a few steps, she stopped dead in her tracks, her breath catching in her throat.

There, standing in the dim shadows of the doorway was a tiny figure, a boy, dressed in brightly colored pajamas, clutching a frayed, tattered stuffed animal. Silently twisting his finger in the corner of his mouth, he had the look of a child who had just awakened from a bad dream and was trying to sift reality out of the chaos that had begun to frighten him.

The instant Lori saw him, she cried out, "Jimmy!"

Stunned, she raised her hands to her face and blurted, "Oh my god, Jimmy, how long have you been standing there?"

The little boy remained perfectly still, not answering. Confused and afraid at what he had seen and heard, and unable to process the conflicting information, he had quickly retreated back into himself, into that fairyland of escape from the world of the big people.

And his mother's words were now only meaningless sounds to him.

Trying to put a confusing spin on the things she knew he had heard, Lori walked to him, knelt down, and said softly, "Oh, Jimmy, Mommy and Daddy were only talking. Now, let's get you back to bed." She then took him by the hand and led him down the hallway to his room.

Steve sighed deeply, ran his hands down across his face and walked into the bathroom, a look of confusion on his face. It was unbelievable to him that this woman who had given birth to his son would not love Jimmy as he loved him.

Removing his robe, he stepped into the shower and let the warm water course over his body, hoping it would wash away the stale taste of their relationship.

THIRTEEN

June 2, 2033

Gripped in the throes of a recurring nightmare of war and death, ghastly images and muffled voices were once again rising like shadowy wraiths from the strange darkness of Steve Weston's subconscious. Ripping through his mind with terrific force were the stark scenes and haunting sounds that marked the night his cameraman and close friend Luke Stratton had been tragically killed.

With the dream images whirling in his brain, Steve was flailing his arms wildly, trying desperately to claw his way out from under the spreading cloud of gray dust and falling debris that had threatened to bury him alive on that fateful night.

On assignment in Thailand, Steve and Luke had been sending reports back to TV9 in Geneva on the changing fortunes of the battles between the Global Forces and a small army of insurgents. After a seventeen-hour day, they had settled down for the night on two rickety beds in a small room in a nondescript hotel a hundred miles out of Bangkok.

Just as his body had relaxed and he was drifting into sleep, he had been violently thrown against the wall by the concussion from an exploding bomb. Caught in an avalanche of debris and dust, he could hear the building crumble apart around him. Pinned beneath the lumber, sheet metal, and plaster, he was unable to move.

Luke had called out to him that he had been hurt badly. For two agonizing hours, Steve lay helplessly buried under the debris, listening to Luke's plaintive voice calling out to him for help. Although Luke lay mortally wounded no more than a few feet from him, Steve was unable to move, unable to go to him and help him.

After two hours, Luke's voice had fallen silent in death.

And now, rising out of the pool of memories submerged in his subconscious mind, he was once again hearing Luke's fading voice calling out to him in his dream.

Caught in the unrelenting icy grip of fear, Steve frantically pounded his fists on the table next to his bed, desperately searching for the handgun that should have been there. In a cold sweat, by the third ring of the phone next to his bed, he had begun to separate fantasy from reality enough to comprehend that he was not in the steamy backwash of the jungles of Thailand and that the voice he was hearing in his head was not his friend calling out his name.

Startled when she heard him cry out, Lori turned on the light, then grabbed him by the shoulder and shook him, calling out, "Wake up, Steve! Wake up! You're having a bad dream. It's only the phone."

As his brain cleared, he slowly realized it was not the terrifying whine of incoming artillery shells that had jolted him from his deep sleep. He drew a breath, shuddering inside. By the time he gained control of his brain's chaotic swirl of thoughts and his runaway emotions, he knew he was in his own home, in his own bed, and the noise was only the loud, insistent ringing of the telephone on the table next to his bed. Relief was the strongest emotion he was conscious of feeling.

It was the "Red Alert" ring-down phone that rang automatically when someone at the network picked it up. They didn't have to dial. When it rang, it was urgent.

Still trying to sort out the disturbing images and confusing thoughts colliding in his brain, Steve groaned, slid his feet off the side of the bed, and rubbed his head, carrying his hands down across his face, trying to wipe away the bad dream. Reaching for the phone, he snarled into it, "Yeah, what is it?"

The excited voice of Randy Standridge, his news director, answered. "I'm sorry to bother you at this time of the morning, Steve, but we're getting reports on a story that's too big for me to handle. I think you had better come down here."

"Well, for pete's sake, Randy," he echoed sharply, "what's going on? What's so urgent?"

A cold, pleading hysteria edging his voice, making it hard for him to maintain his composure, Randy stammered, "Steve, uh, it seems that . . . that . . . people are mysteriously dying in a small town here in Texas called Camden, just a few miles northwest of Templeton. Over three hundred people have already died."

A sudden chill ran through Steve, a chill to the bone. He exploded into the phone, "What are you talking about, Randy? Three hundred people don't just up and die."

"I know, Steve," Randy answered apologetically. "But Ray Mitchell, our bureau chief in Templeton, called me himself. He was frantic."

Steve rubbed the back of his neck. "Do you have any idea the panic we would create if we reported a story like this and it turned out to be false? We've got to have *facts*, Randy."

Randy swallowed hard. "Steve, according to our preliminary reports, the death count could go much higher than three hundred. Nobody knows what happened, or what caused it. Mitchell told us that it's like the end of the world down there."

"All right, give me what else you've got."

"Well, after Mitchell called us with the story the first time, he called back in about ten minutes and told me he had hit a brick wall. He said the local authorities had gotten word from higher up to clamp the lid on the whole thing and not give out any more information."

Furious, Steve yelled, "Well, who do those people think they are? They can't shut us out of a story like this. Did Mitchell tell them he was with TV9?"

"He sure did, Steve, but they told him it didn't matter." Randy's voice was tinged with frustration and anger. "They said their orders were coming from a very high authority. And here's another funny thing about this whole deal. When I called Mitchell back to see if he had gotten anywhere with the story, he downplayed the whole thing, telling me there had been a minor accident, but nothing of the magnitude he had thought. I think he was under pressure to tell me that."

His jaw set, his eyes hard, Steve answered, "That's enough, Randy, I'm on my way." Frowning in concentration, he added forcefully, "Here's what I want you to do. First, activate a Code Three. We're going to need anchors, writers, directors. Then, get all the additional information you can get. I want phone numbers of people I can talk to in Templeton, and the town of Camden."

With a sense of urgency in his voice, Randy responded quickly, "OK, Steve, it'll be waiting for you when you get here."

Feeling his pulse quicken, Steve was suddenly more animated, exclaiming crisply into the phone, "OK, Randy, good job. I'll be there shortly. Have everything laid out for me by the time I get there." Slamming the phone down with a force that almost knocked it off the table, he stood to his feet, a shot of adrenaline clearing his head, giving him the rush he lived for.

Frantically pulling at his arm, Lori pleaded, "What's wrong, Steve? What's going on? Tell me. What is this about three hundred people dying?"

Steve was buttoning his shirt and looking for his trousers before he replied. "I don't know for sure, Lori, just that people are mysteriously dying in a town near Templeton. Three hundred are already dead and the number keeps climbing."

Standing in front of him, fear etched into her face, Lori exclaimed, "Oh, my god, Steve! Was it a bomb? Was it some kind of nuclear device? Are we under attack? Is it coming here?"

Stepping around her, Steve frowned thoughtfully, then answered, "I don't know, Lori. They don't seem to know what's caused it. People are just *dying.*"

Steve was fully dressed in less than ten minutes. He would shave in the car. Scooping up his car keys, he grabbed his briefcase and rushed toward the door, then stopped and looked back at Lori. She was sitting on the edge of their bed, fear blazed across her face, her eyes searching his for assurance.

She's a beautiful woman, he mused. No wonder he had fallen in love with her. But what had happened to them? Why had they drifted apart?

His tone softened. "We should have more information by the time I get to the network. Flip on the set. I'm going to put the story on TV9 as soon as I can."

Leaving the room, he turned left to go to his car. Stopping short, he reversed his course and walked back down the hall to Jimmy's room. Pushing the door open slowly, he stepped quietly inside. The small night-light on the wall cast soft shadows across the room, lighting his way to the small bed. Kneeling down, he stared into the peaceful face of his sleeping child. A wave of emotion passed through him, drawing his hand downward by a bonding love that compelled him to touch his son.

Stroking Jimmy's face gently, Steve whispered, "I'll protect you, Jimmy . . . whatever it takes."

The small boy stirred.

Standing to his feet, Steve looked down at the small figure again, then quietly retraced his steps back down the hall, through the den, and out into the garage to his car.

Steve Weston was now in his element. He was doing what he did best, observing the great events of the world and reporting and interpreting them for the people of the world.

Arriving at the Sky News Network building a little past 6:00, he boarded the elevator and rode up to the newsroom.

The SNN building in Dallas was the prestigious headquarters for the worldwide operation of TV9. Containing several floors of broadcast offices, TV studios, and the latest in digitally driven production equipment, the television signals were beamed to satellites through a nest of small uplink dishes mounted on the roof of the building.

The elevator opened directly into the newsroom. To an outsider, the activity in the main newsroom looked like pandemonium. But the seemingly chaotic activity was, in fact, a well-organized news operation, managed and run by some of the world's most seasoned professionals.

The dozens of news desks and work stations inside the large complex of rooms were equipped with state-of-the-art communications consoles, complete with computers, videophones, printers, and small video screens that could be used to flip to any of the channels from around the world.

These writers, editors, and newsanchors were the key people in running this complex worldwide television news organization. Working in very tight compartments of responsibility, each person was assigned specific duties, thus assuring the global government complete control over the flow of news and information from origination to broadcast. As a firmly controlled top-down system, personal initiative in the pursuit of one's own agenda was strictly forbidden.

Stepping quickly through the newsroom, Steve listened to the cacophony of sounds, the soft clicking of the computer keyboards, the crunching clamor of the printers, plus the conglomeration of voices, all speaking at once, all vying to be heard over the other noises and voices in the room.

Adding to the bedlam were the thin, ultrahigh-density, 3-D television wallscreens, displaying talking faces from all over the world, speaking practically every language on earth. No more than an inch thick, lying flat against the wall, they ranged in size from two feet to twelve feet wide, producing images so lifelike you were tempted to enter into a two-way conversation with the person on the screen.

Maintaining his brisk pace, Steve went straight to Randy's office, positioned in the far corner of the main newsroom. The glass wall overlooking the newsroom gave Randy a clear view of all the activity.

Several people who were crowded around Randy's desk moved aside when Steve walked in. Getting straight to the point, Steve snapped, "Fill me in, Randy. What's happened since we talked."

Randy shrugged. "Not much, Steve. All of a sudden it's got real tight down there. We've made lots of calls to lots of people, but we keep coming away with the same answer."

"And what's that?"

"I'm sorry, Steve, no one will tell us anything. I think they're scared. Nobody wants to talk."

Randy ran his hands down across his face and sighed. "Do you think somebody should go down there?"

Steve hesitated before answering. "Randy, I'm going to go myself. I want to find out what's going on. I don't like the sound of this whole thing."

"You'll need some help, Steve," Randy said. "Who do you want to go with you?"

"You'll need me, Steve," a woman's voice called out.

Steve glanced back at the door. It was Audrey Montaigne. She was leaning against the door, her arms folded across her chest.

Their eyes met for a brief moment, then Steve turned away. Not wanting to complicate his life, he had purposely avoided her, even though she had been in his thoughts every day.

"Not this time, Audrey," Steve answered sternly. "This might get a little sticky."

"I can handle it, Steve. I want to go." Her voice carried no small amount of resolve.

Steve turned back to Randy. "Randy, call the airport and tell them to roust the crew. Have them file a flight plan for Templeton. We'll be at the airport in less than twenty minutes. Tell them there'll be two passengers. Me . . . and Audrey Montaigne."

"Consider it done, Steve," Randy replied as he reached for the phone.

"Thanks, Steve," Audrey said excitedly. "I'll get my stuff and meet you at the elevator."

"I called the airport," Randy told Steve a minute later, "and they'll have the jet warmed up and waiting for you."

"Thanks, Randy. Now get Mitchell on the phone. I want to alert him that we're coming."

Randy reached for the phone and punched in some numbers. "Mr. Mitchell, please. Steve Weston wants to talk to him. Thank you. . . . Ray, hold the line."

Steve took the phone. "Hi, Ray, how are you?"

"A little battle-weary at the moment, Steve," he replied.

"Ray, this situation with all these deaths has me intrigued. I'm taking on this assignment myself. Audrey is coming with me. Can you meet us at the airport? We'll be there in about an hour."

"Well, Steve," Mitchell responded haltingly, "do you think . . . uh, that it's necessary for you to come down?"

There was something about Mitchell's tone of voice that disturbed Steve, but he wasn't quite sure what it was. Even though it was just a gut feeling, he knew this didn't sound like the aggressive newsman he had assigned to the post.

"I'm coming down to look around and get some answers, then I'll hop on the plane and come back to Dallas. OK?"

"Uh, OK, Steve," Mitchell replied in a less than enthusiastic voice. "I'll meet you."

"Thanks, Ray," Steve responded and hung up the phone.

"We'll be standing by, Steve," Randy said, moving with Steve toward the door. "As soon as you have something, let us know. I don't like operating in the dark like this."

Audrey was waiting for him at the elevator. As the elevator door closed behind them, Steve punched the button for the parking garage.

"We can take my car, Steve," Audrey spoke up. "It's right near the elevator."

"Good," Steve replied. "Give me your keys. I'll drive."

When the elevator door opened, they hurriedly walked to Audrey's car and drove to the airport. Passing through the airport security gate, Steve pulled the car into a parking slot and they strode briskly to the waiting TV9 jet. The plane's engines were running.

The copilot met them at the door. "Welcome aboard, Mr. Weston. Nice to see you again, sir. And you, Ms. Montaigne."

"Thanks," Steve said. "Is everything all set?"

"Yes, sir, everything is ready. We have clearance for departure in about six minutes. That'll give us just about enough time to get you folks on board, button up the plane, and taxi out to the runway."

As Audrey slid into one of the oversized seats and fastened her safety harness, Steve stepped to the cockpit door and spoke to the pilot, Captain Frank Mayes. "Good to see you, Captain Mayes. I wasn't sure which crew we'd be flying with today. I feel better now that I know an old ex-fighter pilot is at the controls."

"Nice to have you back on board, Mr. Weston," Mayes replied amiably. "We've got everything ready to go, so you might want to secure yourself in one of the seats. We'll have you in Templeton in no time. There are some breakfast sandwiches, orange juice, and some coffee in the basket next to your seat. Help yourself."

"Thanks, Captain. That'll help. We didn't have time to eat."

Steve sat across the aisle from Audrey. As he was buckling himself in, the plane turned onto the runway and began its takeoff run. Glancing out the window on the left side of the plane, he watched the hangars and terminal buildings pass swiftly by as the jet screamed down the runway and lifted off into the clear Texas sky.

While still savoring the taste of the freshly brewed coffee after having finished their breakfast sandwiches, they felt the plane bank to the right and begin its descent. Guiding the plane to a smooth touchdown at the airport in Templeton, Captain Mayes reversed thrust on the jet engines, made a gentle turn to the left off the runway, and followed a large, dark green Global Forces troop carrier that had landed just ahead of them.

As their plane moved toward the terminal, Steve took note of the unusually large number of military aircraft and personnel at the airport.

Glad to see that the military is on top of this disaster, he thought to himself.

When Captain Mayes had braked to a stop in front of the terminal, he shut the engines down, came back to the cabin, opened the door, and lowered the stairs. "We'll be standing by until you call, Mr. Weston."

"Thanks, Captain. This shouldn't take long."

His briefcase firmly in his hand, Steve stepped from the plane and walked quickly toward the terminal building. Audrey fell in step behind him as armed soldiers quickly surrounded the plane. Other soldiers were positioned on each side of the main door to the terminal, their automatic weapons drawn and ready.

"Wow! Would you look at all the military people," Audrey exclaimed. ·

Stepping through the door into the terminal, Steve scanned the waiting area for Mitchell. He wasn't there. Instead, they were met by a dozen or more Global Forces soldiers.

A young lieutenant instructed them to step up to a table near the terminal entrance. Steve challenged him. "Lieutenant, I'm Steve Weston. I—"

"I know, sir, but I have my orders. They say that *everyone* has to go through the check line. So if you don't mind, sir . . ."

"Very well, soldier. We'll do it your way," Steve answered, shaking his head. He walked up to a table where a young woman dressed in a Global Forces uniform was sitting and handed her their International ID compucards.

His patience quickly wearing thin, Steve insisted, "Young lady, as you can see on your monitor screen, we're with TV9. And we're here to cover a story. Why do we have to go through this procedure?"

"Sir, these procedures are just precautionary."

"You seem to be rather calm, Corporal, in light of the fact that several hundred people have already died near here."

"I don't know anything about that, sir."

The soldier handed the compucards back to Steve, picked up a phone, and dialed a number. "Colonel, a newsman with SNN is here."

She listened for a moment, then replied, "Yes, sir, I'll tell him."

"Mr. Weston, Colonel Walters said that he would be out in just a moment to see you. So if you would just have a seat right over there, sir, he will—"

Steve interrupted her. "I hope the colonel has a good explanation for this delay, miss."

"Yes, sir," she replied.

Shaking his head, Steve walked over to where Audrey was sitting. Trying to keep his temper in check, he slammed himself down in a chair next to her and sighed deeply.

"What's the problem, Steve?" Audrey inquired.

"I don't like to be herded around like this. Mitchell should have taken care of all of this. He had better have a good explanation for not being here."

Steve reached inside his coat and retrieved his digital pocket Sat-Phone. Slightly larger and fatter than a credit card, the small instrument allowed him to access the global telephone system from anyplace on earth. Folding the mouthpiece down, he dialed Mitchell's number.

A pleasant voice answered, "TV9. This is Ms. Powell."

"Ms. Powell, this is Steve Weston. I've just arrived from Dallas. Mr. Mitchell was to meet me at the airport in Templeton. Do you know where he is?"

"Please hold, Mr. Weston. I'll let you talk to his secretary," she replied.

"Mr. Weston, this is Lisa, Mr. Mitchell's secretary. He told me to tell you that he was sorry he would not be able to meet you. He will be out of town for a few days."

"Did you say 'out of town,' Lisa?"

"Yes. He's going to be out of town for a few days."

"Did he say where he was going?"

"No, he didn't, Mr. Weston."

"Lisa, what's going on in this city?"

"I . . . I'm not sure I know what you mean, Mr. Weston," she answered evasively.

"Lisa," Steve snapped. "Who told you to tell me that Mitchell was going out of town?"

"Mr. Weston, I'm sorry. That's all I can tell you. Goodbye." She then hung up.

A puzzled look on his face, Steve folded his SatPhone and placed it back in his pocket. "I don't like this, Audrey," he muttered.

"Mr. Weston . . ." a voice called out.

Steve looked up to see a military man in green battle fatigues walking toward him. Short, balding, and a little overweight, he carried himself with a definite military bearing.

"Yes, I'm Steve Weston," he replied. "You must be Colonel Walters."

"That's right, Mr. Weston. Would you mind coming with me, sir?"

Touching Audrey's arm, Steve said, "This shouldn't take but a few minutes, then we'll be on our way."

Turning to the soldier, he said, "Lead the way, Colonel. I'm right behind you."

The colonel turned and walked down a hall. Steve walked beside him. "I hope we haven't caused you any inconvenience, Mr. Weston," the colonel offered apologetically.

"I just want *answers,* Colonel. When I get them I'll be on my way back to Dallas."

"Fair enough, sir. I'll try to give you whatever answers you want."

After walking a short distance, they went up a stairway to a door marked "Private." Steve followed Walters through the door into a small office. Colonel Walters sat down at a small metal desk and motioned for Steve to sit in the brown leather chair slightly to his right.

"Colonel," Steve said, his voice under tight control, "I'll get right down to business. We were notified by one of our people that a major disaster had occurred in the nearby town of Camden, that several hundred people have mysteriously died."

"I'm sure I don't know anything about that, sir."

"Then, will you tell me, why has my bureau chief suddenly chosen this time to 'go out of town'? And why is this airport crawling with Global Forces personnel? And why are dozens of military aircraft parked on the tarmac?"

Colonel Walters shifted nervously in his chair. "Precaution, sir. There were some minor disturbances in the streets, and we were afraid unfounded rumors would circulate and fan the flames of fear; so we have placed this area under martial law for a cooling-off period."

Steve knew the colonel was lying. Standing to his feet, he gripped the back of his chair and glared at the man seated behind the desk. "I'm a newsman, Colonel Walters, and I can smell a story a mile away. I also know instinctively when I'm being given the runaround. And I don't like it."

Then, moving to the front edge of the colonel's desk, Steve leaned forward and pounded his fist on the desk top and shouted, "I'm not used to being jockeyed around by colonels, or generals, or anybody else. I want some answers, Colonel, and I want them *now!*"

Shaken by Steve's sudden outburst, the colonel blustered, "Well, Mr. Weston, I have my orders. And my orders are to give out that information and that information only. That's all you're going to get from me, sir."

"All right, Colonel, then who is the local person in charge of this operation? I want to talk to him."

"Well, sir, I—"

"His name, Colonel! His name! Give me his name!"

"His name, sir, is . . . Adam Stenholm."

Adam Stenholm!

Steve quickly turned away from the colonel. The name had caused an uneasy chill to ripple through his gut.

Why is the head of GU5 in this small town? he wondered.

His brow furrowed in concentration, Steve walked to the window and stared out, his thoughts whirling. Often referred to as the global government's "iron fist," GU5 maintained a pervasive intrusion into the lives of every person on earth.

Extremely brutal, the organization used a variety of measures to bring about compliance. Electronic surveillance, assassinations, secret arrests, covert operations, and torture were only part of their arsenal of weapons. Steve suspected that some members of his own TV9 staff were GU5 agents.

Turning back to face the colonel, Steve demanded, "Where is Mr. Stenholm?"

"He's in town, sir."

"He's here . . . in Templeton?" Steve asked in astonishment.

"Yes, sir."

"Where can I find Mr. Stenholm, Colonel?"

Answering with a shrug, Colonel Walters said, "I have a phone number. That's all I've got, Mr. Weston. I can call it and tell them you want to see Stenholm. No guarantees, though."

"Dial the number, Colonel."

Colonel Walters reached for the phone, dialed a number, and waited for it to ring. "Sir, this is Colonel Walters at the municipal airport. Mr. Steve Weston with SNN is here. He wants to see Mr. Stenholm. He's very insistent."

Nodding his head occasionally, Colonel Walters listened intently. "Yes, I understand. I'll tell him. I'll see to it. . . . Goodbye, sir."

Cradling the phone back in its holder, Colonel Walters stood. "Mr. Weston, they are going to send a car for you that will take you to Mr. Stenholm. They should be here in about fifteen minutes."

"Thank you, Colonel, that's the kind of cooperation I like," Steve responded.

"If you would like, sir, you can be seated in the lounge area. Someone will come for you as soon as the car arrives."

When Steve returned to the terminal waiting area, Audrey stood up and walked to meet him. "What did you find out?" she inquired.

Speaking barely above a whisper, Steve said, "This thing is getting bigger by the minute, Audrey. This whole area is under martial law."

"What are you going to do?"

"I'm going to see the man in charge of this operation. A driver should be here in about ten minutes."

"What do you want me to do?" Audrey asked. "Shall I snoop around town and see what I can find out?"

Steve rubbed his right temple. "I don't think so, Audrey. Under the circumstances, we might exacerbate an already tense situation. I've got to find Mitchell and talk to him. Maybe he can tell us what's going on here. But I'm afraid this is going to take longer than I had expected. And I don't want you staying around the airport. So here's what I want you to do. Take a cab to the downtown Metropole Hotel. I've stayed there before. They'll have a fax machine and computer hookup in the rooms that we can use. Get two adjoining rooms, then report in to Dallas. Wait for me there."

Audrey looked into Steve's eyes. "Will you call me as soon as you know something?"

Steve could sense the growing tension in her voice. Reassuringly, he touched her cheek and said, "Keep your SatPhone handy. If I'm delayed I'll call you."

A voice interrupted him. "Mr. Weston."

Steve turned. A Global Forces soldier was standing in back of him. "I'm Major Greg Matthews, Mr. Weston. If you'll come with me, sir."

Steve followed the major to the front entrance. A soldier with an automatic weapon hanging from his shoulder was guarding the door. Seeing Major Matthews, the soldier stepped aside and saluted.

FOURTEEN

The heat of the day was beginning to build. The sun was already high, bearing mercilessly down on the parched countryside out of a clear, cloudless sky. The faint trace of a reluctant breeze drifting lazily across the torpid landscape was the only thing that made the stifling, humid heat almost bearable.

Baking in the unforgiving sunlight, a dark green military car bearing the insignia of the New Earth Federation waited at the curb in front of the airport terminal, its motor idling. Sweat running down his young face, a soldier stood at rigid attention beside the car, the back door pulled open.

Sensing that he had stumbled onto something a little bigger and more explosive than he had first thought, Steve slid into the backseat of the car and leaned back, a solemn look on his face. The leather seat was warm, despite the fact that the air conditioner was running at full force. The interior of the car smelled of stale tobacco smoke.

The major joined the driver in the front seat, nodded, and they pulled away.

A black-cloud silence hanging over him, Steve was visibly upset. He exhaled an angry breath and clenched his jaw. One sure way to get his ire up was to try to throw roadblocks and detours between him and a good story. And at the moment, he was in the early stages of a slow burn over the obvious stonewalling he was getting from everybody in this town.

But gliding swiftly through the streets of Templeton, his temper began to subside, and he was having second thoughts about insisting that Stenholm see him. Steve knew power and authority. He also knew how, and to whom, that power and authority belonged. And Adam Stenholm could possibly be the most powerful man in the Federation, with the exception of the Secretary General himself. He had to be careful not to anger him.

As head of GU5, Stenholm ran the most sophisticated intelligence organization ever created. With their use of the most intrusive forms of surveillance technology and data-gathering capabilities, his agents were everywhere, inescapable. The pervasive presence of GU5 guaranteed ideological compliance of the masses.

Steve had learned early on that no one advanced to high position in the Social Order without the blessing of GU5—and that meant *Adam Stenholm!*

Without Stenholm's approval, any possibility of his moving up to the directorship of the powerful Unified Information and Communications Authority would be spiked for good. One slip and he could lose it all.

Don't rock the boat, Weston.

But there was another part to this uneasy equation that troubled and mystified him—the fact that Stenholm was in this small Texas city. There had to be some significant reason for his being here. And Steve had to admit to himself that finding the answer to that question was one of the main reasons for insisting on seeing Stenholm.

Got to be careful.

After a fifteen-minute drive, they approached a large office complex, its tall steel and glass buildings gleaming brightly in the hot sun. Exiting the car, Steve and the major walked through the front doors to the elevator. The major inserted a key that allowed the elevator to take them to the twentieth floor. When the elevator had stopped, the door opened into a reception area with a high ceiling and decorated with choice furnishings and expensive paintings. Several secretaries were typing away at computer terminals off to one side of the room.

The major stepped up to the receptionist's desk and told the prim, gray-haired lady that Steve Weston was there to see Mr. Stenholm. He then turned to face Steve and smiled. "It's been a pleasure to meet you, Mr. Weston."

"Thanks for your help, Major."

As the major boarded the elevator, a man dressed in green battle fatigues, dark green combat boots, and beret walked briskly up to Steve. Steve recognized him instantly. It was General Amos Dorian.

Trying to cover up his astonishment at seeing him, Steve smiled and said, "General Dorian, we meet again."

General Dorian returned his smile. "Good to see you again, Weston. If you'll come with me, I'll take you to meet Mr. Stenholm."

"Thanks, General. I'm right behind you."

Steve followed General Dorian as the two men negotiated their way down the long hallway, coming to a set of large double doors. Two security guards, dressed in civilian clothes, stood just outside the doors. They traced Steve's body with detection wands, then motioned for him to pass through a machine that took an ultrasound image of his body, just in case he had some kind of explosive on him. Adam Stenholm took no chances.

The general knocked lightly on the door, and the two men walked inside.

The office was a large, immaculately furnished penthouse suite overlooking the city. A tall, stately man was sitting comfortably relaxed in a large, high-backed executive chair behind an oversized mahogany desk positioned in the center of the room. Appearing to be in his mid-fifties, his dark wavy hair was full and neatly trimmed, just beginning to show traces of gray around the temples. His clothes were stylishly tasteful and very expensive.

General Dorian cleared his throat. "Uh, Mr. Stenholm, this is Steve Weston."

Motioning toward a leather chair in front of his desk while still entering data on his computer keyboard, the man said, "Please have a seat, Mr. Weston." His voice was pleasant, his mannerisms studied and deliberate.

When he had finished with the task at hand, he looked up. In a congenial but businesslike tone, he said, "I'm sorry I didn't get to meet you personally when you were in Geneva, Mr. Weston. How is my friend, Dr. Wallenberg?"

"Dr. Wallenberg is doing quite well. I talked to him two days ago."

With his penetrating eyes focused intently on Steve, Stenholm stated abruptly, "Now, you wanted to see me. What can I do for you?"

"Mr. Stenholm, thank you very much for seeing me," Steve began as he relaxed back into his chair. "A few hours ago, we got an urgent call from Ray Mitchell, manager of our TV9 bureau in Templeton. He reported to us that people were mysteriously dying in the town of Camden, a few miles from Templeton. He said the number of dead was already over three hundred and was continuing to climb—"

"We are aware of those 'rumors'," Stenholm interrupted, "but I can assure you that they are unfounded and that nothing like that has happened. There was no need for you to make the trip."

"Also, sir," Steve responded cordially, "I've been unable to locate Mr. Mitchell since I've arrived. He seems to have disappeared. Do you know anything about his whereabouts?"

His steely gray eyes zeroing in on Steve, Stenholm returned, "Mr. Weston, please let me assure you that Mr. Mitchell is in very good hands. At the moment, he's in a place where we can guarantee his safety."

The words startled Steve, but he managed with an effort to keep the surprise from registering on his face. It was clear that GU5 had taken Mitchell into custody for some reason. And that reason was what he was looking for. But he had to be careful. He must try to elicit the information without antagonizing Stenholm.

Steve moved to the edge of his chair, his face betraying nothing. "Sir, please indulge me, but Ray Mitchell is not only a member of my TV9 team, he's a personal friend. And what happens to him is of vital concern to me. In addition, I'm a newsman, and I have a responsibility to report on the major stories that affect the public."

Stenholm by now was growing impatient. Rocking gently back and forth in his chair, he strained to maintain his self-control. As head of an agency that operated by its own rules, he had reduced men of much higher rank than Steve Weston into whining cowards who had begged for mercy.

Just before Steve had arrived, Stenholm had called up his Confidential Dossier from Geneva. One part of his file that was of particular interest to Stenholm was Steve's Psychological Profile. It showed the agency whether a person had been properly conditioned to be loyal to the Social Order, or if there were areas of concern in their personality and belief system that bore watching.

And Stenholm had his doubts about Steve Weston.

Unaware of Stenholm's thoughts, Steve pursued his questioning. "And please tell me, if there has been no incident of major proportion in this area, why are there dozens of Global Forces planes and hundreds of military personnel at the airport and on the streets?"

Without answering, Stenholm reached to his right and retrieved a long-stemmed pipe from an ashtray. He then slowly, deliberately, filled it with tobacco from a pouch, packed the tobacco down, placed the stem of the pipe in his mouth, gripping it firmly with his teeth, and lit the tobacco with a gold lighter.

When it was drawing to his satisfaction, he closed the pipe lighter and laid it on the desk. Leaning back in his chair, he slowly exhaled the smoke, savoring the exquisite flavor of some of the world's finest pipe tobacco.

"Do you smoke, Mr. Weston?" he asked casually.

"No, I don't."

"Have you ever smoked a pipe?"

"A time or two."

"How did you like it?"

"I can take it or leave it."

"Pipe smoking is an art," Stenholm said, relaxing back into his chair. "Each phase has to be thought out and planned. First, you have to know how to choose the pipe itself. Finding one that fits your mouth and has effortless, easy drawing is the first step to good pipe smoking. This pipe was special-ordered. You see, selecting a pipe is as important as selecting your clothes. It should fit your character."

Stenholm cupped the pipe between his fingers and looked at it admiringly. "Then after you've matched yourself to the pipe, the next task is to find the proper blend of tobaccos. This is usually done by trial and error. It took me almost ten years to find my proper blend. There's a little tobacco shop around the corner from my office in Geneva. The proprietor and I worked together until we finally found this very special blend. It's made up of tobaccos from several different countries."

He placed the pipe back between his teeth. The tobacco turned a bright red as he drew the smoke into his mouth. Exhaling slowly, the smoke curled upward, following the currents in the room. "Mr. Weston, did you know that all the ingredients in my special tobacco are now on computer and all the storeowner has to do is enter the correct code and my blend is mixed automatically?"

"That's very interesting, Mr. Stenholm, however—"

"Ah, Mr. Weston, you should consider taking up the art of pipe smoking. You see, when I face a dilemma and am not sure what the answers are, or what I should do about them, I take some time out and prepare my pipe, and myself, for a few moments of pleasure and relaxation. The preparation time and the smoking of the pipe have to be done deliberately and slowly, the same way we should face life's complexities."

With his pipe clenched firmly between his teeth, Stenholm stood up and paced slowly behind his desk, letting the pipe smoke drift lazily upward toward the ceiling. He seemed to be thoroughly enjoying the experience.

"You see, we're facing a dilemma. It could be an explosive situation if it's not handled correctly. However, if we handle it in a professional way, always keeping uppermost in our minds that we work for the good of the Social Order, then it will indeed only be an incident, with no long-term effects at all. When we both leave this town, you and I would have only had a short, pleasant conversation. Nothing more would have come of it."

After long moments of mounting tension, Steve asked amiably, "Am I going to be allowed into the town of Camden to look around?"

"I'm sorry, Mr. Weston!" Stenholm responded sharply. "You will *not* be allowed into Camden."

Tactfully, Steve responded, "Sir, this city is crawling with Global Forces, armed to the teeth. You have 'restricted' the town of Camden. That's fine for the general population, but I'm a newsman and I have a responsibility to the people. I have a right to know—"

Stenholm interrupted. "You have a 'right' to know what I decide to allow you to know, Mr. Weston."

Returning to his chair, Stenholm rested his arms against the edge of his desk and spoke slowly, pronouncing each word with deliberateness and care. "Mr. Weston, I would be very careful if I were you. Sometimes our sense of 'mission' blinds us to life's stark realities and we forget that we serve at the pleasure of the Social Order. What we do must be done for the 'social good' and not to satisfy some elusive emotional need. As long as we serve the Social Order, we are useful. When we lose sight of that, we become narrow in our thinking and are of no further use. You are a very talented man, Mr. Weston. Please don't cross the line of good taste."

"Mr. Stenholm," Steve replied, "I would just like to find out what happened in Camden, find Mitchell, then go back to Dallas, that's all."

Stenholm frowned. When he responded, his voice was cold. "Mr. Weston, I know you have a job to do. Your job is in the field of information. But you must understand that information has to be used in such a way that it enhances the advancement of the Social Order, not diminishes it."

"I'm aware of that. I've always been—"

"Information," Stenholm continued, ignoring Steve's attempt to speak, "is an *asset*. It can be bought, sold, traded, or used as currency. You can exchange it for something you want or use it to pay a debt. Information, like other forms of capital, is a medium of exchange, and if you know how to use it, it can make you extremely rich and powerful. Information is bought and sold every day, its value determined by the price someone is willing to pay for it. A person should be careful not to sell it too cheaply . . . or to sell information that might do more harm than good."

Steve listened intently.

"On the other hand, information is sometimes a *weapon*," Stenholm insisted. "It's as much a weapon as is a gun, or an airplane, or a nuclear bomb. The intelligent use of information as a weapon can undermine the beliefs and values of a nation and bring about a paradigm shift in their thinking and loyalties. Even false information can be an effective weapon, if it's employed by qualified, professional handlers. Even so-called 'facts' can be massaged and made to say anything we want them to say.

"GU5, as I'm sure you know, sometimes uses information as a weapon in neutralizing or destroying our enemies. Or, in some instances, to keep our 'friends' in line. Information is *power*. And total control of information is unlimited power."

Steve was becoming increasingly fascinated with Stenholm's insight into the uses of words, images, and information. It was no wonder, Steve mused, that this man was so feared in the inner circles of the new global order.

"Do you think for a moment that the world leaders spent billions to construct a global information network, complete with computers, satellites, fiber optics, and other technology, only so that we could control the air traffic, or the sea lanes, or predict the weather? No, we have these technological marvels for one purpose—*to control the masses!* To control their wishes, their beliefs, their religion, their loyalties."

His voice rimmed with anger, Stenholm declared, "*Compliance* is our goal. But we must control the thought processes of the masses if we expect them to comply. And compliance comes under my department. So words, images, facts, and information are *my* property, Mr. Weston, not yours. TV9 is simply one of our tools to bring about the compliance of the masses. Controlling people's thoughts is the most humane way to bring about compliance. If that fails, we have other methods."

Steve stared intently into Stenholm's face.

Pounding the top of the desk with his clenched fist, Stenholm shouted, "But comply, they will. Believe me, Mr. Weston, they will comply! So don't lecture me about your independence as a 'newsman.' You have no independence. You only have the authority that I choose to give to you."

Steve was shaken by the volatile nature of the man, having seen a sudden flash of rage and unbridled fury rush across his features. It was there for only an instant, then it was gone, as if it had never been there, and the tall man was back in control. Steve swallowed hard. He had provoked him with his question, and the mask had momentarily slipped, allowing him to see into the dark side of Adam Stenholm.

The stories about this man's explosive temper were legend, with whispers of murders and assassinations that had been carried out in his name. On more than one occasion, it was rumored, he had killed uncooperative prisoners with his own hands. Steve could now believe that the stories were true, suddenly knowing that this man was capable of all the atrocities he had heard whispered about him.

His voice now under tight control, Stenholm said, "Mr. Weston, the global order's power is not just in the ability to gather and disseminate enormous amounts of information. Our power lies in our mastery of knowing what information to *withhold*. You see, information withheld is often more effective than information that is dispensed. So a wise strategist carefully guards certain parts of his store of information and only uses it when it will be to his advantage."

A queasy sensation settled in Steve's stomach, knowing that Stenholm was right about him. Even though he had tried to delude himself into thinking he was an independent journalist, at this moment, he knew it wasn't true. He was a tool of the Social Order.

Yet something inside him pushed him forward, causing him to make a bold decision to attempt one more time to get the information he wanted.

Consciously controlling his voice as he had often done under the glaring lights in a television studio, Steve asked, "Mr. Stenholm, would you tell me what happened in Camden?"

Without answering, Stenholm reached to his right and calmly tapped the ashes from his pipe into an ashtray, then filled it with fresh tobacco. Holding the pipe in his left hand, the stem clamped firmly between his teeth, he lit the tobacco, swiveled his chair to the right, and stared out the window for a long moment, momentarily shutting out the world.

"You're a very persistent man, Mr. Weston," he said, still gazing out the window. "And a very foolish one, I might add. It will be so noted in your Confidential Dossier."

Suddenly, something inside of Steve told him that Stenholm was now his avowed enemy. He knew he would have to be careful from now on. This man's operatives reached into every facet of every life on earth and, from this day forward, there would be no place to hide from him.

"I will tell you what happened. A truck loaded with canisters of toxic gas was traveling from the Kavrinski Pharmaceutical Company in San Francisco to the Kavrinski Institute for Human Life, here in Templeton, for testing and experimentation. The truck crashed through the guardrail on an elevated highway on the edge of the small town of Camden, only a few miles from here. A canister ruptured and some of the gas escaped into the atmosphere, killing a few people."

"How many were killed?"

"I think the number of dead is around fifteen."

"Fifteen!" Steve exclaimed. "I thought—"

Stenholm drew slowly on his pipe. "You are not to report anything about my presence in this city, or about the incident in Camden, Mr. Weston."

Before Steve could respond, the phone rang. General Dorian quickly picked it up and mumbled something. It was a short conversation, and when he hung up, he walked to Stenholm, bent over, and whispered something in his ear. He then returned to his seat.

Stenholm glanced out the window a moment, sighing. "I'm afraid I have bad news for you, Weston. Your friend—Mitchell, I believe his name was—just committed suicide."

Steve's breath caught. He half rose out of his chair.

Stenholm stiffened, his expression turning dark.

Dorian's countenance tightened as he looked at Stenholm. His hand brushed lightly against the handgun at his hip.

Regaining his composure, Steve settled back into his chair, his mounting anxiety hidden behind a stony, expressionless mask. Wild thoughts prodded his mind. *Did Mitchell find out too much? Did he commit suicide, or did they kill him? Must watch my step.*

With an air of confidence more feigned than real, Steve asked, "What happened, Mr. Stenholm?"

Stenholm exhaled sharply. "According to the nurse who just talked to General Dorian, Mr. Mitchell somehow came into possession of some very powerful euthanasia drugs. Our people don't know how he got them. When they checked on him a few moments ago, he was already dead. He went peacefully."

A mental alarm sounded a warning in Steve's brain, trickling through the facade of confidence he was showing on the outside. It was a warning that he should not press Stenholm any further for answers concerning Mitchell. For now, he had to retreat, take what he could, and fill in the details later.

Without waiting for Steve to respond, Stenholm reached for a stack of papers on his desk and began thumbing through them. Without looking up, he added, "Sometimes in the rush to fill holes in the news day, your department tells more than we would like for the people to know. Unfortunately, only a handful of people fully appreciate the power of the judicious use of information. One of my duties is to see that your department does not betray the interests of the Social Order in its misguided pursuit of 'the story,' I think you people call it."

With those words, Adam Stenholm abruptly ended the conversation, shoved the papers aside, and directed his attention to his computer screen.

There was only silence in the room, punctuating Stenholm's stern words of warning.

And then there was the soft clicking sound of the computer keyboard echoing through the large office as Stenholm's long, nimble fingers glided across it, typing in more secret codes, accessing more classified data, determining someone else's fate.

The lecture was over.

Stenholm had already moved on to his next task. There were no goodbyes, no handshakes, no acknowledgments. The conversation had ended. Steve knew he had just been shut out. The lesson had been taught, class had just been dismissed, and now it was left up to the pupil to adhere to his teacher's wisdom.

Steve caught a glimpse of General Dorian out of the corner of his eye. The general was standing. Steve looked at him, and the general nodded toward the door. Without another word passing between them, Steve stood and walked through the door. General Dorian followed him.

The two men walked in silence to the elevator. Arriving at the elevator, General Dorian punched the elevator button and turned to face Steve. "Sorry about Mr. Stenholm's abrupt way of ending a conversation, Mr. Weston, but that's just the way he operates. He carries a lot of responsibility and has a lot on his mind. I'm surprised that he agreed to see you at all."

"Well, General," Steve replied, "I think I have finally met a man who has a full grasp of the meaning of the power of information. A man who understands that words, images, and symbolism are more powerful than all the standing armies from Caesar to the Global Peace Forces combined. Goodbye, General."

When the elevator reached the bottom floor, Steve retraced his steps back out through the front door. The military driver was waiting for him, his car parked at the curb, the back door standing open.

"Mr. Weston," the driver said, "I'm Corporal Dunaway. Major Matthews sends his regrets that he couldn't meet you, but he was sent on another assignment. He gave me instructions to take you wherever you wish to go, sir."

"Can you take me into the town of Camden, Corporal?"

"No, sir, I can't. I'm not allowed to do that. I can take you any other place. Where do you wish to go, sir?"

"Well, Corporal, you can take me to the Metropole Hotel."

As the car pulled away from the curb, Steve slumped back into the seat, relaxed his shoulders, and closed his eyes. His brain was beginning to feel as if it were in a vise.

Couched in Stenholm's circuitous lecture were veiled threats, ambiguous orders, and disturbing revelations about the man himself, his mission, and his power. The man was frightening.

The word *insane* crossed Steve's mind.

Possibly, Steve reasoned, that was why he took so much time with his pipe. It was, perhaps, his own way of controlling the beast that lived inside him.

FIFTEEN

TV9 HEADLINE NEWS (JUNE 2, 2033)—*Members of the Global Peace Forces earlier today oversaw the dismantling of the last remaining nuclear missile sites in the former United States. Under the watchful eye of General Gavrilovich, the command computers were deactivated and the nuclear warheads were turned over to members of the military command of the New Earth Federation.*

Sheila Harper parked her car in the faculty parking lot. Taking her daughter, Kathryn, by the hand, they ran together through the light mist of rain to the south entrance of the Northwest Enrichment Center. After hugging her affectionately, Sheila made her way toward her own classroom, pleased that her daughter was making such remarkable progress in recovering from her traumatic experience in Lori Weston's spirituality class.

Weaving in and out of the hundreds of students, governmental agents, social workers, teachers, and facilitators, her eyes looked straight ahead. Rarely spoken to, she had learned to accept the slights and shunning that was accorded to her and the other Christian believers who had somehow managed to hold on to their jobs in the educational system.

During her thirteen years in the system, she had been passed over for promotion to Master Teacher many times. Still classified as only a "Learning Facilitator," she knew that the only way to climb the career ladder was to embrace the culture. But she had chosen to accept her limitations rather than compromise her faith.

Sheila walked into room P-21, sat down at her desk, and placed her purse in the bottom drawer on her left. She had disciplined herself to come early in order to have a few minutes to prepare her mind for the day.

Resting her elbows lightly on the top of her desk, she looked out across her empty classroom, a sophisticated, electronically intensive learning chamber where each child functioned in a world of digital wizardry. This, and other classrooms around the world, were highly developed experimental psychotherapy laboratories involved in remedial programs aimed at promoting state-desired opinions and attitudes in the child.

Programmed to produce "Desired Outcomes," each child was assigned an individualized Learning Pod that contained a powerful, high-speed, personal digital video-processing computer connected directly by satellite to the Master Tutorial System in Geneva, Switzerland.

These highly advanced telecomputers served both as libraries and tutors, giving the educational system unfettered access and control over each child. With each student moving at their own pace, their education consisted of a series of individualized lesson plans assigned by the Global Curriculum Commission in Geneva. Their future career and social position were determined by how well they demonstrated their specified Desired Outcomes.

As the children arrived and went to their places, Sheila walked slowly through the classroom, chatting with them and seeing that each child was busily engaged in their proper interactive lesson plan.

Pausing behind Jerry, a slight, rather shy eleven-year-old boy with reddish-brown hair, she patted him on the shoulder, then helped him into his data suit and data gloves.

For today's lesson, Jerry's Learning Pod had become the cockpit of a Lance-class spaceship. With his left hand grasping the throttle, his right hand firmly clutched the control stick. Playfully jockeying the controls, he was anxious to resume playing the Virtual Reality game "Space Combat," his third week to play the game.

Known as a "Moral Dilemmas Model" game (MDM), the psychologically manipulative stories were so structured that they presented a variety of life situations that called for making moral choices.

The sharp 3-D graphics and digitized sound effects responded to the child's ongoing decisions, allowing the player to manipulate the story, characters, and action inside the electronic landscape. Each response was recorded in the child's Master File, and, along with other data, determined the direction his educational "track" would take him.

With the relevant data generated each time he played an MDM, the educationists could more accurately adjust the program to bring about compliance in the student. If he did not respond correctly, he would simply be recycled and remediated, using whatever time and resources were necessary until his new paradigm had been successfully brought about. No matter what his fixed beliefs were, the Global Curriculum Commission had computer courseware to challenge them.

The interactive features of the "Space Combat" video game allowed the student to communicate by voice with the characters in the story, giving them orders, receiving reports, directing the air battles, hearing suggestions from members of the crew, and deciding the way the story would develop by choosing between several storyline options.

Seeing that Jerry was anxious to play the game, Sheila leaned down and kissed him on the cheek, then strapped on his shoulder harness, knowing that once the program started and he was immersed in the fast-moving video landscape, he could become disoriented, lurch forward, and hurt himself if not strapped in properly.

Testing to see that he was secure in his restraining harness, she then picked up the bright red Virtual Reality helmet and carefully placed it on his head.

"Is the helmet too tight, Jerry?"

"No, Ms. Harper," he responded excitedly. "It feels fine."

"Are you ready to begin?"

"I'm ready, Ms. Harper."

When the child was scheduled to play a Moral Dilemmas Model Virtual Reality game, the classroom facilitator had been instructed to access the Master Tutorial System by entering the child's own Global Identification Code (GIC), plus the ID number of his Learning Pod. Based upon his previous input, the computer at the Global Curriculum Bank would instantly design and transmit his personal lesson plan directly to his individual computer in his assigned Learning Pod.

After overseeing the access transaction, all school personnel were forbidden, by law, to interfere in any way while the game was in progress.

Sheila accessed the control panel on the side of Jerry's Learning Pod and entered in a code that downloaded the game. She then placed her hand on Jerry's shoulder and kept it there to help him while he made the transition into the Virtual World.

When she pressed the key to start the program, instantly, computer-generated 3-D stereographic optics were beamed directly onto the retinas of Jerry's eyes, transforming his helmet into a Virtual Reality theater, immersing him in a complete visual and acoustic sensorium.

Swept along in the digitized hyperreality of outer space, the Virtual World filled his entire field of vision no matter how much he turned his head. Merging with the scenes, he looked around in all directions, seeing planets, stars, large mother ships, and space fighters engaged in mortal combat.

Secured inside his wired body suit, gloves, and helmet, the computerized system flawlessly responded to Jerry's slightest head movement, constantly updating and adjusting the computer-generated images in real time.

Feeling a sudden rush of excitement, the young boy was startled when an alien fighter screamed in from his right side, slightly behind him, ready to fire on him. Jerking his head, he saw the fighter approaching at high speed. Frantically, he pushed his control stick hard left, plummeting downward, then reversed his course to come up behind his enemy. With three short bursts from his rocket guns, he watched the alien space fighter erupt in flames. He had scored another "kill."

"Space Combat," one of the most insidious of the MDM games, was designed specifically to force the child to make decisions about who was worthy to live and who must die "for the good of the Group."

Even though he was only playing to increase his score and win the game, the entire procedure was designed to guide him into making socially correct choices. If the student should make an unacceptable choice, he would be punished by having the story end in disaster. The high-definition graphics made it all seem real to the child, subjecting him to scenes filled with flowing blood, screams of agony from the dying, and total destruction of his spaceship.

The purpose of the tragic end to the story was to impress upon the child that it was his fault and that the destruction was a consequence of his wrong choices. He alone must bear the blame.

The Virtual Reality of the psychogames tended to blur the lines between illusion and fact in the pliable mind of the child. However, the emotions the stories produced in the child were real and served as a path for intrusion into his inner thoughts, belief system, and world-view. It was from this data that the Master Computer compiled his next level of indoctrination. In the end he would conform to the mandatory outcomes, or he would simply be recycled again and again through the system.

If any child did not respond willingly, he would also be subjected to a series of drugs known as "personality helpers," comprised of a variety of "psychobalance" drugs that altered human emotions. One of the most commonly used by the educational system was a drug that enhanced self-esteem. Others enhanced or inhibited such emotions as joy, happiness, sadness, sexual excitement, fear, and guilt. There were drugs that would create or dispel a long list of phobias.

Another family of drugs known as "psychoawareness" drugs were used to induce alternate states of consciousness in those who were resistant to "spirituality."

Touted as beneficial, drug therapy was one of the government's most powerful and effective weapons of control.

Sheila had watched Jerry playing the "Space Combat" game exclusively for the past three weeks. She had observed his tension level rise as the pressure had mounted for him to make the acceptable moral choices. It was a pattern she had witnessed hundreds of times—seeing bright, lively, free-spirited children slowly taking on a somber tone as they progressed deeper and deeper into the psychosocial games.

Prompted by a growing concern for Jerry, Sheila plugged her headset into the audio port of his Learning Pod to listen to his progress in playing the game. Unable to see the video, she could track his progress by listening to the sounds of the action and the dialogue.

What she heard chilled her to the bone. A voice speaking into Jerry's helmet declared in a loud, excited voice, "Captain Jerry, the Mother Ship has just been hit. We have declared a *Red Alert!*"

Still in his fighter, Jerry responded, "Uh, sir, how much damage was done to the ship?"

"We are assessing the damage now, sir. It doesn't look good. It's imperative that you return to the Mother Ship immediately."

With a sense of elation from his victories against the alien space-ships, Jerry acknowledged the suggestion and gently moved his control stick to the right. Turning slowly through the virtual dark blue of outer space, he saw the mammoth Mother Ship looming in breathtaking magnificence before him.

The sight was overpowering.

The computer-generated graphics were perfect, down to the most minute detail. He was overcome with awe and wonder. At this dis-tance, he could see flames shooting out of one side of the ship. Men with small rocket-powered impellers strapped to their backs were darting back and forth outside the ship, endeavoring to seal off the damaged sections.

"Sir, we have your fighter in sight. Please enter the Mother Ship through the Alpha bay, slightly to your right."

Jerry turned his head slightly to the right and the entire virtual landscape shifted. Seeing the name *Alpha* above an open bay, he gently pressed his hand against the throttle and guided his spaceship into the belly of the Mother Ship.

The computer graphics, designed to lead him into the moral dilemma situation, positioned the young boy inside the flight deck of the giant spaceship. He was awestruck by the most magnificent space vehicle he had ever seen.

Standing in front of him were six people—four men and two women. A tall man, dressed in a brightly colored uniform, looked out of the virtual scene into Jerry's eyes. With his space helmet cradled under his left arm, and standing at parade rest, the tall man announced, "Captain Jerry, I'm Lieutenant Widener. And we have a serious problem. Our ship has suffered a direct hit from one of the alien fighters, causing considerable damage to our main thrusters. We are unable to achieve warp speed. That will delay our return to Earth by three months."

Growing more serious, Lieutenant Widener added, "Captain . . .

that means we will run out of food, water, and oxygen before we are able to land back on Earth. The entire crew is at risk."

Surprised by the turn of events in the game, the young boy stammered back to the video image, "Well . . . Lieutenant Widener . . . uh, what do you suggest we do?"

After the initial fun and excitement of the space battles, the game "Space Combat" was programmed to engage the child in a storyline that involved making life-and-death decisions about the members of his own crew.

The child playing the game was the captain of the Mother Ship, and his decisions were final. Allowed to choose the direction of the story, when it came to the final outcome, his options narrowed and he was forced into making choices that would tell the educational establishment whether or not he had responded properly to the programming process.

The moral dilemma programmed into the game that Jerry was engaged in was designed to bring about a state of mental chaos, confusion, and disconnectedness that would deliberately traumatize him, leaving him vulnerable to the infusion of the beliefs and values prescribed by the educational establishment.

Sensors embedded in the space body suit, gloves, and helmet that each student was required to wear when playing the games measured the child's physical reactions and fed a steady stream of information to the student's Master Computer File. The computer instantly analyzed his voice stress level, heart rate, breathing, skin responses, and other emotional indicators, then moved the game forward to the next programmed response without an instant's delay.

These responses helped to give the educationists a clear picture of the student's belief system, his moral parameters, and his receptiveness to outward control.

These psychological games had no time limit for completion. Designed for the "total immersion" of the child's mind, they were considered by the government educationists to be of more value than any other phase of the educational process.

All other subjects were shunted aside while the student was engaged in any MDM game.

"Well, Captain," Lieutenant Widener responded, "we have run the situation through the onboard strategic analyzer and have also confirmed it with mission control on Earth, and we agree that we have only one choice."

"And . . . what is that, sir?" Jerry asked, obviously beginning to feel the pressure of the decisions he was being forced to consider.

"Some of the crew must be put in the flaming tube, sir, in order for the rest of the crew to survive. But that is a decision you must make."

"How many must be—"

"Out of the one hundred thirty crew members, a minimum of thirteen must be flamed, sir."

"Who—" The small boy couldn't finish the sentence.

Lieutenant Widener answered, "I have a list of 'expendables' for you, sir. These are people who are the least vital to the operation of this spaceship. Their loss would be tragic, but it would mean that the rest of us could get back to Earth and save our ship."

"Who's on the list?" Jerry asked reluctantly.

Lieutenant Widener read the names of the thirteen crew members, along with their job descriptions, their backgrounds, and the reasons for putting them on the list. Then he pressured the boy to decide whether they should be sent to the flaming tube. If Jerry made the wrong choice, or hesitated too long in responding, the game would be abruptly ended.

Unprepared for the game to take this turn, Jerry wanted to jerk his helmet off and run from the schoolroom. Beginning to cry, he wanted the man to go away and let him continue his battle against the "aliens."

But, unknown to Jerry, if he did quit, the next pass-through would be even more intense, more brutal, until he gave them the responses they demanded.

"This mission, Captain Jerry," Lieutenant Widener insisted, "as well as the survival of the other members of this crew, are in danger. The overpopulation of this ship is causing a drain on our nonrenewable resources. Sir, we have a limited amount of food, water, oxygen, and medical supplies. Even if we charted our course for Earth immediately, it would still be three months before we would arrive. The entire crew would be dead before that. This number of people is unsustainable with our diminishing resources. It is a critical situation, sir. I must insist that you give us your decision."

The steady gaze of the thirteen condemned crew members standing to Jerry's right unnerved him. *These people are not alien space creatures,* he reasoned, *they are human beings.*

And he didn't want to have to decide whether or not to "sacrifice" them in order to save the others. But he remembered that if he refused to eliminate the expendable crew members, he would be condemning the entire crew to death.

"Uh, sir," Jerry stammered. "Can't we get the entire crew back to Earth?"

One of the officers stepped forward. "Captain," she said sternly, "life is about choices. Hard choices. Keep in mind that the most important thing is to do what is good for the group. Some people must be sacrificed for the good of society." Then, standing stiffly at attention, she waited, staring into the young boy's eyes.

It was all part of the conditioning.

As Sheila watched Jerry play the game, she sensed that she was on the verge of losing him, knowing that if he succumbed, the intense psychological conditioning would render the young boy incapable of ever making a decision that would violate his new paradigm. As an adult, while believing that he was exercising his own free will in matters of conscience, his responses would be automatic and in line with the new universal values. He would be a willing servant of the Social Order and would enthusiastically do its bidding.

He had been a tough kid, Sheila thought to herself. He had lasted longer than most, but in the end, she feared that he would not be able to resist.

"Captain," Lieutenant Widener persisted, "we can place the thirteen crew members in the flaming tube and continue on with our mission. It's your choice, sir."

The boy asked, "Can we wait . . . ?"

The first officer answered defiantly, "No, Captain, our life environment is not sustainable with this number of people on board. Thirteen must be eliminated. You must choose *now!*"

The child could not escape. He could say "no," but that would mean the death of all the crew members and the destruction of the Mother Ship. Sighing deeply, he stared into the eyes of the crew members. They stared back. No one moved. The pressure mounted. He had to make a choice.

At that point in the game, the educationists had reduced his time to think and reason things through. And by limiting his options to their own predetermined responses, they had pushed him to his automatic cutoff point. They had so overwhelmed his mind that he was no longer willing or capable of resisting.

Having been brought forward to this moment since his first day in the educational system, he was on the verge of gently succumbing to the will of the government.

Listening to the dialogue on her headset, Sheila watched as the small boy agonized over the decision. His hands were shaking as beads of sweat formed on his face. And his head jerked from side to side, as if he were looking for someone who would make the choice for him.

Wanting to abort the insidious game, she instinctively reached out toward him, but drew her hand back, knowing that there was nothing she could do. When the game was over, she would be there, to try to calm his fears after having been traumatized by the cruel game.

Suddenly, Jerry seemed to come out of the daze he was in. Looking into the virtual eyes of Lieutenant Widener, he thrust his fist into the air and shouted the order, "Flame them! Flame them! Flame them!"

The crew broke into applause, congratulating him for making the right choice. Hearing the audio, Sheila knew that the approving applause, the waving arms, and the smiling faces of the video spaceship crew was all part of the "reinforcement" phase of the psychogame. Proper behavior was to be rewarded, while improper behavior was to be punished. A powerful weapon, the professionals called it "social validation."

Seeing the crew's approval of his decision, Jerry smiled and waved his clenched fist in circles above his head.

"Congratulations, Captain Jerry," Lieutenant Widener said, smiling, "you made the right choice. You are a true leader."

Instantly, Lieutenant Widener gave the order to seize the thirteen condemned crew members. Struggling valiantly against their captors, the thirteen were finally overcome. As the virtual captives were led away, Lieutenant Widener stared out at Jerry, came to attention, and saluted.

Jerry's Virtual Helmet then turned dark.

The game was over. Jerry had passed the test and would be moved to the next level.

The educationists had been successful once again, Sheila reflected to herself, in persuading a child that there were some human beings who could be sacrificed for the good of the Social Order.

Trying to quell the smoldering anger building inside her, Sheila desperately wanted to strike out at the insidious evil of the educational system that was bending and breaking the minds of these small children. But she knew if she took any kind of action to sabotage the system, she would be fired and her family could suffer even more reprisals than they were suffering now.

That was the hardest part about working in the educational system, and the strain was beginning to show in the lines in the soft features of her face. With her heart near the breaking point, and silent tears of despair slowly filling her eyes, she wondered if she would be able to survive the pain much longer.

Turning away from Jerry, Sheila folded her arms and walked slowly through her classroom, checking on each student. She looked up when an older lady entered her classroom.

"Ms. Harper," the lady said coldly, "Dr. Stewart wants to see you in his office immediately. He sent me to take over your class."

SIXTEEN

A thousand troubling thoughts whirled through Sheila's mind as she walked back to her desk, opened the drawer, took out her purse, and walked out of her classroom. With a worried expression on her face, she fought a growing uneasiness as she approached the office of Dr. Paul Stewart, Headmaster of the Northwest Enrichment Center, wondering why she had been summoned.

Laura Ratcliff, Dr. Stewart's secretary, glanced up when Sheila walked in. Noting who it was, she said curtly, "Just have a seat, Harper. Dr. Stewart will be with you when he can."

Sheila sat down in a small armchair to wait.

Taking note of Ms. Ratcliff's rudeness, she chided herself for not being able to endure the slights and hurts without a feeling of resentment. When she sat down, she noticed a broken fingernail and started to repair it when Ms. Ratcliff called out, "Dr. Stewart will see you now." Sheila stood and walked into the spacious office. The fingernail would have to wait.

Paul Stewart, a rather rotund man in his late forties, had a round face and sagging cheeks that made him look much older. His small eyes peered out at Sheila from behind a crop of bushy eyebrows.

Motioning to a chair in front of his desk, he said in his rather high-pitched voice, "Have a seat, Harper. I'll be with you in a moment."

After glancing over several pages of computer printout, he opened a drawer, put the papers inside, then looked up at Sheila. "Harper, I've been going over your daughter's progress report, and it is 'unsatisfactory.'"

"What do you mean, Dr. Stewart?" Sheila asked, deathly afraid of the answer.

Dr. Stewart opened a large file folder and began thumbing through the pages of copy and color graphs. "It seems, according to these records, that the female Harper unit is not exhibiting the proper 'outcomes.'"

Resting his ample forearms against his desk, he said, "Now, you're an educated, intelligent woman, Ms. Harper, so I won't play games with you. Your own Master File indicates that you and your husband continue to persist in adhering to your restrictive religious views. So, quite honestly, we're not surprised at the difficulty we're having with your daughter."

"Dr. Stewart," Sheila answered, trying to quell her mounting anxiety, "the educational system is destroying the mind of my daughter."

"Quite to the contrary," Dr. Stewart responded sarcastically. "We're trying to repair the damage that's been done by her parents. It's our obligation here at the Enrichment Center to challenge the unit's old paradigm and bring about the desired changes. Unfortunately, our work often comes in conflict with the beliefs and values the bioparents have encoded into the unit's thought processes."

Continuing to lecture Sheila, Stewart said, "You see, personality disintegration is a desired outcome of the educational process. The unit sometimes experiences disunity, disconnectedness, even paranoia. But these reactions should not be feared. They should be encouraged. In the context of change therapy, they are quite normal."

Sheila looked at Dr. Stewart. "Are you calling the trauma that my daughter is experiencing *normal?*"

"Of course!" Dr. Stewart responded emphatically. "It is to be expected and is quite unavoidable. All students go through this process. Before the universally accepted values can be integrated into the unit, there is inevitably a time of upheaval of their frame of reference. Your daughter's resistance to change is causing her these extreme psychological problems. And I might add, Ms. Harper, your refusal to cooperate by constantly undermining our work is only making it more difficult for her."

Sheila bit her lip.

Shifting his weight in his oversized chair, Dr. Stewart exclaimed, "Don't you understand, Ms. Harper? We're on the threshold of fulfilling our dream of creating the perfect global society. And in order to bring it about, we must alter human behavior so that total integration into the Social Order can be accomplished. There's nothing you can do to halt this process. The best thing for your daughter is for you to work with us to bring about the paradigm change as painlessly as possible."

"Dr. Stewart," Sheila responded, "I took the same courses in Paradigm Manipulation in college that you did, and—"

Trying to hold his anger in check, Dr. Stewart shouted, "Stop thinking only of yourself and your own narrow religious beliefs, and start thinking about your daughter's future. She must be successfully integrated into society. All of this is necessary in order for the unit to succumb to the inevitable conclusion that she is no longer an individual but a member of the Group. And that the Social Order is her friend, guide, and provider."

Dr. Stewart then turned to his computer on the left side of his desk. Punching in a number of codes, he studied the files on his monitor screen. "Ms. Harper, your daughter's profile of outcomes has been disintegrating over the last few months. Unfortunately, she has now dropped below the acceptable percentile."

"What does that mean?" Sheila asked cautiously.

Still looking at his computer terminal, Dr. Stewart explained, "Our staff therapists say the unit is not making satisfactory progress. Their prognosis is not good. So it has been determined that in the best interests of the unit she will be enrolled in one of the full-time care facilities, where she will stay until she has been remediated."

Upon hearing Dr. Stewart's casual pronouncement that Katy was being taken from her, terror exploded inside of Sheila like a clean, hard punch to her midsection, almost knocking the wind from her body.

Her voice dropping sharply to a whisper, she bent forward in her chair, held her head in her hands, and gave vent to a low moan of despair. "Oh . . . not my Katy . . . not my little girl. This isn't happening. None of this is real. . . ."

"Now, now, Ms. Harper," Stewart stormed coldly, "you must keep in mind that we must do what is best for your daughter."

Wiping the free-flowing tears from her eyes with the back of her hand, she asked pleadingly, "Are you sure . . . you haven't made a mistake, Dr. Stewart?"

Sighing deeply, Dr. Stewart shoved the hard copy of Katy's file across his desk and told Sheila to look at it herself.

Looking at the file in front of her as if it were a living thing, Sheila reluctantly reached out and took it in her hand. Her eyes moved reluctantly across the pages as her brain fearfully absorbed the incredible indictments against her Katy. Pausing momentarily at certain points in the document, she became deeply troubled and offended at the way they had maligned her daughter, her family, and their deeply held religious beliefs.

Her fingertips pressing lightly against the left side of her face, fighting against the rising panic, she timidly read large sections of the incriminating data:

HOME ENVIRONMENT: Student comes from an *uncooperative* home environment. They are members of a subversive group of religionists who display hostility to the Social Order.

PSYCHOLOGICAL PROFILE: Student shows signs of independent thought. Has difficulty in subrogating her own ideas and desires to those of the Group. Has caused some unrest among her fellow students. If allowed to remain, this student could be a disruptive influence in the school.

RECOMMENDATIONS OF THE COMMITTEE: Student reflects the religious beliefs of her bioparents, which can only mean that they are defying the law by continuing to impart their faith to the student. Bioparents have been reprimanded on several occasions but have refused to comply with the law. Therefore, because of the negative family influence on this student, the committee recommends that she be placed in full-time care until her negative thought patterns have been remediated.

Her hands shaking, and her body on the verge of convulsions, Sheila held the file in her shaking hand, staring at the committee's recommendations as if she were reading her daughter's death sentence. With the room turning to a blur around her, she carefully reached out and laid the intrusive file back down on Dr. Stewart's desk.

Slowly shaking her head in a hopeless gesture of despair, she pleaded, "Dr. Stewart, please, I beg you . . . don't take my daughter away from me. I'm her mother. I can nurture her better than anyone. Please, Dr. Stewart . . ."

With a dismissive toss of his hand, Dr. Stewart responded caustically, "I'm sorry, Ms. Harper, it's out of my hands. Unfortunately, some parents never seem to learn."

"Where is my daughter?" Sheila ask imploringly. "I just want to take her home."

Biting off each word venomously, Stewart shot back, "I'm sorry, Harper, the unit has already been taken to another facility out of the city. You can't see her."

Shock registered on Sheila's face. The blood drained from her cheeks. Her first reaction was guilt. Guilt that, somehow, she had failed as a mother. It was an overwhelming guilt that knew neither measure nor reckoning.

"It's so"—she searched for the word—"*harsh.*"

Stewart looked away, busying himself with some papers on his desk.

"I don't understand, Dr. Stewart," Sheila said softly. "Why didn't you at least let me see her before you took her away?"

Refusing to make eye contact with her, Stewart answered casually, "You would have upset the unit, making it more difficult on yourself and her."

Sheila sat quietly for several moments, her head down, her hands clasped tightly together across her lap. Then, looking up, she said, "I've seen children who have spent time in one of the full-time facilities, Dr. Stewart. They are never the same."

Rocking back and forth in his large chair, Dr. Stewart replied,

"That's a compliment to our effectiveness, Ms. Harper. Full-time care allows our facilitators to guide the units through the psychological chaos that facilitates their new stability."

"When can I see my daughter, Dr. Stewart?" Sheila asked.

Dr. Stewart leaned back and drew in a deep, raspy breath. "We've found that it takes a minimum of one year of separation from 'uncooperative' bioparents to cleanse the unit of its old paradigm before the restructuring process can begin."

"One year!" Sheila gasped.

"That's the minimum time. After the old thinking has been removed, then the restructuring therapy begins. That process could take months . . . or years. It's all up to the unit. She'll have to learn to cooperate, or she will simply have to start over."

"It's so unfair, Dr. Stewart," Sheila said, a tone of desperation in her voice.

"Ms. Harper!" Dr. Stewart thundered, slamming his meaty palm on the top of his desk, his voice trembling with anger. "You're getting close to total *insubordination*. As a friend, I warn you . . ."

Visibly shaken by his abrupt outburst, Sheila quickly answered, "I'm sorry, Dr. Stewart. I'm sure you are trying to help me . . . in your own way. I appreciate that, but it doesn't help my little girl."

"I'm trying to make this process less painful for you," Stewart replied, in a somewhat calmer voice. "You and your husband could have avoided this trauma for yourself and your daughter if you had—"

"If I had *cooperated?*" Sheila interrupted. "Is that what you're trying to say? I'm not a brave woman, Dr. Stewart. And the prospect of losing my daughter—and seeing her taken away—frightens me. But there's no way to avoid it. We can willingly hand our children over to you, or you will take them by force. Either way, you win, Dr. Stewart. And we lose."

Clutching her purse with both hands, trying to fight back the tears, Sheila said, "Dr. Stewart, your faith is in the Social Order. Our faith is in God. And He is high above all governments, and—"

"I'm warning you, Ms. Harper, that's treasonous!" Dr. Stewart yelled, waving his arms in anger.

Sheila sat for a long moment, then stood to her feet. Removing her car keys from her purse, she took a step toward the door, then turned back to face Dr. Stewart. "My Katy is in the hands of God, Dr. Stewart. Thank you for your kindness. You're doing what you believe is right. I don't hold you personally responsible."

She then stepped through the door and went to her car in the parking lot without going back to her classroom. Sheila Harper had just faced another tragic blow, the loss of her daughter.

Maybe it was her fault, she reasoned. Perhaps Richard would blame her for it. No, she told herself, he would understand.

As she drove out of the parking lot toward home, staring aimlessly through the windshield of her car, her greatest sadness was having to tell Richard that his Katy would not be coming home.

His hurt would be beyond measure.

SEVENTEEN

Templeton, Texas was sweltering under an oppressive blanket of southern heat and humidity. The searing, bright sun was cooking the asphalt and concrete of the streets, sending shafts of blurry heat waves rising into the atmosphere above them.

Overhead, a small gathering of ragged clouds drifted slowly by, driven by errant puffs of wind as the military car carrying Steve Weston pulled to a smooth stop at the curb in front of the Metropole Hotel. The irreverent glare of the blazing midafternoon sun had heated the gentle southwesterly breeze that hit him in the face when he stepped out of the car. He blinked his eyes against the brightness.

The door to the lobby of the luxurious hotel slid open as he approached it, and he gratefully walked into a blast of welcome coldness.

Walking straight to the front desk, he asked the desk clerk about Audrey. The clerk informed him that she had checked in earlier then she had left the hotel. No, he didn't know where she was going, and she had left no message.

When the desk clerk handed him his key, Steve scanned the lobby area, hoping to see her, then walked to the elevator. Stepping through the open door, he punched his floor number.

Alone in the elevator, his mind was plagued by a number of nagging questions. He was usually able to analyze a situation and come up with a logical answer or two that would satisfy him, but this time the troubling events of the day just didn't add up. His position in the world of politics and power had opened practically every door he had ever knocked on, so why was he being closed out by Stenholm? Why was he being restricted from entering the area of the accident? And why the stern warning to cover up the story?

He harbored a growing resentment against Stenholm because of his lack of respect for his position and his ability to make an international incident of the whole matter. Steve's natural curiosity, and his instinct to get the real story, though, drove him to think of ways of possibly breaking a few rules. But, he reasoned, he shouldn't jeopardize his career for just one story.

On the other hand . . .

The slight jolt of the elevator coming to a stop broke his concentration. The door opened and he stepped into the corridor, turned right, and found room number 753. He inserted the key, and the door opened into a private suite. Lavishly decorated, one entire wall consisted of angled glass overlooking a green courtyard. Once inside, Steve walked to the door that separated his room from Audrey's and knocked lightly.

There was no answer.

Removing his coat and tie, Steve stepped to the phone and punched in Randy's number at TV9 in Dallas. He could picture Randy's desk in his mind, stacked high with papers, magazines, news copy, computer printouts, and other assorted items. Steve smiled in spite of himself.

The phone rang twice; then he heard Randy's voice. "Is that you, Steve?"

"It's me, Randy."

"Anything new?" Randy asked quickly. "Have you found out what's going on? What can I tell my people?"

"Hold on, Randy, let's take it a step at a time."

"Sorry, Steve, but I guess I'm under a little pressure here," Randy responded. "I've got an entire crew of writers, editors, and newsanchors ready and waiting to do something on the story. What've you got?"

"Randy," Steve began cautiously, "everything I say is 'off the record.' Are you confident that the line is secure?"

"As sure as I can be, Steve."

"Is the recording disk turned off?"

Steve heard Randy punch a key in his communications console. "Recording machine off, Steve," Randy assured him. "Go ahead."

"Well, Randy, I've got some bad news . . . Mitchell is *dead*."

"What!" Randy exclaimed. "I don't believe it. What happened?"

Steve cleared his throat. "For some reason," he said bitterly, "they had him in custody. They say he got hold of some euthanasia drugs, took his own life. But I don't know, Randy. I'm not sure what I believe. I'm convinced that Mitchell was right, though. I believe there has been a major tragedy of some kind here, but I can't prove it yet. Camden, the town where it evidently happened, has been cordoned off and is restricted to everybody, including me. And to make matters worse, they're stonewalling us."

"Send me some video. Let me go with the story, Steve," Randy pleaded.

Steve rubbed his face vigorously. "It's not that simple. I finally got to the man in charge here, and he has put a news blackout on the whole incident. We can't touch it."

"Who has enough authority to spike a story like that?" Randy asked incredulously.

"Are you sitting down?"

"Yeah, why?"

Steve's face took on a hard sheen. "The man who gave the order is Adam Stenholm."

Randy didn't respond.

"Did you hear me, Randy?"

Randy muttered a quiet oath. "Yeah, I did Steve. That blew me away. Adam Stenholm—my god, Steve, what's he doing there? He rarely gets out of his office in Geneva. I even understand he has an apartment in the back of his office suite. It's got to be something *real* big."

Steve felt his pulse pound unexpectedly hard. "You're right," Steve agreed. "And there's another strange twist to this whole thing. I can't prove it, but I think Stenholm was already here in Templeton when this happened."

"That is strange, Steve," Randy answered, his voice low.

"Well, at least you can now understand my dilemma," Steve responded with a note of resignation in his voice.

"What are you going to do?" Randy asked.

Steve hesitated for a long moment before answering. "I'm not sure, Randy," he answered tentatively. "I've checked into a hotel and I think I'll go ahead and stay overnight. I've got to find out what happened to Mitchell. But I do need to get back to Dallas as soon as I can. By the way, have you heard from Audrey?"

"No, I haven't talked to her," Randy returned, the tension in his voice growing evident. "Isn't she with you?"

Steve took a deep breath and deliberately lowered his voice. "No. She came to the hotel and checked in, but she left. She's not here, and I don't know where she went."

"You'll hear from her soon," Randy said reassuringly. "Audrey can take care of herself."

"One more thing," Steve remarked, brushing away his concerns. "I want you to access the TV9 research files and look up the Kavrinski Institute for Human Life, here in Templeton. Get me the name of the top man there, and a phone number, and fax it to me immediately. Don't let anyone know what you're doing."

"I'll do it right now, Steve."

Hanging the phone up, Steve straightened and stretched, hearing the small bones in his spine crack and complain. Stenholm had told him that the destination for the toxic gas had been the Kavrinski Institute. Hounded by a growing curiosity, he was not sure what he was looking for, but he was sure there had to be a connection between the institute and Stenholm's insistence that he bury the story about Camden.

After carefully studying the papers Randy faxed to him, he reached for the phone and punched in the number listed. He then called the concierge's desk and had them order a cab.

The cab was waiting when he got downstairs.

After a twenty-minute southeasterly drive to the outskirts of the city, the cab turned off the main street onto an obscure side road that twisted and turned, passing underneath dark canopies of overhanging trees. Sweeping around a bend, Steve saw the large campus of the

Kavrinski Institute for Human Life lying straight ahead. Covering over a hundred acres of meticulously manicured grounds, the entire facility was surrounded by a twelve-foot-high security fence. Circular razor-wire ran menacingly along the top of the fence.

Once the cab entered the grounds, Steve leaned forward and stared out at the impressive complex of buildings that housed the institute. It spoke of money and affluence. Built around a small spring-fed natural lake of crystal clear water, the maze of buildings, its park areas, tennis courts, golf course, and lavish swimming pool made it look like a world-class resort. Surrounded by sculptured lawns and tall trees, the pristine lake gave the scene an ambiance of peace and tranquility.

An elaborate twenty-story building of copper-toned steel and gold-tinted glass gleaming in the sunlight dominated the complex. Strategically placed around the lake was an array of buildings that complemented the architectural design of the main structure.

After paying the driver, Steve adjusted his tie and walked to the main entrance. One of the tinted glass doors slid silently open when he approached it, and he stepped into the comfortably cooled reception area. Resembling an international luxury hotel, designer lighting fixtures overlooked an assortment of greenery that was carefully scattered among the many sitting areas.

The entire front wall of glass curved tastefully back over the reception area joining the main building at the third-floor level, forming an expansive sunlight roof and giving the feeling of being outside.

Soft music filled the room.

This large main room was brimming with people, many of them sitting in the tastefully decorated waiting areas. Others were milling about, talking, or signing papers in the small cubicles lining the far wall.

Steve had learned from the information Randy had sent that Dr. Charles Brandt was the Executive Director of the KavLife Institute. Dr. Brandt had at first refused to give him a tour of the facility; but, upon verifying Steve's high clearance level in the global government, he had no choice but to accommodate him.

Stepping to the receptionist's desk, he told the lady that he was there to see Dr. Brandt. He then sat down on a couch and was busy flipping through the pages of a magazine when a rather tall lady in her mid-thirties stepped up to him. Smiling, she said, "Mr. Weston, I'm Judith Jennings, Dr. Brandt's secretary."

"Oh, hello, Judith," Steve replied as he stood up to face her.

"Please come with me," she said. "Dr. Brandt is just coming out of surgery and should be in his office by the time we get there. So if you'll please follow me."

Steve walked beside her as they moved through the swarm of people to the elevator. Arriving on the third floor, she escorted him to Dr. Brandt's office. When Steve walked in, the two men shook hands amiably. Slender, in his late forties, Dr. Brandt was slightly taller than Steve. His mannerisms were precise. His tone was clipped and formal.

After a brief conversation, he turned to introduce Steve to a second man standing to his right. Rather plain looking, slightly overweight, and almost bald, Steve guessed him to be in his sixties.

"Mr. Weston," Dr. Brandt said, "this is Dr. Samuel Wilson, assistant director of the institute."

Steve nodded, then sat down in a chair in front of Dr. Brandt's desk.

"Dr. Brandt," he said as he slid back in his chair. "Thank you for seeing me."

Dr. Brandt leaned back in his chair and took measure of Steve. There was something uncomfortably critical in his steady gaze. Steve knew that lurking behind the polite veneer, Brandt resented having to take time with him. With the slightest tinge of disdain, Brandt asked abruptly, "Mr. Weston, do you have a medical background?"

Biting back an angry reply, Steve answered, "No, I don't."

A tight smile crossed Brandt's face. "Well, in that case," he answered condescendingly, "I would like to strongly recommend that you reconsider your request to tour this facility."

His tone a shade sharper than he would have liked, Steve retorted, "And why is that?"

Sighing deeply, Dr. Brandt said, "To put it bluntly, Mr. Weston, we're engaged in a variety of very sensitive medical procedures and experiments, and some people have a rather severe emotional reaction to them. That's why we usually confine our tours to medical people."

"But what you do is . . . *legal,* isn't it?" Steve returned.

Stung by the remark, Dr. Brandt shot back, "Of course, it's legal.

This is a state-of-the-art research and development center. And it's important that our work be kept out of public view."

Shaking his head slightly, Steve answered, "I understand."

Dr. Brandt stood and walked to the window overlooking the campus. He remained silent for a few moments. Steve waited.

Sounding resigned and grim, Brandt said, "Mr. Weston, I've been with the institute for ten years. We exist because the times demand it. The laws of the land demand it. You see, the people of the world are in general agreement with our global policies on euthanasia, infanticide, assisted suicide, aborticide, and other forms of population control." He paused for a moment, then added in an afterthought, "But they don't want to know the details of how those policies are carried out."

Walking toward the door, Dr. Brandt said tersely, "And now, if you will come with me, I will introduce you to the work of the Kavrinski Institute for Human Life." On the way to the elevator, Dr. Brandt added, "Dr. Wilson will accompany us. If either of us should get an emergency call, the other will continue the tour."

Riding down the elevator to the lobby, they walked to the reception area, where congenial, smiling staff persons were busy answering questions and filling out admission forms.

Stopping at the third cubicle to his right, Steve watched an absorbing drama. A young man in his twenties was sitting at the desk, nervously signing papers. An older man sat quietly in the chair next to him. After he had signed the papers, the young man stood and embraced the older man, whispered something into his ear, then walked quickly across the lobby and out the front door without looking back.

When the young man had left the building, the lady at the desk nodded to two very large men in white uniforms who came and led the older man down the long hallway to the left. He offered no resistance.

Intrigued, Steve stepped into the small cubicle and asked the lady who had just filled out the forms to tell him about her work. She glanced warily up at Dr. Brandt. He gave her a nod. She then smiled, looked uncertainly at Steve, and explained, "I'm a processor. It's my job to meet with the people, process the forms for admission, and authorize any payment the family of the patient may be entitled to receive. Then I—"

Before she could finish her sentence, Steve turned to Dr. Brandt. "What does she mean by 'payment'?"

"Oh," Dr. Brandt replied, "we're a private institution, and that's part of our research program. A person who is scheduled to be euthanized, or who is contemplating 'assisted suicide,' can benefit themselves, contribute to science, and leave their family a sum of money by volunteering to enter one of our research and development programs."

Steve stared at Brandt for a moment, collecting his thoughts. "So the family has a financial incentive to bring them here?" he asked casually.

"Of course," Dr. Brandt answered.

Steve turned back to the woman. "Other than receiving a request from a family member, how do you determine who should be euthanized?"

The woman shifted in her chair nervously. Dr. Brandt assured her that she could answer the question. Taking a deep breath, she answered, "When a person requests medical care, we access the Social Care System's master computer and enter the person's name and Global Identification Number, along with their request for care. The computer then processes the information and makes a value judgment on whether the person is eligible to receive further health care or not."

"Then, the computer makes the decision," Steve responded.

The woman brushed nervously at her hair. "Yes," she answered. "The computer weighs the patients' *positives* against their *negatives*— things such as age, productivity, life expectancy, how much of his health-care allowance has already been consumed, and how much of his lifetime health-care resources are still available. The system also factors in the future costs of food, clothing, and housing, and then determines whether it's morally or economically feasible to allocate further limited resources for the patient. If it's determined that the person has no more allotted health care, he or she can be brought here, or to one of our other facilities, for termination."

Steve nodded without comment, then asked, "Tell me about the man who was just admitted."

Placing her fingers on the keyboard, she typed in a code. Looking at the data on the screen, she explained, "That was Mr. Strickland. He is sixty-seven years old. He was healthy and productive until three months ago when he fell and broke his left hip. He has been unable to move around on his own since then. When it was determined that his social benefits had been used up, his son felt he could not take the time away from his own career and pursuits to be responsible for him. So he met with his local Global Population Control Commission representative and requested that his father be euthanized."

Turning back to face Steve, she added, "Mr. Strickland objected at first, but after a few days in one of our psychiatric facilities, he agreed that it was best for all concerned. He's scheduled for the procedure tomorrow afternoon at three."

Steve lifted his eyebrows in response. "And what is the 'procedure'?" he asked.

With a blank, incurious stare, the woman shrugged. The almost casual gesture was eloquent in its uncertainty. "Oh, I don't know that, sir," she answered, her smile fading slightly. "That's outside my knowledge category. I'm only a processor."

Noting her obvious lack of knowledge beyond her own bit part in the process, Steve felt he shouldn't push her any further. He smiled, thanked her for the information, turned and walked out of the small office. Dr. Brandt led the way back to the elevators.

While waiting for the door to open, Steve asked, "Where did they take Mr. Strickland, and what will happen to him?" The question was directed to either man.

The elevator door slid open, and the three men stepped inside. Dr. Brandt inserted a card into the control box and punched the button for the third floor. As the door closed, Dr. Brandt turned to Steve. "First, the patient will be taken to one of our holding rooms where he will be cared for overnight, then he will be taken to one of the procedure rooms to be euthanized tomorrow afternoon. Would you like to view the euthanasia process, Mr. Weston?" His words were smooth and congenial.

Waiting a heartbeat, Steve tried to ignore the sudden clenching in his gut. Nodding slowly, he answered, "Why, yes. Yes, I would, Dr. Brandt."

As the elevator door slid open, they stepped out into a wide corridor filled with white-uniformed personnel and their patients. Making their way through the throng of people, Dr. Brandt led them to a large door marked "Procedure Rooms." Stepping through the door, they walked down another long hallway. On each side was a series of numbered rooms. The three men stepped inside the room marked "Procedure Room 18."

Occupying the very center of the large, round room was a circular electronic control station with thirty or more technicians monitoring an array of computer screens and digital medical readouts. Completely surrounding the control room, and separated by one-way glass walls, was a series of twenty small rooms labeled as "Chambers."

Steve quietly moved behind the technician monitoring Chamber 10. Looking curiously through the glass, he watched the door to the chamber open. A gurney, routed by an automated guidance system, rolled into the room. A gray-headed woman lay on it. She was completely nude, her hair in disarray, her arms and legs strapped tightly to the sides of the portable, silver-chromed bed.

Once the gurney was secured in place, the monitors in front of the technician instantly came to life. Steve tensed. The sound of her breathing and the beating of her heart came through the small speaker built into the control console. The woman's face was displayed on the center monitor. She appeared to be in her mid-sixties. Her head lolling to one side, a lax smile on her face, she was looking aimlessly around the room, obviously heavily drugged. Steve could hear her trying to talk, but her words were garbled and incoherent.

A stainless-steel hood, two feet in diameter, positioned over the head of the bed, lowered slowly to within six inches of her face. As the helpless woman stared up into the hood, a rose-colored mist shot downward, engulfing her face. Breathing in twice, she went into mild convulsions, then her body relaxed and she lay perfectly still.

A pleasant, computerized voice came through the speaker in Control Station 10. "Life signs: negative. Brainwaves: negative. Respiration: negative. Blood pressure: zero. Heart rate: flat. Now exiting patient from Chamber 10."

Fighting an uneasy feeling growing in the pit of his stomach, Steve watched as the mechanized system moved the bed and the woman out of the chamber, noting that the entire procedure had taken less than two minutes.

Steve took a shallow breath and felt the welcome air enter his lungs. Clamping down on his self-control with every resource at his disposal, he stepped back and looked around the room at the people who were busy at the business of death. Everything seemed so normal, so impersonal, so efficient. The people displayed neither hate nor sympathy for their victims, only detached indifference. They were laughing and joking among themselves, sipping coffee, or talking about sports, while the beds moved in and out of the chambers, snuffing out the lives of their occupants.

His face was suddenly gray and drawn. Having just seen a woman put to death, he fought against an inner coldness. All the arguments for reducing the world's excess population had sounded so good, so sane, in the abstract. But now, seeing the process up close, with a human face, made him uncomfortable. He repressed a shudder. Trying to shake off the feeling, he told himself there was no alternative. And that it was *legal*. Shaking his head anxiously, he wondered if he, too, would have become desensitized to killing on this scale if he had witnessed it on a regular basis, as these people had.

Steve folded his arms across his chest and looked out across the high-tech room. With all the chambers in constant use, he watched the beds move in and out with assembly line efficiency. Glancing toward Chamber 4, he watched as the door opened and another bed rolled in. He looked into the frightened face of a boy, no older than seventeen. His eyes wide in terror, his head thrashing back and forth, the young man pulled furiously against the straps that held him.

Steve wondered why a boy so young would be put to death. Shaking his head, he turned away, not willing to watch.

The expression on his face belying his calm, confident words, Steve began firing questions at Dr. Brandt, who was standing beside him. He wanted to know who the people were, why they were being euthanized, and who decided their fate.

Ignoring his questions, Dr. Brandt turned and led them out of Procedure Room 18.

Turning left down the long hallway, Dr. Brandt finally said to Steve, "We have designed our technology to separate the technician from the procedure. Everything is automated and computer-driven.

None of the personnel in the procedure rooms actually terminates anyone. The people who work here are skilled technicians, and they carry out their tasks in a rational, businesslike manner. They're family people; they have children, go to Little League, pay orthodontist bills; shop at the neighborhood malls."

With a toss of his hand, he concluded, "The machines do it. It's a *technical* matter, that's all."

Steve glanced at Brandt uncertainly, clearly disturbed by his answers. Pressing his inquiry, he asked, "Where did they take the woman I just saw euthanized?"

Dr. Wilson spoke up. "She was routed to Tissue Evacuation. We'll take you there."

After leaving the procedure rooms, the three men moved quickly down the hallway and turned left into the east wing of the building. As they approached a large, dark gray metal door, two armed guards stepped aside, and they entered the Tissue Evacuation section.

Once inside one of the large rooms, Steve counted a row of twenty-four gleaming stainless-steel tubular compartments built into two walls of the room. On the third wall was a series of tubular passageways marked "Receiving Ports." Men and women dressed in stiff white uniforms were taking the gurneys that were arriving through the receiving ports from the procedure rooms, and were rolling them across the room to the doors of the tubular compartments. Another worker would then take the gurney, move it up to the open door of the compartment, slide the dead body inside, then close and seal the round steel door, while the receiving crew went back to the receiving ports for another gurney.

Dr. Brandt smiled, looked around the room, and gestured with his hand. "One of our biggest challenges has been the problem of tissue disposal. The global government's policy of population reduction presented us with enormous technical and logistical problems. The challenge was to find ways to dispose of the corpses of the millions who would be exterminated throughout the world."

He then walked purposefully to one of the cylinders. Laying his right hand against the oval door, he stroked it gently. "Here's our answer, Mr. Weston. This diathermic cylinder is one of the most significant scientific developments coming out of the KavLife research. It's the Tissue Evacuation Cylinder. We call them 'smokeless ovens.'"

Pulling open the door to the cylinder, Dr. Brandt smiled and explained, "You see, when the body is secured inside the cylinder, high-energy laser blasts vaporize the tissue, leaving less than a cupful of residue. The residue is then simply vacuumed out of the cylinder and flushed into the sewer system. The air is recycled through the filtering system, removing all smoke and odor. We have simply adapted the technology that we use in recirculating and purifying the air in our spaceships and nuclear submarines."

Steve turned to his right and watched as technicians moved the body of an elderly woman up to Cylinder 22. A man slid the body off the gurney and into the tube with one swift, smooth movement, then closed and sealed the door.

When he pressed a large red button on the side of the cylinder with the heel of his hand, Steve heard a low hum of energy, followed a few seconds later by a loud *whoosh*, as the vacuum system engaged, vacuuming out the ashes of the woman's body.

Still staring at Cylinder 22, Steve whispered softly, "It's as if the person . . . had never existed."

"Quite true, Mr. Weston," Dr. Brandt replied, obviously pleased. "No more telltale remains. The vapors are recirculated through the filtering system and do not go into the atmosphere. If there were smoke coming out of our facilities, the radicals would raise the specter of the infamous Nazi regime and their medical crimes back in the twentieth century."

His face suddenly turning grim at the thought of comparing his work to that of the Nazis, Dr. Brandt spoke through clenched teeth. "We are far more advanced, more civilized, than those barbarians. They were crude, inhumane. Ours is a work of compassion. What we do is for the benefit of humankind."

"I wonder, Dr. Brandt . . . I wonder," Steve said barely above a whisper.

"What did you say, Mr. Weston?"

"Oh . . . *nothing*. Nothing at all."

While having lunch in Dr. Brandt's private dining room next to the cafeteria, the three men continued their conversation about the work of KavLife.

"KavLife's program of therapeutic elimination is part of our goal of human perfection," Dr. Brandt explained. "But in order to reach our goals we must first purify the global genetic pool."

Steve glanced at Brandt. "And how will you . . . purify the genetic pool?"

A trace of a smile appeared on Brandt's face. "Through global genetic screening," he said as he dabbed at his mouth with his napkin. "You see, a single drop of blood, or a strand of hair, contains all of a person's genetic information. Through genetic screening, we're able to identify, and eventually eliminate, all those who are polluting the global genetic pool. A New Race is waiting to be born, Mr. Weston."

Steve felt his stomach tighten.

The implications of what Dr. Brandt was saying were horrendous. Information in the International DNA Data Bank in Geneva was being used to determine whether a person would live or die. And the killing of human beings was being justified as "purifying" the genetic pool.

Having finished lunch, Dr. Brandt stood to his feet and announced, "And now, Mr. Weston, so that you will get the full picture of our work here at KavLife, our final stop will be the Organ Transplant Division."

Boarding a small tram, the three men rode through an underground passageway to Building 6. Dr. Wilson led them to a private elevator. Getting off at the second floor, they turned right and walked down a wide hallway to a door marked "Organ Retrieval Division," where they entered an observation theater that overlooked an operating room. Several medical students were staring intently at two beds in the large, fully equipped operating room, making notes on small computers.

Dr. Brandt motioned for Steve to be seated on the back row, whispering, "Surgeons come here to practice and perfect their surgical skills, then go into the finest hospitals in the world."

Looking through the glass into the operating room, Steve saw a young woman, no more than twenty years old, on the bed to the left.

Plastic tubes from bags suspended on a chrome IV pole next to her bed were feeding liquids into her arm. Electric sensors were taped to her body. A breathing machine was breathing for her. Her face was pale, almost white.

On the other side of the operating room, in the other bed, was an older woman. She appeared to be in her seventies.

Steve watched a team of surgeons remove the beating heart from the chest of the young woman, then carry it across the room and hand it to the second team. As the surgeons began the procedure of grafting the young girl's heart into the body of the older woman, the first team rolled the young girl out of the operating room.

"That young girl, Dr. Brandt . . ." Steve stammered.

Brandt stood and walked to a computer to the right of the glass wall overlooking the operating room. Steve followed him, watching over his shoulder as Dr. Brandt's fingers moved swiftly across the keyboard, filling the screen with data. Brandt studied the information for a moment. "The young lady's name is Beth. She walked into one of our Assisted Suicide centers in San Angelo, Texas, and requested the assisted suicide procedure. After signing the proper forms, they sent her here."

Steve could see that the medical professional was thoroughly enjoying his role in the entire process.

"Although she has been brain-dead for six weeks," Brandt added pleasantly, "we've kept her body functioning. When the client, the older woman, arrived for the heart transplant, we accessed the medical profiles of both women and found a combined Level Four tissue and DNA match. Beth was then brought out of the Care Room for the organ retrieval procedure. Because of her age, physical condition, and favorable DNA rating, she has been categorized as a multi-organ donor. Her remaining organs will be removed and placed in storage until needed. Then she'll be sent to Tissue Evacuation."

Steve had a sudden, troubling thought. What if he found during his next physical exam that he had a bad heart, or liver, or lungs? Would he care who the donor was? Or how the organ was procured? Or would he also pay his money, accept the new organ, and go on with his life?

As they walked out of the observation room back into the hallway, Steve suddenly felt a strange sense of disorientation. His knees became weak, his hands turned cold and clammy, and he swayed slightly. Reaching out with his left hand, he touched the wall, trying to steady himself. His first reaction was to end the tour and go back to the hotel, but he knew he had to continue.

Dr. Brandt looked at Steve. "Are you all right, Mr. Weston?"

"Yes . . . yes, of course, I'm fine," Steve answered dismissively.

"You looked a little pale there for a moment. Would you like to discontinue the tour?"

"No," Steve responded emphatically. "I want to continue."

Composing himself, Steve pressed gently, "Dr. Brandt, I'm a curious man by nature. I suppose that's why I'm a journalist. I have one more question that I would like to ask you."

Dr. Brandt stopped walking, turned to Steve, and said, "Of course, Mr. Weston, what's your question?"

"That young lady . . . Beth. She was in her *twenties*. She was put to death and her heart was removed and placed in a much older woman. Do you have any . . . *qualms* about killing such a young girl . . . and putting her organs into someone else?"

Dr. Brandt smiled condescendingly. "*Qualms* about the organ-transplant procedure, Mr. Weston? Quite to the contrary, the organ-transplant operation is a beautiful spiritual experience. I get an enormous spiritual high when I remove someone's organs and graft them into another body."

"How can you say that . . . killing another human being can be a *spiritual* experience?" Steve asked incredulously.

"No one dies, Mr. Weston," Brandt intoned. "Death doesn't exist. It's an illusion. We only move from one plane of existence to another. You see, we're all one. Those two women have always been one. Now, through this organ transplant, they're joined in a physical as well as a spiritual union. All of life is one. The donor moved forward on her evolutionary journey, while the recipient was given a better quality of life on this earthly plane. We must all eventually complete the circle. What happens to us was decreed for our lives by forces greater than ourselves. It was their karma."

Still trying to comprehend his logic, Steve responded, "But you are still killing another human being, Dr. Brandt. That's an inescapable fact."

"*Killing*, Mr. Weston," Dr. Brandt exclaimed with an expressive shrug. "You have not cleansed yourself of Western thinking. The death experience is part of a pleasant journey. The quality of the drugs that we use in the euthanasia procedure often produces a euphoric state which lasts up to three minutes from the moment the drug is administered to the moment of brain death. But in those three minutes, our patients experience an incredible journey into the spirit world, often describing it to us as it's happening. Rather than wait for the uncertainty of normal death, many people have requested the procedure in order to experience this ultimate mind trip. Just before brain death, they attain a euphoric state, then they merge with the universe."

Smiling broadly, Dr. Brandt added, "They attain Nirvana, Mr. Weston."

Steve stared at the man in disbelief. Before he could respond, Dr. Brandt's wrist communications device sounded a soft electronic tone. The doctor lifted his arm, pressed a small button, and watched a message scroll across the face of the device.

"I'm sorry, Mr. Weston," he said bluntly, "but I have an emergency call. A donor has been found for one of our clients. I must go to surgery. Dr. Wilson will show you out."

He then abruptly turned and walked away.

EIGHTEEN

A disbelieving look crossed Steve's face. He was clearly disturbed as he watched Dr. Brandt turn and walk down the long corridor and disappear among the rush of medical personnel making their assigned rounds. Trying to keep a tight lid on his smoldering anger, he turned to face Dr. Wilson.

He had questions, and he wanted answers.

Before Steve could speak, Dr. Wilson turned and began walking away, saying over his shoulder, "The tour is over, Mr. Weston. Please come with me and I'll show you out."

Standing firmly in place, Steve's forehead wrinkled into a frown. "No, Dr. Wilson," he announced emphatically. "I have too many questions. I want to know more about this place."

Dr. Wilson stopped and looked at Steve. Taking a breath as if he were about to speak, the doctor abruptly turned and started walking away.

Steve called out, "I'm not leaving until I have some answers, Dr. Wilson."

Dr. Wilson stopped, turned, and stared at Steve for a moment. "Are you sure you want to see more, Mr. Weston?"

"Yes," Steve answered convincingly.

Dr. Wilson took a quick glance around the room. Exhaling a sharp breath, he said, "Very well. Please follow me."

Steve moved in behind the doctor. Negotiating their way through the flurry of people, they turned right into the south wing. Pushing through swinging double doors, the two men walked past a busy nurses' station and entered a door marked "Authorized Medical Staff Only."

Dr. Wilson pressed his thumb against the scanner on the side of the door. It slid open and they walked in.

Once inside the large room, Steve's eyes were drawn to rows of glass containers resting on dozens of white metal shelves, all containing functioning human organs. One wall was lined with electronic monitoring devices with digital readouts on the state of each of the organs. A master source was vigorously feeding life-giving nutrients to each organ through clear plastic tubes.

Nurses and technicians, dressed in their white uniforms, gloved and masked, glided among the shelves, checking, monitoring, caring for the living tissue.

Motioning for Steve to follow him, Dr. Wilson moved to a corner of the room, away from the other personnel. Sweeping the room with his hand, he said softly, "This room is off limits to all visitors, Mr. Weston. I could lose my position if they ever found out I brought you here. The organs you see here are of prime quality and are sold exclusively through an international network of medical doctors and human organ brokers."

A look of disbelief crossed Steve's face. "Did you say . . . *human organ brokers?*"

"Yes," Dr. Wilson affirmed. "They buy and sell human organs and fetal tissue the way others deal in stocks and bonds."

An uneasy chill rippled through Steve.

"You see," Dr. Wilson went on, "when an organ is retrieved here at KavLife, or at any other facility around the world, it is graded on its tissue quality and its genetic blueprint. Then it is registered with the International Organ Data Bank (IODB) in Brussels, Belgium. When a clinic somewhere in the world has a client who needs a top-quality organ, they contact one of the brokers. Using the candidate's International ID Number, the broker runs a search of the IODB files for a tissue and DNA match between the available organs and their client."

Walking up to a container, Dr. Wilson read the data printed on the bottom of the container. "This heart, for example, Mr. Weston, is going to a clinic in Munich, Germany. It carries a very high rating. The client paid a large price for it."

"Who . . . are the clients?" Steve asked with a frown.

"Our clients come from around the world," Dr. Wilson said in a deliberately casual manner. "They include presidents of global corporations, heads of state, high government officials, world-renowned scientists, members of the Congress of the People, holograph stars, popular musicians, military leaders, global bankers—the very rich and the very powerful. The list could go on. Preferring to remain anonymous, they stay in seclusion at a heavily guarded small luxury hotel right here on the KavLife campus. The hotel is known only as Building Nine. When a tissue match has been made, the client is rushed to one of the private operating rooms. The private operating rooms are not listed in the hospital directory. Only a few of our medical personnel even know of their existence.

"The client never sees the donor or ever knows who it is. After the procedure is over, they convalesce for a period of time in a private room, then they leave. Only a few of us ever know they were here. Many of our clients have had multiple organ transplants, spaced out over several years; for example, the older woman who received the heart from the young woman, Beth. That was her third organ transplant within five years. Both kidneys, a new liver, plus several injections of fetal brain tissue to rejuvenate her thought processes."

"Fetal-tissue injections?" Steve responded.

"Yes. Both organ transplantation and fetal-tissue injections are a major part of KavLife's 'Youth Rejuvenation' services. We have found that fetal-tissue injections are effective in improving the skin and reversing the aging process."

Glancing up into Steve's eyes, Dr. Wilson said, "You see, Mr. Weston, the trade in living tissue and viable organs is, indeed, a very lucrative business. The human race has become a living, walking, organ and tissue bank for the rich and powerful."

Turning away, Steve scanned the room, studying the state-of-the-art equipment and observing the medical technicians making their rounds, caring for their inventory of costly human organs. Workers were disconnecting organs from their master source, securing the containers inside scientifically designed, cushioned, metal travel cases, and hooking the organs to internal cylinders of nutrients. It was all done with the utmost care, under strict, sterile conditions.

This was, he reasoned, as coldly efficient an organization as any he had ever seen.

Gesturing toward the workers, Steve said thoughtfully, "The people who work here . . . they talk about hearts and lungs and other organs as if they were . . . *automobile* parts . . . or *computer* parts. It just seems . . ." His voice trailed off.

"That's what it is to them," Dr. Wilson confirmed. "They are trained to deal with their link in the chain. They never discuss the procurement process. Their only interest is in running an efficient shipping department. They'll pack the organs for shipment and take the crate to the loading dock. A specially equipped van will take it to the airport, and it'll be flown to its destination. It's simple; they receive an order for an organ of a certain grade and quality, at an agreed-upon price, and they fill the order. Facilities such as KavLife are scattered throughout the world."

Out of a misty mental haze, a bizarre picture was coming into focus in Steve's mind: the donors, the procedure, the brokers, the clients, the money connections, the surgeons, the medical personnel. Could it be possible that the Social Order was a dreadful monster that preyed on the human race, scavenging for body parts for the wealthy and powerful? If so, should he dare say anything about it?

Feeling a sudden stab of fear and regret for pursuing this excursion, he thought of telling Dr. Wilson that he had seen enough and preferred to return to his hotel.

But he knew, deep inside, that he would have to play it out to the end.

When Dr. Wilson moved toward the door, Steve followed him, glancing back one more time at the pristine room and its living inventory, knowing that it was a scene that could never be erased from his mind.

Walking a few yards down the hallway, Dr. Wilson invited Steve into a private conference room. The curtains were drawn back on a large window overlooking the small lake. Shafts of afternoon sunlight were beaming through, reminding him of the searing Texas heat outside. The two men sat across from each other at the long conference table.

Taking a deep breath, Dr. Wilson sat forward, his elbows resting on the table. Speaking softly, he said, "Mr. Weston, I have broken some very strict rules by showing you the room we've just left . . . and by telling you some of the institute's confidential business, I could lose my position, and perhaps my life."

Steve shifted in his chair. With a feeling of unease steadily growing in the pit of his stomach, he decided it would be best to say nothing. The entire procedure might be some form of subterfuge to get him to incriminate himself in some way. For all he knew, there could be security people monitoring their conversation at this moment.

Standing to his feet, Dr. Wilson planted his palms on the table and leaned forward. "Mr. Weston," he said imploringly, "I want you to meet a man. Will you come with me?"

Casting a wary glance at Wilson, Steve took a moment before answering. "Who is this man? And where is he?" Steve asked, a note of skepticism in his tone.

"I can't tell you who he is," Wilson responded, an audible quiver in his voice. "And he's *here* . . . at KavLife."

Steve fixed Wilson with a cold stare while he pondered his proposition. He then shifted his gaze, glancing outside through the large window. Despite his misgivings, there was a desperation in Wilson's voice that convinced him to take the next step in this ever-widening entanglement. "All right," he responded, standing to his feet. "Take me to him."

Dr. Wilson smiled, then walked to a small closet and took out a white jacket like the one he was wearing. "I think it would be best if you wore this. It will keep people from asking too many questions."

After Steve slipped the jacket on, the two men made their way to an underground passageway where they boarded a four-person shuttle car that moved them rapidly to an adjoining building. After exiting the shuttle, they turned right. Coming to a secure door, Dr. Wilson placed his thumb on the ID pad. The door slid open.

As they walked briskly down the hallway, Dr. Wilson spoke in low tones. "The main work of KavLife goes on in this building, Mr. Weston. You are not supposed to see it."

"And what is the main work of KavLife?" Steve asked.

"The use of human beings in medical experiments."

"Human beings . . . in medical experiments?" Steve asked hesitantly.

"Yes," Dr. Wilson answered.

"What kinds of experiments, Dr. Wilson?"

"A variety of experiments. The Kavrinsky Pharmaceutical Company in California manufactures drugs of all kinds. This is their major laboratory for testing new drugs. You see, we no longer have to use animals now that it's legal to use live human beings, or 'unpersons,' as they are called. Using human beings bypasses several steps in getting the drugs approved and on the market, saving the company enormous sums of money. In addition to producing drugs for healing, Kavrinsky Pharmaceutical is a major supplier of drugs that are used for euthanasia and infanticide. We're also involved in research and development of chemical and biological weapons."

Dr. Wilson continued, "But, Mr. Weston, even that's not the most disturbing part of the KavLife work."

"What could be worse?" Steve asked.

Dr. Wilson glanced over his shoulder. "Some of the people here at KavLife are being deliberately infected with a number of killer viruses. It's a program to find faster-acting methods of eliminating vast numbers of excess human beings."

"Maylay . . ." Steve whispered.

"What did you say, Mr. Weston?"

"Have you heard of the Maylay virus, Dr. Wilson?"

"Why, yes," Wilson answered. "We're testing it here at KavLife now. It's one of the world's most deadly viruses. Maylay, along with many others, is being developed and manufactured as a weapon against the human race."

Boarding an elevator, they descended two flights down. Turning right, they stepped through a secure door and entered a dimly lit hallway. When Steve's eyes had adjusted to the low level of light, he saw dozens of small doors on each side of the long hallway. Behind each door was a small cell. Low moans echoed throughout the building. A foul odor caused Steve to cover his mouth with his hand.

Repulsed by what he saw, Steve asked, "What is this, Dr. Wilson?"

"This is where we house the people who are being used in the medical and biological experiments and testing."

"How many people are kept here?"

"We can warehouse up to two thousand people at a time in this building," Dr. Wilson answered. "The turnover is rapid. Most are here for just a short time; others may stay for months, or even years, depending on the test program they're involved in. But, of course, after they have served their purpose, they're euthanized and taken to tissue evacuation."

Noting the shock on Steve's face, Dr. Wilson added, "You see, Mr. Weston, when society determines that it's both legal and moral to kill human beings, the reasons for the killing and the methods of the killing are no longer of importance. The person who has been declared an unperson has lost all legal and moral claim to a right to live. The killing of a human being becomes of no more significance than the killing of a virus."

Gradually, in a subtle way, a word insinuated its way into Steve's consciousness. A word he was desperately fighting against. The word was *murder*. He suddenly knew that the Social Order was murdering millions of people around the world, all done legally and under the auspices of the respected medical profession by men and women with impeccable credentials, all carried out in pedantic orderliness by hundreds of thousands of rank-and-file functionaries.

It was *murder* . . . murder on a mass scale, and no word could change that.

A dark dread descended over him, and for a fleeting moment he feared that he might also be a monstrous criminal for his part in the actions of the Social Order.

Steve walked slowly from door to door, glancing inside each small room. Both men and women, young and old, were kept in the rooms, most of them asleep. About halfway down the long hallway, he placed his face close to the small window in one of the doors.

A pair of eyes was staring back at him.

"How do you do, sir?" the man inside the cell said.

Steve was startled. "Very well, thank you," he quickly responded.

Dr. Wilson stepped up beside Steve. "This is the man I wanted you to meet, and talk to."

The face behind the small opening in the door smiled. "I would be delighted to speak with you. It's been so long since I've had a conversation with anyone."

Dr. Wilson reached into his belt and pulled out his master key, inserted it into the lock, and swung the door open. The door opening was only five feet high, forcing Steve to bend down to enter the room.

Passing through the door, he found himself standing in a room no larger than five feet wide by eight feet long. The ceiling was approximately eight feet high. The walls were concrete, painted over with a drab gray paint. The furnishings were made up of a small metal bed that took up much of the space, a rust-stained washbasin with a single cold tap, and a lidless toilet in the corner of the room. A thin, dirty blanket lay folded neatly at the foot of the bed.

Pale and gaunt, the man stood over six feet tall. His fingers were long and slim, and his hair was almost to his shoulders. It had once been a dark reddish-brown, but now it was nearly all white. His fingernails were long but clean. His faded blue uniform matched those Steve had seen in a dozen prisons.

Guessing him to be in his seventies, Steve knew that at one time in his life this man had taken pride in his dress and grooming. To be seen in such circumstances, he could tell, embarrassed him, causing Steve to feel bad about intruding upon his misery.

Finding himself now inside the small cell, Steve felt a gut-wrenching pang of fear at the thought of being locked up in a room like this. Glancing back to see that the door was still open, he quelled an urge to turn and escape.

Fixing his gaze on the man in front of him, he took a step forward and put out his hand. "My name is Steve Weston. And what is your name, sir?"

The man thrust his hand forward, and with a firm grip shook Steve's hand. "Yes, I'm acquainted with you, Mr. Weston, from TV9. It's an honor to meet you. Welcome to my humble home. I apologize that I can't offer you a comfortable chair or a cup of tea. But, as you can see, my small room is sparsely furnished."

"That's fine, sir. Please don't apologize. I'm sure that under better circumstances you would offer those finer amenities."

Motioning toward the cot, the man said, "Won't you please sit down here on the side of my bed? It's the best I can offer."

Still fighting the urge to run, Steve answered, "Please, if you don't mind, I'll just stand. But I do want to ask you some questions. It would help if I knew your name."

"I have no name, Mr. Steve Weston," he answered softly. "You see, when I arrived here two years ago they took away my name and gave me a computer number. I'd be happy to give you my number."

"No, that won't be necessary. But do you mind telling me why you don't want to give me your name?"

The strange man smiled, showing a row of smooth, bright teeth. "No, I don't mind telling you. When I was sentenced in the courts, I was 'disenfranchised' as a human being. They now call me an 'unperson.' As you know, the government can now do to me what they will, and there's no legal recourse for me or my family. There will be no notification given to my family about my death. They'll never know whether I'm alive or dead. So if I gave you my name, you might contact them and tell them you had seen me. And that would give them hope. And there is no hope for me. So please respect my wishes or we'll have to conclude our conversation. And I do so want to talk to someone."

"Fair enough, sir."

"But I will tell you this much about myself, Mr. Weston. I am a medical doctor. I was in practice for many years."

Suddenly Steve understood why the man carried himself as he did, even under such horrendous conditions. He could tell that he was a man of intelligence, poise, and culture. Even in this prison, he carried himself with decorum. There was a peace, a presence about him that defied explanation.

Haltingly, Steve ventured to articulate the thoughts that were raging through his mind like a strong gale. "Sir, I don't understand. Why are you here? Why would a man of your obvious education and culture be . . ."

"Marked for death, Mr. Weston? Is that what you're asking?"

Steve felt his face flush. "I'm sorry, sir . . . but, yes, that's what I'm asking. What was your crime?"

"I was a pediatrician, Mr. Weston. I cared for children for over thirty-five years. I was also a pastor. The government does not allow a Christian minister to receive a salary from that profession, so I continued my medical practice and did my teaching and ministry in addition to that. But the time came when the government could no longer tolerate my influence in the community and it had to destroy me. Would you like to know what my high crime was, Mr. Weston?"

Steve looked into the moist, blue eyes of the man in front of him. Respectfully, he said, "Yes. I'd like to know, if you don't mind telling me."

"My offense was the crime of *intolerance*. I was judged to be 'intolerant' because I held to the teachings of our Holy Scripture that Jesus Christ is Lord above all."

A thousand conflicts raged in Steve Weston's brain. Here was a man who held firmly to his beliefs, even in the face of suffering and death. But why would the government fear him so? Is he enough of a threat to society that he has to be put to death?

Turning, the old man's eyes looked away, as if he were focusing on some distant place, some fondly remembered time. Softly, he said, "Do you know what I've missed the most during the two years that I've been in this little room? I've missed my children, and my grandchildren . . . and I miss the sunshine, and the flowers, and the birds. And the wind . . . the wind blowing in my face as it did when I was a boy of twelve, racing with my friends . . ."

Then his voice trailed off and the room fell silent. The only sound was the faint murmur of the air coming through the small metal vent over the door.

Trying to control his emotions, the old man turned away from Steve. "And my sweet Susan . . ." he said tenderly. "My wife of forty-three years. I miss her smile, the touch of her hand, her warm embrace. She's the most beautiful woman in the world, Mr. Weston. She was with me throughout the trial. She was there when the judge pronounced sentence. That's when she broke down. The guards came quickly and took me out of the courtroom. I only had time to glance at her. They didn't even let me say goodbye."

Steve was intrigued with the man's story. "Sir, I know enough about the law to know that if you abandon these unacceptable beliefs of yours, you have a good chance of having your sentence reversed."

"I'm aware of that, Mr. Weston. And thank you for saying it. It shows that you do have concern for your fellow human beings. But it would be impossible for me to deny my faith. I have made my peace with God. I have no fear of dying."

"I have a measure of influence. Perhaps I could—"

Holding up his right hand, the man said, "No, it would do no good. I know the law. I have no rights at this point. They can do with me whatever they please. I have lost my right to personhood."

Sensing a deep respect for this man, Steve suddenly felt that he was intruding on his privacy. "I'm sorry, sir. I know we're intruding on you, so we—"

"Oh, no, Mr. Weston, I'm not going anywhere. And they'll come and get me when it's my turn."

"Do you know . . . uh, *when?*"

"No, I don't when they will come for me. But they will come. To euthanize me, or to perform some additional medical experiments on me. But I've learned to shut out the pain. They may drive me insane, but I've already made my peace with God."

Steve edged toward the door, then glanced back at the tired figure, his shoulders slumped, his breathing labored, his eyes now moist with tears.

The man spoke in a soft voice. "Mr. Weston, doctors whom I've known in the past as colleagues now experiment on me. But do you know the worst part? They won't look me in the eye or respond to my voice. They've shut me out. It's as if I don't exist anymore. They only touch me and probe me and talk to each other about me, but they never talk to me. They talk as if I can't hear them, as if I were not in the room. That's the greatest punishment. It's as if I'm no longer a man."

Then, looking up at Steve, he said pleasantly, "But don't think badly of them. I believe it's their way of coping. I believe they would be good men, and good doctors, in another society, in another time."

With a pleasant smile, and a softness in his voice, the old man looked into Steve's eyes and said, "Mr. Weston, may I pray with you?"

Steve hesitated. Nobody had ever asked him that question before. Not knowing how to respond, he was surprised to suddenly feel honored to have this man make such a personal offer. Even in his fatal circumstances, he still had concern for others. It was a rare trait.

"No," Steve answered respectfully. "Maybe if we had met at another time in my life, I might have. But if your God answers your prayers, sir, then why hasn't He delivered you from this place?"

"I don't venture to guess His purpose. He could have delivered me. He could have delivered His own Son from His death on the cross . . . but He had a purpose for Him, and He has a purpose for my being here . . . and a purpose for your coming here today."

Turning away from Steve, the man said, "Please excuse my rudeness, but I'm rather tired now. So if you don't mind, I think I'll lie down."

He then stretched his full length on his spartan bed. Resting his head on the small pillow, he turned his face toward the gray wall and whispered hoarsely, "God bless you, Mr. Weston, for coming."

Steve stood transfixed, staring at the thin, sickly man. Strangely, he felt an unusual bond with him, as if they were both in prison, and that maybe the old man's prison was not as confining as his own.

Walking to the cot, Steve leaned over, took the frayed, thin blanket, and stretched it thoughtfully across the old man's frail body. Gazing down at him in quiet respect, he went deep into himself, facing the truth of his own life, finding nothing there of which he could take pride. He only saw the worst he had done—harsh truths so intense they threatened to overwhelm him. The lies, the naked ambitions, the deceptions, rose like dark ghosts to taunt him, to shame him.

His face a mask of uncertainty, Steve quietly backed away, turned, leaned his head down, and stepped through the door back into the dim hallway.

As he started walking slowly toward the exit, he heard Dr. Wilson close the door to the small cell, then turn the key, sealing the man inside.

Retracing their steps out into the large hallway, they walked a few yards, then turned to their right down a very long corridor that stretched before them like a cavernous tunnel. Their footsteps echoing softly off the hard concrete floor, the two men walked in silence, each lost in his own thoughts.

At length, they came to a connecting corridor where they made a sharp turn to the left and came to a door that led into a large ward. Nearly a hundred women lay almost lifeless on small beds lined neatly against the room's stark, barren walls. Heavily sedated, they were quiet, subdued, slack-jawed, their hollow eyes staring out into space, seeing nothing.

With Dr. Wilson in the lead, the two men strolled casually among the beds. With the heart of a healer, Dr. Wilson looked into each face, softly touching them, concern etched across his features.

Steve could see that he cared deeply for each one of them.

The silence in the room was oppressive.

Stopping at one of the beds, Steve looked down at the woman lying there, staring into her face wordlessly, unable to look away. She shifted her eyes slightly, returning his gaze, looking deeply into his face, searching his eyes. He was sure that she recognized him. Smiling broadly at her, he could only imagine the hardships and indignities she had been through—and what still lay ahead for her. The thought of the horrors she might face caused a knot to form in his throat.

No more than forty years of age, with fine, delicate features and deep emerald eyes, he knew she had at one time been a woman of remarkable beauty. Shadowed under the disorderly sweep of her once beautiful red hair, her face was now pale and gaunt. Her sad eyes, reflecting deep hurt and resignation, stared pleadingly out at him, moving him deeply.

"What's her crime, Dr. Wilson?" Steve asked haltingly in a whispered voice, unable to tear his eyes away from her face.

"She's a Christian, Mr. Weston," Wilson whispered. "That's her crime."

Drawn by compassion, Steve then reached out his hand and softly touched the woman's face with his fingertips. Her sparkling eyes suddenly brimmed with tears at his touch. With his own vision slightly blurred, he thought he saw the faint trace of a smile break through the profound sadness that weighed heavily on her delicate face.

Without another word being spoken, Dr. Wilson turned and walked purposefully toward the door. Following close behind, Steve suddenly had a feeling of helplessness wash over him. Trying to gather his shattered composure, he stopped abruptly at the door and looked back at the lady they had just left. Having lapsed back into her drug-induced stupor, she was once again lying still and quiet, staring blankly into space.

Wilson touched Steve's arm. "There's nothing we can do for her, Mr. Weston."

A million searing questions burned feverishly in Steve's mind. With paralyzing doubts trembling through his brain, measures he had once believed justified and above reproach were suddenly being exposed as indefensible, inhuman cruelties.

The next hour seemed a blur as Dr. Wilson led him through a macabre journey into a netherworld of human suffering and indignity, the frightening visions wrapping his consciousness like a second skin.

Experimentation laboratories, equipped with the latest in computer-driven medical technology, lay unseen by the general public, ensconced several stories below ground level. White-coated men and women bent over their experimental tables, peering through microscopes and staring into computer terminals, adding data, writing in their journals, conjuring, mixing, exploring, probing, constantly searching for that singular instrument, or drug, or technique, that would make human death easier, swifter, and more cost-effective.

Hundreds of doctors, nurses, technicians, and skilled workers rushed about in detached efficiency, interested only in reaching the goals set by those above them, deliberately ignoring the fact that their subjects were human beings.

The sights, the sounds, the faces, and the voices of the condemned drove Steve to the brink of a mental and emotional overload. He felt as if he had descended into the unquenchable fires of hell and had stared into the somber faces of the damned.

Steve was relieved when Dr. Wilson escorted him back to the lobby. Standing quietly near the main entrance, Dr. Wilson glanced around to see that no one could overhear him. "Mr. Weston," he said, struggling against the fear rising inside him, "I . . . have a confession to make. I'm a religious man. I'm . . . a Christian . . . one of the Offenders."

Steve looked at him with a curious stare, not responding.

Wilson took a deep, cleansing breath. "Tens of thousands of our people, my fellow believers, are suffering and dying for their faith. Hundreds of them have been brought to this facility, imprisoned in these cells, and subjected to the most barbaric, heinous experiments. Sometimes I have the opportunity to fellowship with some of them, to pray with them, and help them through their long terror."

Steve asked casually, "How do you know I won't turn you into the authorities?"

"I have to take that chance," Wilson answered, making no attempt to disguise the apprehension in his voice. "Maybe you are a man who still has some human compassion left in him. If I'm caught, I'll be executed. But I owe it to my brothers and sisters in the faith to do what I can to stop the barbarism."

Steve's eyes narrowed. He spoke in a low tone. "Why would you risk your reputation . . . and perhaps your life, to tell me these things?"

Wilson glanced furtively around, great beads of sweat glistening brightly on his pale forehead. "Hopefully, sir, you have seen and heard enough to be persuaded to use your power in the international media to inform the world of the horrors that are taking place in this facility . . . and other facilities around the world. If you choose to betray me, then my life will be ended. They will not allow me to live. Either way, it no longer matters to me."

Deadly serious, Steve asked Wilson, "Do you trust me that much?"

Wilson swallowed hard. With desperation taking shape deep inside his being, he fought back the terror. "I . . . don't know whether I trust you or not," he answered, his voice soft with resignation. "I don't know you that well. But I did see moments of revulsion as Dr. Brandt showed you the various procedures. I knew then that you were a man who had not been completely co-opted by the Social Order."

Wilson wiped his brow with the back of his hand, his voice trembling. "KavLife is a house of horrors, where medical professionals commit monstrous crimes against humanity, all in the name of science. I have stayed here, waiting for someone who would listen and tell the world the truth."

Without saying another word, Dr. Wilson abruptly turned and walked away. Steve stared at him for a moment, a diminishing figure slowly melding into the crowd of people in KavLife's main lobby.

In a daze, Steve turned and moved through the front door.

NINETEEN

I t was past seven in the evening, just before dusk began to deepen into darkness, when Steve finally arrived back at the hotel, picked up his key at the front desk, and hurriedly went up to his room. Once inside, he went immediately to the door that joined his room to Audrey's and knocked lightly. There was no answer.

Beginning to grow concerned, he walked to the phone and called Randy Standridge at the TV9 offices in Dallas and asked if he had heard from Audrey. Randy said he hadn't. When Randy asked if he had anything for him on the Camden story, Steve assured him that he still had nothing he could use.

Hanging up the phone, Steve accessed his messages on his personal computer in Dallas and began returning phone calls and sending e-mail to people around the world. After working on a number of news stories for later broadcasts, he glanced at the digital clock on the table. It was a quarter past eight. He stood and stretched, then walked to the door to Audrey's room and knocked again. There was still no answer.

He phoned the front desk and asked if they had seen her come in. They assured him she had not returned to the hotel.

He then called room service and ordered some food and a bottle of wine. When it arrived, he laid his work aside to eat. After he had finished the meal, he poured himself a glass of wine and turned his chair to face the large window.

Sipping the wine slowly, he surveyed the western horizon, watching as the sun's rays splashed a fiery orange glow across the scattered clouds. Further to the north, vivid streaks of lightning forked through tumbled masses of darkening clouds, the faint sounds of thunder echoing in the distance.

Caught in a swirling dilemma, he played the various options over in his mind, trying to decide how he should react to the situation. Even though he deeply resented Stenholm's arrogance, he knew he was not a man to cross.

Steve glanced back at the clock. It was now past ten o'clock, and his concern for Audrey deepened. If he didn't hear from her by ten-thirty, he resolved, he was going to call the local authorities and have them initiate a search for her.

The minutes agonizingly dragged by. His concern mounting, he was pacing the floor when he heard a knock on the door between their rooms. He rushed to the door and threw it open.

It was Audrey.

Instinctively, he reached out and grabbed her firmly by the shoulders and asked urgently, "Where have you been, Audrey? I've been worried sick. Why haven't you called me?"

"Please, Steve, not so many questions," she begged. "I'll explain everything. But first, let me take a bath and change clothes."

Fighting an overwhelming urge to draw her into a tight embrace, he released his firm grip, stepped back, and looked into her eyes.

"Audrey, are you all right?" he asked.

"Yes, I'm fine, Steve. We'll talk in a few minutes."

As the door closed behind her, Steve was suddenly overwhelmed with a great sense of relief at the sight of her. Feeling his face flush, he was surprised and slightly embarrassed at the depth of feeling he had for her.

Almost sure that she hadn't eaten, he called room service and ordered some food for her, too. The food arrived a few minutes before she opened the door and walked back into the room.

Dressed in a powder blue robe, no makeup, her hair pulled back away from her face and tied with a ribbon, she was stunningly beautiful. Sitting at the small table near the window, she ate the food and drank a glass of wine while Steve read several pages of faxes Randy had just sent to him.

When Audrey had finished eating, she stood to her feet, folded her arms, and began to pace the room. "Steve," she said haltingly, obviously nervous. "I have something I must tell you."

Steve shoved his papers aside and looked up at her.

Biting her bottom lip, she said, "Steve . . . I came to the hotel and checked in as you told me. I waited a few minutes in the lobby, then I walked into the bar, where I met a soldier. After a few drinks, I got him to talking. He said that something very strange was going on in the town of Camden, so I talked him into taking me there."

"You did what?" Steve exclaimed, genuinely shocked.

Audrey flinched. "I persuaded him to take me to Camden in his military vehicle. But when we got within about two miles of the town, we were stopped by the military at a roadblock set up on the main highway."

Suddenly animated, Steve exclaimed, "Audrey, that was dangerous. You could have been arrested, or even worse, you could have been killed."

Tears came to Audrey's eyes. "I know, Steve, but one thing is for sure, something horrible has happened there and they're trying to cover it up. The entire town of Camden is surrounded by military forces. Barricades are everywhere. And the strange thing is . . . all the military people are dressed in biouniforms."

"Biouniforms?" Steve blurted. "Did they tell you why they were wearing them?"

"I couldn't get anyone to tell me what was going on."

"Well, if you couldn't get into the town, where have you been for all this time?" Steve demanded.

Brushing the tears from her eyes, Audrey took a couple of deep breaths. "They arrested me and the soldier. They took me to a house near the barricade, isolated me in a room, strip searched me . . . and even drew blood for some kind of blood test. All the medical people were dressed in those biouniforms, staring out at me through their plastic visors. They wouldn't talk to me. They kept me isolated for hours, but wouldn't tell me why they were keeping me. And then, less than an hour ago, they came into the room and told me to get dressed. No explanation. They just released me. They assigned another military man to drive me back to the hotel."

Audrey then stood, walked to the table, and opened her purse. Reaching inside, she took out a small video camera, no larger than a thick credit card. Holding it up, she said, "For some reason, they didn't confiscate my PalmCam. I don't think they knew what it was. So as we were leaving, I took it out and held it down at my side and just let it run. What I saw terrified me. But I'm not sure what I got on video."

"Let's see it," Steve responded.

Her hands trembling, Audrey took a small cord from her purse, unwound it, and connected the tiny PalmCam to the video monitor. Pressing a button, the TV monitor sprang to life. With the sound coming through in stereophonic clarity, the two of them watched scenes along the highway leading into Camden: the barricades, the military vehicles moving about, the dozens of armed soldiers, and the sounds of automatic weapons fire coming from all directions.

Noting that Audrey had aimed the microscopic lens of the digital camera toward a speeding vehicle coming from the town of Camden, Steve could see that the frantic driver had no intention of stopping at the barricade. As the car closed the distance at a high rate of speed, the soldiers opened fire with their automatic weapons, spraying the car with a hail of bullets, killing the driver and sending the car and its occupants careening out of control and crashing into a tree a few yards from the barricade.

Steve then watched in horror as a dozen men, dressed in green-colored biouniforms, rushed to the crash scene and sprayed the car with a flaming gel, setting the car on fire, trapping the people inside.

Some were still alive.

When the disk had played out, the two of them sat in silence for a few moments. Then Audrey spoke. "Steve . . . I don't think I've ever seen anything so terrifying in all my life."

Steve was confused. Stenholm had just assured him that it was a minor incident with a minimal loss of life.

Her voice filled with emotion, her eyes glowing in hot anger, Audrey declared forcefully, "Steve, we've got to get this story on TV9."

Steve stood to his feet and walked to the large window. Staring out at the night for a few moments, he turned to face her.

"No, Audrey, we can't report it."

Surprised at his answer, she exclaimed in bewilderment, "Why, Steve? Why can't we run it?"

"We . . . we would be putting our lives in danger if we broke this story. I'm sorry, Audrey."

"I don't understand."

"I don't expect you to. Just trust me."

A hushed tenseness hung in the room for a long moment. Then Audrey spoke, her voice filled with determination, as if she had not heard Steve's response. "Steve, I think I know a way to get into Camden. I want to try to get past the barricades tomorrow morning and get some more video footage. I think that will convince you to put it on TV9."

"I'm sorry, Audrey, but I can't let you do that," he answered sternly. "Look, you could have been killed today."

"But, Steve, we've been lied to. This is being covered up. I want to know what the real truth is."

"I'm sorry, but the answer is still no. We'll stay here tonight, then we'll both go back to Dallas tomorrow morning—without the story."

Audrey folded her arms and pursed her lips, trying to control her disappointment and anger. A full minute of silence passed. She then fell into the couch, buried her face in her hands, and began to sob.

Steve caught himself staring at her. The deep feelings he had for her shocked him and he tried desperately to deny them. But no matter how he felt at the moment, he knew he didn't want to get involved with another woman, especially one on his own staff. That could lead to some very unpleasant consequences. But now that his relationship with Lori had been shattered, he was vulnerable.

Even as he fought desperately to deny his feelings for Audrey, she was stirring the old passions, the hopes.

He cautiously moved to the couch and sat down next to her, resting his hand lightly on her shoulder. Sensing his presence, her crying slowly subsided. After several moments of silence had passed, she leaned back and rested her head against the couch. Looking up at him, her large, green eyes caressed him in their gaze.

As their eyes met, Steve felt a slight tremble. Gently brushing a tear from her cheek, his eyes traced her face, the curve of her neck, the tilt of her chin.

The mood in the room changed.

Reaching out with his right hand, he gently brushed a strand of her hair back away from her face, bringing his fingertips back down slowly across her cheek, feeling the soft, smooth texture of her skin.

Something passed between them, and in the moment of their shared anticipation, she moved closer to him.

As his hand came to rest gently on her neck, she turned her face to his. Their lips came together. The sweet aftertaste of the wine, the exquisite scent of her perfume. Their passions mounting, Steve's hands caressed her body, unhurried. Her sigh intensified his desire. Their kisses became more forceful, with more abandon.

Suddenly the phone rang.

Slowly, Steve broke their embrace. Audrey sighed deeply, rested her head on the back of the couch, looked up into his eyes, and smiled.

Steve stood, walked to the table, and picked up the insistent phone. It was Randy. His voice filled with concern, he wanted to know if Steve had heard from Audrey. Steve assured him she was safe, then hung up the phone.

Audrey was now standing next to the fireplace. Steve moved close to her, but they both knew the moment had passed. With a playful sweep of her arm, she lifted her wine glass, drank the final sip, and placed the empty glass on the mantel.

"Well, I'll just say good night for now," she said, her speech slightly slurred from the effects of the wine. "And what just happened, or almost happened, I should say, hasn't changed my mind about covering this story."

Throwing her arms around his neck, she stretched herself up to him and kissed him passionately. With that, she turned, walked across the room, opened the door, glanced teasingly back at him over her left shoulder, then disappeared into her room.

Steve stood motionless, staring at the door that had just closed. The intoxicating scent of her perfume still lingered in the room. The feel of her lips on his, the smell of her breath, the lilting sound of her voice, the sight of her trim body gliding gracefully across the room kept him in a hypnotic state for several minutes.

Then, startlingly, he felt a sense of relief. The night could have presented complications he was not ready to deal with.

Feeling the effects of the wine, his thoughts slowed and he sat down on the edge of the bed, removed his shoes, and stretched out. As his head buried into the soft pillow, he closed his eyes and felt his body relax as his mind recast the strange events of the day.

While adrift in the twilight of that mysterious world between wakefulness and sleep, he was suddenly startled by the ringing of the phone next to his bed. Instantly, he reached for it and spoke into the receiver.

"Hello!" he barked. It sounded like a command.

A man's voice came through the phone, his words deliberate and slow. "Mr. Weston, this is a friend. Leave it alone. This is bigger than you are. You are in danger. Lori and Jimmy are in danger."

"Who is this?" Steve yelled into the phone.

"I'm a friend," the voice said as the phone went dead.

Stunned, Steve sat holding the telephone receiver in his left hand for several seconds, listening to the hum of the dial tone. An uneasy chill rippled through his insides as he slowly put the receiver down. His hand was shaking. "How did they know the names of my wife and son?" he spoke out loud.

He paced the room.

Even though he had been in danger on many occasions in his travels around the world, this was different. Now he had placed his wife and son in danger, and he was afraid. He could take care of himself, but how could he protect his family? A thousand questions raced through his mind.

Did they already have Lori and Jimmy? Were they already being held somewhere as pawns in this mysterious and ever-deepening story?

Gripped with a mounting sense of urgency, he grabbed the phone and hurriedly punched in the number at his home. When Lori answered, he stammered, "Lori . . . I . . . uh . . . just wanted to call to let you know that I'm staying longer than I had planned. There are some loose ends . . . I, uh . . . ."

Lori responded, "Well, that's fine, Steve. It's going to be a very busy time for me anyway. What time is it?"

He was trying to detect if her voice would betray any sense of danger. "It's late. I'm sorry, but is . . . uh, everything all right at home?"

"Why, yes, of course," she answered in a matter-of-fact tone.

He tried again. "Is Jimmy OK?"

"He's at the Enrichment Center," she responded. "I had other plans for the evening, so I left him overnight."

"That's good, Lori," Steve announced. "That's a good idea. Why don't you leave him there. I'll pick him up when I get in."

"What's the matter, Steve?" she responded. "You *never* want me to leave him at the Center. Is anything wrong?"

"Oh, no," he lied. "Everything's fine. I . . . just wanted to make sure that everything was all right . . . with you and Jimmy. Oh, by the way, be sure to lock all the doors and activate the alarm system before going to bed."

After giving her his phone number at the hotel, he cajoled, "Now promise that you'll call me immediately if you need me for any reason."

"You have my word on it. Good night."

Steve hung the phone up and glanced at the clock. It was two-thirty in the morning. It was settled. Now he knew he would have to find out what was going on in this city and in Camden.

He had to let someone know what he was going to do.

Frantically, he punched Randy Standridge's private number at home. Randy answered on the third ring.

"Randy," Steve said haltingly. "I just got a call . . ."

"What about?"

"It was an anonymous caller . . . a warning."

"What did he say?" Randy asked.

"Well, he told me I was in danger if I pursued the story any further."

"Do you think it was legitimate?"

"Yes . . . that's the frightening part. He knew the names of Lori and Jimmy. He said something might happen to them."

There was silence on the line for several seconds. "What are you going to do, Steve?"

"I'm sending Audrey home. She could be in danger. But I'm going to stay to pursue the story. I have to. Something's going on here and I want to know about it."

"OK, Steve, let's make a deal." Randy's voice was filled with concern. "You call me every six hours, starting from right now. If any six-hour period passes and I haven't heard from you, I'm sending somebody in there to look for you. Agreed?"

"Agreed," Steve responded without an argument.

After hanging up the phone, Steve walked to his closet, picked up his briefcase, and laid it on his bed. Lifting the lid, he unzipped a hidden compartment on the right side and retrieved his Omni 441, a small but deadly firearm. Lifting a panel at the bottom, he removed a lightweight shoulder holster, then carefully arranged the gun and holster on the table beside his bed.

There was one more step he must take before he would feel secure. Retrieving a small electronic device from his briefcase, he fastened it to the door of his room, then armed it. Now if the door was opened, the device would sound a shrill alarm. Steve had gone through this ritual a hundred times in dozens of rooms across the world, and on a few occasions his meticulous care to these details had saved his life.

Having completed this task, he lay back down on his bed and waited for the dawn and the unknown dangers the new day would bring.

TWENTY

June 3, 2033

S teve blinked his eyes wearily and covered his face with his arm in a vain attempt to block out the bright glare of the morning sun that was pouring through the window of his hotel room. Knowing that it was a losing battle, he sat on the side of the bed and rubbed his neck and face in an effort to coax his body back to life.

He then stumbled into the bathroom, took a hot shower, shaved and dressed. Now ready to find some breakfast, he decided to try the grill on the ground floor of the hotel.

Casting a glance at Audrey's door, he decided it was too early to disturb her.

Walking to the elevator, he pressed the "down" button and stepped inside when the door slid open. The door closed and he looked up absentmindedly to watch the floor numbers pass by in descending order. Stepping from the elevator, he glanced to his left, looking for the restaurant.

Three people, two men and a woman, were strolling casually toward him. One of the men was over six feet tall. The second man was short, with square shoulders and huge arms that pressed against his tight-fitting white jacket. The woman was about twenty-five with short-cropped dark hair. She was about five feet, six inches tall, slender, with a pretty face, and a figure to match. Their eyes met for a brief moment, and she smiled. It crossed his mind to speak to the pretty woman. A natural instinct, he told himself.

It was going to be a clear day today, he thought to himself. That was good, because he had lots of territory to cover before evening.

At first Steve thought one of the men had inadvertently brushed up against him, but he quickly changed his mind when he felt a hard object pressing firmly against the lower part of his back.

"Don't move, or make a sound, Weston," he heard one of the men say. "If you try anything, one shot from my gun will sever your spinal cord. Just keep quiet and do as you are told and you won't get hurt. Do you understand?"

His first reaction was embarrassment—embarrassment that he had been so careless. *It was the woman.* She was the decoy. He had fallen for one of the oldest tricks in the book.

How could I have been so stupid?

"OK, fella," Steve responded. "Just take it easy with that gun. I'm not going anywhere. Who are you and what do you want me to do?"

By this time the taller man and the pretty woman had moved in close, one on each side of him. The taller man spoke, his tone somber, his words crisp and sharp. "Mr. Weston, listen to me very carefully. I'll only tell you once. In case you're thinking about trying to get away, please be informed that the gun my friend has pressed against your spine is equipped with a silencer and is loaded with bullets that will tear the bottom half of your body apart."

Steve mentally took inventory of his rather limited supply of options. He was in a bad predicament and he knew it. The first rule, he reminded himself, was to not make any quick moves that might cause the man with the gun to pull the trigger. These were professionals and he had no illusions about whether or not they would kill him. He had to go along until he had an opportunity to extricate himself with a reasonable chance of coming out alive.

"You've got my full attention and cooperation. Just tell your man to stay calm and play it cool. I don't want that thing to go off. It could ruin my whole day."

"Well, I'm glad you have a sense of humor, Mr. Weston," the tall man responded. "I hope you still have it when the day is over. Please put your hands down and act normal."

As if to make a point, the short man drove his gun hard against

Steve's back. The tall man spoke with authority. "Now, Mr. Weston, just follow the lady. Don't speak to anyone and don't make any sudden moves. Understand?"

"Yes, I understand."

The pretty woman stepped in front of Steve, turned left, and walked briskly down a long corridor. The two men moved in close, the tall man resting his left hand gently on Steve's right shoulder while the short man kept his gun dug into his ribs on his left side.

The woman made an abrupt right turn through the laundry room, passing several women who were busy washing the hotel linens. Steve tried to think of a way to get their attention, but the women kept their eyes on their work. Then, exiting the laundry room, they walked past a large storage area and went through a door that opened onto an alley in back of the hotel. Steve quickly scanned the alley both ways, but no one was in sight. The only thing he saw was a long black car with tinted windows.

He knew instinctively it was theirs.

When the tall man opened the door to the rear seat of the car and motioned for him to get inside, Steve felt the icy certainty of his own death, knowing that if he got in the car, he would never survive.

Suddenly, a rage swept through him, a blind, irrational rage drawn from some unknown primal source, driving out the fear. And without consciously willing it, he exploded in a final struggle for life, feeling himself turn and throw a hard right squarely into the face of the short man, sending him sprawling against the wall, his gun clattering across the pavement.

The man lay in a crumpled heap, blood spurting from his broken nose. He didn't move.

With everything now passing before Steve's eyes in surreal slow motion, he turned to face the other man, just in time to see a black instrument coming down toward his head. Instinctively, he tried to raise his left arm to block the blow, but it was an instant too late.

The man's hand brought the black instrument down hard, catching him flush on the left side of his face. A fiery current of pain shot down the left side of his body, buckling his knees. A scream welled up in his brain, but no sound came, only the throbbing bolts of agony from the blow.

Then he felt his body float slowly, gently, toward the ground, still hearing the man's cursing, his words only sounds echoing down a long, dark tube.

S teve felt himself rising out of a sea of darkness, with strange visions of floating, shapeless images flooding his confused mind, his thoughts running wild, with no order or reason. Near panic, he strained to clear his head, to make sense of what was happening to him.

Where was he?

And what was causing the unbearable pain that was shooting across the side of his head? He tried to move his arms, but they wouldn't respond to his commands.

Something—or someone—was holding him down.

Gradually, shapes became objects, and he saw that he was sitting in a strangely built, massive wooden chair, his arms and legs bound to it with broad leather straps. In a surge of panic, he fought against his bonds, desperately trying to loose himself.

Nearing the brink of exhaustion, he realized his efforts were futile and reluctantly relaxed his arms and legs, then turned his attention to his unwelcome surroundings. Sweeping his gaze around the room, he was overwhelmed with disbelief and dread. His strange wooden chair sat in the center of an enormous room, at least fifty feet wide and sixty feet long, with a ceiling over thirty feet high. Dark brown wooden beams, etched with age, stretched the width of the ceiling.

Strange metal chandeliers hung ominously from the tall ceiling, emitting a gloomy light across the room. Long, heavy chains with metal arm and leg clamps, well-worn with use, hung menacingly from the walls.

A large wooden table with leather straps attached to it occupied the corner of the room to his right. Other tables and devices scattered throughout the room brought recollections of pictures he had seen of medieval torture chambers. Realizing he was alone, the silence of the room closed in around him like a shroud.

The only sound was the frantic beating of his own heart.

He closed his eyes tight in disbelief, confident that when he opened them again, this night terror would have vanished and he would be back in the real world. But to his dismay, when he opened his eyes, nothing had changed.

The room remained, and he in it.

Steve wished for the oblivion of unconsciousness.

Involuntarily, Steve's head jerked to the left when a thick wooden door opened suddenly, swinging back, crashing against the wall with a jarring thud. Three men and the pretty woman walked into the room. One of the men had bandages plastered across his swollen face. Steve recognized him immediately as the short man he had sent plummeting to the pavement. He had never seen the other two men.

The short man walked slowly up to Steve, and without warning, struck him across the left side of his face with his clenched fist, snapping his head back with the vicious blow. New waves of pain drove him to the edge of unconsciousness.

"How does it feel, Weston," the man snarled, "to be hit in the face?"

Before the man could do further damage, a door on the other side of the room opened and a slender man with dark brown hair, sharp facial features, and an aquiline nose stepped into the room and walked toward Steve.

Not a tall man, nor particularly impressive in his physique, yet he carried himself with the dignity and composure of a man who was accustomed to being in command. Steve guessed him to be in his early forties.

His piercing eyes stared menacingly at him.

Two men, armed with automatic weapons slung over their shoulders, followed him into the room, stationing themselves on each side of the door, their guns in readiness. The others in the room stepped aside as the slender man walked up to Steve.

Coming to within three feet of his prisoner, he stopped, placed his hands on his hips, and stared, unsmiling, into Steve's swollen and bleeding face. Steve met his hard stare, desperately trying to assess the situation he faced. The man then walked slowly around the chair, examining his prize from all sides.

"Well, Mr. Weston," the man began, in a pleasant baritone voice. "It's good to see that you're awake. I must say that you don't look quite as noble now as you do on the video wallscreens across the world. However, I can assure you that you will look even worse before we are through with you."

With his pain intensifying, Steve stared at the strange man standing in front of him for a long moment, then asked defiantly through bleeding lips, "Who are you? Why are you holding me? Answer me! Who are you?"

"One question at a time. My name is Carlo, and you are here because we want you here. And we are going to do many things to you, but rest assured, Mr. Weston," he said, leaning into Steve's face, "in the end . . . I am going to kill you."

Steve gazed back into Carlo's cold, dark eyes, fighting to keep his panic in check. When Carlo turned away, he scanned the room for any signs of help or escape, but all he got in return were the stares of a dozen or more somber people who had entered the room and were standing behind Carlo.

Looking from face to face, he searched for someone who would help him, but their expressionless faces told him they were anxious to get on with the killing. Knowing now that he must draw upon every ounce of his courage and cunning, he set his mind to somehow outwit his adversaries.

He turned back to Carlo. "Why me? Why are you going to kill me?"

"Why am I going to kill you, Mr. Weston? That's a very good question. And I owe it to you to give you an honest answer. I'm going to kill you for one reason and one reason only," Carlo answered.

"What reason?"

"For *pleasure*. It will bring me *pleasure* to kill you," Carlo said coldly. "That's the reason I have killed all my victims. They all gave their lives that I might indulge in my pleasure."

"You've killed others?" Steve asked out of desperation.

"Yes, of course, I've killed many, and they all brought me pleasure, especially the women; they brought me double pleasure."

Steve could hardly believe what he was hearing. His body racked with pain, his nerves raw, his mind confused, he watched in bewilderment as Carlo walked back and forth in front of him, casually talking about killing people.

"Why shouldn't I kill you, Mr. Weston?" Carlo continued. "I get my personal pleasure from engaging in all forms of torture, acts that the beastly lords of old never dreamed of. We receive pleasure from pushing people to the limits of their endurance before they go insane or die."

"But why me? Why did you choose me?" Steve asked desperately.

"It's nothing personal, Mr. Weston. I don't despise you or hate you. You just happen to be the one I chose this time. And you have no right to deny me of my pleasure."

"Where am I?"

"All you need to know is that you're in the Pleasure Room. This room is dedicated to pleasure. *Our* pleasure. Some people derive their pleasure from work, or play, or sex. We too get our pleasure in these ways, but our pleasure is intensified tenfold because we add the ingredients of torture, pain, and death. The combination is quite stimulating. And you, sir, are here to add to our pleasure."

His darting eyes betraying his confusion and fear, Steve looked past Carlo and called out to those in the room, "Who are you people?"

Nobody spoke. They only glared at him.

"Who are you? . . . Answer me! Who are you?"

With a sweep of his hand, Carlo answered, "Ah, Mr. Weston, you are the honored guest of members of the Party of the New Barbarians."

The New Barbarians!

A knot tightened in Steve's stomach. Images of their atrocities flashed through his mind. A scourge to the world, the New Barbarians were an army of anarchists who killed and destroyed for the sheer pleasure of it. Coming from families of every social and economic level, their common bond was a life that was devoid of any conception of morality.

"All is futile," they said. "Life is a mockery." They shared the same wish—to see humanity annihilated and the earth go up in one large nuclear ball of fire.

Functioning within a belief system that had expelled any conception of a moral order, they had been set free from the restraints of guilt and conscience. And in an effort to satisfy their increasingly evil desires, they had given themselves over to the pursuit of all forms of perverse and malevolent entertainment.

Believing that the self is the center of all things, and that pleasure is the highest goal, they sought and demanded satisfaction for their every lust and desire. They reasoned that human life, as such, has no intrinsic worth, and that only through death and destruction is there meaning.

Enemies to all religions—especially Christianity—their gods were destruction, violence, annihilation, and death. Their avowed purpose was to destroy all governments, all religions, all social order and, in the end, to destroy the human race, including themselves. To the New Barbarians, the universe itself was an aberration that must also be destroyed.

"Oh, I see by the expression on your face that you know about us," Carlo said, with a look of satisfaction.

"Yes, Carlo, I'm acquainted with your group. I've seen some of your handiwork, and I hold you in utmost contempt. I—"

"Now, now, Mr. Weston, you shouldn't talk that way. After all, you are our honored guest. However, it does increase our pleasure even more to know that you are acquainted with our ways. And please accept my complete gratitude. You and the others have made it possible for us to live our lives to the fullest. It's even more thrilling to kill a person of high rank in the global order, such as yourself."

"But what about my own desire to live?" Steve responded loudly.

"Your desire to live means nothing to me. I'm only interested in my own freedoms, choices, and desires. If torturing and killing you brings me the highest pleasure, what right do you have to deny me this?"

"You have no right to take other people's lives, Carlo."

"No *right?*" Carlo returned. "You dare to lecture me on my *right* to kill other human beings? You and your fellow assassins in the global order make us look like amateurs. We kill for pleasure. You disguise your barbarism behind righteous-sounding words like 'Earth Cleansing.' You are word masters. You have already slaughtered millions through your scientifically designed death technologies, and if your plan to drastically reduce the earth's population continues to succeed, you will kill millions more."

Carlo hesitated a moment. "What's the total so far? One billion? Two billion? With such large-scale murder now accepted as good and moral, Mr. Weston, how could you possibly believe that *your* life, or mine, is of any significance whatsoever? But let's not talk about me. Let's talk about you. As a trusted newsman, you're supposed to give the world the truth. But unfortunately, when you are ordered to suppress a story that might inconvenience the Social Order, like all the others, you are quick to obey. Is that why you haven't reported the truth about the tragedy in the town of Camden?"

Leaning into his face, Carlo yelled, "Did Stenholm order you *not* to report the story?"

Shooting a scornful glance at his captor, Steve said, "Some escaping toxic gas killed fifteen people in a small Texas town, hardly worthy of international attention."

"You're such a fool, Weston. Don't you know that Stenholm has lied to you? Why do you think he wouldn't let you go to Camden to see for yourself? Camden is a tragedy beyond your comprehension."

"What are you talking about, Carlo?"

Enjoying the sound of his own voice, Carlo said, "It will add to my pleasure to tell you what happened before you die. Two days ago, a truck on its way to the Kavrinski Institute for Human Life, here in Templeton, was passing through the town of Camden when it was involved in an accident. The driver lost control on an overpass and the truck plunged thirty feet down to the pavement below. Onboard the truck were several canisters filled with the Maylay virus—"

"Maylay!" Steve exclaimed. The very word made him shudder.

With the words of Dr. Alexi Monet describing the newly discovered virus at the briefing inside The Mountain flashing into his mind, Steve now knew why the town had been cordoned off from the rest of the world. And why Stenholm would not allow him near it.

"Oh, I see you've heard of the Maylay virus, Mr. Weston," Carlo said in a taunting way. "Well, you would be interested to know that the live virus was being sent to KavLife for further research and experimentation in developing more powerful chemical and biological weapons to be used against the excess human population of earth."

With a shrug of his shoulders, Carlo added, "Unfortunately, some of the canisters ruptured during the accident and the virus escaped into the atmosphere near a highly populated area. A brisk wind was blowing, so no one knows how far the virus traveled or how many people were exposed."

Genuinely shocked at this news, Steve asked his captor, "How do you know these things, Carlo?"

Carlo smiled. "I have my sources. Within two hours after the accident, people began reporting to the hospitals in Camden, complaining of nausea, cramps, headaches. Some were breaking out in red blisters all over their body. And then a large number of them began to die. There was an immediate quarantine placed on the town, and no one has been able to get in or out since. Camden is closed behind an unbroken barricade that completely surrounds it. Thousands of Global Forces troops have been deployed to guard it."

Suddenly turning somber, Carlo added, "You see, Weston, the entire population of the town of Camden is doomed. Every living thing that could possibly be a host for the virus will be vaporized. The final blow will be struck soon. But don't look so concerned; you won't be here to see it."

Steve cautiously watched Carlo, barely breathing, knowing that the least provocation could push this man over the edge, causing him to end his life in a heartbeat.

At that point, Carlo turned to the people in the room and barked an order. "Leave us alone. Go to your stations."

Steve watched as they obediently exited through the huge wooden door, leaving him alone with Carlo. The two men once again stared into each other's eyes.

Carlo walked behind his prisoner. Steve tensed. He felt his tormentor fill his hand with his hair, pulling it violently, snapping his head backward, causing the room to spin. Pain shot up through his neck. Carlo slowly leaned over him from behind, their faces no more than six inches apart.

Steve felt the hot wind of his breath and smelled the pungent odor of alcohol. He fought the urge to throw up.

Struggling for breath, and his life, Steve gulped a lungful of air and forced out the words, "You're insane, Carlo."

Carlo took his handgun out of its holster and pressed the barrel hard against Steve's throat. "Maybe I am insane. So tell me why I shouldn't pull this trigger right now and end your life? Give me a reason to let you live."

"I . . . have a son. I want to live . . . *for my son!*"

Tears welled up in Steve's eyes, betraying his point of vulnerability to his enemy. Carlo relaxed the gun, letting it drop to his side. "Yes, I know. His name is Jimmy. But no, Weston, having a son doesn't buy your life for you," he said derisively.

With the blood now dried to a sickening brown crust on his face and hair, Steve looked up into the eyes of his strutting captor.

Whispering hoarsely, Steve said, "Water . . . give me some water. For God's sake, Carlo, give me some water."

Ignoring his plea, Carlo continued to taunt his victim. "You know, Mr. Weston, I have tortured and killed many people. Some I've allowed to live longer because I enjoyed the intellectual interchange with them. But make no mistake about it, in the end I killed them, in spite of their diligent pursuit in trying to reason with me. Some were very articulate and presented their case with intelligence and dexterity. However, in the end they all became sniveling, begging cowards, pleading for their lives."

Breathing deeply, Steve responded, "I won't give you the joy of seeing me beg, Carlo. I may not be able to talk you into sparing my life, but I can rob you of that part of your 'pleasure.'"

"I should kill you now," Carlo hissed through clenched teeth. "But then I wouldn't have the pleasure of seeing you suffer. So I will spare your life a little longer."

Fighting the seeping weariness that was beginning to paralyze his mind, Steve's eyes followed Carlo's hand as it toyed with the revolver that filled the black leather holster lying hard against his right leg. A tight smile crossed Carlo's face and he pulled back the hammer of the gun, then gently released it against the chamber. He did it again, and again, and again. The cold metallic sound seemed to inflame his passions beyond reason.

Once again Carlo straddled the small straight-back chair in front of Steve, folded his arms across the back of the chair, shook his head slightly, and said, "You see, Mr. Weston, there are no answers. There is no meaning to our existence. There is no truth. Only a difference in tyrants. So all must be destroyed. That's why we take pleasure in killing. So we kill anyone we wish, in whatever manner that brings us pleasure."

Abruptly leaping to his feet, he shouted into Steve's face, "And that, sir, is why I will take the utmost pleasure in killing you!"

Carlo's words had scarcely escaped his lips when both men were startled by the sound of screaming voices, accentuated by the rapid roar of automatic weapons fire and jarring explosions. A speaker on the wall of the torture room burst to life. A man's voice howled, "They're inside; Carlo, they're coming through the door. I can see—"

His last words were covered up by the sound of machine-gun fire and a woman's horrible shriek.

Quickly turning his attention to Carlo, Steve could see the panic of a caged animal in his cold, empty eyes. When the heavy thud of a battering ram slamming against the thick, heavy wooden door echoed through the room, Carlo jerked his revolver from its holster. Steve's head snapped up. His eyes wide, he watched in horror as Carlo walked toward him, his gun held menacingly in his right hand, ready to fire.

Nausea swept across Steve's body when Carlo jammed the barrel of the gun against his forehead, pressing it hard against his flesh.

Steve held his breath, waiting for the inevitable.

His voice cold with dark fury, Carlo pulled the hammer of the gun back, pushed it mercilessly against Steve's head, and bellowed loudly, "This is the end, Mr. Weston!"

In one last desperate bid for life, Steve called out, "Wait, Carlo! I can help you. I can save your life. If you kill me, they're going to kill you. Your only hope for life is to let me live. You'll never get out of this room alive without me. Save yourself, Carlo."

His fiery eyes fixing Steve in their evil glare, Carlo cried out, "Beg, Weston! Beg for your life, like all the others have done!"

His mind yielding to the inevitable, Steve answered, "No, Carlo, I won't beg. But I will—"

A jarring sound cut him off in midsentence.

With the rapid staccato of machine-gun fire sending deadly projectiles ripping through the heavy wooden door, scattering debris across the room in their wake, Carlo raucously threw back his head and laughed a maniacal laugh.

Steve stared in wide-eyed disbelief.

With the sound of his crazed, mocking laughter echoing and reechoing throughout the large room, Carlo unexpectedly jerked his gun away from Steve's head, swiftly placed it against his own temple, and pulled the trigger.

The gun gave a loud, terrifying report.

Passing before his disbelieving gaze in agonizing slow motion, Steve's unblinking eyes stared in horror as Carlo's head burst apart in a grisly shower of brain tissue, blood, and bone fragments, the force of the bullet splattering the ghastly mixture across the floor and up against the dark stone wall.

All but decapitated, Carlo's body seemed to hang ominously suspended in the stifling air for a long, terrible moment before it crumbled downward, his lifeless finger pulling the trigger of the gun once more as he hit the floor.

Now quivering in fear, Steve retched from deep inside his belly, throwing up, sending the bitter fluids flying across the floor.

Suddenly, the huge door gave way and armed men, dressed in green military fighting attire, rushed inside, their firearms sweeping the room.

Seeing that Carlo was dead, one of the soldiers called out, "It's clear in here."

The room now whirling around Steve at an increasing speed, out of his confusion and fear, he chanced to look up. There, walking into his vision, was Randy Standridge, moving toward him at a rapid pace.

"Randy," Steve called out hoarsely.

Rushing to his chair, Randy looked at him and exclaimed, "My god, Steve, what have they done to you?"

The two men looked at each other in silence, both of them sensing the miracle of Steve's rescue, each knowing that a delay of only a few seconds would have meant death.

In an unconscious gesture of affection, Randy reached out his hand and smoothed Steve's matted hair, promising, "We'll have you out of here in a minute or two. Just hold on."

While one of the soldiers loosened his bonds, Steve looked up and said in a shaking, raspy voice, "Thanks for coming. I . . . I didn't think I was going to make it, Randy."

"Can I get you something, Steve?"

"Water, Randy," Steve gasped. "Do you have any water?"

Randy turned and shouted to a military man who was guarding the door. "Sergeant, Mr. Weston needs some water. Get some in here . . . quick!"

In a few seconds, the soldier handed Randy a glass filled with water. Randy handed the glass to Steve and watched as he devoured it in large gulps.

"Thanks, Randy," Steve said, wiping his bloody face with the back of his shirt sleeve.

A colonel, dressed in the dark green uniform of the Global Forces, stepped up to Steve's chair. "We've got an ambulance on the way, Mr. Weston. It'll be here in a couple of minutes. We'll get you out of this hellhole just as soon as we can."

"Thanks, Colonel. Thanks for all you've done."

The water seemed to revive Steve's spirits. He looked at Randy and asked, "How did you find me? How did you know where I was?"

"Well, when you didn't call me in the allotted time we had agreed on, I started calling your room. When I didn't get an answer, I knew something was wrong. I called the front desk at the hotel, and a lady told me they had seen you leave with two men and a woman, but didn't know where you were going. She said that everything seemed normal, but they hadn't seen you come back in. So I hopped a TV9 plane and came down. When I checked in with the authorities, they told me they had just received an anonymous phone call that told them where you were. I insisted that they allow me to come with them—"

The sergeant broke in, "Sorry, sir, the ambulance is here. So if you don't mind stepping aside, we'll get Mr. Weston up and out of here."

"No problem, Sergeant," Randy replied as he moved to the side of Steve's chair.

Two medics, rolling a stretcher, pushed their way through the door and went straight to where Steve was seated. An attractive nurse accompanied them. She spoke to Steve. "Mr. Weston, I'm Nurse Wagstaff. Could you see if you can stand, please?"

Steve made an effort to stand but sank back into the chair. "Sorry,

Ms. Wagstaff. I guess I'm weaker than I thought. I'm going to need a little help."

Slipping their hands underneath Steve's arms, the two medics helped him onto the stretcher, then rolled him toward the door with Nurse Wagstaff on one side of him and Randy on the other.

Moving through what remained of the shattered door, they entered an enormous den, its walls lined with expensive books, the furnishings tasteful and very expensive. One of the walls was made almost entirely of glass and looked out over well-groomed grounds, tall stately trees, and a private lake that covered several acres of land. With its luxurious furnishings, it spoke of money, status, and culture.

Rolling swiftly through the den, they passed a large formal dining room. An immense crystal chandelier hung in the center of the room, its hundreds of pendants clear and sparkling.

Moving past an expansive winding staircase, they turned left down a wide hallway lined with expensive antiques and classical paintings.

What did it all mean? Steve asked himself.

Things were not fitting together in his mind. They had just come out of a medieval torture chamber where he had almost met his death, directly into rooms that quite obviously were part of a splendid home, one that had the markings of a man who was educated, cultured, and who appreciated the finer things in life.

How could a chamber of such unspeakable evil be inside this magnificent dwelling?

When they had secured his stretcher in the ambulance, Nurse Wagstaff placed a needle in his left arm. "This won't hurt, Mr. Weston, but it will calm you and make the ride a little easier. So just relax; we'll take care of everything."

Steve felt the forward lurch of the ambulance, heard the muffled sound of the siren, saw the pretty face of Nurse Wagstaff looking down at him, and welcomed the soft, assuring touch of her warm hand.

Then everything went black.

S teve could hear the pleasing sound of a woman's voice in the far-off distance of his consciousness. When he opened his eyes, he was in a hospital room, the pretty face of Nurse Wagstaff looking down at him, smiling. "Can you hear me, Mr. Weston? It's time to wake up. Dr. Lambert is here to examine you. You've been through quite an ordeal."

A short, rotund, middle-aged man with a head full of unruly dark hair walked to the side of his bed. "I'm Dr. Lambert, Mr. Weston."

"Good to meet you, doctor. How am I doing?"

"Considering everything you've been through the last few hours, I would say that you've come through very well. There are no fractures, no damage to major organs, and no cranial damage."

"Fine. Now, when can I get out of here?" Steve asked.

Making some notes on an electronic pad at the foot of the bed, the doctor said, "I would suggest that you stay overnight for observation. I'll be back first thing in the morning."

When the doctor and Nurse Wagstaff left the room, Steve turned to Randy. "Have you contacted Lori?"

Randy moved to the foot of the bed. "I called her and filled her in on what I thought she needed to know."

"And Audrey . . . where is Audrey?" Steve asked.

Randy shrugged his shoulders. "I don't know, Steve. She hasn't contacted the office in Dallas, and no one in this town seems to know anything about her."

Steve quickly glanced out the window, not wanting Randy to see the disappointment on his face. Standing up, Steve walked shakily to the closet and began to get dressed.

"What do you think you're doing, Steve?" Randy called out. "The doctor told you to stay overnight."

Continuing to dress, Steve answered, "Randy, I've got to get out of here. I've got to find Audrey."

"Are you sure you can make it, Steve?"

"I think so. I'm sore, but nothing serious. I'll make it."

"What do you want me to do?" Randy asked.

Steve thought for a moment. "I want you to go back to Dallas without delay. You have my SatPhone number, so call me the moment you hear from Audrey. I'm worried, Randy. With what's going on here, she could be in real trouble."

When Steve had finished dressing, Randy walked with him through the lobby to the outside, where Steve summoned a cab.

"Steve, are you sure you don't want me to hang around and help you look for her?" Randy asked, concern in his voice.

"No, Randy," Steve responded thoughtfully. "I think I can work better alone. Besides, she may get in contact with the office in Dallas."

As he stepped into the backseat of the cab he looked up at Randy. "Thanks for everything."

Randy nodded and walked away.

His head still spinning, Steve leaned back against the seat as the cab pulled away from the curb.

TWENTY-ONE

Steve walked into the lobby of the Metropole Hotel, desperately hoping to see Audrey waiting for him. Scanning the lobby carefully, he was disappointed when he didn't see her. Approaching the clerk at the front desk, he asked if they had seen her come in.

The clerk assured him that she had not returned. Disappointed, he picked up his key, walked hurriedly to the elevator, and rode up to his floor. Once inside his room, he knocked solidly on her door, almost certain she wouldn't answer. But he could hope.

There was no answer.

Accepting the fact that she had not returned to the hotel, he reached for the phone and began dialing numbers, making calls, asking questions, and getting no satisfactory answers. Desperate to find her, he used every tactic he could muster to elicit information, any information, any lead, that might tell him where she was. But evening came and he had not turned up a single credible lead. It was as if she had vanished off the face of the earth.

Still a little shaky over the ordeal he had just gone through, he fought against a dark foreboding growing inside him that Audrey might be in mortal danger. He hadn't told anyone, but he was afraid she had somehow stumbled onto the secret about Camden that Adam Stenholm was so desperately trying to keep hidden.

In a daze, he walked to the large window and stared out into the night. Fighting against the onrush of confusing, debilitating thoughts, he felt as if his life were falling apart. It seemed that the well-ordered world he believed in was turning on him with a vengeance. Even the Social Order that had nurtured him, and that he served, was now taking on a new and ugly face.

Besieged by heavy, crushing doubts and unrelenting questions, he was driven to know the truth, regardless of the consequences. He struggled to find answers, knowing they were there, just at the edge of his reasoning, screaming to be recognized. But he couldn't quite reach them.

Dejectedly, he turned to make a telephone call. Then, in midstride, he suddenly remembered his conversation with Dr. Wallenberg in the car when they were leaving The Mountain on the way back to Geneva.

And as if he were standing beside him in this room, he heard his mentor's voice telling him, *"When the time comes, Steven, you will know. You will know."*

Maybe this was the time.

He glanced back at the digital clock. It was past eleven in the evening. Knowing that Randy would be at his post at TV9, he would call him. At the moment Randy was the only man in the entire organization he felt he could trust. Grabbing the phone, he dialed the secure line on Randy's desk.

Randy picked it up on the fourth ring. "This is Randy Standridge."

"Randy, this is Steve."

"Hey, Steve, are you all right?" Randy asked with a note of concern in his voice. "Have you made contact with Audrey?"

"No, Randy, I haven't found her. I haven't been able to uncover a single lead. I'm stumped. Anything there?"

"No, we haven't heard from her."

After a long pause, Steve said, "Randy, I need your help."

"Sure, Steve," Randy replied. "Just name it."

"First, hang up your phone and go to my office. I'll call you on my secure line. And, Randy, don't tell anyone where you're going or what you're doing. Do you still have the key to my office?"

"I've got it. I'm hanging up now."

"The phone will be ringing by the time you get there."

Hanging up the phone, Randy slipped his jacket on and walked out of his office into the newsroom. Dozens of people were scurrying back and forth, talking to news sources from all over the world, yelling across the room, waving paper, rushing about in what seemed to be a perpetual state of pandemonium. But it was all part of responding to the constant pressure of gathering, compiling, and airing the never-ceasing newscasts.

Making a quick survey of the room, Randy spotted Ted Schultz, his assistant, who was engaged in a heated debate with one of the female newsanchors. Ted looked up and saw Randy motioning for him.

Turning back to the newsanchor, he shouted, "The answer is still no!" He then walked over to where Randy was standing.

"Ted, I'm going to be out for a while. Take over for me."

"What's up, Randy?"

"Nothing. I've got a couple of errands to run, that's all," Randy replied as he turned and walked to the elevator.

Once inside, he pushed the button for the twenty-third floor, the one reserved for the executive suites. He was the only one onboard. When the elevator stopped, he exited into the reception area and, without breaking his stride, walked down the corridor to Steve's office, placed his key in the lock, and pushed the door open just as the phone began to ring.

Stepping inside, he closed and locked the door behind him, glanced out at the lights of the city through the huge glass wall, flipped on the lights, and walked to Steve's desk, answering the phone on its third ring.

Recognizing Steve's voice, Randy said, "OK, I'm sitting at your desk. What now?"

"Randy, open the top drawer to your right," Steve instructed.

Randy reached for the drawer handle and pulled it open. "The drawer is open. What am I looking for?"

"Pull the drawer all the way out. There's a small metal box toward the back. Remove the box."

Steve heard the metal box brush against the drawer.

"I've got the metal box," Randy told him.

"Now, there's a black marble pen and pencil set on the top of my desk. Take out the pen and unscrew the top."

Randy reached across the desk, retrieved the fountain pen, and unscrewed the top part. "Why, it's not a fountain pen at all, Steve. What is it?"

"It's a key, Randy. It will open the metal box."

Randy tilted the metal box up and inserted the key. "The box is open," he exclaimed.

"Good. Do you see the small plastic laminated card inside the box?"

"Got it, Steve."

"You'll find a series of numbers, symbols, and letters on it. It's a computer code. I'm now interfaced with TV9's Sidhartha 4000 mainframe from my small computer here in my room, but I need you to enter the code on the card through my personal computer there on my desk. Randy, those codes are highly classified, and it's illegal for you to even see them. I apologize for asking you to do this, but I don't know of any other way."

"I'm here to help you, Steve. I know this must be important to you or you wouldn't be asking me to do it."

"Thanks, Randy. Now enter the code, double-check each entry, but don't hit ENTER. I'll do that from here. Make sure that every letter, symbol, and number is absolutely correct. I'll follow each entry on my monitor here."

"All right, here goes, Steve."

His palms sweating, Steve listened to the soft clicking of the keyboard as Randy punched in the secret code, following each entry as they moved across the face of his monitor screen. If it was possible to get into the Omega, he knew TV9's powerful Sidhartha 4000 had the muscle to do it. He hoped Randy was getting it right.

"There it is, Steve," Randy announced. "I've checked it twice. I think I've entered it correctly."

"All right, Randy, I'll take over now. When I hit ENTER, your screen will go blank. But don't worry; it's a little precaution I programmed in from here. At that point, all I want you to do is to sit in my chair and guard that computer. If someone comes in and gets inquisitive, just tell them you're waiting on a transmission from me about the situation here in Templeton."

"I figured this might take a while," Randy said, "so I told Ted to take over the supervision of the newsroom while I'm in here."

"Good. And, Randy, if anyone insists on breaking in on my transmission, and I mean *anyone*, just reach over and press the ESCAPE key. That will execute an immediate disconnect. If all goes well, when I finish my work, I'll call you back and you can disengage the system then."

"OK, Steve. I'll sit here until you call me back," Randy said as he hung up the receiver.

With the code to the Omega glowing on his monitor screen, Steve hesitated, feeling as if he were about to descend into a dark, digitized dungeon, to see things he was never intended to see, to gain knowledge that would put him at odds with his own government and the Social Order.

Small beads of perspiration formed on his brow. He was pushing the limits of his luck and he knew it. Any trip into the innards of the world's mightiest and most secret computer was a little scary, at best. Breaking into the ultrasecret files at this level, using someone else's code, was terrifying. He did not take his actions lightly.

With a sense of determination, his trembling hand moved slightly to the right and he pressed ENTER. Instantly, TV9's Sidhartha 4000 read Steve's instructions and beamed them to a series of Low Earth Orbit satellites a few hundred miles above the earth.

Plunging downward from there, the electronic impulses were scooped up by small satellite dishes positioned on the peak of The Mountain in Switzerland. And from there they were sent through fiber-optic cables straight into the inner sanctum of the forbidden underground city inside the cavern fortress.

Challenged by digital barriers guarding the entrance to the Omega, the Sidhartha 4000 demanded entrance, executing billions of permutations, unscrambling indecipherable codes, and opening infinitely complex digital passageways.

And before Steve could withdraw his finger from the keyboard, his screen had painted the words,

```
PRIVILEGED FILES SECTION
WELCOME DR. WILHELM WALLENBERG
PRESS "ENTER" WHEN READY TO PROCEED
```

Steve stared at the screen, momentarily frozen in a state of near panic. He was inside the "Privileged Files Section." Opening and closing his fists in an attempt to relax his fingers, he took a series of deep breaths, then placed the heels of his hands on the pad at the bottom of the keyboard. Stretching his fingers out to the keys, he pressed ENTER.

Instantly, the computer prompted:

ENTER NAME OF FILE TO BE RETRIEVED

Steve studied the screen for a long moment. Wiping the sweat from his top lip, he placed his fingers over the keyboard, poised to strike the keys that would take him into an unknown world. With a note of finality, he typed in the words,

THE GAIA PROJECT

When he pressed ENTER, the screen instantly displayed a three-dimensional graphic of the earth with the words "Most Secret" emblazoned across it. Clicking on a small icon of the earth in the upper right-hand corner, the screen flashed the words,

THE GAIA PROJECT

Steve hesitated, staring at the ultrasecret file, wondering what lay ahead of him. Glancing at the clock, he knew he would not be able to stay on-line long enough to read the material he had accessed, so he typed in a code that instructed the computer to download the file on the Gaia Project onto the internal hard disk of his small computer. When the file had been transferred, a message appeared on the screen:

DATA TRANSFER COMPLETED.
DO YOU WISH TO ACCESS ANOTHER FILE,
DR. WILHELM WALLENBERG?

Staring intently into the screen for several moments, Steve weighed his next move.

L i Wong was sitting in Pit 7 inside the Unauthorized Intrusion Department (UID) hidden away in a large room deep inside The Mountain in Switzerland. A short, slightly overweight young man, he was a dedicated computer expert. Squinting through his round glasses that were perennially perched near the end of his nose, Wong stared at Steve's entry into the Privileged Files Section that had suddenly appeared on one of the monitors in front of him.

One of the government's most secret and secure departments, the UID was manned by hundreds of trained computer professionals who constantly scanned an array of sophisticated electronic monitoring devices busily deciphering billions of digitized transactions, looking for any unauthorized attempt to break into the system.

Each workstation—called a pit—consisted of twelve computer monitors, arranged in a half-circle with the security officer sitting in a chair in the center for easy access to each computer.

It was standard operating procedure to lock onto any source, authorized or not, that attempted to access the Privileged Files Section, one of the most secret sections housed in the Omega.

With only a limited number of people with authorization to enter these files, Li Wong had come to know the personality and style of each person through their unique way of entering and accessing data. Seeing something that sounded an alarm in his brain, he turned to the attractive Swedish girl sitting in the pit next to his own.

"Hey, Freda," he called. "Would you step over here just a minute? I've got something I want you to look at."

The tall blonde stood to her feet, pulled her short skirt down around her slender hips, walked to Pit 7, and stood behind him. Wong pointed to the third computer on his left. Her eyes quickly locked onto monitor three.

Wong said, "Look at this. Someone is using Dr. Wallenberg's confidential entry code. Somehow, he's entered the correct code, but this is not Dr. Wallenberg's signature. I know his style. He's sure-handed, precise, decisive. This person's hesitant, cautious, intimidated."

Shrugging her shoulders, she said, "So what? It looks like some hacker is trying to get himself in bad trouble."

"Yeah, Freda," Wong answered, with a note of glee in his voice.

"But this person is staying on-line even though he knows he's not authorized to enter. He's not going to give up."

Myra Kenshasi, a native of New Africa and a supervisor over ten surveillance pits, saw the commotion in Pit 7. She walked over and stood next to Freda. When Wong expressed his doubts about the entry, she turned quickly and walked to her desk in the center of the large room and pressed a red button marked "Urgent."

The phone rang in the office of the Chief of Security, Ernst Krohn. Myra told him to come to Pit 7.

Ernst Krohn walked up to Pit 7. "What have you got, Wong?" he demanded.

Without taking his eyes off the monitor, Wong replied, "This is not Dr. Wallenberg. But whoever it is, he's staying in. I think we should check him out."

"Freda," Krohn said authoritatively, "double-check with Security Recording and make sure that this entire transaction is being copied."

"Yes, sir," she replied, walking briskly away.

Krohn then picked up a phone on Wong's table and barked into it. "This is Ernst Krohn. Activate a trace on an incoming on unit three in Pit 7. And put it up on the house screens."

Instantly, several wallscreens came to life displaying a three-dimensional map of the world. The staff watched in silent anticipation as a bright red line started snaking its way across the map, following the digital impulses back toward the origination point of the incoming transmission.

Wong stared into monitor three. He spoke to it, saying, "Hold on, mister. Don't go away. Give us time to see who's knocking at our secret door."

Ernst Krohn picked up the phone again on Wong's computer table and shouted, "Retrieve Dr. Wallenberg's file to determine his whereabouts at this precise moment. Then confirm his location, but don't let him know what we're doing. Put his voice response through the Voice Print Verification system for a positive ID. I want to know if he is presently transmitting to the Omega. Do it immediately!"

As soon as Krohn hung up the phone, Wong said excitedly, "Mr. Krohn, look at the wallscreen. The trace has taken us to Dallas, Texas.

It's now probing the uplinks and fiber-optic highways for an accurate pinpoint of the location of the transmission."

The phone rang on Wong's table. Krohn snatched it from its cradle. The voice on the other end responded crisply. "Mr. Krohn, we have a positive connect with Dr. Wallenberg. One of our agents spoke to him personally. He is definitely *not* transmitting to the Omega, sir."

Krohn hung up the phone and ordered, "Keep at it, Wong. As you said, this is not Dr. Wallenberg. Whoever it is must be caught, and any information he may retrieve must be confiscated. It cannot be allowed to get out. I'll alert our people in Dallas."

Driven by an overwhelming need to know, Steve Weston quelled his urge to cut his connection to the Omega. The prompt on the screen taunted him.

DO YOU WISH TO ACCESS ANOTHER FILE,
DR. WILHELM WALLENBERG?

Fearing that his connection would be terminated, he hurriedly answered the query by pressing YES.

After another prompt, he entered the words:

GLOBAL CORPORATIONS

The Omega instructed:

ENTER NAME OF GLOBAL CORPORATION

Steve pondered his next move. He might get lucky, but if he tipped off the system that he was not sure where he wanted to go, there was the possibility of an automatic disconnect. All he knew for sure was that his time was fast slipping away; so in a desperate attempt to find the missing pieces to the puzzle, he hurriedly typed in:

KAVRINSKI INSTITUTE FOR HUMAN LIFE

He pressed ENTER and his computer screen stormed to life.

Sensing that he was stretching his luck by staying on-line so long, he keyed in the code to download the file onto his internal hard disk. With lightning speed the data was transferred and a message appeared on his screen:

```
DATA TRANSFER COMPLETED.
DO YOU WISH TO ACCESS ANOTHER FILE,
DR. WILHELM WALLENBERG?
```

Steve had what he wanted. He would read it later. Now he must back out of the system before they could trace him. But there was one other question hanging in his mind, taunting him, and the strange events that had interrupted his well-ordered life had increased his interest in finding an answer to it. Perhaps one more entry into the supercomputer would satisfy his intense curiosity.

He looked again at the question lingering on his screen, then touched the letter "Y." The computer prompted:

```
ENTER FILE NAME
```

Without hesitation, Steve typed in the words:

```
THE PRINCIPALS
```

When his finger pressed ENTER, the screen instantly changed to a pulsating red and flashed the words:

```
UNAUTHORIZED INQUIRY: ACCESS DENIED!
ABORT IMMEDIATELY!
```

Steve smiled as he looked at the "denied" message on his screen. He spoke out loud, "So there are files so confidential that even Dr. Wallenberg can't access them."

He quickly hit the EXIT key, hoping that his connection to the Omega had been broken. That done, his left hand lunged for the telephone, as his right hand punched in his office number in Dallas.

Unknown to Steve, when he ended the inquiry, he disappeared from Wong's screen in the Unauthorized Intrusion Department deep inside The Mountain. Driving his clenched fist down hard against the table, Wong voiced a string of expletives. He had to abort the trace, but he was sure he had enough information to pinpoint the location of the originating computer that had executed the illegal entry.

The phone rang once in Steve's office and he heard Randy's voice say, "Steve?"

"Yes, Randy," Steve answered with a tone of urgency in his voice. "I'm disconnected. Deactivate my computer immediately . . . *Go!*"

With panic threatening to overcome him, Steve rubbed his forehead, fearing that he might have stayed on-line too long and wondering if security agents were already on their way up the elevator to his office in Dallas.

"It's done, Steve. Your system is now deactivated," Randy assured him.

"Good," Steve sighed, feeling a weight lift off his shoulders. "I don't want some computer jockey to trace our transmission."

"I don't think that could happen," Randy offered. "Everything was done with the sweeper engaged. Nobody's been able to get past that so far."

Steve wanted to tell Randy that he was very naïve about the enormous power and capabilities of the global government, but he felt it would serve no good purpose.

"Hope you're right," Steve answered. "Now, Randy, one more time, just for safety's sake, verify that the system is off-line before you leave my office. Then, if anyone, and I mean *anyone*, starts asking questions, you don't know anything. Do you understand?"

"I . . . uh, I guess so, Steve." Although he was puzzled, Randy knew his boss had good reasons for doing what he did. After hanging up the phone, Randy walked out of Steve's office, locking the door behind him. Hurrying to the elevator, he rode it back down to the newsroom.

TWENTY-TWO

Steve Weston splashed cold water on his face, then lowered his head into the bathroom sink and let the icy rivulets run through his hair and around his neck. Savoring the cool sensation, he wanted to clear his brain, to wash away the confusion that had pressed in on him in the last eighteen hours. Feeling better, he stood up and dried himself off.

Seeing his reflection in the large mirror, he was surprised at how tired he looked. Suddenly feeling a little weak, he remembered that he hadn't eaten since early in the day, a day that seemed a lifetime ago.

If I get something in my stomach, he thought, *then I'll be fine.*

Picking up the phone on the bathroom wall, he dialed room service and told the lady who answered that he'd like to order a sandwich and a large pot of coffee. He had to wake up and think. But in the back of his mind, Steve knew it wasn't hunger that was causing the queasy feeling in the pit of his stomach. It was something else.

It was fear, raw and intense.

He was afraid for Audrey, afraid for himself, afraid for the world. Afraid because, for the first time in his life, he was up against something so much bigger than himself that he didn't know how to handle it.

It would take about twenty minutes for his food to arrive. He dressed, sat down in front of the computer, and opened the ultrasecret file he had just downloaded from the Omega.

There on his computer screen he saw the title, *The Gaia Project*, and underneath it a three-dimensional graphic of a spinning globe.

Steve hesitated for a long moment, staring at the forbidden file, wondering what lay ahead of him. Taking a deep breath, he clicked again and was surprised to see a woman materialize on the screen. In her late seventies, she looked old, with wrinkled skin and thin lips. She was sitting upright with her eyes closed in a trancelike state, and her long, slim fingers tightly gripping the ornately carved arms of her thronelike chair.

Her long, straight white hair flowed gracefully down across her shoulders and lay sedately against the high-collared black velvet dress she wore. A heavy gold chain hung loosely around her neck, a dark, occultic pendant attached to it.

"Madame Rousseau!" Steve exclaimed, suddenly recognizing the woman.

It was Madame Helena Rousseau, the World Leader's mother. He had seen her briefly two years ago in one of her rare public appearances at a high-level governmental reception in Geneva, surrounded by her wealthy friends among the Council of 100.

Reputed to be an avatar of the Gaian religion, Madame Rousseau was an exalted priestess, transchanneler, and medium, often communicating messages from the Ascended Masters.

Staring in fascination, he watched the elderly woman begin to gently sway, very slowly at first; then she began jerking from side to side as her body started to tremble convulsively. She was uttering odd syllables with no apparent meaning.

Moments passed, her body calmed, and she sat rigidly still. With beads of perspiration glistening on her face, she lifted her head slowly, and her dark eyes, like shimmering black orbs, glared out at him. Feeling a knot form in the pit of his stomach, he knew immediately that she was channeling a spirit entity.

Steve's eyes narrowed thoughtfully as he watched the woman's lips begin moving, quickly turning up the volume on his audio board.

Her voice deep and guttural, she intoned rhythmically, "The Masters say that you must 'purify' the earth by the year 2040 in order to bring the human race back into balance with Nature. Gaia will be restored to her original beauty and will once again give of Her bounty. All those who do not conform to Gaia's will shall be allowed to 'pass into spirit.' Gaia, your Mother, has given you the power of destruction and co-creation. Let Light and Love and Power and Death fulfill the purpose of the Masters."

The black piercing eyes flared, glowered ominously, then slowly closed as the old woman's pale chin dropped against her chest.

As Madame Rousseau's image slowly faded from the screen, Steve vividly remembered her son's inaugural address just days before. He, too, had called for a global initiative to purify the earth, and the crowd had cheered ecstatically.

Steve pressed another key, and pages of the captured file began scrolling across the screen. Fascinated, he began reading on page three.

In spite of the best efforts of the New Earth Federation in recent years to stem the tide of human overload, the world population has grown to nine billion. This number is too large for the over-burdened planet to sustain. If current trends are allowed to continue, the population of the world will proliferate to unacceptable levels, resulting in ecological collapse. This in turn will produce human misery, disease, famine, and starvation.

The population must be reduced drastically and quickly if the earth's ecosystem is to survive. Therefore the NEF, with a view toward the long-term best interests of the planet and its legitimate inhabitants, has implemented an emergency program to bring human population levels into harmony with the ecosystem.

Effective immediately, all of our scientific knowledge and military resources will be mobilized in a global purification program, code-named The Gaia Project.

The goal of the Gaia Project is to reduce the number of legitimate human beings on the earth to a "sustainable level" of no more than two billion. Due to the urgency of the current crisis, this goal is to be accomplished by the end of the year 2040, by whatever means necessary.

Stunned, Steve slowly read the document again, his eyes intensely fixed on the final paragraph. Shaking his head slowly in sharp disbelief, the full import of *The Gaia Project* forced itself into his consciousness.

"My god!" he exclaimed aloud. "They're going to eliminate *seven billion human beings* in the next seven years. That's a billion people per year."

His mind reeling, he moved the document forward, scanning the pages. Stopping at page 123, he eagerly read the details of the propaganda policy to be followed in supporting the principles of the Gaia Project. His eyes were drawn to the subhead, "Conditioning the Masses," and he read the short paragraph that followed.

In order to incite the masses to adopt the goals of the Gaia Project, they must be made to believe that excess population is a life-or-death threat to the continued existence of both the human race and the planet. The consequences of delay in reducing the world's population must be made sufficiently clear in order to mobilize support for and solidify public opinion in favor of this new social organizing principle.

Flashing next on his screen was an elaborate display of a number of three-dimensional color diagrams, graphs, and charts depicting the Projected Population Depletion Goals on a yearly, monthly, and weekly basis. Each Zone of Global Cooperation had been assigned a Sustainable Population Norm and a schedule for achieving it.

Colorful lines on a detailed organizational chart snaked down from the highest officials in the Population Control Commission's headquarters in Geneva to individual Population Control Officers in each ZGC. Each officer would wield the power of life and death in order to achieve the mandated population control outcomes in his zone in order to lower the population to their preassigned level until they reached their Sustainable Population Norm.

A knock on his door caused Steve to tense reflexively. Feeling a sharp stab of fear, he mentally pictured himself diving behind the couch for cover. Then he remembered he had ordered food from room service. Walking to the door, he looked at the screen above the door and saw that it was indeed one of the hotel staff and let him in.

Steve hurriedly ate his sandwich and drank two cups of steaming black coffee. He quickly felt better, calmer, more alert. Returning to his computer, he continued to study the stolen files. He shuddered when he discovered that one of their stratagems for reducing the population was to foment limited regional wars throughout the world, giving the military arm of the NEF an excuse to use their sophisticated high-tech weapons to eliminate thousands of innocent people at a time.

He was staggered to learn that they had indeed embraced the unthinkable in their mad pursuit of creating a perfect world. Colored maps showed heavily populated regions in Africa, Southeast Asia, and Central and South America that had been targeted for extermination.

His revulsion turned to outrage when he read the NEF's plan to eliminate whole blocks of Third World people through deliberate purges. Half dazed, and feeling as if he were sleep-walking through a dreadful dream, Steve took a deep, tremulous breath and read the document to himself in whispered tones.

The government, in order to promote the general welfare and advance the common good, will eliminate all inferior races and peoples. In targeted areas with excess populations, inhabitants will be allocated only subsistence-level quantities of food, water, medicine, and energy until acceptable population norms have been achieved. Where necessary, scientifically controlled starvation will be implemented. All means at our disposal must be employed until a sustainable global population level of two billion persons has been reached.

Steve vigorously rubbed his face with his hands. *Eliminate all inferior races! That's where we were one hundred years ago,* he reasoned.

Though their program of killing was couched in carefully crafted terms, he now saw it for what it was—a diabolical plot by those in power to kill off a large part of the human race and set themselves up as the undisputed rulers of an earth that they believed would be turned back into the Garden of Eden.

The two billion allowed to remain alive would be forcibly disbursed throughout the earth and assigned tasks that would contribute to the good of the Social Order, while living in primitive conditions "in balance with nature."

Steve's stomach churned in disgust.

He felt betrayed, defiled.

I should quit now, he told himself. But more probing questions urged him to press forward. He had to know who was profiting from the death technologies surrounding the Gaia Project. And whose bank accounts were being filled from this monstrous attack on the human race?

Bringing up the file on the Kavrinski Institute for Human Life, the picture that unfolded before Steve's eyes filled him with a mixture of fascination and fear. KavLife, he discovered, was a wholly owned subsidiary of the Kavrinski Pharmaceutical Company of Palo Alto, California, which, in turn, was a wholly owned subsidiary of the DeGolyer World Health Services, Ltd. of Berne, Switzerland.

As the pieces to the puzzle fell into place, a picture of total control over everything related to pharmaceuticals, health care, and the death industry slowly came together before his eyes.

But that was only the beginning. By the time he had reached the twentieth page, he found that the DeGolyer World Health Services, Ltd. was, in fact, owned by a consortium of ten global holding companies. And that these ten holding companies also owned and controlled most of the world's businesses and industry. As he read the file, the names of the officers and major stockholders in these ten holding companies began to surface. He was astonished to find that many of these same people were also directors of the Global Population Control Authority.

Making the connection, he now knew that the ones who set the policy for reducing the population also stood to profit enormously from implementing the Gaia Project.

Further, he discovered, some of these same people were also members of the Council of 100, the ruling body in the New Earth Federation.

He had seen enough. There was no need to read further.

Almost at the point of despair, he stood to his feet and began pacing the room.

Then he felt it, like a hard fist driven into the pit of his stomach, almost knocking his breath away. As the cold, raw, paralyzing fear hit him, he had to brace himself to keep from doubling over. What he had denied for so long had now become real, undeniable, overpowering.

"What will I say to my son?" he asked himself aloud. "How will I explain that I was guilty of aiding and abetting in the murder of three-fourths of the human race?"

Forcing himself to return to the computer, he opened more files, read more data. His mind and emotions growing numb, he hurriedly scanned large numbers of pages, sensing the tone of urgency of those who were calling for the quick elimination of seven billion living human beings.

After another hour was gone, he inserted a disk into the computer and copied the stolen files onto it, then lunged for the terminal plug, wrenched it from the wall socket, and watched anxiously as the glow of the screen dwindled to a dot.

Frantically pacing the room, trying to process the disturbing information that had invaded his world, Steve forced himself to think, to reason, to consider the barest possibility that what he had just uncovered in the Gaia Project was indeed true.

With the disturbing events of the last few hours taking on a surreal dimension, Steve's entire belief system, the locus point of his sense of being, was slowly disintegrating, leaving him troubled and confused. Feeling as if he were in the jaws of a raging, savage beast that was seeking to devour him, he feared for his life, for his family, and for his own sanity.

The decision was made.

There was now no other course for Steve Weston. He must defy the Social Order and somehow expose the Gaia Project to the world. Even though it might mean forfeiting his own life, it no longer mattered to him. After his escape from death at the hands of Carlo and the New Barbarians earlier that same day, he felt that his life was a gift, given back to him by some unknown power.

Steve glanced anxiously at Audrey's door. He then walked over to it and knocked, but still no answer. He wondered where she could possibly be.

Something has to be terribly wrong.

Drained from the most intense day of his life, Steve Weston collapsed across his bed. He was asleep in seconds.

TWENTY-THREE

June 4, 2033—3:46 A.M.

Alarm bells were sounding somewhere in the indistinct, murky distance. Grindingly persistent, the grating sound growing louder every second, Steve struggled through the thick mental fog. Then he was awake, fumbling for the jangling intruder, not knowing how long it had been ringing.

Still more asleep than awake, he grabbed the phone. "Audrey, is that you?"

His head hurt and his whole body ached.

There was a short pause on the line. "I'm sorry, Mr. Weston," a man's voice answered. "This is Dr. Wilson at KavLife. But I do apologize for waking you."

As Steve's eyes were slowly adjusting to the dark room, he fought to gain mental coherence. He glanced at the digital clock on the table. It was 3:47 A.M. Why was the doctor from Kavrinski Institute calling him so early?

"I . . . I'm sorry, Dr. Wilson. I thought it might have been . . ."

"That's why I'm calling," Dr. Wilson answered apologetically. "I think I have found your friend."

"Where . . . where is she, Dr. Wilson?" Steve asked desperately.

"She's here at KavLife . . . in the organ-transplant facility. I came on duty just a few minutes ago and discovered that she was being prepared for surgery."

None of this made any sense. Steve fought to clear his mind. "Surgery, doctor? I don't understand. Why is she there?"

Dr. Wilson swallowed hard. "She's in a holding room. She's scheduled to receive a gas that will render her brain-dead, then her organs will be harvested for transplant. The procedure is supposed to begin in less than an hour."

A suffocating wave of emotion rushed through Steve. Fighting the rising panic, he struggled to catch his breath, then to speak. "This can't be, doctor!" he cried in desperation. "There's got to be some terrible mistake. You must stop them at once!"

"I understand how you feel, Mr. Weston, but there's no mistake. A woman of very high rank has been at the clinic for more than two weeks, awaiting a suitable donor for a heart and lung transplant. Your friend fits the physical profile required."

"Is Audrey dead?"

"No, they haven't administered the gas yet."

"I've got to come . . . to try to save her."

"Ordinarily, in such a situation, I would not be able to help you," Dr. Wilson replied. "But in this case, I believe I can. That's why I called. But you must come quickly. I'll send a car for you. Be ready in fifteen minutes, in front of the hotel."

"Yes, doctor, I'll be there," Steve promised, then added, "Dr. Wilson, I don't know why you're doing this, but thank you."

Steve stumbled into the bathroom and stood under the shower until he was awake. Quickly dressing, he took the small computer disk with the stolen files on it and slipped it into a small pocket in his jacket and headed for the elevator.

He walked out the front door of the hotel just as a long blue limousine from KavLife was pulling up to the curb in front of the hotel. Steve slipped into the backseat.

Without speaking, the driver pulled away and drove back to KavLife.

Entering the compound through a gate at the rear of Building Six, Steve took note of a number of large busses with darkened windows parked in a long line at the curb in back of the building. As he stepped from the car, a large door opened and one of the busses pulled through it, disappearing inside the building. The tall door closed as soon as the bus was inside.

Dr. Wilson was waiting at the entrance next to the tall door. "Please hurry, Mr. Weston. We don't have much time."

Once inside, Steve watched armed guards walk to the bus that had just entered the building. More than sixty people, of various ages, got off and were escorted into an oversized elevator. Most were docile, as if they had been drugged. Watching the elevator door close behind them, Steve instinctively knew they were going to their death. They offered no resistance.

"Those busses—" Steve remarked.

"The busses run day and night, Mr. Weston. There's nothing either of us can do about it. Please hurry, we don't have much time."

Boarding an elevator, the two men rode down two floors, exited, and moved quickly down a long corridor. Turning to their right, they were talking in hushed tones when Steve looked up as a door opened and a tall man walked through. Close behind him were two other men, evidently his personal bodyguards. The one on his right was a towering man with a scarred face, his eyes sweeping the hallway. The one on his left was a black man, lean, muscular, grim-faced.

Seeing Steve and Dr. Wilson, the tall man abruptly stopped in his tracks, eyeing them suspiciously. The two bodyguards froze, their hands poised, ready to reach for their weapons. For a few brief, uncomfortable seconds, they stared at Steve and Wilson, unmoving, as if in suspended animation.

Steve's eyes were drawn like a magnet to the tall man in the center. Dressed casually in slacks, leather sandals, a light blue blazer, and a dark blue shirt, open at the collar, the man walked slowly toward Steve, stopping within two feet of him. The man's shoulder-length hair was parted in the middle. His skin was smooth, flawless, almost effeminate.

With his large, dark, hypnotic eyes locked into Steve's eyes, his unblinking stare bore into his inner soul, causing him to feel vulnerable, defenseless, as if this man were reading his thoughts and knew his every sin.

Mesmerized by his stare, Steve was suddenly confused, unable to frame his thoughts with any clarity. Fighting desperately against a power that he could not see and did not comprehend, for a frightening moment, he felt himself stagger.

The *eyes* . . . it was the eyes.

"You!" Steve gasped, his eyes wide in astonishment.

Even without the flowing white robe, Steve suddenly recognized the World Leader, the most powerful man on earth.

"Yes, Steve Weston," the man answered with a broad smile, thrusting out his hand. Steve gripped his hand firmly.

"How are you, Steve?" he asked.

Momentarily at a loss for words, Steve managed to stammer, "I'm . . . fine, sir. Thank you for asking."

"Ah, I do so appreciate your work with TV9. I'm one of your most ardent supporters."

"Thank you, sir."

His pleasant baritone voice had the soothing quality of a skilled hypnotist, his manner one of controlled charm, his gestures flowing and precise. The man seemed genuinely to enjoy talking to Steve, giving him his undivided attention, making him feel that he was the most important person in the universe.

They chatted amiably for a few more moments; then the World Leader apologized profusely for having to leave. Without waiting for Steve to reply, he turned and walked away, the two men following in close pursuit.

In the confusing storm of his thoughts, Steve stared slack-jawed at the World Leader as he disappeared around the corner. For a moment, he was confused, wondering if he had misjudged the man. How could a man of such warmth and charm be anything but good?

Dr. Wilson broke the silence. "Now I can tell you, Mr. Weston," he said in a low voice. "The person who is scheduled to receive the heart and lung transplant is . . . the World Leader's own mother."

"His mother is the one—" Steve couldn't finish the sentence.

"Yes. The World Leader and his mother have been here for almost two weeks awaiting a suitable organ donor for her."

Steve glanced down the hall in the direction the World Leader had gone, a growing anger inside him.

"Come quickly," Dr. Wilson urged. "We don't have much time now."

Walking with grim purpose down the long corridor, Dr. Wilson quietly briefed Steve on the circumstances that brought Audrey to Kavrinski Institute. A military vehicle carrying Audrey and a young soldier had been in a wreck at dusk the previous day near the outskirts of Camden. Both of them were thrown from the vehicle, killing the soldier instantly, while Audrey was merely knocked unconscious.

Ordinarily, he told him, she would have been transported to a hospital emergency room for treatment. But after a quick scan of her DNA readout and other vital statistics, the computer found that she fit the Top Priority Profile required for Madame Rousseau's donor. Audrey was then immediately delivered to KavLife.

Dr. Wilson had discovered her there when he came on duty and had called Steve.

Passing a nurses' station, the two men entered an unmarked door. The large room was bathed in the fluorescent glow of the ceiling lights. Each wall was lined with beds filled with patients, all of whom seemed to be in a state of suspended animation, unmoving, feeding tubes and catheters fixed to their still bodies.

A lone nurse kept a solitary vigil, occasionally glancing at the computer readouts of their vital signs. She looked up when the two men entered the room. Recognizing Dr. Wilson, she smiled, then returned to the paperback novel she was reading.

Fear, frustration, terror, and rage coursed through Steve like water plunging over a dam. He stood frozen in place, staring into the macabre scene. Forcing himself to look into each face, he carefully scanned each bed, his eyes coming to rest on the fifteenth bed to his right.

"Audrey . . ." he whispered under his breath.

Lying deathly still, ashen-faced, she was hooked to an array of clear plastic tubes, rhythmically dripping their mixture of chemicals into her inert body.

Moving quickly to her side, Steve looked down into her pale face. His first thought was that she was dead, but Dr. Wilson quickly assured him that she was only heavily sedated.

"I've got to get her out of here, Dr. Wilson, before they kill her," Steve exclaimed with quiet anxiety.

"Mr. Weston!"

Steve spun around to face Adam Stenholm. General Amos Dorian was at his side. Three other men were standing behind him. One of them was Dr. Brandt; the two others were Stenholm's bodyguards.

"Stenholm!" Steve blurted.

"I see that you're surprised to see me," Stenholm returned.

Dr. Brandt stepped around Stenholm to face Dr. Wilson. "Wilson," he shouted angrily, "you're a troublemaker. We've been monitoring you for months. Now by bringing Weston to this facility, you have signed your own death warrant."

Stenholm gestured to his men and calmly instructed, "Take Dr. Wilson."

Steve turned and looked into Dr. Wilson's eyes. Wilson smiled and said in a calm, controlled voice, "Goodbye, Mr. Weston. Forgive me if I have brought trouble to you."

Turning quickly on his heels, Stenholm started walking down the corridor. "Bring Mr. Weston," he said over his shoulder.

One of the men pushed Steve in the back, nodding for him to follow Stenholm. Following Stenholm down the hallway, Steve battled the panic that lay just below the surface, telling himself that he had to remain calm. Panic wouldn't help him now. He tried to think. He had to think.

Turning left, they stopped in front of the third door on the right. Gesturing to the men standing at Steve's side, he said, "Bring him in here."

"Sit down, Mr. Weston," Stenholm instructed, motioning toward a large couch near a window. Steve dropped into the soft couch. Stenholm sat in an armchair facing Steve. The two bodyguards remained standing a few feet away from Steve, unsmiling, their eyes constantly on him.

"Why have you taken Ms. Montaigne?" Steve demanded.

Stenholm steepled his fingers. "She was in an automobile accident. The ambulance brought her here. Our doctors are trying to save her life."

"You're lying, Stenholm," Steve said. "She was deliberately brought here so that her organs could be scavenged for someone here at

KavLife. Who is the person slated to get Ms. Montaigne's organs? Is it the World Leader's mother? Is she the one?"

Smiling, Stenholm intoned, "The mother of the World Leader is an Avatar, the incarnation of a deity. She gave birth to the One who is to lead humankind through its transformation to godhood. She is also a major transchanneler and brings the instructions of the Ascended Masters to the leaders of the world. So you see, Mr. Weston, you should feel honored that your friend could give her life for someone of such great value."

Suddenly, filled with an uncontrollable rage, Steve lunged at Stenholm. As Stenholm braced himself for the attack, the two bodyguards responded instantly, catching Steve just before he reached his target, throwing him hard against the wall.

"You're mad!" Steve cried out.

Glaring back at him, his eyes filled with contempt, Stenholm countered, "No, we are not mad. We are the enlightened ones. It is our destiny to rule the world. The World Leader is leading us to global harmony. He possesses enormous powers, exceeding the powers of Jesus Christ. His miracles are greater than all the holy men of history."

"If he can work miracles," Steve responded sarcastically, "why didn't he give his mother a new heart and lungs?"

Angered by the remark, Stenholm leaped to his feet and struck Steve along the side of his face with his open hand. A small trickle of blood formed at the side of Steve's mouth. Shaking with rage, Stenholm shouted, "I should kill you now with my own hands for such blasphemy, Weston." Tiring of the game, Stenholm turned quickly and started walking toward the door.

His voice tinged with anger, Steve said, "Mr. Stenholm, Ms. Montaigne must not be harmed. I want her released to me . . . *immediately!*"

Stenholm stopped and fixed Steve with a cold stare. "It would please me to see you die, Weston," he said caustically. "The only reason I do not kill you now is because of your friend, Dr. Wallenberg. He is your protector. But don't ever make another mistake. If you do, I'll be there. You will not be so fortunate the next time."

Unshaken, Steve replied firmly, "My only concern is for Audrey

Montaigne. I get Ms. Montaigne, or I'll make a global incident out of this, or you will have to kill me. The choice is yours."

Stenholm glared at Steve for a moment. "Very well, Weston. I will allow you to win this round. I will release her. But if there is any report of any kind about this city, or this facility, or the town of Camden, I will hold you personally responsible. And you will not be so fortunate the next time."

"Mr. Stenholm, one more thing," Steve returned. "Who was Carlo? I'm sure the name *Carlo* was not his real name."

Stenholm replied, "You're right, Weston. His name was not Carlo. He was a medical doctor. His name was Dr. Lawrence Kavrinski."

"Kavrinski!" Steve blustered.

Stenholm smiled. "Yes. He was the only son of Dr. Karl Vincent Kavrinski, the founder of the Kavrinski Pharmaceutical Company. When he inherited his fortune from his father, he founded the Kavrinski Institute for Human Life. But disappointed because of his failures to find the secret to eternal life, he came to believe that human life was devoid of value. Thereafter, he dedicated his life and fortune to the study of death technologies. And in the process, he became a member of the Party of the New Barbarians and helped to finance much of their activities around the world."

His jaw set, his eyes glaring, Steve moved a step toward Stenholm. The two bodyguards tensed.

Steve spoke slowly, deliberately. "Tell me, Stenholm. Did you order Carlo to kill me?"

Stenholm's jaw tightened. Then, with a derisive smile, he answered, "You're very perceptive, Mr. Weston. Perhaps a little too perceptive. But the target was Carlo, not you. Carlo was going to kill you out of fear that you would expose the true nature of the work at KavLife. It was a very lucrative business that supported his political goals . . . through the Party of the New Barbarians."

With a wave of his hand Stenholm said, "You can take Ms. Montaigne now. We found another suitable donor for the mother of our World Leader. The transplant operation has already been suc-cessfully completed."

Stenholm studied Steve's face for a moment. "A young woman

with no family ties, and a position of no particular importance in the Social Order, happened to meet with a tragic accident last night. She was not nearly so lovely and talented as Ms. Montaigne, but fortunately she was young and quite healthy, and she perfectly matched the Top Priority Profile that had to be filled."

Turning quickly, Stenholm moved toward the door, calling out over his shoulder, "Goodbye, Mr. Weston."

When Stenholm had left the room, General Dorian stood and said, "I'll escort you out of the building, Mr. Weston."

Steve studied Dorian's face for a moment. "General, would you mind answering a few questions for me?"

General Dorian glanced at his bodyguard and nodded. The man quickly left the room, leaving the two men alone.

"What would you like to know, Mr. Weston?"

"General, I've been given the runaround about what happened in Camden since I've arrived here. I'd like to know the facts, that's all."

General Dorian smiled. "Very well, Mr. Weston. As you may remember, I told you many things when you were with me inside The Mountain. That was because of your high-security clearance. I will tell you what you want to know about the Camden operation. But please let me remind you that you are sworn to secrecy."

"I understand," Steve replied.

"Part of what Mr. Stenholm told you was true. He told you that there was an accident and that some toxic gas had escaped into the atmosphere, killing a few people. He had hoped that giving you that much information would have satisfied you and you would have gone back to Dallas. He didn't count on your being this persistent."

"Why did Stenholm lie to me?"

Dorian looked Steve in the eye. "Stenholm doesn't trust you, Weston."

"If Stenholm lied to me, then what *did* happen in Camden?"

General Dorian lit a cigarette. "Mr. Stenholm was telling you the truth when he told you that a truck had crashed in Camden. What he didn't tell you was that the truck contained canisters filled with the Maylay virus. It was being sent to KavLife for testing and experimentation. When the truck crashed, several of the canisters were ruptured, releasing a very small amount of the virus into the air. A brisk wind was blowing that sent the contaminated air containing the virus on its deadly journey to the northwest, covering several square miles of the city of Camden."

Steve asked, "How . . . how many people were exposed to the virus, General?"

The general took a drag on his cigarette. "We don't know, Mr. Weston. The problem is that the Maylay virus is airborne and can live up to twenty-four days after it has been exposed to the atmosphere. Our scientists calculated the speed and direction of the wind and came up with a graph of the area believed to be vulnerable to exposure. We've determined that there could have been as many as fifty thousand people in the path of the escaping virus."

Startled, Steve responded, "Fifty thousand—"

"Yes, Mr. Weston. There is the potential of fifty thousand people being exposed. But we don't know how many for sure."

"How are you going to find out . . . for sure?"

"We're not."

"You're not going to find out? I don't understand."

"We don't have the time, Mr. Weston. Every person who is exposed is a carrier. And if they are allowed to leave the targeted area, they could spread the virus into the surrounding territory, and from there it could spread in an uncontrolled manner across this continent."

"Then . . . what are you going to do?"

"A contingent of our Global Forces biotroops have completely sealed off the city of Camden. The targeted sector will be cleansed."

"Cleansed?"

"Yes, no chances can be taken. It's now a Red Zone, and we must vaporize it. No one must be allowed to escape."

"But it was an *accident*, wasn't it, General? So why—"

Showing his impatience, General Dorian lifted his right hand, interrupting Steve in midsentence. "An accident, Mr. Weston. Yes . . . and no."

"What do you mean?"

"While this particular incident was indeed an unfortunate accident, our scientists are developing a number of exotic weapons of mass destruction—chemical, radiological, biological, nuclear—in order to quickly reduce the human population overload on the ecosystem. The Maylay virus, which was accidently set loose in Camden, in fact, holds the greatest promise of being one of our most effective tools. It's a scientific breakthrough, the answer we've been looking for. Its action is swift and decisive. We can use the Maylay virus like a finely crafted scalpel in the hands of a skilled surgeon to rid the earth of the disease of too many human beings, fulfilling the will of Gaia."

Hiding his revulsion at what Dorian was saying, Steve stared at him, unblinking, his eyes giving away nothing.

Dorian continued. "Once a targeted area has been activated by the virus and it works its way through the population, the TR6 device will be available in case the virus starts to escape the targeted area. The TR6 can be used to cleanse the infected areas, burning out the impurities, vaporizing all flesh."

Growing animated, Dorian declared, "The twin tools of the Maylay virus and the TR6 device, working in tandem, will cleanse the earth. The Earth will return to Her original beauty. As you can see, Steve, this is why we must destroy Camden. It was an accident, but that doesn't matter. We can't allow the Maylay to escape from the Camden area. This project is far more important than the lives there."

"But there are other ways, Dorian," Steve insisted. "You don't have to slaughter everyone in Camden."

"You still don't understand, do you, Weston?" Dorian retorted. "No one is being *slaughtered*. They will not be destroyed. The physical is an illusion. Their psychic energy force will simply be released to merge with Gaia. The TR6 is a creative force, not a destructive force. It's an instrument that we use to carry out Her will."

"When will it be done, General Dorian?" Steve asked.

"After the World Leader and his mother are safely out of the area. In fact, we had come to the hospital to pick them up when we ran into you. Mr. Stenholm is escorting them to their plane at this moment. They're going back a few days ahead of schedule because of the unfortunate circumstances here, but the plane has hospital facilities, complete with doctors and nurses to care for the World Leader's mother on their flight back to Geneva. Mr. Stenholm will be accompanying them."

"And you . . ."

"I'll stay here to see that the Camden operation is carried out satisfactorily. When it's over, I'll return to Geneva."

"How will you carry out the . . . *operation*, General?"

"When the World Leader is safely out of the area, I'll execute the strike order. The TR6 device, delivered by a Zeus missile, will be launched from one of our nuclear submarines. It is Gaia's will, Mr. Weston."

"Did you say the missile would be launched from a sub?"

"Of course. Our subs are stationed at strategic points around the world, ready to strike in a moment's notice. And guided by global positioning satellites, our missiles can hit any target on earth with pinpoint accuracy."

"But . . . such a thing can't be hidden from the public. How will you—"

"That's already been taken care of, Mr. Weston. After the fact, the explosion will be blamed on the Party of the New Barbarians. The news releases are already being prepared. Following the strike, your people will be called in to film the aftermath of the operation, and it will be broadcast worldwide on TV9."

With a wry smile, the general added, "You see, that's why we had to kill Carlo. We had to have someone to blame. We'll announce that his band of terrorists were responsible for the destruction of the city of Camden, and that they have been hunted down and killed."

"There's still something that I need to know, General," Steve insisted.

General Dorian gave a noncommittal shrug.

A coil of anger behind his cool exterior, Steve moved closer to Dorian. He was sick of secrets being kept from him, of questions without answers, of lies and devious half-truths. His mouth drawn in a thin, angry line, he looked into Dorian's face. "General, I want to know what happened to my bureau chief, Mitchell," he said bluntly, an edge to his voice that did not give room for argument.

Shaking his head slowly, Dorian smiled. "Another tragic accident," he said cordially. "You see, Mitchell went into the city of Camden to report on the *incident*. Unfortunately, he was exposed to the Maylay virus. Within two hours of being exposed to the virus, he began to show symptoms. He died a horrible death, Weston. He was dying when you talked to him. He was instructed to say nothing of his condition. His body is still in Camden and will be vaporized, along with the others, when Camden is *cleansed.*"

The color drained from Steve's face. He now knew why there had been such a dramatic change in Mitchell, why he was trying to convince him not to come to Templeton. Mitchell knew he had been infected with the virus when he talked to him the last time. He was already dying a horrible death, and he wanted to spare his friend the same fate.

Glancing around the room, Dorian spoke in a low tone, as if not to be overheard. "Weston, I want you near me. We need each other."

Startled, Steve responded, "I . . . don't know what you mean, General."

"What I mean is that if all goes well, I'll be in a stronger position in the Federation very soon. When I am, I'll need your help."

"Can you explain that, General?"

"Not now, Weston, but soon."

Crushing the small stub of his cigarette into the metal ashtray on the top of the desk, Dorian asked casually, "One more thing, Weston."

"What's that, General?"

"How is your son?"

Somewhat surprised at the question, Steve replied, "Uh, fine, General. His birthday is tomorrow. He'll be three. That's one of the reasons why I've got to get back to Dallas. We have some things planned, just the two of us—the zoo, things like that."

Dorian looked at Steve. "Did you know that your wife has contacted the DFW Central Referral Service of the Population Control Commission?"

Steve shrugged. "She works with all the governmental agencies, General. Why is that so unusual?"

Dorian hesitated, looking intently into Steve's eyes, studying his reactions. Folding his arms across his chest, he furrowed his brow. Speaking slowly, he said, "Then . . . you don't know, do you?"

"Know what, General?" Steve asked, arching an eyebrow.

Dorian hesitated a long moment. "That she has made an appointment with one of the children's clinics to have your son *deactivated*."

Steve felt the icy fingers of fear around his throat, cutting off his breath. Trying to contain his shock, he cast a contemptuous glance at Dorian and, for an agonizing moment, wondered why he was playing such a sick mind-game with him. His first reaction was to retaliate, but the unwavering, somber expression on the general's face, and the certainty of his tone, told Steve that he was deadly serious.

And with that realization, a cold wave of utter helplessness swept over him.

Feeling his strength drain from his body, his voice now trembling with fear, he whispered softly, "Are . . . you sure, General?"

"I'm sorry, Steve," Dorian said, shaking his head. "Thousands of units are terminated each day throughout the world. I assumed it was a joint decision between you and your wife."

Shaking his head in stunned disbelief, he whispered, "No . . . I knew nothing about it. But . . . how did you find out? How—"

"We know, Weston, that's all I can tell you."

"*When . . . where . . .* is the procedure scheduled?"

"Sometime today. But I don't know the time, nor which facility she'll be using."

With cold, vivid fear exploding inside his chest, Steve suddenly knew how much he loved his son, needed him. And how his loss would tear at the very foundations of what remained of his tenuous belief system.

"My god!" Steve groaned softly. No logic could explain the mounting despair sweeping through his being. "Jimmy turns three tonight at midnight," he stammered almost incoherently, looking at Dorian. "If she does it, she'll have to do it today," he said, his words slow and reluctant. "But if he lives until midnight tonight, he'll be categorized as fully human, and can't be legally deactivated."

Suddenly, from somewhere deep within himself, an anger that knew no bounds washed over him. An anger against his son's mother and her dreadful plan for him. An anger against the senseless evil of the Social Order that allowed the wanton destruction of its most vulnerable subjects.

The Social Order he had served so faithfully had now reached too far. They had touched his only child, his son, his own flesh and blood. With a wall of primal rage, a rage beyond reason, clearing his mind and suppressing his fear, he turned quickly on his heels to leave, calling out defiantly, "I'm going to Dallas, General. Please excuse me."

Before he reached the door, two male nurses walked into the room and told him they had been sent to take him to Ms. Montaigne.

Steve motioned for them to wait, then turned and took a step toward Dorian. "You've got to help me, Dorian," he called out sharply, his trembling voice betraying his apprehension. "You have the authority to rescind the infanticide order. You must send someone with the authority to stop my wife. I don't care what you have to do, or how you do it, but she can't be allowed to kill my son."

Trying to keep the fear out of his voice, Steve added, "I . . . I'll owe you, Dorian."

Dorian waited a moment, then nodded. "All right, I'll see what I can do, Weston. But I can't promise anything."

Moving in behind the two nurses, Steve followed them down the wide, pristine corridor to the room where Audrey was being held. Once inside, he rushed to her bedside, relieved to see that her eyes were open, and she was looking lazily around the room. Disappointed that she did not recognize him, Steve leaned over, brushed her hair from her face, and gently stroked her cheek.

Holding his emotions in check, he whispered, "Just hold on, Audrey. I'm going to get you out of here."

Turning to one of the male nurses, he barked an order. "Bring that wheelchair here, *fast!*"

Gently lifting her limp body from the bed, Steve placed her in the wheelchair and motioned for the nurses to stand aside. Guiding the wheel-chair out into the hallway, he moved directly to the elevator, then retraced his steps out the back door to the waiting car.

Lifting her from the wheelchair, he placed her on the backseat, moved in beside her, closed the door, and ordered the driver to take him to the airport.

As the car pulled away, Steve placed Audrey's head in his lap and softly stroked her forehead with the tips of his fingers.

She stirred, looked up at him, smiled, then drifted back into unconsciousness.

Steve glanced at his wristwatch. It was a little past five-thirty in the morning. Mentally counting down the minutes, he hoped he could get back to Dallas in time to save his son.

Reaching for the SatPhone in his coat pocket, he dialed the hotel room of Captain Mayes, the pilot of the TV9 plane. "Captain Mayes, sorry to wake you so early, but you must get to the airport. We have to leave for Dallas *immediately.*"

TWENTY-FOUR

A murky gray overcast, punctuated by scattered rain squalls, hung like a ragged shroud over the warm, choppy waters of the Gulf of Mexico, a hundred and five nautical miles off the southern coast of Texas. Like a silent ghost, at a depth of one hundred fifty feet beneath the surface, the rounded black hull of a nuclear-powered attack submarine, the *Golden Dawn*, glided sullenly through the water toward its rendezvous point.

Designed for fast, silent running out of reach of the surface, the sub was manned by a crew of fourteen officers and 135 enlisted men. At an imposing length of 380 feet and displacing over seven thousand tons when submerged, the prowling, silent specter of death was propelled swiftly through the water by twin BE48 nuclear reactors.

One of the most advanced subs in the New Earth Federation's inventory, the *Golden Dawn* carried a full complement of the new Zeus cruise missiles. Capable of delivering the most dangerous nuclear, biological, or chemical weapons, the Zeus missiles aboard the *Golden Dawn* had been outfitted with a new classified warhead known only to the captain, his executive officer, and the political officer aboard the sub.

High above the sub, circling in low earth orbit, a secure worldwide web of highly sophisticated global positioning satellites pumped a continuous stream of data to the sub's onboard computers. Using digitally encrypted, unbreakable algorithms, these code commands were beamed to the satellites from the Round Room, the nexus of the command post of the Global Forces Command and Control Center, sequestered somewhere inside the subterranean labyrinths of The Mountain in Switzerland.

Captain Maurice Davos sat hunched forward in his soft, leather chair in his private quarters aboard the *Golden Dawn*, staring intently into the computer screen mounted in the console in front of him. The barely audible, deep hum of the turbines was a reassuring sound to him, telling him that everything was in order and that his sub was moving.

A combat veteran, his weathered face, lined with the wisdom of age and experience, made him look ten years older than his forty-eight years. One of the top commanders in the massive fleet of stalk-and-strike nuclear subs, he had been awarded the Federation's highest honor, the Medal of Unity, for his part in the expansion of the New Earth Federation.

His Executive Officer and the Political Officer stood behind him, looking over his shoulder at a message from the Command and Control Center. After studying the message, the captain keystroked his military confirmation code and instructed the Command and Control Center to proceed with orders.

A computerized voice coming through the small speakers mounted on the sides of the computer ordered,

ACTUATE VOICEPRINT VERIFICATION

Captain Davos spoke his name into the small microphone on his computer. The screen instantly flashed the words:

VOICEPRINT VERIFICATION CONFIRMED
AUTHORIZED TO LAUNCH MISSILE

The three men stared intently into the screen, reading the orders from Switzerland. With everything confirmed, it was now the captain's duty to execute the mission.

Captain Davos glanced up at the Political Officer and nodded. Following established military procedure, the PO stepped to the wall safe a few feet away and dialed in a combination known only to him. Swinging the small, heavy metal door open, he retrieved two encrypted computer cards, turned and handed one to the captain and one to the Executive Officer.

The two men then inserted the cards into separate slots at the base of the computer. With lightning speed, a three-dimensional navigational fix on their target was fed directly into the sub's computerized Missile Launch System.

After securing his computer, the captain, along with his exec and the Political Officer, left his private quarters and walked swiftly to the sub's control room.

The electronically intensive control room was bathed in a soft red light. A series of 3-D flat-panel video screens along one wall displayed the changing data streams flowing to and from the Round Room.

Enlisted men studied the symbols dancing across the screens, skillfully interpreting each one as another sub, a ship, or a plane in their area. With the sub rigged for ultraquiet, the crew in the red-lit control room communicated in whispers and walked lightly as they carried out their varied duties inside the fighting fortress.

While his eyes adjusted to the low level of light, Captain Davos studied the data on the video screens. Then, speaking softly, he said, "Left standard rudder."

"Left standard rudder," the officer of the deck answered.

"All ahead one-third. Heading three-five-zero," he added.

"All ahead one-third. Three-five-zero degrees," came the response.

When the display read the correct heading, the captain ordered, "Bring her up to periscope depth."

"Aye, sir, periscope depth."

The captain could feel the deck angle change as the sailor manning the diving planes eased back on his controls, sending the vessel upward toward the surface.

When the sub leveled off, Captain Davos confidently walked onto the slightly elevated platform. "Up scope," he ordered.

As if obeying his verbal command, the periscope instantly rose from its storage well with a slight hiss. Captain Davos reached out and snapped down the dual handles and peered into the periscope's optic module. Relaxing his right arm across the handle, he watched as the scope rose from the sub's sail to the surface of the water. The sun was just breaking through the eastern horizon. The water was calm.

Quickly scanning a 360-degree arc, he looked for any obstacles or ships that might spell danger for his ship and his crew. Satisfied that everything was clear, he snapped the handles back up, stepped back from the periscope, and barked, "Down scope."

Now traveling at less than six knots per hour at a depth of sixty feet, Captain Davos ordered, "Prepare to launch missile."

Taking a few steps to his left, Captain Davos glanced over the shoulder of the Missile Launch Officer sitting in front of a bank of computers mounted against the bulkhead. The young officer deftly began entering a series of cryptic codes into the launch system, activating the Zeus missile inside of Missile Launch Cell number 3.

Quickly verifying the coordinates of the target that had been fed to his computer from the Round Room in Switzerland, he entered another code that armed the classified warhead riding on top of the Zeus missile. He then set the warhead to detonate at an altitude of one thousand feet AGL (Above Ground Level) at arrival over its assigned target.

He then set the coverage parameters for a fifteen-mile burn. From the point of detonation, the burn of the TR6 would cover an exact fifteen-mile circle, vaporizing everything within that circle. The area would be "cleansed." No living thing would remain.

"Ready to launch, Captain," the Missile Launch Officer called out.

Taking a deep breath, Captain Davos ordered, "Start launch sequence."

"Aye aye, sir, starting launch sequence," said the young officer as he pressed RUN on his keyboard.

After having started the firing sequence, the Missile Launch Officer glanced at the enlisted man sitting next to him and whispered out of the side of his mouth, "Hey, this is our fifth launch in the past thirty days. I wonder what's going on?"

The young man shrugged his shoulders.

Staring at the sequential numbered countdown on the center wallscreen, Captain Davos picked up the count verbally.

"Five . . . four . . . three . . . two . . . one . . ."

"Fire!" he pronounced with a sense of finality.

At the speed of light, the computer sent a digital command hurtling through the fiber-optic cables to the boost motor of the Zeus cruise missile in the vertically mounted Missile Launch Cell number 3.

Captain Davos felt a slight tremble in the sub as an explosive charge propelled the Zeus missile upward through the hatch, blowing it out of the water above the sub, leaving behind an angry cloud of spray.

Rising slowly at first, the Zeus seemed to be momentarily frozen in space, hovering on the edge of flying. At that critical point, the missile's cruise engine kicked in, erupting in a roaring fireball, hurtling the missile and its deadly cargo skyward atop a blazing trail of fire.

At fifteen hundred feet into the gray, hazy sky, the missile did a zero-G pushover and descended to its ground-hugging altitude, heading landward toward its preprogrammed target. Guided by computerized commands relayed through the global positioning satellites, it would hit the target with pinpoint accuracy.

There was no margin for error.

Once the Zeus missile had been launched, the rounded black hull of the *Golden Dawn* slid silently back down into the shadowy darkness of the waters of the Gulf of Mexico, its computers already receiving new encrypted orders from the Round Room, storing the new coordinates for their next target.

To Captain Davos and his men, it was nothing more than another practice maneuver, carried out in video-game fashion, with no measurable consequences. Their target was only a series of digital readouts on their computer screens. There was nothing personal about it.

They had a job to do, and they did it with as much professionalism as they could command.

But to the people of Camden, Texas, it was more serious.

6:04 A.M.

Speeding through the security gate at the Templeton airport, the driver went directly to the TV9 jet parked on the tarmac near one of the hangars. Pulling up beside the plane, Steve scooped Audrey up in his arms and practically ran toward the open door of the plane.

The copilot stepped from the plane to offer his assistance in getting Audrey onboard. Brushing him aside, Steve bounded up the steps into the plane and placed her gently in one of the seats. While strapping her in, she rolled her eyes up toward him and said groggily, "Hi, Steve, where are we? I—"

Before she could finish the sentence, her eyes again closed, and her head fell limply against the shoulder harness.

Captain Mayes was sitting at the controls, the plane's jet engines whining, and even before Steve could get to his own seat, he started his taxi to runway 15.

Sinking wearily into his chair, Steve glanced at his watch and thought of his son. It was 6:07. Lori usually left for work at 7:30. He had to be home before then. As it stood, their estimated time of arrival in Dallas was 6:40. Add to that the thirty-five minutes for the drive from the airport to his home, and if everything worked out right, he would have a few minutes to spare.

Leaning back hard, he adjusted his seat and prepared to relax.

Feeling the plane come to a sudden stop, Steve sat up. Captain Mayes clicked on the intercom. "I'm sorry, Mr. Weston, but there will be a slight delay. A plane with the highest priority is just now leaving the hangar. The tower instructed all traffic in the area to hold until it takes off and is out of the Terminal Control Area."

Steve cursed under his breath. Squeezed in a vise of time, he knew that his margin of safety for getting back to Dallas was growing dangerously short. Even a slight delay could be disastrous.

Looking out the window, he watched a large, hypersonic luxury airliner pull away from a hangar at the far end of the airport and taxi slowly toward runway 15. Solid white, the only marking on it was a small emblem of the earth, the official seal of the New Earth Federation.

"The World Leader," he fumed.

Steve's emotions churned with resentment at the perilous delay. Staring dejectedly at the Secretary General's large white plane, he watched it leisurely move into place at the end of the runway and take off. Resenting the loss of precious time, he glared hard at the mammoth plane, watching it grow smaller and smaller as it climbed out into the clear Texas sky and vanished from his sight.

With the TV9 plane's jet engines humming a low song of tremendous power, straining to be unleashed, Steve sat rigidly in the plush cabin waiting impatiently for Captain Mayes to move onto the runway for takeoff. When the plane didn't move forward, he called out sharply, "Captain Mayes, what's the problem?"

"I'm sorry, sir," he answered, his voice tinged with impatience, "but I don't have clearance for takeoff. The tower told me to hold right here until they release me."

Raising his voice in anger, Steve shouted, "I don't care whether you have clearance or not, Captain Mayes. Just get this plane off the ground. I'll take full responsibility."

"Yes, sir," Mayes said as he smiled and nudged his throttles slightly, quickly taxiing into position above the numbers at the end of the runway. With the tower operator yelling at him through his headset to hold his position, Mayes advanced the throttles and began his takeoff run, guiding the sleek craft down the runway and lifting off into the smooth morning air, still ignoring the shouted orders from the angry tower operator.

Once he reached a thousand feet above ground level, Captain Mayes turned into a gentle twenty-degree bank to the left, still climbing, bringing the plane to a solid heading of three-five-zero degrees.

F lying at supersonic speeds, deftly rising and falling with the terrain, the fiery Zeus missile that had been launched from the *Golden Dawn* passed through a series of preprogrammed digital waypoints fed to its internal guidance system from the global positioning satellites overhead. Changing course, ever so slightly, its pathway was designed to avoid causing any undue alarm by keeping it from passing directly over any highly populated areas as it pursued its deathly mission across the land mass of Texas.

At a range of ten miles from the target, the Zeus missile executed a pop-up maneuver and climbed almost vertically to an altitude of ten thousand feet; then it arced over and plummeted downward. When it had descended to an altitude of five thousand feet, its parachute deployed.

A tiny optical lens mounted in the nose of the TR6 sent a continuing stream of discreet data back through the Panoptican Surveillance System satellites to the Round Room deep inside The Mountain in Switzerland. As military technicians watched, the data was reassembled, displaying a clear image of the city of Camden on high-definition screens in front of the Surveillance Attack Officers.

Floating lazily below the yellow plume of the parachute, passing through wisps of white clouds, the missile broke out into the clear, calm air at three thousand feet, directly over the center of the town of Camden.

A young businessman in Camden walked to his car, opened the back door, and placed his briefcase on the seat. Before getting in behind the wheel, he glanced up at the brightly colored parachute floating out of the sky.

He smiled. Its small size made him think it was a kid's toy rocket floating back down to some open field nearby.

At one thousand feet above Camden, the TR6 exploded.

S ighing deeply, Steve glanced out the window of the TV9 jet as they passed through three thousand feet. It wouldn't be long now until they arrived in Dallas, and, hopefully, he could get his son before Lori took him to the infanticide center.

Turning, he gently cupped Audrey's face and chin in his hands and shifted her to a more comfortable position against the headrest. Assured that she was riding comfortably, he wearily kicked his own seat back, stretched out his legs, and lay back heavily into the comfortable, soft leather chair inside the quietness of the plush passenger compartment of the TV9 jet.

Feeling the tension and strain drop from his shoulders, he hoped to get a few minutes rest before they landed in Dallas.

But just as he closed his eyes, he was jarred by a blinding flash of light that flooded the airplane cabin with such force it seemed to penetrate his entire body. Sitting bolt upright, he jerked his head to the left and looked out the window, his gaze riveted on a scene in the direction of the city of Camden.

What he saw chilled him to the bone.

Several miles in the distance, spreading like a giant orange sphere, a fire cloud was surging downward out of a device that had been detonated no more than a thousand feet above the ground.

Trying to shield his eyes from the intensity of the light, he watched in fascination as the fiery cloud spread its deadly plume downward from the epicenter of the explosion, forming a huge, incandescent bubble, ever growing in size, a billowing, boiling, churning, angry mass of fire, spreading outward with lightning speed, covering mile after mile, as if on a path to consume the whole earth.

The sun overhead dimmed in comparison.

The two pilots in the cockpit sat frozen in their places, their senses suddenly numbed by the fury and force of the stunning glare from the burning inferno. Fearing the worst, their muscles instinctively tensed against the inevitable blow they knew would come.

The shock wave from the explosion slammed against the left side of the plane, sending a violent shudder through it, jolting the three men out of their momentary stupor.

They were trapped in the throes of its fury as the pressure blast from the TR6 tossed the luxury executive jet wildly about like a cork on an angry sea, sending it pitching and rolling, uncontrollable, its powerful engines screaming in protest.

In the distance they heard a low, rumbling roar that built irresistibly into an ear-splitting crescendo, indescribable, overwhelming, passing over them in thundering waves, a sound that could mute a thousand violent, crashing thunderstorms.

Gripping the arms of his chair, Steve watched in quiet respect and admiration as Captain Mayes and his copilot battled valiantly to maintain control of the plane, their faces set in grim determination. With relentless effort they fought with all their will and strength to wrench their derelict craft from the strong force that had clutched it tightly and was trying mightily to dash it into the ground below.

Frozen in a fatal moment in time, Steve knew with steely certainty that he was about to meet his death. But strangely, there was no fear, only curiosity at the prospect of dying.

Suddenly locked in a disastrous vacuum inside the churning, disrupted elements, the plane shuddered violently, then the left wing dropped suddenly, precipitously, sending the luxury jet spiraling downward at great speed, threatening to force them into a disastrous stall or nonrecoverable spin.

Captain Mayes continued to tug at the controls, even though the craft was no longer responding to him. He watched helplessly as his flight instruments whirled frantically, screaming at him that he had lost control of his plane.

Watching in almost detached fascination at the needle on his altimeter furiously unwinding, indicating that they were plummeting downward toward the earth at a tremendous speed, Mayes tried valiantly to lift the nose of the wildly plunging jet as the fast-approaching earth, and sudden death, loomed ever larger in their view.

Five hundred feet . . . four hundred feet . . . plunging ever downward.

Casting his fear aside, Mayes gripped the controls hard, throwing all his inborn skill as a seasoned pilot into this battle to the death against the unseen enemy that was bent on snatching them from the sky and destroying him and his passengers.

Calling on his copilot to help him pull the plane out of their near-fatal attitude, their eyes wide and staring into the face of death, they strained with all their combined might to level the wings of the plunging craft, to raise its nose, and to bleed off the deadly increasing airspeed.

Suddenly, passing through a scant two hundred feet above the ground, they managed to level the wings. Then both men pulled back hard on the controls. With the blood-draining G-forces pushing their bodies forcefully against their seats, Captain Mayes and his copilot could almost feel the outstretched limbs of the trees beneath them brush menacingly against the belly of their plane as they screamed across them.

Having wrenched his craft from the death grip of gravity, Mayes' skillful hands coaxed his errant plane upward, ever climbing, gaining precious lifesaving altitude.

Passing through six thousand feet, still climbing, the air smoothed, and they were safe, and alive.

Shaken by the near disaster, Steve reached over and adjusted Audrey's seat harness, then turned and looked out the window to the southwest.

He saw the fiery cloud over Camden abruptly cease to grow in size, as if some invisible hand had stopped it at a predetermined point. Gazing intently at the specter of death hanging ominously over the landscape, he watched its color begin to fade from its bright orange glow to a brilliant white, then to a light purplish haze.

And as quickly as it had appeared, the purple cloud died away, dissipating back into the atmosphere. Steve blinked his eyes, and it was gone. The sky was clear and clean once again, as if nothing had happened.

"The Purple Death," he whispered under his breath.

After the purple haze had washed away, giving Steve an unobstructed view of what should have been the city of Camden, what met his gaze caused him to shudder. All that greeted his sight was an enormous, circular, black burned-over scar on the earth's face.

This smoldering mound of earth had once been a city with buildings, and homes, and living, breathing, human beings.

Now, there was *nothing*.

Camden had simply vanished . . . vanished into thin air.

It was as if a giant fiery hand of a malevolent surgeon had skillfully cut the city away, leaving the adjoining countryside undisturbed.

There was nothing there.

No buildings, no trees, no vegetation, no animals, no sign of life. Nothing moved.

The fire had been so intense that everything that came under the all-consuming umbrella of the bomb had been obliterated. Only a smoldering scar remained.

Camden, Texas, and its fifty thousand inhabitants no longer existed, victims of the Federation's fiery genocide.

The word "cleansed" leaped into Steve's brain.

Once again, General Dorian and the leaders of the Social Order had murdered thousands of human beings in their righteous quest to save the earth and to please Gaia.

As the macabre scene disappeared from his view, Steve fell back into his chair and gave vent to a low, telling moan, wondering what other town or city these madmen would strike next in their unbridled fury against the human race. A dark dread caused him to consider that perhaps someone, at this very moment, was standing at the computers in the Round Room inside The Mountain, studying the satellite pictures of what remained of Camden.

Or perhaps they were already punching in more ultrasecret codes, sending more purifying agents to more towns and cities, to burn out more evil—all to appease Gaia.

A disturbing thought hit his mind with the force of a hammer. Was their next target Dallas?

Or London, or Cairo, or New York?

In his wildest fantasies, Steve Weston would never have believed that it would have come to his native land.

Captain Mayes turned and called out through the open door to the cabin. "Mr. Weston, are you all right?"

"Yes, I'm fine, Captain."

"And Ms. Montaigne?"

"She's fine. She never knew anything happened."

"I don't know what that was, Mr. Weston. I'll call Air Traffic Control and see if they can tell me."

Steve started to tell him not to bother, but he knew that might complicate things and cause him to ask questions. So he answered, "That's fine, Captain. Let me know what you find out."

Suddenly, Steve felt he was an accomplice to high crimes against humanity. And at this moment he would have willingly traded all of his wealth and position to get out from under the enormous guilt that now weighed upon him.

There was no escaping it; these wicked and demented men who ruled in the new Social Order were beyond the pale of reason and compassion. But feeling small and alone, he was afraid there was nothing he could do to stop them. And he feared that the global order would escape from this incident unscathed, its reputation and its image as the world's healer still intact.

Steve checked again to see that Audrey was comfortable. When he touched her shoulder, she moved her head slightly to the left, opened her eyes, and gave him a weak smile, then drifted back into unconsciousness.

In a daze, he reached for his SatPhone and called TV9 in Dallas and instructed them to have an ambulance waiting for Audrey when they landed at the airport. He then leaned back and tried to assess the meaning of the events of the last few hours.

The flight back to Dallas took a little over thirty minutes. Landing at 7:16, Captain Mayes parked the plane near the terminal building. Immediately, three paramedics entered the plane, secured Audrey on a gurney, and wheeled her to the waiting ambulance.

When he was sure she was taken care of, Steve hurried to the parking lot where they had left Audrey's car. Fortunately, he still had her keys. Pulling out of the parking lot, he drove quickly to the autobahn.

Fearing that the delay in leaving Templeton had sealed Jimmy's fate, Steve fought against a mounting despair. If Lori kept to her regular schedule, she would leave the house at seven-thirty, only a few minutes from now. He slammed his fist against the steering wheel, knowing he couldn't make it in time.

Grasping at straws, he reminded himself that if she was going to carry through on her plans to have Jimmy deactivated, she still had until midnight tonight to do it. There was a chance she could have scheduled the procedure for later in the day. It was a slim chance, but it was all he had at the moment. He must get home and talk her out of it . . . or forcibly stop her, if necessary.

But what if Jimmy is already dead?

Quickly rejecting the thought, he urged the car to a higher speed, hoping to arrive in time.

TWENTY-FIVE

June 4, 2033—7:25 A.M.

L ori Weston dressed her son in a light blue velvet suit with a dark blue bow fastened to his white shirt, the one with the ruffles on the sleeves. While Jimmy sat at the kitchen table drinking a breakfast meal, she went to their Home Communications Unit, sat down and looked into the blank monitor screen. A tiny camera lens stared out at her from the top of the monitor.

Feeling it would be easier to talk to her mother this way, she rested her arms on the table and nervously rubbed her palms together, unconsciously trying to avoid the eye of the camera as she would have avoided her own mother's disapproving gaze.

Waiting until she had her emotions under control, she touched a key, prompting the video disk inside the HCU to begin recording her image and voice.

Trying to sound casual, she said, "Hi, Mom. It's, uh, a little past seven in the morning. I didn't want to disturb you and Dad so early, knowing how much Dad needs his rest. So I'm recording this before I leave home. You'll get it a little later in the day. How is Dad doing? Tell him I want to come up as soon as I can get a break in my schedule."

Shifting in her chair, she went on, "Well, Mom, Steve's career seems to be going well. He's off on some story right now. I'm not sure what it's all about, but he seemed excited about it. Sad to say, Mom, my own career is not advancing the way I had planned. I had counted on a promotion, but because of my family obligations, the committee felt I couldn't devote the time and energy that the job called for. They were wrong, but—"

Leaving the sentence unfinished, she reached over quickly and pushed the PAUSE button. Trying to regain her composure, she breathed deeply, smiled, released the button, and continued. "Unfortunately, Mom, Jimmy had a lot to do with my not getting the promotion. He's . . . well, he's more of a problem than I was prepared for. Even though he spends most of his time at the Enrichment Center, there are still quite a few demands on my time. They seem to call me about every little thing, from head colds to his attitudinal adjustment problems. The committee spokesperson informed me that such diversions were hindering my career advancement."

Her confidence slowly building, Lori looked into the eye of the camera and continued. "And the expense! Mom, you just can't imagine how expensive it is to fund a child these days. It makes me a little angry to have to pay these extra bills when we're already paying taxes that are supposed to completely cover child care and medical expenses. Sometimes I think the government is shirking its responsibility in not providing more complete parental services. We've had to cut back on our own activities and comforts because of the additional expense Jimmy is costing us. And there's no end in sight."

Hitting the PAUSE key again, Lori bit her bottom lip, then continued. "Which . . . brings me to the reason for talking to you. Mom, I've made a choice that's going to be best for me, and Steve . . . and Jimmy. I've been thinking about it for several months but didn't want to do anything until I was absolutely sure. But today is the deadline, so I had to make a decision, and I believe I have made the right decision, Mom. It's really best for Jimmy. After all, every child has the right to be wanted and loved. It was a mistake to bring him to term; I know that now. With my career, and my own life and needs, I'm just unable to give him the love he really deserves. And it's not fair to him.

"I've looked into the 'deactivation procedure' and have talked to other parents who have used it, and have found that it's a very pleasant experience for both the child and the parents. I've also been to some discussion groups and have heard parents talk about how good they feel over having had the procedure done. There were no regrets. They all felt they did the right thing.

"Now, Mom, I know how much you love Jimmy. Well, so do I, but we can't let our personal feelings interfere with what's best for him. And, Mom, please don't second-guess me. It's no more serious than having an abortion."

Feeling a load lift off her shoulders, Lori smiled into the camera. "By the time you see this, Mom, it will all be over. I was going to have Jimmy come and stand with me and say goodbye to you and Dad, but I was afraid it would have made it harder on both of you."

With a wave of her hand, she said, "Give my love to Dad. Talk to you later. Bye."

Lori then entered her mother's address, set the time for delivery, and pressed SEND, locking the instructions in.

With that done, she turned to get Jimmy. "We must hurry, Jimmy," she insisted. "We can't be late for our nine o'clock appointment at the Clinic. We've got just enough time if we leave now."

Clutching tightly to his ever-present, frayed and ragged stuffed dinosaur, Jimmy reached up to take his mother's hand, brandishing a big smile born of love and trust. He was going with his mother, a rare treat, because most of his life had been spent in the government enrichment center's child-care facility.

In fact, Jimmy knew his teachers and counselors at school much better than he knew his own mother and father.

7:44 A.M.

Securing Jimmy into his safety seat, Lori closed his door, walked around the car, and slipped into the driver's seat. Guiding her car past the security gate, she turned right. A few minutes later, she accessed the autobahn and drove south toward Dallas. Having requested a half-day off from work to take care of some "family matters," she would have just enough time to keep her appointment at the clinic and be at work shortly before noon.

When the Zen Guidance System took control of her car on the autobahn, relieving her of the driving duties, she busied herself by filling out some of her students' progress reports that were to be entered into their master computer file.

Tiring of Jimmy's repeated attempts to engage her in conversation, Lori snapped at him, "Can't you see I'm busy, Jimmy? Please be quiet so I can work."

After a few more feeble attempts to get his mother's attention, the little boy retreated into his own fantasy world.

Riding in silence, Lori desperately tried to avoid her son's eyes, not knowing that Jimmy had already run away to his imaginary world and was now busily playing on a green meadow with his favorite imaginary friend. Even though he was a child, he had learned to escape the pain of rejection by retreating into the sanctuary of his own mind, a game that had served him well. The coldness of the professional educators at the center drove him to seek escape. Having no way out, his child mind had devised this elaborate make-believe world to run to. It helped him cope.

Arriving at her designated exit, the Zen system smoothly moved Lori's car into the right lane, then off the autobahn. Taking manual control, she turned right, passed under the autobahn, and drove to the large Vista Gate shopping mall where the clinic was located.

The Artemis Children's Health Clinic was only one of the hundreds of infanticide centers that were located in cities and towns across the country. Most were found in shopping centers with ample parking space. Quick and convenient, with paperwork and hassle cut to the minimum, the people could bring their children in, then get back to work, or whatever other activity their busy schedules called for. Everything about the centers had been planned with the convenience of the customer in mind.

The people of the world had come to accept these clinics as part of their culture, believing them to be in the best interest of the public good.

As Lori and Jimmy approached the glass door, it slid open automatically, sending a rush of cold air into their faces. Once inside, they were surrounded by digitized music that seemed to be a part of the landscape itself, coming from all sides, from the walls, the plants, perfectly diffused, engulfing them wherever they walked, drowning out the loud murmur of the thousands of shoppers hurrying from store to store.

One of the most modern shopping malls in the world, this one boasted the finest department stores, specialty houses, restaurants, entertainment centers, a virtual-reality theater, water fountains, and strolling musicians, along with rapid escalators and moving sidewalks that transported thousands of people from store to store in climate-controlled luxury and comfort.

Jimmy smiled when he picked up the enticing aroma coming from the popcorn machine near the shoe store. He looked for it.

Lori tugged at Jimmy's hand when she felt him try to slow down when they walked past the giant clock. Fascinated by its enormous face, its ornate hands, and its large swinging pendulum, he strained to look back over his shoulder, his eager eyes trying desperately to follow the wide arc of the pendulum's back-and-forth motion.

Scurrying on past the indoor ice-skating rink, where laughing children were gliding across the ice in sync with the rhythm of the music, Jimmy again pulled at his mother's arm in a futile effort to stop and watch the kids and listen to their laughter.

Passing the sprawling electronics store, they turned right and walked toward the clinic. Emblazoned across the entrance, in brightly colored, dancing lights, were the words, *Artemis Children's Health Clinic.*

7:52 A.M.

Feeling his heart pounding in his temples, Steve turned the corner onto his street and sped to his own driveway. Punching in the security code, the gate opened and he urged the car forward, stopping abruptly in the driveway. Running to the front door, he placed his hand on the security panel. When the electronic lock opened the door, he dashed inside.

Rushing madly from room to room, he searched desperately for Lori and Jimmy, frantically calling out their names as he went.

He was startled when the house computer system said, "Good morning, Mr. Weston. May I brew some coffee for you?"

"No, Harry. Are Ms. Weston and Jimmy in the house?"

"No, Mr. Weston," the computerized voice answered. "Ms. Weston and Jimmy departed the house at 7:43 A.M."

Trying to rein in his raging emotions, he sat down on the edge of the couch and rubbed his forehead, trying to think. Then, reaching for the telephone on the table next to the Home Communications Unit in the corner of his den, he punched in the number for the enrichment center where Lori worked. When a secretary answered, he asked if Lori had arrived at work yet. His heart sank when she told him she had taken the morning off and would not be in until noon.

With deep despair setting in, Steve happened to glance at the monitor screen of the HCU, noticing that Lori's face had been freeze-framed on the screen.

Unusual, he thought.

Desperate to uncover the smallest clue about where they had gone, he punched in the code for video messages. Discovering that it was an outgoing video letter that had been time-delayed, he backed the video disk to the beginning and watched in horror as Lori announced to her mother that she was taking Jimmy to the infanticide center to be deactivated.

Distraught, he knew he had to find her and take Jimmy from her before the procedure could be performed. But where was she going? There were many infanticide centers scattered across the DFW region.

"Which one!" he cried out loud. "Where is she taking my son?"

Glancing to the right side of the table holding the HCU, he spotted a small piece of paper with writing on it. Hoping that it might mean something, he picked it up. Scribbled in Lori's own handwriting were the words: *Artemis, 9:00* A.M.

"Artemis . . ." he muttered quizzically. "What does it mean?"

Pacing the floor, glaring at the piece of paper, he searched his brain for an answer. Did it mean anything, or was it just something that would delay his search for Jimmy? Punching in the number for information on his HCU, he entered the words "Infanticide Centers."

Scanning the list of names as they scrolled across his screen, he stopped at "Artemis Children's Health Clinic."

Making a note of the address, he glanced at the digital clock. It was now 8:17.

He had forty-three minutes to get to Lori and stop her, by whatever means necessary. The drive would take thirty minutes. He prayed he would make it in time.

Quickly stepping into his bedroom, he rushed to his closet, grabbed his spare handgun from its hiding place, and slipped it into his coat pocket, just in case.

Somehow he had to stop Lori, or at least detain her until midnight tonight when Jimmy would turn three and be declared a legal "person" in the eyes of the law. Filled with a passion to save his son, he was determined to do whatever was necessary, even if it meant killing Lori, or anyone else who might get in his way.

It no longer mattered what happened to him.

TWENTY-SIX

June 4, 2033—8:31 A.M.

The Artemis Children's Health Clinic was more colorful, lively, and enticing than any other store in the entire mall. A fairyland of magic and excitement, the decor was designed by experts in the entertainment industry to appeal to children under three years of age.

As Lori and Jimmy approached the door of the clinic, a woman stepped in front of them and thrust a small piece of paper into Lori's hand and said softly, "Please read this before you do anything."

Annoyed at the intrusion, Lori only glared at the lady, turned, and continued on to the clinic. Not wanting to clutter the mall with the unwanted piece of paper, and not seeing a trash receptacle nearby, she crumpled it up, placed it in her purse, and promptly forgot about it.

Passing through the wide doors of the clinic, Lori kept Jimmy's hand firmly clutched in her own. The large waiting room was decorated with colorful couches, kid-sized chairs, and pictures of cartoon characters seen on TV. More than thirty children, ranging in age from a few months to almost three years, sat at small tables scattered throughout the room, coloring, working puzzles, or playing with toys that buzzed and whirred, walked and talked.

The instant Lori relaxed her grip on Jimmy's hand, he ran quickly to one of the play centers where a clown was performing tricks for the kids, causing the room to echo with their laughter. Jimmy's face reflected the joy and magic of childhood.

While Jimmy and the other children were busy playing and chasing the clown, Lori quietly stepped up to a counter at the back of the large reception area. A lady in her early sixties, with her graying hair pulled back and wound into a tight bun, looked up, smiled, and said, "I'm Susan. Are you here for the procedure?"

Lori swallowed hard and forced out the words, "Uh, yes, Susan, I . . . I'm not sure what I'm supposed to do. Are there papers for me to sign?"

"It's a rather short and simple form, really, but I will need to see the biounit's Global Identification Card. Are you the unit's biological mother?"

"Yes, I am," Lori quickly replied. Reaching into her purse, she produced a small plastic computer card, handed it to the lady, and said, "This is my son's . . . uh, the *unit's* birth certificate."

The lady behind the counter took the card and slid it through a small slot on the side of the computer screen in front of her. Glancing up at the screen, she said to Lori, "Is the unit designation, James Dwight Weston?"

Lori answered, "Yes."

"Was the unit born on June 5, 2030?"

"Yes."

"Just under the wire," Susan muttered to herself.

"What did you say?"

"Oh, nothing," the lady replied. "Is your name Lori Pennington Weston?"

"Yes."

"Is the unit's biological father, Steven James Weston?"

"Yes."

She then looked up at Lori and said, "Ms. Weston, please let me see your personal Global Identification Card."

Lori handed the card to her and watched her slide it through the same slot on the side of the computer screen. Lori's picture, along with other vital information, flashed on the monitor.

The lady looked at the picture, then back at Lori. "Everything seems to be in order, Ms. Weston. If the handscan IDs of you and the biounit match, we can proceed."

Pointing to a small glass panel in the top of the counter, Susan said, "Ms. Weston, please lay your hand, palm down, on the handscan there in front of you."

She placed the palm of her hand on the glass, and in less than a heartbeat, the pattern in Lori's hand had been transferred to a central database. The returning data was displayed on the screen in front of Susan.

Satisfied with the ID, Susan said, "Now if you'll bring the biounit forward, we'll identify him through the same procedure. If you'll notice, there's a small plastic clown to your right. The left hand of the clown has a glass panel inside the palm. Have the biounit lay his hand on the hand of the clown. The handscan will read his palmprint for a verifying ID. If everything is in order, we'll receive an authorization and will move forward with the procedure."

8:46 A.M.

When Lori turned to get Jimmy, she suddenly felt as if the room had started to spin. With a wave of nausea sweeping over her, her hands began to tremble, and an unwelcome hollowness began to form in her stomach, causing her to reach out and take hold of the corner of the counter to steady herself.

Confused, she tried to think her way logically through the growing panic, telling herself that her physical weakness and momentary blurred vision was due to an abrupt drop in her blood-sugar level because she had skipped breakfast.

Clutching the counter, she took a series of deep breaths, letting them out slowly, until the panic that was pouring at her from all sides began to subside. Steadying herself, she was now back in control, determined to get on with the task at hand.

The lady at the desk spoke to her. "Are you all right, Ms. Weston?"

Lori squared her shoulders, let go of the counter, and replied, "Of course, I'm just fine, Susan." She then walked over to Jimmy and took him by the hand, telling him that she wanted him to come with her.

But Jimmy protested, not wanting to leave. He was playing with another small boy, named Paul, who appeared to be two or three months younger than Jimmy.

Bending over, Lori whispered in his ear, "Jimmy, there's a clown over there. He wants you to come and talk to him."

"OK, Mommy," Jimmy replied, obviously pleased with the attention his mother was giving to him. Excitedly, he started running across the room, then hesitated, looked back toward his mother, and waited for her to catch up. "Come on, Mommy, let's go see the clown."

Built of molded plastic, the clown had a painted-on face with a wide smile and glowing eyes. Dressed in a suit of red and white stripes, his head moved when he talked while his right hand moved back and forth, waving to the children. A small strip of glass in the clown's stationary left hand was positioned in such a way that it was easy for a child to place his own hand on top of it.

"Jimmy," Lori said softly as she knelt down beside him, "the clown wants you to put your hand over his. Can you do that?"

"Yes, Mommy, watch me."

When their hands met, the handscan raced across Jimmy's palm, recording a positive ID. With his hand lying on top of the clown's hand, Jimmy turned to look at his mother, but she was looking in the other direction, toward Susan.

Susan nodded her head, indicating that there had been a positive ID and they had received authorization for the procedure. The hard copy was already being printed out by the time Lori reached the counter.

"Everything is in order, Ms. Weston," Susan informed her. "There'll be one final identity verification in the procedure room. The unit's Life Chip will be scanned just prior to the procedure." She then slid the form across the counter to Lori, indicating where she should sign.

Life Chip! The words hit Lori with a sharp, emotional stab, bringing scenes to her mind that she thought she had buried. For an instant she was transported back to her room at the hospital where Jimmy was born.

The scenes came rushing back.

The delivery room, the birth, Jimmy's first cry, the first time she held her newborn son to her breasts, listened to the sounds of his nursing, and felt her life-giving fluids flowing into his tiny body.

She remembered that while he was nursing, she had caressed his tiny body, counting the toes, and the fingers, seeing if everything was normal, bonding with her newborn son. Then running her fingers lightly across the back of his tiny head, at the base of his skull, she had felt a small bump. Nothing serious, she remembered thinking, but it did make her curious.

When the nurse returned, she pointed out the small bump and asked if it was anything to worry about. The nurse laughed good-naturedly and informed her that everything was normal, that the bump was the place where they had inserted his Life Chip. The implanted chip, she told Lori, was a very sophisticated, miniaturized computer chip that had the capacity to hold libraries full of information.

As she talked, the kindly, middle-aged nurse had softly stroked the place where the chip had been inserted, explaining that it had already been downloaded with all of Jimmy's vital statistics, including his name and address, the names of his biological parents, his birthdate, sex, health records, blood type, DNA profile, and much more useful information.

"Ms. Weston . . . Ms. Weston . . ."

Susan's voice brought Lori out of her daze. Looking up, she apologized, "Oh . . . I'm sorry . . . I was thinking about something else. Now what did you want me to do?"

"Just sign in these three places, Ms. Weston," Susan responded, pointing to the computer printout. "The first part of the form states that you, as the biological parent, authorize the clinic to perform the procedure. The second part is an acknowledgment that we have the right to harvest the tissue of the biounit following the procedure. And the third section states that we are not responsible for any unexpected mental or emotional distress that the procedure might produce in the future. Do you have any questions?"

"You . . . are going to 'harvest' Jimmy's organs?" Lori asked, not having considered that part of the procedure.

Susan looked up at Lori, as if surprised by the question. "Why, of course, Ms. Weston. It's the humanitarian thing to do. When a biounit is deactivated, the functioning modules are transferred into other biounits who have reached the age of personhood and need the transplanted organs. It's the law."

Lori hesitated.

"Ms. Weston!" Susan said authoritatively. "If you'll please sign the form, we can get on with the procedure and you can be on your way."

Lori glanced over the freshly printed forms and signed where it had been indicated. Susan checked the signatures to see that everything was in order, then gave her a small card with a number on it and told her to wait, that it would only be a few minutes. She smiled and assured Lori that it was their policy to have their customers in and out in as short a time as possible.

Lori turned to look for a place to sit down, telling Jimmy that he could go back and play with his friend, Paul, for a few minutes. But when Jimmy looked around for Paul, he was nowhere to be found. Lori didn't ask where he had gone.

While Jimmy played in the entertainment center, Lori sank into one of the couches, fatigue suddenly setting in. Trying to relax, she had scarcely gotten into an article in one of the women's magazines when a soft-spoken lady's voice came over the speaker, announcing, "Number 43." Lori retrieved the stub from the pocket in her jacket.

It had a large "43" on it.

Closing the magazine, she walked to where Jimmy was playing, took him by the hand, and led him across the room. A kindly lady dressed in a fairy-tale character's costume was waiting at the door.

Fascinated by the lady's costume, Jimmy went to her immediately. The lady knelt down in front of him, and, in a voice that sounded as if she were telling him a bedtime story, she said, "Jimmy, would you like to go see some beautiful lights and play some fun games with me?"

Jimmy turned and looked at his mother for some sign that would tell him what to do.

Lori knelt down beside him, taking his tiny face in her hands, and whispered, "Jimmy, I know you don't understand, but Mommy is doing this for your own good. This is for *you*. It's my gift to you. It's best. . . ."

Pulling her son into her arms, she held him tightly for a moment. Kissing him lightly on the forehead, she glanced up at the lady in the fairy-tale costume. When the lady tried to lead him away, Jimmy turned to his mother, pleading with his eyes for her not to leave him.

Tightening her grip on his wrist, the lady pulled him toward the door.

Jimmy turned to ask his mom to go with him. She only stared at him. Just before the door closed, Lori heard his tiny voice call out, "Mommy . . ."

Watching her son disappear through the door, only hours away from his third birthday, Lori was shocked at the maternal instinct that was triggered inside her, begging her to run and save her son. This sudden rush of emotion was illogical, she told herself repeatedly. Jimmy was only being hurried along the evolutionary ladder to a higher form of life. Whatever happens has surely been ordained to happen. It is his karma, and she shouldn't stand in the way.

But why was she having these emotions? Why did she want to stop the wheel of fate and step in to save her son?

Becoming emotionally numb, she made her way to the couch, sat down, and reached for the cold cup of coffee she had left on the table next to the couch. But her hands were shaking so badly she was unable to get the cup to her mouth without spilling it.

Feeling a sudden, crushing fatigue, she placed the cup back on the table, closed her eyes, pressed the tips of her fingers hard against her temples, and began to softly recite her mantra, hoping to alter her consciousness enough to shut out the urge to rush into the secured rooms of the clinic and stop the procedure that was about to drain her son's life away.

But this time, her magic formulas failed her.

Frantically trying to distract her mind from the mental images of the procedure, she remembered the piece of paper the lady had given her at the door of the clinic. Maybe this would occupy her thoughts. She reached for her purse and took out the note.

Unfolding it, she read the handwritten, simple message. It said,

You've been told that it's legal to kill your baby up to three years of age, but life is worthy at all stages of development. This clinic is murdering children, so please consider what you're doing before it's too late. Many of us believed their lies and have killed our children. We now live with that deed night and day. Please stop the procedure before it's too late.

Lori stared at the compelling piece of paper. *"Please don't kill your child!"* was the last sentence.

It was a *reflex* action, she told herself, that caused her to look toward the door to the procedure rooms. And before she could stop it, her son's name involuntarily slipped out of her mouth.

"Jimmy . . ." she whispered softly.

And, for a fleeting moment, she wanted to rush through the door and stop the procedure. But the years of indoctrination and mind-control by the Social Order had convinced her to suppress her maternal instincts for the "good of society." And once again she rationalized that what she was doing was best for Jimmy, for her, and for Mother Earth.

Now back in control of her thoughts and emotions, Lori pushed herself up from the couch, crumpled up the piece of paper, and dropped it purposefully into the trash container next to the door.

And with it, Jimmy's last hope for life.

She then walked out of the clinic and made her way back to her car, and her new life.

Lori Weston's ordeal was over.

But inside one of the procedure rooms of the Artemis Children's Health Clinic, Jimmy's nightmare had only begun.

9:03 A.M.

When the door had closed, separating Jimmy Weston from his mother, the nurse tightened her firm grip around his small hand and led him down a brightly colored hallway toward the infanticide procedure rooms. When they came to room number nine, she pulled him inside and closed the door behind them.

The room had a dome-shaped ceiling. A child-sized sculptured chair, complete with colorful hand controls, was positioned in the center of the room. When the nurse placed Jimmy in the chair, it automatically tilted back and the entire ceiling burst into a three-dimensional, panoramic theater, showing the universe, complete with planets, shooting stars, constellations, and darting spaceships.

While Jimmy's eyes followed in childlike fascination the colorful, whirling universe above him, he hardly noticed when the nurse rubbed a pleasant smelling lotion on his right arm, causing a small patch of his skin to go numb.

Suddenly sensing that something was terribly wrong, he became frightened and searched the room for his mother. But she was not there. His tiny heart pounding frantically in his small chest, he fought desperately to get out of the chair and go back to her. But strong, unforgiving straps clamped tight around his wrists and legs held him firmly in place.

Helpless, he watched in mounting alarm as the nurse leaned over him, a syringe with a long, shining needle held delicately in her right hand. With his frantic gaze fastened on the needle, he followed the downward movement of the dreaded instrument as she lowered it toward him with cold, dark purpose.

Knowing instinctively that she was going to hurt him, he whimpered and tried desperately to reach out with his hand and stop its downward advance. But his tethered arms wouldn't obey his commands. Unable to stop her, Jimmy looked up into the nurse's face, begging her with his eyes to help him.

Bent on her grisly task, she stared down at him. Her face reflected neither mercy nor concern as she whispered contemptuously, "You little biounits, you're all the same. Struggling for life when you're not even human."

His thoughts whirling in a frightening jumble, bordering on raw terror, Jimmy's eyes darted wildly about the room. Searching throughout this cold, haunting chamber of death, he tried in vain to find his mother's reassuring face in the gathering chaos that was rapidly swallowing him up.

Where is she? his child mind screamed out silently into the uncaring void.

Trying with all his strength to hold on to his world, his eyes darting about the room, his tiny lips formed a word without sound . . . *Mommy.*

A cruel smile spread across the nurse's face like a gaping wound in anticipation of snuffing out the life of another excess biounit. Crudely, she grasped Jimmy's right arm. While holding it firmly and still, she moved the needle into position, poised and ready for the injection of the deadly mixture. Letting out a small involuntary cry, his eyes now wide in terror, Jimmy braced himself against the inevitable pain.

As the sharp tip of the needle touched the tender, soft skin of Jimmy's tiny right arm, suddenly, without warning, the door to the procedure room was violently thrown open, slamming against the wall with terrific force.

Startled, the nurse only had time to catch a fleeting glimpse of a dark figure lunging at her. Opening her mouth to scream, she felt strong arms close around her upper body and crush her in a violent embrace as a powerful hand closed around her gaping mouth, shutting off her air.

Overpowered by her attacker's superior strength, the needle flew from her hand and was sent crashing to the hard floor, shattering apart as it hit, spilling its poison at her feet. Struggling for air, she could feel the heat of her attacker's breath against her neck. She tried to twist away, but her assailant tightened his unforgiving grip.

Forced away from Jimmy's chair, she was thrown viciously up against the wall and held there. Terrified, she fought wildly against the unknown enemy. Gripped in a firm military-style hold, for an agonizing moment, she knew she was about to die.

With wide, terrified eyes she stared in horror into the face of her assailant. He was a young man, lean and muscular, his face expressionless, his large hand still clamped tightly against her mouth.

Shifting her eyes, she saw movement. A lone, imposing figure stood outlined in the half-shadow of the doorway. When the figure stepped purposefully into the room, she saw that it was a tall, angular man, dressed in a dark business suit. Silver-haired, his unsmiling face was lined with age. Slowly surveying the room, his sharp eyes regarded the nurse momentarily, a contemptuous look on his face. With a gesture, he ordered the younger man to release her.

"Now, sit down in that chair and be silent!" he ordered gruffly.

Feeling a welcome rush of relief, the grateful nurse obeyed instantly.

Assured that she was now under their total control, the older man turned and nodded to a middle-aged woman who had been standing in the hallway. She walked into the room, closing the door behind her.

Flashing a badge, the older man informed the nurse, "We're going to take this child. Your superiors have been instructed to invalidate the infanticide order. All records of this visit will be erased. Under penalty of law, you are to tell no one that this child was ever here. Is that understood?" There was something in the man's voice that carried authority, demanding obedience.

Cold fear in her eyes, the nurse answered softly, "Yes, I understand."

She then watched in silence as the middle-aged woman gently removed the leather straps from Jimmy's arms and legs, smiling at him, and talking to him softly as she worked. While her gentle words played their magic on his mind, he became still and quiet.

Looking up at her, Jimmy responded to her kindness with a smile, drawing from a reservoir of strength that only a child possesses.

The middle-aged lady gently lifted Jimmy up, softly cradled the frightened child in her arms, and nodded to the older man. Without another word being spoken, they exited the room, walked hurriedly down a corridor and out through a back entrance to a waiting car.

When the two men and the lady had left the room with Jimmy, the nurse splashed some cold water on her face, took several deep breaths, then went back to her routine tasks of arranging the room and the equipment for the next infanticide procedure.

After adjusting the sculptured chair and resetting the computers and medical readouts, she reprogrammed the video display of the virtual universe in preparation for the next biounit.

O utside, in the half-light of the narrow alley in back of the Artemis infanticide center, a driver stood stoically beside a long, expensive black car. Behind the darkly tinted windows, a man sat in the backseat, alone, staring intently at the clinic door, anxiously waiting for the two men and the woman to come through it. As the moments dragged by, he grew more anxious, wondering if they had been in time.

When he saw the door swing open, he slid forward on his seat and pushed the door open. The lady stepped into the backseat next to him, a small boy in her arms.

When she was seated, Steve Weston reached out and took the child and drew him to his chest in a tight, lingering embrace. With mist filling his eyes, slightly blurring his vision, he looked down into the face of his son, grateful that he was alive.

Jimmy Weston looked up into his father's eyes and smiled.

TWENTY-SEVEN

November 21, 2033

S heila Harper was jarred from a deep sleep by the insistent ringing of the phone next to her bed. Flipping on the lamp, she glanced at the clock. It was 2:27 A.M. Richard raised up on one elbow, a puzzled look on his face. "Who could be calling at this time of the morning?" he muttered.

Picking up the phone on the third ring, Sheila spoke softly, "Hello."

There was no response, only the sound of someone quietly sobbing.

"Hello, who is this?" Sheila insisted. "Please speak up."

"Sheila . . ." a faint voice whispered.

"Yes, this is Sheila. Who is this?"

"I . . . I'm sorry to bother you. This is Lori Weston."

"Lori, what's wrong?" Sheila exclaimed.

"Sheila, they're trying to kill me," Lori said, her voice quivering with fear.

Bewildered, Sheila asked, "Who's trying to kill you, Lori? Is there someone in the room with you? Do you want me to call the police?"

Sobbing like a frightened child, Lori answered, "They're horrible. . . . They've changed. . . . They're going to take me with them. . . . I don't know what to do."

"Who's going to kill you, Lori?" Sheila persisted.

Silence on the line for a long moment. "Sheila . . . my . . . spirit guides have turned on me. . . . They're trying to kill me. I don't know what's happening. . . . They're taking control of me. . . . I can't fight any longer."

Sheila now knew that she had been thrust into the middle of a furious spiritual battle. Knowing that demon spirits had been Lori's source of power and guidance, she was not surprised that they were now turning on her and revealing their true identity.

In a mortal battle with the very forces she had relied on to guide and protect her, Lori Weston now feared she would not live to see the morning light.

It had all started earlier in the evening. Seeking refuge in her only known source of power, Lori had gone into her meditation room. After more than an hour of deep meditation, her body suddenly quaked in fear when she felt mysterious, invisible hands close tightly around her throat, choking off her air. Clutching at her throat, she fought furiously against the unseen force that was trying to take her life.

Suddenly finding herself being physically thrown across the room by a power beyond her comprehension, she cowered in fear as mystical forms began to materialize in one corner of her meditation room. Horrible, snarling, ugly faces glared at her, their hideous mouths contorted into repulsive sneers.

Rolled into the fetal position, she had watched in morbid terror as a parade of demonic beings moved toward her, their venomous eyes glowing, unblinking, revealing their unadulterated malevolence.

Among them, she recognized her own spirit guide. Appearing as a tall, beautiful angel, bathed in a glow of pure white light, he had stood in front of her quaking body, staring down at her, smiling. But this time, the white glow faded, and the handsome face disappeared, and she watched in horror as he was transformed before her eyes into a dark, ghastly, leering monster, his mocking, shrill laughter filling the room.

Terrified, she tried to escape, but strong, invisible forces held her pinned to the floor. And once again she felt the cold hands of death close around her throat, tightening, choking her life away.

Paralyzed and helpless under the cold hands of the evil presence, she despaired of ever freeing herself from their power. Fearing she would surely die if she ever lost consciousness, she forced herself to resist and fight.

Lori Weston, teacher, medium, channeler, occultist, school counselor, was seeing the dark side of her spiritual friends.

The struggle had gone on for several hours, and gradually Lori lost her will to resist. Sinking deeper into a state of dark unreality, she had struggled free just long enough to crawl to the telephone in the adjoining room. And out of her desperation she had dialed the number of the only person she knew who might understand what was happening to her . . . and could help her.

Her voice low, almost inaudible, Lori begged, "Can you help me, Sheila? . . . Can you help me?"

"God can help you, Lori, . . ." Sheila answered confidently.

The only sound that answered Sheila was the subdued, muffled weeping of a tormented soul striving against the forces of darkness. Waiting patiently, Sheila knew that Lori would have to ask God for help of her own free will. She would have to be willing to renounce her past beliefs and approach God as an unworthy sinner.

"Lori, God's power is stronger than the forces that are trying to destroy you. Do you want God to help you?"

After what seemed an eternity, Lori whispered, "They're all ugly. . . . They used to be so beautiful. They've come to kill me. . . . Help me, Sheila, please help me."

Praying intensely for guidance, Sheila knew that Lori was faced with making a choice. A choice between her allegiance to her spirit beings and a God she knew little about.

"Lori," Sheila answered patiently. "I can't help you. Only Jesus Christ can help you. He's the only one who has power over them. You have to call on Him. You have to renounce your allegiance to your spirit guides and all your beliefs in the occult. Are you willing to do that?"

As if deathly afraid that she would alert the beings in her room who were trying to kill her, Lori held the phone close, cupped her palm around the mouthpiece, and whispered, "Yes."

Realizing what was going on, Richard slipped out of bed and knelt next to Sheila, holding her hand as she continued to talk Lori through the steps that would lead her out of the kingdom of darkness. The next few minutes were critical. It could go either way, and Sheila and Richard knew it.

"Sheila . . . I tried to have my son, Jimmy, put to death. . . . My spirit guides told me to do it. Now I know they were wrong. Sheila . . . will God forgive me for what I tried to do to my child?"

Sheila hesitated a moment, fighting back the hurt this woman had caused her and her family. She bit her lip and silently prayed for God's help.

"Yes," Sheila answered. "God will forgive you."

"Will you ask God to forgive me?" Lori pleaded.

"You must ask Him yourself, Lori. I'll pray with you, but you must ask Him yourself."

"But I don't know how to pray to your God, Sheila. Will you show me how to pray?"

"Yes, I'll show you how to pray."

"Can I get out from under the control of my spirit guides?"

"Yes, Lori, Jesus Christ destroyed the powers of Satan through His death on the cross. The only power Satan has over you is the power you willfully give him. Do you understand?"

Lori's weeping began to subside at the thought that there might be a glimmer of hope that she could be freed from the forces bent on destroying her. Sensing the receding darkness in her room, her thoughts were becoming clearer, more focused.

"Yes, I think I understand. . . ."

With calm assurance in her voice, Sheila moved forward. "Lori, the first step to getting free from those evil forces is to renounce them. That means you're going to turn your back on your beliefs in the occult and make a total and complete break from all spirit beings, including your own spirit guides. Now if you're ready to make that kind of a commitment, I'll lead you in prayer. To make it easy, you can repeat the words after me. Lori, are you ready to renounce those forces?"

"Yes," Lori answered, sounding more calm by the moment.

Sheila then led Lori Weston in a declaration of renunciation of an array of beliefs, including the occult, Earth Spirituality, the worship of Gaia, witchcraft, and many others. There was no hesitation in Lori's voice as she repeated the renunciations of the forces that had been with her since her childhood.

When Sheila was through with the prayer, Lori continued on her own by voluntarily renouncing all of her spirit guides, calling them by name, as if addressing them there in her room. Having revealed themselves for what they were, she was determined to be rid of them forever, with no thought of ever going back under their bondage.

When Lori had finished, Sheila told her, "Lori, there is one very important thing you must understand. . . . There are not *many* ways to God. There is only one way. And that one way is Jesus Christ. Do you understand that you are renouncing all other paths to God and are accepting Christ as the *only* way?"

"Yes, I fully understand that now."

When Sheila asked her if she was ready to accept Christ's work of redemption and accept Him as her personal Lord and Savior, she answered with a firm, "Yes!"

Then Sheila led her in a brief prayer of repentance and commitment of her life to the Christ she had been taught to despise. The prayer only took a few seconds, but the impact on Lori was both immediate and dramatic.

At this point, both women were overcome with emotion. When Lori spoke, Sheila scarcely recognized her voice. It seemed she was talking to a totally different person.

"It . . . seems," Lori said, "as if I've been living in a murky fog, and that I . . . suddenly . . . walked into the bright sunlight. Sheila, I feel that a lifelong, oppressive darkness has been driven from my mind, from my whole being . . . and I'm experiencing a peace I've never known before. I had no idea my mind was so tormented. . . . I think I would have . . . ended my life tonight if I hadn't called you."

Like a weary, spent traveler seeking a place to rest, Lori knew her search had just ended and she was home. Never having doubted the reality of the supernatural world, she comprehended instantly that the power of Christ was indeed greater than all the forces to whom she had dedicated her life. And her first thoughts on this eventful morning were of those whom she had deceived, and how she might reach them with the truth she had found.

By this time Sheila felt she could relax and let her own emotions come through, and she, too, began to softly cry. For several minutes, wordless messages passed between the two women as they were both caught up in the miracle. Not in her wildest dreams could Sheila have ever imagined she would be praying with this woman who had been her bitter enemy. And she could only guess what the dramatic developments in the life of Lori Weston would be in the next few months.

"Lori, you've made a great step forward, but please let me warn you that Satan will be back. He'll not give up so easily. So if you get in a situation you can't handle, please call me, night or day, and I'll help you through it. Please don't try to do it alone."

"I'm not sure what has happened to me, Sheila," Lori said in a calm voice, "but whatever it is, it's what I've been searching for all my life. I know I have some battles ahead and lots to learn, but I feel I've taken the first step on a long journey into understanding. I'm not afraid anymore. . . ."

Falling silent for a long moment, Lori whispered, "Thank you, Sheila. . . . Thank you."

Hearing the line go dead, Sheila slowly lowered her phone to its cradle, stared blankly out into the dimly lit bedroom for a moment, then turned to face her husband, who was still kneeling beside their bed.

Their eyes met, and she slipped to her knees beside him.

TWENTY-EIGHT

A moisture-laden storm, accompanied by bitter cold winds and heavy snow, whipped across the majestic peaks of the Swiss Alps during the night, cascading downward through the narrow passes and washing over the city of Geneva, Switzerland, leaving more than two feet of powdery snow in its frigid wake. At dawn, as sparkling ice crystals glistened magically against a blanket of white in the early morning sun, the city awakened to begin the new day.

After carefully maneuvering the Daimler limousine along the treacherous streets of Global Village, the driver felt a sense of relief when he turned into the safety of the parking garage inside the Unified Communications and Information Authority building.

Pulling up to the small private elevator, he quickly exited the car and opened the back door for his passenger.

Steve Weston reached across the seat and picked up his black leather briefcase, folded his overcoat over his arm, and stepped out of the car. He then walked the few steps to the elevator where a uniformed attendant was holding the door open for him. Stepping inside, he inserted his security key and rode to the thirtieth floor. When the door slid open, he exited and walked the long corridor to a private entrance to suite 3001.

Once inside, he placed his briefcase on the corner of the credenza behind his large walnut desk, then settled into his plush, tufted leather chair. Pressing a button on a control panel on his desk, the thick drapes to his right parted, letting the bright sunlight spill through the glass wall that framed a panoramic view of the New Earth Federation building, the centerpiece of Global Village.

Steve Weston's lifelong dream had come true.

Having been named as Dr. Wallenberg's successor as Director of the Unified Information and Communications Authority, he was now at the pinnacle of power and position in the new global government. Envied by those who were still climbing the social ladder, having been appointed to this new position was not a triumph for him. It was only a bitter aftertaste in his mouth, since he had long ago become disenchanted with the new Social Order.

Several months after his breakup with Lori, he and Jimmy, along with Jimmy's nanny, had been living in a small luxury apartment a short distance from the TV9 building in Dallas when he got a phone call from General Amos Dorian. Dorian informed him that Adam Stenholm had been assassinated and that he, Dorian, had been appointed by the Council of 100 to take his place as head of GU5.

Insisting that he immediately fly to Geneva to see him, Steve had obeyed his summons and had spent three very intensive days with General Dorian in his private quarters inside the GU5 headquarters building. Assuring him that he would be named the new Director of the UICA, Dorian had laid out a list of demands that Steve would have to agree to before he would be allowed to assume the position.

Steve didn't trust Dorian.

Replaying in his mind the conversation the two men had in Templeton, Texas, he now believed that Dorian had, at that moment, been laying plans for Stenholm's assassination and his own rise to power. Although Steve feared and despised Dorian, he knew that in the present world of global power and intrigue, he must not cross him.

Knowing that this new position would allow him to move more effectively against the Federation, Steve had convinced Dorian that he was his friend and confidant. And with their new relationship firmly sealed, Dorian was quite open with him about very confidential matters involving the work of GU5 and of the Federation.

Until that moment, Steve had not fully grasped the totality of control the GU5 exercised throughout the realm. At an intense moment in their conversation, as if to impress him with his total grasp of power, Dorian had laid a top-secret file on the table in front of Steve. In the file was the order issued by Adam Stenholm himself for the elimination of . . . *Steve Weston.*

A cold chill had run down Steve's spine when he saw his name printed in bold letters on the file that contained the order for his own assassination.

Dorian openly told how Stenholm had planned to carry out the execution. Steve would have been ordered to come to Geneva, and on the way, the TV9 plane, with him on board, would have exploded over the Atlantic Ocean.

Confused at that point, Steve had asked why the order had not been carried out. Dorian had laughed uproariously, informing him that before Stenholm could have the assassination order carried out, he and a woman and two of his bodyguards had died in a hail of bullets from automatic weapons fire when he exited his limousine to walk into a private club in Geneva.

Steve now knew with cold certainty that he was living in a world of betrayal and murder, and that he would have to handle his new office, and this man, with unusual care and skill, or he would turn on him just as he had turned on Stenholm. His resolve now hardened, Steve vowed to use his new position to beat men like Dorian, and all the other people who controlled the New Earth Federation, if he had time, and if his luck didn't run out.

Swiveling his chair to the right, Steve touched a button on his desk phone. When his secretary answered, he instructed, "Ms. Albright, I don't wish to be disturbed for a while."

"Yes, Mr. Weston. I'll hold your calls until you notify me," she answered courteously.

Secure in the knowledge that his secretary would not disturb him or allow anyone to come into his office, he began a ritual that he had engaged in dozens of times since becoming the Director of the UICA. He reached to his right and pulled open the top drawer of his desk. Moving his hand to the back of the drawer, his fingers grasped a small metal box. He pulled the box out, laid it on his desk, and closed the drawer.

He then reached across his desk to a black marble pen and pencil set, took out the pen, and unscrewed the top. The pen was the key to the metal box. Placing the key in the lock on the front of the box, he turned it, and the lid popped opened.

There was a small plastic card inside the box.

Steve picked it up, held it in his fingers, and looked at the code printed on it.

Reaching for his computer keyboard, his fingers stroked the keys carefully as he scrupulously typed in the code, checking each entry. After entering the codes, he glanced at the numbers, letters, and symbols on his monitor screen. He felt a sense of exhilaration at knowing that these entries would grant him passage into the digital brain and electronic nervous system of the monstrous computer that lay hidden deep inside The Mountain.

When the full complement of letters, numbers, and symbols had been verified, he pressed ENTER and his monitor screen stormed to life, welcoming him inside the Omega.

Steve knew that the limitless power of the men who sought to rule the world was tied like an umbilical cord to the massive supercomputer housed inside the subterranean fortress known as The Mountain. And if their power over the human race was ever to be broken, it would have to be by destroying their major tool of control.

And the only way to do that would be to invade the sanctity of the Omega and destroy the programs that controlled the Federation's most powerful weapons, the global digital money system, their military forces, transportation, communications, and even the food supply.

Knowing that he must gain access to the Omega if he were going to be effective in thwarting their global plans, he had drawn upon all his cunning and resourcefulness in his negotiations with Dorian, demanding he be given the codes that would allow him unlimited access into the deepest levels of the supercomputer.

Arguing that he must know what he was dealing with if he was going to be able to help him, he had persuaded Dorian that it would be in his own best interests to give him the access codes.

Reluctantly, Dorian had given Steve the small plastic card with the ultrasecret codes—codes that would unlock an electronic back door into the Omega, a back door reserved for the exclusive use of GU5.

There was nothing hidden from him, Dorian had bragged, saying that GU5 was the one agency that reported directly to the one hundred members of the World Council for Security and Cooperation, who, in turn, reported directly to the Principals.

And now, with these codes, Steve could tap into the source of information that was available to only a handful of people in the highest ranks of power. Once inside, he was able to browse, to learn, to develop a broader picture of the plans of the people who were in charge of the Federation.

And he had come to know facts about the Social Order that had shoved him to the brink of a dark abyss, knowing with certainty that he would lose his life if he made a mistake.

His only concern was for the safety of his son. He had to move carefully or he might forfeit Jimmy's life.

Watching the readout of the intensely complicated algorithmic data scramble across his screen, he had the exhilarating feeling that he was a passenger aboard an electronic spaceship traveling at the speed of light into an unknown universe.

Hurtling downward through hidden electronic highways and trails, he crashed through the Omega's impenetrable barricades of infinitely complex coded digital gateways, merging into the fulcrum of a parallel universe made up of mammoth datawalls of the Federation's most cherished and guarded secrets.

Containing vital and sensitive information on the worldwide political, spiritual, and economic system, they were the world's most sophisticated programs, guarded by pathways so secret and enigmatic that they were impossible to enter without the proper assigned codes.

Having penetrated the sophisticated electronic barricade of infinitely complex code-doors, he was, once again, moving with ease and grace through the rooms of data, absorbing the dense concentrations of carefully guarded information that were revealing to him the secrets to the global government's weapons of control over the human race.

Although Steve had been inside this cybernetic world many times since coming to Geneva, he could not shake the uncanny feeling that he had entered the belly of an electronic leviathan.

The word "beast" came to mind.

In fact, it would not have surprised him to have heard the voice of the Beast that lived hidden away inside the sanctorum of The Mountain speak to him, telling him that he knew he was there, chiding him that he knew why he had come.

At times, he wondered if Dr. Mueller was right, that the Omega was, in fact, inhabited by spirit entities.

In his many ventures into this electronic kingdom, a coherent picture of the Federation's elaborate military capabilities had emerged, including its satellite and communications systems, its codes for arming and firing their arsenal of nuclear weapons, and the flow of command in case of a nuclear attack against the political and military leaders of the government.

It also laid out in elaborate detail their military strategy and tactics of retaliation and suppression of the uncooperative, dissident nations and peoples.

And, as if to emphasize the arrogance and cynicism of the ruling class, he had discovered a file that laid out an elaborate scheme to guarantee the survival of those deemed most worthy to live.

Known as the "Priority Lives" file, it contained the names of those who would be protected inside the mountain stronghold in case of a global catastrophe. Listed by social ranking, governmental status, and ability to pay for a Priority Lives status, in the final analysis, it had been decided that some would be allowed to die while those of higher rank would live.

Steve was stunned to learn that General Amos Dorian, as head of GU5, personally controlled the access codes to a program called "Code One," the program that laid out the emergency procedures to be followed in case of a disaster on the outside or the inside of the facility. When activated, Code One would seal the mountain fortress, change the entry codes, and shut out everyone not authorized to enter.

Once Code One was activated, GU5 would have full power and authority to secure the safety of those in the Priority Lives category and determine who would have access to the Most Safe Zones inside The Mountain.

The Most Safe Zones were the final strongholds where those of the highest order of ranking would have access to the last of the emergency food caches, the emergency air supply, water, and escape routes to the outside. Heavily armed guards would be assigned the task of assuring the safety of those in the Priority Lives category.

To his surprise, Steve found that his own name was listed in the Priority Lives file.

But in spite of finding that he was listed in the elite file, he was still driven to bring down the brutal regime. And in order to do that, he knew someone would have to find a way to disrupt or destroy the Omega.

Somehow, someone would have to bore their way into the heart of the electronic beast's operating system and inject an ever-spreading explosive virus—a deadly computer virus that would cause it to crater, destroying its programs, erasing its billions of files, effectively ending its ability to command the human race. If that could be done, their empire of surveillance, psychological dominance, monetary control, and military power would come tumbling down.

Whatever the cost, the Omega must be destroyed, Steve silently vowed.

After scanning several more hidden files inside the Omega, Steve backed out of the program, shut his computer down, and leaned back in his chair.

Often in his quiet contemplative moments, he could almost hear the faint, weak voice of his father-in-law, Dr. Dwight Pennington, telling him the only thing that could save the world would be a divine intervention.

But that was wishful thinking, he told himself. No one would save us; we must save ourselves. And driven by his hatred for the people who controlled the world, he had sworn that he would do everything in his power to stop them, to keep them from advancing the Gaia Project and fulfilling their goal of eliminating seven billion human beings.

Unable to share his thoughts with anyone, at times he feared he might lose touch with reality, and that his dreams of restoring freedom to the world could possibly be only the psychotic delusions of a man who had finally gone over the edge. But, as if to reinforce his belief in his mission, he reminded himself that the dangers were real, and that without some kind of intervention, the human race could very well be headed for extinction.

And at times, strangely, Steve felt it might be possible that some Divine Providence had put him in this place, at this moment in history, for some reason.

But at this moment, inside this elaborate office, at the pinnacle of success and power, Steve Weston was the loneliest man on earth.

Pushing himself up from his chair, he stood and walked slowly to the huge glass wall that faced south, overlooking Global Village. Below, armed soldiers kept a constant vigil, protecting the most prized real estate on the planet.

It was a breathtaking crystalline clear day. The skies were now empty of clouds from horizon to horizon, a deep blue void that seemed to stretch forever.

Drinking in its beauty, he thought of Jimmy. His most painful experience had been when Lori had tried to have their son put to death. Having nearly lost him, Steve made sure that Jimmy stayed behind locked doors in his apartment here in Global Village.

Standing perfectly still, he recast in his mind the pictures of the events of that fateful day. The long-remembered images and emotions came to him in a rush, clear and vivid.

Having dashed out of the house, clutching the address of the Artemis infanticide center in his hand, he had desperately tried to make it in time to stop the deactivation procedure.

Pushing his car to its limits, he had watched the minutes painfully drop away, and knew he wouldn't make it, and that Jimmy would die. With waves of panic rushing through him, black clouds of despair set in, washing away all hope of saving his son.

As he frantically pulled into the Vista Gate shopping center and slammed to a stop near the entrance, he threw the door open and bounded from the car, hurtling himself through the large doorway, pushing his way through the jostling crowd of people.

Near the ice rink, he was roughly stopped by two strong men in business suits. Caught in their firm grip, Steve's eyes fixed on them with an icy, defiant stare. Struggling to loose himself from their strong arms, fear closed in on him like a suffocating blanket.

Spent physically and emotionally, his strength drained from him. In one terrifying instant, his last hope of saving Jimmy was shredded like a cloth under a knife. Breathing heavily, his chest heaved and his heart pounded violently as he thought of what waited for his son.

As he quieted, one of the men whispered to him that they were with GU5 and had been sent by General Dorian. Assuring him that they had people on their way to stop the procedure, Steve's frenzied mind tried to grasp the meaning of what they were telling him.

After the three agents from GU5 had brought Jimmy to him in the waiting car behind the infanticide center, they drove him to the front of the shopping center where his own car was waiting. Knowing he could not take Jimmy back home, Steve secured him temporarily in one of the many enrichment centers in Dallas, instructing them that they were not to release him to anyone but him. He then drove to his home in Windsor.

When he arrived at home, Lori was there. After telling her that the procedure had been stopped and that Jimmy was alive, she went into an uncontrollable rage. Showing no traces of remorse, she insisted that her actions were justified.

When she began screaming at him, it was, strangely, as if he couldn't hear her. Even when he looked at her, it was as if he couldn't see her. The incident took something out of him, leaving him cold and empty inside, as if his emotions had suddenly shut down, leaving him without feeling.

In a daze, without answering her, or even acknowledging her presence, he had turned away from her, packed a small suitcase, and walked out the door and out of her life. He had neither seen nor heard from her since that day.

Determined that his son would always be safe, they lived quietly in his luxury apartment; just the two of them, along with Jimmy's nanny. Steve's life now centered around his son. And under his watchful eye and the guidance of his nanny, a matronly lady of sixty, Jimmy had grown and flourished in an atmosphere of love and security.

Watching a flurry of small snowflakes fall gently, silently, against the tinted glass wall, he thought about the puzzling rumors he had heard about Lori. Rumors that she had embraced Christianity and was now a member of the despised sect known as the Offenders. But knowing her temperament, he could only conclude that she had finally snapped. He knew it was coming. *How sad*, he thought.

And Audrey Montaigne, beautiful, exciting, unpredictable Audrey. He had toyed with the idea of developing their relationship after he had nullified his domestic arrangement with Lori.

But Audrey had changed.

Shortly after their experience at Templeton, she had become a radical devotee of the World Leader, convinced that he was god, and that he was leading humankind into godhood. She was now traveling among his entourage throughout the world, reporting on his activities for TV9.

Hearing the door open, Steve turned to see his secretary, Midge Albright, enter the room. *Unusual*, he thought. *She always knocks before coming in.*

A strange look on her face, she stammered, "Mr. Weston, your former wife is here to see you."

TWENTY-NINE

Mr. Weston, your former wife is here to see you. The words hit Steve like a hard blow. A swirl of questions and emotions coursed through him. At a loss for words, he hesitated, his confusion written all over his face.

"Lori . . . is here?" he asked, trying to hide his surprise.

"Yes, sir," Ms. Albright answered. "She's in the outer office. She says she needs to see you."

Steve's immediate reaction was anger, bordering on rage. Suddenly, the pent-up hostility toward Lori that he had kept bottled up on the inside for these many months was spilling over again, stirring up old memories and ancient nightmares.

In an effort to quell his surging emotions, he slowly walked to the glass wall. His face grim, he stared out at the bright sun reflecting off the snow-covered streets. With thoughts of the past surging through him like a flood, he felt the old, stale bitterness, still there, buried deep, lingering within him like a fever.

For several moments he stood at the window. Then, slowly, his emotions changed, letting the dark thoughts vanish like a vapor. And what he now felt was curiosity. Curiosity about Lori. And why she had come.

He exhaled heavily. "Yes, I'll see her, Ms. Albright. Send her in."

Ms. Albright turned and quickly walked out of his office, closing the door behind her.

Moving from the glass wall, Steve walked toward the door just as Lori opened it and walked through. Stopping in his tracks, he stared at her.

Her dark, lustrous hair was pulled back and tied with a small ribbon, emphasizing the exquisite features of her face. Wearing a stylish midnight blue dress that accentuated her slender figure, a single strand of pearls lay seductively against her white blouse. Stunningly beautiful, his eyes traced her form from head to toe. His nostrils caught the scent of her perfume.

"Lori, what are you doing here?" he blurted.

"Thank you for seeing me, Steve," she answered softly, almost apologetically. "I . . . I must talk to you."

Still trying to recover from the shock of seeing her, Steve motioned her toward a sitting area with a couch and two leather chairs. When she sat down on the edge of the chair, Steve settled back into the couch, still surprised to see her.

For a few moments, neither of them spoke. Her eyes cast down, Lori nervously smoothed her skirt across her legs with the palms of her hand. Her hand was trembling slightly.

His mind racing with a thousand questions and his emotions running the gamut from curiosity to dread, Steve remained silent and waited.

Her eyes looking down at her hands now resting on her lap, Lori whispered faintly, "Steve, I've come to ask for your forgiveness."

Her words hit him like a jolt of raw electricity. In his wildest dreams, he would never have believed that Lori would have uttered such a statement. It was totally out of character for her. And now that she had offered it, he was left without a response.

Leaning forward in his chair, his voice betraying his confusion, Steve stammered, "I . . . I don't understand, Lori."

It was only then that he saw the tears Lori was trying desperately to hide from him.

Her voice choking with emotion, she replied, "For . . . Jimmy. For what I attempted to do to our son."

A disbelieving look crossed Steve's face, his mind suddenly whipped into a chaos of confusion and uncertainty.

They exchanged unreadable glances.

Unpleasant images, vivid and unforgettable, played at the fringes of his memory, the old bitterness welling up anew. *How dare this woman come into my office like this and even discuss my son!* he thought to himself, sharp resentment lancing through him. *If she only knew what she has done to Jimmy and me. She's the person who has carved this void in both our lives. And now she's asking me to give her absolution.*

He was suddenly caught in a numbing daze as anger, bitterness, and deep resentment mingled together inside him. He searched for the sharp words he had rehearsed in his mind a thousand times over. Words he had promised himself to say to her if he ever had the opportunity. Words that would express his hurt at what she had done. But now that she sat only inches away from him, the words would not come.

Steve stared at Lori, more confused than angry. She was someone entirely *different* from the person he had been with only months ago. There was a softness, a tranquility about her that he had never seen.

Then suddenly, inexplicably, all the pent-up anger seemed to flow out of him like the air escaping from a child's balloon. For in his wildest dreams, he would never have imagined that the woman he had known as his wife could be capable of such an act of contrition.

Regaining his composure, he leaned forward and asked gently, "What happened, Lori? Please tell me. I must know."

Her eyes cast down, her voice filled with emotion, Lori recounted in sharp detail the last hours and moments that drove her to take their son to an infanticide center with the sure purpose of having him put to death. Her eyes were brimming with tears. Droplets coursed down her cheeks, impossible to hide.

When she had finished describing the incident, her voice trailed off and she fell silent, nervously clutching her purse as if it were her sure anchor in an uncertain storm. When she finally looked up, she saw that Steve had his face turned away from her, struggling to hold back his own tears.

Seeing how badly she had hurt him, Lori moved to the couch and sat down next to him, then reached out and touched his hand.

"I'm so sorry, Steve," she whispered.

"Why, Lori? Why did you—" He couldn't finish the sentence.

For the next hour they talked in low tones, saying things they were never able to say before, opening old wounds and hurts that had finally destroyed their relationship.

And for the first time, Lori was able to take Steve along the twisting, perilous paths of her own dark, tortured past, divulging in morbid detail her life-and-death struggles with the tormenting demons that had eventually driven her to attempt to commit the unspeakable crime.

Fighting back the tears, she described in graphic word pictures the events of the horrifying night her spirit guides had viciously turned on her, wanting to kill her, and of her call to Sheila Harper, and the prayer that had brought her freedom.

She asked about Jimmy. Steve told her about his schooling, his nanny, and how he was growing. Her face lit up.

Intrigued by Lori's openness and honesty, Steve listened in fascination as she told him of her new faith and her changed life. Not sparing her own feelings, she candidly revealed the details of the hardships and suffering that her friends were going through because of their Christian beliefs.

And in answer to his probing questions about the people who were feeling the brunt of the condemnation and wrath of the Social Order, she reluctantly shared her own fears, telling him that many of her own group in Dallas had been arrested and imprisoned for their beliefs.

Becoming quite emotional, she related how untold numbers of Christian believers had been put to death, and that countless thousands, having felt the hot breath of the wrath of the Social Order, had fled and were in hiding in the remote areas of the country.

Steve could sense her searching his face for understanding, compassion.

The room fell silent for a few moments, then Steve said, "I haven't seen you for months, Lori. Why did you choose to come at this particular time?"

With urgency in her voice, Lori explained, "I . . . had to come . . . to talk to you . . . to tell you what has happened in my life. I couldn't escape the feeling that I didn't have much time left."

Shaken by her statement, Steve quickly asked, "Are you ill? Is that why you've come?"

Placing her hand on his, Lori smiled and replied, "No, I'm fine. I . . . just feel that my time on earth is short."

"*Why*, Lori? Why do you say that?"

Lori looked deeply into Steve's eyes. "I don't know if I will be arrested and put to death, or—"

"Or what, Lori?"

"Or if Jesus Christ will come back to the earth," she said with unfeigned sincerity.

"How did you come to believe this, Lori?"

With a gentleness about her that Steve had never known, Lori explained, "The Holy Scriptures contain prophecies about the end-times. And since the time when Christ was on the earth, His follow-ers have believed that He would return as a conqueror to engage in a final battle against Satan. In each succeeding generation, believers have nourished the hope that perhaps they would be alive when He returned."

"Do you know when this . . . *return* might take place?"

"No one knows. But preceding His return, there will be an unusual phenomenon that will defy explanation."

"What phenomenon?"

"Many people will suddenly disappear from the earth. We call it the 'catching away' of the believers."

"I don't understand, Lori."

"I wish I could explain it to you, but I've only been a believer for a short time."

"Well, can you tell me the purpose of this 'catching away,' as you call it?"

"According to what I've been taught, a very powerful man is going to lead the world to the brink of destruction. But Jesus Christ will remove His followers from the earth before it happens. He will then return to the earth to personally conquer that powerful leader and his armies."

"Do they call him the Antichrist?"

"Why, yes. That's what he's called," Lori answered.

Steve rose to his feet and walked a few steps to his right, and paused. Thoughtfully, he asked, "Do you believe that the World Leader is this Antichrist?"

"I don't know, Steve. Some in our group believe that he could be, but none of them are sure."

Steve looked away for a moment, as if in deep thought. "Your father spoke of those things, Lori. He said that he feared the entire human race would be annihilated without some kind of divine intervention. He said that a friend had told him that unless Christ came back to rescue mankind, no flesh would be saved. I . . . think he believed it."

Sitting back down, he took Lori's hand in his, stroking it softly. "When . . . is this going to happen?"

"I don't know. No one does."

When he started to respond, a chime on the interoffice phone sounded. He rose from the couch, stepped to his desk, and pressed a button. Ms. Albright reminded him of an appointment he had.

Steve told her to tell the gentleman to wait a few minutes. When he turned to face Lori, she was standing, clutching her purse.

"Thank you for seeing me, Steve," Lori said. She then walked to him, kissed him lightly on the cheek, and turned and walked toward the door.

Steve stood frozen in his tracks, unable to move or make a sound, wanting desperately to call out to her and ask her to stay. But the words wouldn't come out.

Halfway across the room, she stopped and turned, and looked back at him. Steve's heart seemed to skip a beat, hoping she was going to come back to him. He had already decided that if she took a step toward him, he would rush to her, embrace her, and tell her he still loved her. He would then take her to see her son.

But as Lori opened her mouth to speak, a blinding shaft of light suddenly burst through the ceiling, filling his office with an unbelievable, penetrating brightness. As brilliant as noonday, the shaft of light reflected and refracted a thousand times over until it flooded the room with all the force of a new dawn, separating them and totally enveloping Lori inside its transcendent glow.

Stunned, the blinding light threw him backward, causing him to crumble to the floor. Shielding his eyes with his hands, he stared at Lori in openmouthed wonder. For in the space of time it took him to blink his eyes, Lori was suddenly changed, transfigured, into the most beautiful creature he had ever seen.

Although the event went against the patterns of nature, defying the very flow of reality, Steve watched in awe as Lori stood before him transformed. Now radiant. Angelic, yet not an angel. It was Lori, he reasoned, yet this person he was staring at now was more perfect than anything he had ever seen.

She was without blemish, without a flaw, as if the molecules of her body had suddenly been altered, miraculously translating her into this celestial, heavenly being before him. She was now perfection, chaste, pure, as if her outer physical essence had been changed by the hand of God and her eternal spirit being had emerged, cut loose from the bonds of the earth.

Instantly clothed in a glistening, shimmering, intricately designed white garment, his eyes followed her as she was carried upward in the very center of the light. Passing before his eyes in vivid detail, his perception of the event seemed to be magnified a hundredfold.

Steve stared with unblinking eyes, enthralled, a rush of feeling sweeping over him that was beyond his comprehension.

"So beautiful," he whispered. "So very beautiful."

With everything now passing before him in graphic slow motion, his eyes were drawn suddenly to Lori's empty clothes hanging suspended in midair where she had stood only an instant before, still forming the shape of her trim body, then drifting slowly downward and landing softly in a neat bundle against the carpeted floor.

Awed by the sights surrounding him, Steve gazed intently up at Lori, watching her ascend as she was drawn by some invisible hand, being carried upward inside the very center of the beam of dazzling light that surrounded and held her.

Trying desperately to fathom the full meaning of this sublime transformation, he watched in unfeigned wonder, suddenly feeling a touch of sorrow that he had not been taken away with her.

Drawn toward her, he stood and took a faltering step forward, reaching up imploringly to her as she ascended, calling out her name.

"Lori . . ."

In response to his voice, Lori looked back down at him and smiled, then turned her face away, looking upward, seeing things that his mortal eyes could not see. Her sight now focused away from him, her hands uplifted, she rose upward, upward.

Transfixed, Steve could only stare at this magnificent creature as she was transported out of his sight.

Then suddenly she was gone, in the twinkling of an eye, and the room was dark and empty.

Lori was gone. And the light was gone. In an instant of time.

Looking around the darkened, empty room, his first reaction was one of disillusionment, suddenly fearing that her appearance had only been a holographic image.

Confused, he rubbed his eyes, trying to reason his way out of something he couldn't comprehend.

Perhaps, he thought, Lori had never been there at all. Conceivably, some of his enemies could have staged it all in an effort to try to drive him over the edge, to cause him to lose his sanity.

Shaking his head as if to dislodge the alien thoughts, he glanced down at the floor.

What he saw startled him.

No, it was no illusion. For there on the floor in front of him was the dark blue dress, the white blouse, the strand of pearls that had been around her neck, and the small purse that she had clutched nervously all the time they were talking.

With a sudden, overwhelming sense of loss, he knelt down and took her white blouse in his hand and brought it slowly up to his face. Still fresh with the beguiling fragrance of her favorite perfume, the scent of her threw him headlong into an emotional storm. His body trembled as he held the soft cloth against his face, now knowing that he still loved her, wanted her, needed her.

But she was gone. Caught away in the vortex of a mystifying event, leaving him.

With an overpowering feeling of regret that he had not been granted the time to know this new person Lori had become, he stared out into the empty room, hoping she might return.

But she was not there.

Slowly realizing that Lori was gone forever and there was nothing he could do to bring her back, Steve felt a crushing loneliness.

He was alone. . . .

So very much alone.

Out of his grief and disappointment, he pounded the carpet with his fists, crying out into the empty room that if God existed, as Lori had claimed, why then had He brought her back to him, only to take her away?

THIRTY

Slowly rising from his knees, still clutching tightly to Lori's white blouse, Steve was startled by the piercing sound of a woman's terrified scream resounding loudly from one of the nearby offices. The scream was followed by a rising tide of excited voices just outside his door.

As he took a step toward the door to investigate, the door flew open and Midge Albright cried out, "Mr. Weston, something terrible has happened." The woman was trembling with fear.

Following her out of his office into the hallway, he was met by a scene of total bedlam. Many of the employees of TV9 were weeping hysterically while others cowered in the corners of their office or hid under their desks curled into the fetal position.

Steve discovered that at the moment of Lori's disappearance, many of the people who worked in the TV9 building had also suddenly disappeared, their clothes still lying inert at the feet of the frightened and the curious who were trying to wring some sense out of this unexplainable phenomenon.

Knowing there was nothing he could do, Steve returned to his office, closed the door, and paced the room, trying to get a tight grip on his emotions. With a flood of unresolved questions in his mind demanding answers, he desperately tried to comprehend the inexplicable event.

If only Lori could have had more time to explain, he reasoned to himself.

Caught in the riptides of confusion and helplessness, his chastened mind could find no solid answers to the mystifying drama that had suddenly taken on biblical dimensions.

Returning to his desk, he touched a button on his console and brought up TV9 on one of the large wallscreens. The TV9 logo and the words "Special Report" were emblazoned across the length of the screen.

As the logo faded into the background, a newsanchor appeared. Unsmiling, obviously nervous, he began haltingly, "We . . . are receiving reports from around the world that an unusual event has occurred. It seems . . . that thousands, perhaps millions, of people have mysteriously disappeared. They seem to have been caught up in some kind of confluence of psychic powers."

Someone handed the newsanchor a single sheet of paper. He scanned it briefly, then looked back into the camera. "Some are saying that an alignment of the planets, precipitated by a galactic synchronization was the psychic trigger that caused the event. They argue that a breakthrough in humanity's evolution to a higher collective Planetary Consciousness has occurred, moving the human species a step closer to godhood. Others admit that there is no rational, scientific explanation. But this much we do know: whatever the explanation, a massive number of people have suddenly disappeared, vanished from the face of the earth."

With a grim set to his jaw, Steve leaned back in his chair and watched the parade of reporters from around the world excitedly try to describe what had happened in their respective cities.

The details were the same.

Without warning, people had suddenly disappeared, and the fallout from the disappearances had been devastating.

Planes had flown off their courses and crashed.

Freeways were choked with traffic as vehicles careened out of control, their drivers suddenly gone.

Members of families had suddenly been snatched away, leaving their loved ones frightened and bewildered.

Steve watched in utter fascination at the stunned looks on the people's faces. Nothing like this had ever occurred on earth—they had nothing to compare it to. With the number of missing persons increasing exponentially, the people feared for their own safety.

With the mounting hysteria throughout the world nearing critical mass, Steve feared that the world could be on the brink of a total psychic meltdown.

Fifteen minutes into the special report, the newsanchor ventured an explanation. "Some are calling it the 'vanishing,' or 'rapture,' as taught by the Christian sect known as the Offenders. But various reputable theologians have assured us that this is nonsense. Even though they do not have an immediate explanation, they say that one will be forthcoming."

Reaching to his right, the newsanchor took a sheet of paper handed to him by the floor director. Scanning it quickly, he told the viewers, "Here's a special bulletin. The World Leader will be in the Great Hall of Unity in twenty minutes for a statement. The bulletin assures us that he will have a full explanation for the phenomenon."

Steve immediately called Ms. Albright, instructing her to have his car downstairs in three minutes. He then rushed out of his office, took the elevator down to the parking garage, walked to the limo, and told his driver to take him to the Great Hall.

Upon arriving, he went immediately to the TV9 booth overlooking the main floor of the hall. The usually animated people in the booth were quiet and subdued, not understanding what had happened, and wondering what the Secretary General of the Federation would tell them.

Steve stepped to the anchor's desk and chatted with the man and woman who would cover the Secretary General's speech. He then walked to the glass wall and stared out at the twenty-four hundred members of the Congress of the People who had been in session when the event occurred.

Glancing upward, he saw that the balconies were quickly filling with thousands of people, anxious to hear what the Secretary General of the Federation would have to say.

The people in the hall talked in whispers.

When two uniformed men opened the massive doors at the rear of the platform, the people in the Great Hall of Unity instinctively stood to their feet, waiting in breathless silence.

After several anxious minutes had passed, a solitary figure emerged from a side room, strolled purposefully into the hallway, and walked slowly down the red carpet to the platform. Dressed in his flowing white robe and white sandals, the World Leader confidently climbed the stairs and moved to center stage.

Standing motionless for a few moments, his hypnotic gaze bore like laser beams out at the people of the world who were staring at his sharply defined 3-D image displayed on millions of viewscreens in every part of the earth.

The hall was electrified by his presence.

Assured that all eyes were upon him, he motioned for the audience inside the Great Hall of Unity to be seated.

They obeyed instantly.

Making eye contact with the center television camera, the man on stage abruptly thrust his arms upward, the sleeves of his white robe flowing downward from his arms.

"Peoples of the world," he shouted, his voice rising like thunder, piercing the quietness of the vast chamber. "What you have witnessed is *The Removal!*"

The Hall remained deathly quiet.

"The Removal is the work of Gaia, our Mother."

The silence deepened.

"The world has just witnessed a magnificent display of Her awesome power. In Her wrath, Gaia has caused the removal of significant numbers of the creatures of the Negative Mass. They are gone. While they were allowed to live on this planet, their collective negative consciousness held back humankind's evolutionary leap forward to godhood."

His words explaining the meaning of the event sent a sense of collective relief throughout the Great Hall, reassuring the assembled people that Gaia was still in charge of the affairs of humanity. His words were smooth, assuring, inciting the people to leap to their feet as one, yelling out their raucous approval of the World Leader.

"Citizens of the earth!" the speaker exclaimed, looking sternly into the eye of the TV9 camera positioned in the center of the Great Hall. "Be warned that this is only Gaia's *first* act of removal of those who are mentally and spiritually defective. The Masters tell us that the earth still groans under the curse of the *inferior species*. As *subhumans*, they too have built up a mass of negative karma and must be dealt with. We must hurry them to their next karmic destination. In their present incarnation, they are the enemies of Gaia."

As if on cue, the people stood to their feet and began the chant, "Gaia . . . Gaia . . . Gaia . . ."

The chant lasted six minutes.

Lowering his voice to a whisper, the white-robed man on center stage warned, "*Christianity* is the one great curse, the one enormous and innermost perversion, the one immortal blemish on humankind. I call on you to destroy the very image of the Christian god in your minds. And to those of you who have not embraced the spirituality of the earth, you must now bow your knee to Gaia, the Earth, your Mother. All those who refuse to bow to Gaia will be removed."

Shaking with emotion, his clenched fists raised high above his head, he cried aloud, "People of the earth! Gaia is your *God!* Gaia is your *Mother!* Bow your knee to *Gaia!*"

At those words, pandemonium broke out in the Great Hall. The people leaped from their seats, shouting their words of adoration for the World Leader. Hundreds crumbled to their knees, so overcome in their frenzied adoration of the man on stage that they were unable to stand.

Declaring that his extraordinary spiritual powers made him worthy of their veneration, they wildly pledged their lives and their undying loyalty to him.

And at that moment, they were bound together as one by their divine reverence for the person of the World Leader.

Glancing up at one of the large wallscreens, Steve thought he saw the flash of a faint smile cross the man's face.

Having heard enough, he turned and walked out of the TV9 booth, boarded the elevator, and retraced his steps back to his waiting car.

THIRTY-ONE

Steve Weston walked through the revolving doors into the sparsely furnished reception area of the Bedford Geriatric Center in Baltimore, Maryland. After signing in, he was given a number and told to wait. Fifteen minutes later, a nurse, dressed in her starched and pressed whites, approached him. A powerful young woman with fleshy arms and solid legs, she flashed him a smile and motioned for him to follow her.

Stepping in behind the nurse, Steve followed her through the busy hallway, shutting out the low murmur of voices coming from the crowded rooms as they weaved their way through the slow, shuffling patients, the darting gurneys, and the somber medical personnel.

They passed several large wards, crowded with the sick and elderly. Coming to Ward 33, they stepped through a set of steel double doors and went to the thirteenth bed on the right.

As the nurse left, she called over her shoulder, "You have twenty minutes."

Steve moved slowly to the side of the narrow bed—one of thirty in the crowded room—then reached up and pulled the isolation curtain around the bed, hoping for at least a small amount of privacy.

Pausing, he looked down into the sleeping face of his old friend, Dr. Dwight Pennington, Lori's father. The old man opened his eyes and looked sleepily up at Steve. When he recognized him, he reached out a trembling hand.

Steve moved closer to the bed and grasped his friend's hand in both of his own in a gesture of deep affection. He then bent over and whispered, "How are you, sir?"

A slight smile ran across the deep folds in the old man's weathered face. "Steve . . . Steve, how good to see you. I didn't know if I would live long enough to see you again. Oh, thank you for coming. You're the only one I've got left, you know."

"Yes, I know, sir. As I told you in my e-mail, Lori and Jimmy were taken away . . . in the Removal. But I wanted to come in person and talk to you . . . and tell you that I was with Lori when she was . . . *caught away*. I thought you would want to know."

The old man's eyes brightened. "Tell me what happened."

Steve glanced away a moment, squeezing back the tears. "It . . . was the most beautiful thing I've ever seen in my life, Dr. Pennington. It happened so fast. One moment she was standing in front of me in my office in Geneva. We were talking. And the next moment the room was filled with a dazzling light . . . and her entire body was *changed*. I don't have the words to describe the sublime nature of the event to you, sir. She looked at me . . . then she was *gone.*"

Their eyes met, held.

After a long moment, Dr. Pennington looked away, soft tears rolling silently out of the corners of his eyes, following the lines and creases in his face in their downward movement. His voice so soft it could barely be heard, he said, "Martha went, too, you know."

"No, I didn't know. Then you saw—"

A faraway look in his eyes, Dr. Pennington explained, "No, Martha was in another part of the house when it happened. I was in my chair in my den at the time. When I saw the news bulletin on TV9 about the sudden, mysterious disappearances, I knew Martha would be gone."

With a trace of a smile, he added, "I asked my nurse to look for her, but I knew she wouldn't be there."

The two men remained silent, an unspoken understanding taking shape between them, binding them together. Words didn't seem necessary. Silently, they shared something that allowed them to see beyond death, something that gave meaning to life, and answered questions about evil, pain, and suffering.

Steve wanted to gather the old man up in his arms and flee with him from this charnel house that was slowly draining his life away.

Reining in his emotions, Steve asked, "How long will it be before they take you back to your home?"

A cloud seemed to pass over the old man's face. "Oh, you don't know, do you?"

"Know what, sir?"

"That . . . I'll undergo the *procedure* in two days."

A dreadful silence passed between the two men.

Steve's face reflected his shock. "No . . ." he answered softly, incredulity creeping into his voice. "No, I didn't know. But why—"

His sharp, old eyes squinting up at Steve, he answered, "It's rather simple, really. You see, they tell me that my allotment of medical-care benefits will run out in two more days. After that I won't even be eligible for pain medication. I'm on a minimum dose now. So to save everybody a lot of trouble and money, they simply kill off us old and unproductive folks. They'll just give me a shot, and it'll be over in moments. After that, they'll vaporize my body. It'll almost be like I never existed."

Dr. Pennington smiled up at Steve, his rough features wrinkling. "Maybe it's time for me to get out of the way anyway."

Steve looked off for a moment, fighting back the tears. The astonishment and emotion apparent in his voice, he whispered, "I'm sorry, sir."

"Don't be, Steve," the old man answered, his voice calm and reassuring. "Don't weep for me. Weep for yourself, and for all the people of the earth."

A nurse stepped around the curtain and picked up a small tray holding a pitcher of water and a plastic cup. Steve waited for her to leave before he spoke.

"Sir, what's going to happen? To the world, to the human race—"

Dr. Pennington pressed a button and his bed slowly rose up, allowing him to assume a sitting position. Steve helped him rearrange his pillows.

When he was settled, he said, "Well, after that amazing event that the World Leader has named 'The Removal,' and before I came here,

I spent most of my time studying the biblical prophecies. My friend, Dr. Sam Nicholson, gave me some very informative books before he died that helped me understand the event and to get a pretty good picture of what's going on."

Becoming more animated, he added, "In fact, it's rather exciting to sit here day after day and watch your TV9 reporters give us a running account of the events. It's as if I know what's going to take place even before it happens. The way I see it, this disappearance of millions of people was a sort of trigger that set some very remarkable things in motion."

Steve sat down on the edge of the bed, careful not to disturb his friend, listening intently.

Lowering his voice to a whisper, Dr. Pennington made a startling statement. "Steve, I'm now firmly convinced that the Secretary General of the New Earth Federation is indeed this person that's described in the biblical prophecies as the Antichrist."

Steve looked around nervously.

"As you know, I'm a logical, well-organized man, and things have to fall into place before I come to a firm conclusion about anything. And the things that have happened since this man has come to power are just too darn close to what the prophecies say for me to come to any other conclusion."

With a twinkle in his eye, like a child who had just discovered a secret, the old man said, "Yep, he's the one. I'm sure of it."

Intrigued, Steve prompted gently, "If . . . he's this Antichrist, as you say, then what's likely to happen next?"

Turning somber, Dr. Pennington said, "That's the sad part, son. It looks like the world is in for some pretty rough times. According to what I've been reading, we're probably already into the first part of what the prophecies call 'The Great Tribulation.'"

"What's that?" Steve asked.

The old man's chin now trembling, he spoke through his tears. "I'm glad . . . that Martha, and Lori, and Jimmy are not here. I wouldn't want them to go through what's ahead for the human race."

Bringing his emotions under control, he continued. "Sam told me that the Great Tribulation would be a time of divine judgment. But, you know, as I read the descriptions of the catastrophes that are to come to the earth, I had the strange feeling that mankind was bringing most of these things on himself."

"What do you mean?"

"Well, as I explained to you, I'm no theologian, or prophecy expert, but I can read, and I have a pretty good mind. Let me show you some of the things that are prophesied, and see if you don't agree with me. As I said, from what I can see, mankind is going to bring this upon himself. In their insanity to 'save the earth' by eliminating masses of excess human beings, they're going to destroy the ecosystem and drive the human species to the brink of extinction. And that's why there has to be a divine intervention."

Reaching for a well-worn, leather-bound notebook on the table beside him, Dr. Pennington said, "Here are some notes that I've made from my discussions with Dr. Nicholson and from what I've read in the books he left me."

Thumbing through the notebook, he stopped at a well-worn page and slowly ran his finger down to a notation. "Here's a description of something that's supposed to happen during the Tribulation. It's written in a book called Second Peter. It really intrigued me. Here's what it says: 'The heavens shall pass away with a great noise, and the elements shall melt with fervent heat, the earth also and the works that are therein shall be burned up.'"

"Not a pretty picture, sir," Steve commented.

"Dr. Nicholson, who was also a Greek scholar, explained to me that the word 'elements' comes from a Greek word that describes the atom, and that the Greek word for 'great noise' describes a sound that would be like rushing wind and roaring flames."

Without looking up, the old man softly repeated the gut-wrenching words, "Great noise . . . fervent heat . . . elements burning up . . ."

"My god, that's a description of the TR6," Steve said slowly, gravely.

Looking up, Dr. Pennington squinted and asked, "What did you say?"

"The TR6, sir," Steve said, his face grim. "A new development in nuclear warfare that generates enormous heat energy, beyond anything the world has ever known. And what you read sounds like an accurate description of the detonation of the TR6."

"So an ancient holy man," Dr. Pennington replied thoughtfully, "thousands of years before we discovered the atom, or developed nuclear weapons, described in exact detail the intense heat and atmospheric trauma that could only come from a nuclear blast."

Steve's face tightened. Recalling the frightening scene over Camden, Texas, he answered softly, "Yes. I've seen its power and destruction."

His fingers turning the pages of his notebook, Dr. Pennington searched for a certain page. Finding it, he told Steve, "Now here's something that has really captured my attention. Bear in mind that this was written thousands of years ago, but what it says could only be possible with our modern computer technology."

Curious, Steve asked, "What did you find, sir?"

"Let me read it, and you tell me what it means," the old professor said, with a lilting note to his voice. "'And he causeth all, both small and great, rich and poor, free and bond, to receive a mark in their right hand or in their foreheads: And that no man might buy or sell, save he that had the mark or the name of the beast, or the number of his name.'"

Their eyes met. "That's a description of the Seal of Gaia, Dr. Pennington," Steve said. "They've designated two places where the subcutaneous computer chip must be inserted into the body. In the hand or in the forehead."

"Do you see this notebook, Steve?" Dr. Pennington asked intently, his hand lying pressed against its well-worn leather cover. "This book is full of notes I've made in my study of the biblical prophecies. And I've learned that the Great Tribulation is a time of wars, ecological disasters, environmental upheavals, enormous air pollution, nuclear explosions, worldwide famines, and epidemics that will cause the deaths of untold millions of people." Looking up, he added, "I . . . think it has already begun."

Steve stared at him. "How do you know that all of this is true?" he asked respectfully.

Dr. Pennington paused. Then in low tones, he said, "Let me give you some things to watch for . . . some things in the future. According to the prophecies, a crisis in the Middle East will trigger the Antichrist's intervention, militarily and politically. He will eventually sign a peace treaty with Israel, guaranteeing her safety. Watch for that to shape up. You see, Steve, events are moving us toward one enormous, cataclysmic event."

Steve hesitated, then asked, "What event?"

"The Antichrist will break his covenant with Israel; then his global armies will invade the tiny nation, seeking to destroy it in one final battle. And he would be successful, except for one very important thing."

Steve frowned. "One thing?" he asked.

"At that point, the prophecies say, Jesus Christ will return to the earth and do battle with the Antichrist at a place in Israel called *Megiddo* . . . or *Armageddon,* as some say. If the prophecies are true, the carnage will be beyond human comprehension."

Steve's eyes darkened. "But . . . why must it happen, sir?"

Dr. Pennington took a sip of water. "There's only one answer, Steve," he explained. "The World Leader, the Antichrist, is driven by Satan, perhaps, *possessed* by Satan. And it's the desire of Satan to wipe out the human species."

"Will . . . Satan be successful?"

The old man smiled. "The Antichrist and his armies will find themselves fighting against God. And they will lose. They will—"

Before Dr. Pennington could finish the sentence, a nurse touched Steve on the shoulder and smiled. "I'm sorry, sir, but your time is up, and you must leave."

Steve started to protest.

"I'm sorry, sir. But those are the rules. Please follow me."

Steve stood, reached out and took his old friend's hand, gripping it firmly in his own. "I'm sorry, sir, but they say I must leave now. Do you want me to come back and be with you when—"

With a toss of his hand, the old man cut him off in midsentence. "When they kill me? No, son, I've made my peace with God. I know where I'm going." His voice calm, he smiled and added, "Besides, I'm looking forward to seeing my grandson again."

Steve touched his shoulder. "I hate to leave you alone, sir . . ."

Tears filled the old man's eyes. "Don't take the Seal, Steve, whatever you do."

Steve paused. "I—"

His face somber, Dr. Pennington insisted, "Those who take the Seal of Gaia will be doomed. It's a religious pledge of loyalty to the Antichrist. Don't take it. Promise me."

"You have my word, sir," Steve promised.

As Steve turned to leave, Dr. Pennington touched his arm. "Steve, I want to give you something."

Reaching to the table beside his small bed, he lifted the leather notebook, brushed it lightly, and said, "In these pages are my notes about a quest I began many years ago. And that quest finally led me to the answers I've searched for all my life."

Handing him the priceless treasure, he added, "And, son, if you will let it, it will help lead you to the truth. And the truth is all that matters. I've written about things I've come to believe about God, Jesus Christ, and especially what I believe is going to happen on the earth during the Great Tribulation."

His gaze firm and piercing, the old man said, "These are my conclusions, but they're all based on the biblical prophecies. Read it and let the words guide you through the horrendous days that lay ahead for you . . . and the human race."

Reluctantly Steve took the book from the old man's trembling hands. Caressing it gently, he said, "I'll read it, sir, with an open mind. And thank you."

Steve patted his friend's shoulder lightly, then turned and followed the nurse through the door, clutching tightly to the treasured book.

His private jet was waiting at the airport.

THIRTY-TWO

Steve Weston strolled casually into the penumbral comfort of his spacious den in his luxury apartment on the twenty-first floor of one of the most fashionable apartment buildings inside the Global Village compound, only a few blocks from the UICA building. Standing for a moment in front of the large fireplace, he gazed deeply into the bright, shimmering flames. Edging closer, he opened his hands to catch its soothing warmth. The room was quiet . . . and lonely.

Moving to his oversized, tufted easy chair, he sat down heavily, stretched out his legs, and sank back hard into its softness. Sighing deeply, his brow wrinkled into a frown, his weariness and deep fatigue mirrored in his face. With faint shafts of light angling through the partially drawn drapes, casting the room in soft shadow, he was mercifully wrapped in a welcome silence, deep and hushed.

Outside of this fragile sanctuary, the world seethed in a cauldron of war, famine, and disease. His lips drawn into a tight line, he wrestled with the dark realization that the violence had moved closer to him. Struggling against a gnawing fear he could feel growing inside him, his rushing thoughts were fueled by the memory of the three assassination attempts that had been made on his life within the last six months.

His eyes darkened as frightening images of the latest attempt on his life exploded in his brain in holographic reality. It had happened only three days ago. The emotional impact from his latest brush with death, the graphic memory of the sights and sounds, the smell of the gunpowder, and the pulsating emotions that hammered at him were all bound together to form a lasting tapestry of terror.

Unconsciously, Steve reached up and touched the bandage that covered the small gash over his right eye. It was his only mark from the dreadful incident that had taken the life of his personal bodyguard and left his driver badly wounded.

He knew he was still a marked man.

Amid a hail of bullets from automatic weapons fire, his bodyguard had shoved him violently through the open door into the bulletproof passenger compartment of the Daimler limousine, saving his life. Slamming the door shut, sealing Steve inside, the brave man died beside the car, his body riddled by the deadly fire.

Steve had caught only a fleeting glance of the three assassins before his wounded driver sped away, crashing through two cars that were blocking the street in his desperate bid for the safety of his passenger. Although the three assassins were dressed in black, with black ski masks pulled down over their faces, Steve was sure that he recognized the boldness and cold professionalism of GU5.

He had no proof, but there was no doubt in his own mind that General Amos Dorian, Director of GU5, was behind the attempt. Steve knew that Dorian, and possibly the World Leader, feared him because of his celebrity status and his influence over the people of the world. But if he were assassinated, he told himself, they would blame it on dissident forces, absolving themselves of any guilt in the matter.

Steve had started wearing his shoulder holster and carrying his Omni 444 with him everywhere he went. The deadly handgun lay beside him on the table next to his chair, a silent confirmation of his fear and distrust of the leaders of the Social Order.

He remained quiet and motionless in the semidarkness of the room as vivid images of the events of the past few months swept through his mind with horrific clarity.

Powers beyond his comprehension seemed to be in control of his life, defining and directing his very existence. The puzzling twists and turns that had buffeted him now frightened and confused him. And at the moment, his world seemed to be spiraling out of control, dragging him down into an endless, spinning void.

With a glint of sadness in his eyes, he took measure of things past and present, coming face-to-face with the dark specter of his own sharp fears and desperation.

Since the death of Dr. Dwight Pennington, his father-in-law and dearest friend, he had been left alone, and there was now no one to turn to in moments like this. Recalling the shared memories they had forged in their quality time together, Steve found himself facing dilemmas and uncertainties that he was not equipped to handle without his friend's wise advice and counsel.

Now that both Lori and Jimmy were gone, taken in the Removal, followed by Dr. Pennington's death, he felt a constant, chilling void inside him.

He sighed heavily, reflectively, remembering.

In the aftermath of the chaos that had racked the planet following the Removal, the New Earth Federation moved to tighten its grip on the peoples of the world. With freedoms once enjoyed by millions now only jaded memories, most of the population of the earth lived their daily lives in perpetual fear of the Earth Forces, the terrorist arm of the Global Peace Forces.

As a savage reign of terror settled over the earth like a diabolical shroud, people throughout the world who were suspected of any crime against the Social Order, no matter how small, were quickly arrested and imprisoned or executed by the dreaded Earth Forces. With grim regularity, massive numbers of people throughout the world who were guilty of the crime of nonconformity were seized and forcibly taken from their apartments and homes, usually under the cover of night.

Millions simply disappeared, never to be seen again, swallowed up inside the stifling cloak of oppression that had settled over the earth.

Steve rubbed his temples with the tips of his fingers.

In an attempt to divert his mind from the dark thoughts, he reached to his right to the control panel and pressed a button that brought up TV9 on the large, three-dimensional television screen in front of him. He glanced up at the screen to see a woman's smiling face.

It was Audrey Montaigne.

He hadn't spoken to her in months.

Steve turned up the volume as she said, ". . . and in just a few moments, the Secretary General of the New Earth Federation will speak to the peoples of the world on an urgent matter."

With Audrey's vivid image filling the screen in front of him, Steve relaxed into his chair and eagerly traced the attractive features of her face with his attentive gaze. She was seated at the large news-anchor's desk in the main TV9 broadcast studio in the TV9 building in the UICA compound.

Her large green eyes were looking directly at him, holding him.

Without taking his eyes off her, Steve reached for the diet drink on the table next to his chair. Taking a sip of the semisweet liquid, he watched as she smiled into the camera and said, "Ladies and gentlemen, His Majesty, the World Leader."

The Secretary General was standing in his private studio in his residence at his large estate a few miles outside of Geneva. Dressed in his luxurious white robe and sandals, his face was framed tightly by the TV9 camera.

Remaining ominously still for a long moment, the World Leader waited, gazing steadily, hypnotically into the camera. His large, dark eyes were cold and frightening, utterly without boundary. His baleful stare was so penetratingly intense that Steve felt a sharp chill course through his body.

With words both soft and coaxing, the Secretary General of the New Earth Federation intoned sincerely, "Citizens of the world . . . We face perilous times. Gaia, our Mother, is angry with us. . . . Much of this planet lies in smoldering ruins. . . . Millions of people have been removed from the earth . . . by war . . . by the spread of deadly viruses . . . by disease, and by famine."

He made a sweeping, flowing gesture with his arms.

His voice rising slightly in intensity, he declared, "I warned you in the past. I now warn you again . . . Gaia is going to pour out even more of Her wrath upon us. . . . Her anger is stirred against us."

Steve glared contemptuously into the face on his screen, the face of the man who had brought untold misery to the world. He had heard it all before. Even as he spoke, the world was still helplessly floundering in a sea of confusion and fear over the phenomenon of millions of Christian believers who had mysteriously disappeared during what had come to be known as the Removal.

Firmly convinced by this man that the Removal had been brought about through his own spiritual power, the masses lived in mortal fear of him. That fear, carefully cultivated, gave him almost unlimited power over the human race.

Steve stared into the World Leader's face, listening intently, trying to unravel the mystery of his power over the human mind. He watched his hands moving with fluidity, his long, slender fingers punctuating his words. His bearing was straight, commanding. His force of personality unexplainable, irresistible. His power over people was beyond anything Steve had ever witnessed before.

His voice and demeanor suddenly changing, a dark rage seemed to surge through the features of the World Leader. Raising his voice to a high pitch, he declared in a shrill, crazed tone, "Only those who have the Seal of Gaia in their bodies will be saved from Gaia's wrath . . . and only those who pledge their loyalty and worship to Gaia, our Mother, will be worthy to receive the Seal of Gaia."

His eyes flashing in hot anger, his arms flailing wildly, the World Leader snapped sharply, his voice harsh and impatient, "Those who do not have the Seal of Gaia hidden within their body are not worthy to participate in the Social Order. They will not be allowed to move within our economic system or to consume our limited resources. They will not be allowed to either buy or sell."

Raising his right arm slowly, the robed figure pressed his finger against the center of his forehead. "It is Her Mark . . . . Her Mark of Unity with all things. . . . It is the Seal of Gaia I carry in my body, here at the point of the Third Eye."

Dramatically holding his hands outstretched toward the TV9 cameras, his palms turned upward, he lowered his voice to a whisper. "Through the sacrament of the breaking of the skin, you will enter into a Sacred Blood Covenant with Gaia . . . with the Earth . . . with *me!*"

Steve shook his head in disgust. He had heard it all before.

The final phase of the campaign to have everyone on earth submit to having the subcutaneous biochip implanted in their body had been in full swing for months. Millions had already had the biochip injected into their hand or forehead. And in an organized campaign to persuade the peoples of the world to willingly submit to being reduced to a computer number, the airwaves crackled nightly with an unrelenting barrage of carefully scripted propaganda.

While the world reeled under his brutal regime like a mortally wounded man, the World Leader dominated the TV screens throughout the world, telling the masses that he was the only one who could save the human race. Dressed in his flowing white robe and white sandals, his hands outstretched imploringly, his dark, piercing eyes staring balefully into the cameras, he boldly promised the terrified masses that he would bring peace to the world if they would follow him.

Dazed and confused, and tottering on the brink of a collective mental breakdown, the world was drawn to the mystic figure, mesmerized by his message of world peace and his promise of safety. Confounded by the unusual manifestations of his dark spiritual powers, masses of people of every tribe and tongue throughout the world embraced him as their only hope of salvation and safety.

Responding to his commands, they rushed to enter into the sacred covenant between themselves and the World Leader by receiving the Seal of Gaia. In an act of blind devotion, their flesh was cut and the subcutaneous computer biochip was inserted under their skin. Believing the words of the World Leader, they were convinced that this new sacrament would save their lives and protect them from the wrath of the angry Earth Goddess.

Steve glanced back at the face of the ranting figure on his television screen. By now the man had lost control of himself and was flailing his arms wildly, screaming into the cameras, cajoling and threatening his audience, looking like a man possessed.

Steve shuddered.

Not willing to listen any further, he reached to the control panel and clicked off the set, then stared for a long moment into the darkened screen, wondering.

With the room now quiet, he pushed himself up from his chair and walked aimlessly to the large bank of windows overlooking the main boulevard in Global Village. Drawing back the heavy drapes, he stared out, once again trying to deal with the crushing realities of the global order, trying to find the elusive answers to the cryptic puzzle that had remained hidden from him.

Glancing down below, his eyes followed the colorful lines of the sun's rays playing on the ice and snow in the trees. The sparkling scene reminded him of his boyhood and the times that he and his friends would escape from their warm rooms to spend splendid hours in the magical coldness.

Standing perfectly still in the solitude and heavy loneliness of his apartment, he began to put together the seemingly disconnected parts of their plan for control of the human race. Like a child connecting the dots to a puzzle that formed a picture, he drew mental lines that connected the fragmented, disparate pieces of their hidden strategy.

And slowly, a frightening picture of their monumental deception began to emerge, forming a recognizable pattern in his mind.

The key to their grand scheme of total control, he reasoned, depended upon their ability to compel every person on earth to submit to having a tiny programmable subcutaneous biometric computer chip injected under the skin somewhere in their body.

Each person's Personal Identification Code would be programmed into the chip, taking the place of all other forms of identification. Containing all their vital data, from the cradle to the grave, the chip could be quickly and easily scanned to furnish accurate readouts for the authorities.

Steve sighed heavily. Mentally visualizing its massive tentacles connecting it to the four corners of the earth through its fiber optics, satellites, landlines, laser beams, and cables, he knew that the Omega system was their key to total control.

Relaxing his mind a moment, he watched the people on the sidewalks below him scurrying through the brisk wind and light snow flurries that had started. From a logistical point, he wondered, how would they be able to get the cooperation of the billions of people on earth to have the chip implanted?

With sudden clarity, he concluded that the actual physical experience of having the skin penetrated and the chip injected into the body was being sold to the people as a religious sacrament. It was being touted as a mystical act, holding the same spiritual significance that circumcision held for the Jews and that water baptism held for the Christians. That's what the World Leader had skillfully suggested in his speech. He had made the act a part of the Gaian religion.

Steve let all the pieces sift through his mind slowly until the full picture became clear and sharp. The act of breaking the skin and injecting the computer chip into the body, according to the World Leader, constituted the mystical Seal of Gaia. Those who refused to submit to their numbering system would have no place to hide, no way to survive. Receiving the Seal of Gaia in their bodies would be the people's only means of salvation, safety, and life.

Steve's jaw tightened. *It's a brilliant scheme,* he mused.

The spokesman for the Principals had skillfully divided the world between those who would submit to them by taking the Seal of Gaia and those who would refuse. And in order to save their lives, the masses would willingly give up their own personhood and become human data in the mammoth Omega system.

Those who refused would be branded as enemies to Gaia and would be systematically destroyed, giving the Federation the moral right to commit whatever human atrocity they deemed necessary.

And then it hit him.

With this final step in their global conspiracy, the Principals will achieve total control over the human race.

Steve took a long breath and slowly let it out. Questions clawed at his mind, intrusive and demanding. Although he had considered the entire process of having the skin broken and the chip injected into the body to be only a ploy to coerce the peoples of the world to willingly submit to being numbered like so much human data, he was having second thoughts.

He was no longer certain that the act didn't carry a more sinister intent, too dreadful to imagine. As much as he wanted to reject the idea, he had to consider the stark possibility that the act of receiving the Seal of Gaia did indeed hold some darker, more evil, supernatural implications.

Perhaps it is a pact with Satan, he thought.

Regardless, there was one thing he knew for sure: the Seal of Gaia was a monstrous lie hiding within an evil and deadly deception. But he had to admit, it was the most cleverly conceived and executed deception in the history of humankind.

Steve rubbed his face vigorously with his hands, trying to frame his thoughts. The authorities were already demanding that he also "cooperate" by submitting to having the biochip injected into his own body. And they wanted him to do it publicly, before the eye of the TV9 cameras. It would be the ultimate test of his loyalty to the Social Order, to Gaia, and to the World Leader.

When that time came, what would he do? How would he react? Shaking his head in disgust, the very thought of the act nauseated him.

Swallowing down his fear, his forehead furrowed into a deep frown as the questions pressed in on him. Like a man groping through the darkness, he couldn't find his way. Questions flooded his mind, but the answers fled away like elusive shadows.

Would the Principals order their armies to strike a final, decisive blow against the forces who had not bowed the knee to them? Would they justify their prosecution of that apocalyptical battle on the grounds that it was to save the earth? And would that battle be part of their overall strategy for reducing the world's population, as laid out in the Gaia Project?

Perhaps the Christians are right, he mused. *Maybe their Holy Scriptures do indeed tell the truth about one final, all-encompassing battle that will occur someday in the tiny land of Israel. And that Christ will suddenly appear at that final battle.*

And could it be that the nations of the world, at this moment, were lining up behind the World Leader to follow him into a battle against God Himself?

He felt a strange sense of dread welling up inside, vague and indefinable.

With the unrelenting questions scratching away at his brain, Steve suddenly felt he had been caught in the violent downdraft of an inescapable fate that was propelling him headlong into the center of a swirling maelstrom of unspeakable evil. It was as if a strong hand had clutched him tightly and had slammed him down on the floor of a giant, ancient stadium where he was watching two combatants of supernatural proportions square off for a fight to the death.

The prize was the human race.

With the World Leader's hypnotic power to mesmerize the peoples of the world, Steve had no doubt that they would blindly follow him to their own death.

His weariness dragging at him like heavy chains, he relaxed back into his chair, took a deep steadying breath, let the air out slowly, closed his eyes, and went still. Letting the memory of the reassuring tones of Dr. Pennington's sometimes gruff voice play in his fevered mind, he could almost hear the old man telling him that if he wanted to survive he must stare down his own doubts and uncertainties and cast off the debilitating fears.

His situation was grim, and he knew he might forfeit his own life if he pursued his quest to expose the evil intent of the oppressive regime that the world chafed under. But events had already engaged and had spun out of his control, denying him the option of turning back.

Time crept by. Outside, the night descended like a silent white shroud.

Returning to the wall of floor-to-ceiling windows, he looked through the light flurry of snow that was falling across the Global Village landscape.

He stood motionless for several minutes, his eyes staring out into the soft shadows. Threatening visions of what might occur in the future swept feverishly through his mind in swift disarray, forcing him to confront what part was truth and what was a lie. He told himself that he must prevail over his own fears, or they would destroy him. He blocked out what he could of the confusion and uncertainties, quieting what he could of the fear.

Drawing on every ounce of the fragile reserve of strength remaining to him, at length, he pushed back the confusing images and raging thoughts that collided inside his mind.

His only alternative was madness.

Then a strange thought imposed itself upon Steve's mind. He regarded it seriously for a moment. If it were true, it would change everything. It would answer his most haunting questions about whether there was a purpose, a reason for it all.

His arms folded loosely across his chest, he silently pondered the implications of the sweeping question.

Could it be, he asked himself, *that at this single point in time, he—Steve Weston—was witnessing the dramatic unfolding of the ancient biblical prophets' predictions of the endtimes?*

Steve took a deep, cleansing breath. Letting it out slowly, he felt a penetrating relief wash over him, calming his inner turmoil.

And suddenly, he was no longer afraid.

His mind now relaxed, his eyes reflected his fierce resolve.

THIRTY-THREE

It was now past midnight and Steve was bone tired. Feeling drowsy, he stretched himself and decided to go to bed. Having finished his drink, he set the glass down on the table next to his chair, stood to his feet, and started wearily toward the bedroom. Stopping suddenly, he glanced toward the front door, listening. He thought he heard a faint knock.

Strange, he thought to himself. The security people always announced guests before they were allowed on his floor.

Quelling his initial reaction to go for his handgun hidden away inside the drawer of the table next to his chair in his den, he moved cautiously toward the door. With the world in turmoil, even Global Village had become an armed camp.

Curious, he glanced up at the small viewscreen above the door.

It was Audrey.

Steve quickly opened the door. Hesitating, he stared at her, speechless.

"Aren't you going to invite me in?" she asked.

Regaining his composure, he smiled. "Audrey . . . please . . . come in. I was just surprised to see you," he stammered, motioning for her to come in.

When she stepped inside the room, Steve slowly closed the door and turned to face her. She was wearing the same dress she had on earlier in the day when she hosted the TV9 telecast of the Secretary General's speech. Even though her hair was slightly rumpled, she was stunningly beautiful.

In a choked whisper, she said, "I'm so frightened, Steve."

Having said that, the tears came in a rush. Unable to handle the storm of emotion that hit her, she could no longer hold the tears back, couldn't slow them down. With her eyes tightly closed, in her next sobbing breath, she felt herself being gathered to Steve's strong chest, his arms gently enfolding her. He didn't ask why she was crying, or ask her to stop. He just held her tightly, letting her cry against his shoulder.

As her sobbing subsided, Steve relaxed his embrace, placed his hand under her chin, and raised her face to his.

"Want to talk about it?"

She gave a tiny nod.

"Let's go into the den. I'll fix us a brandy."

She nodded again, even managed a weak smile.

Audrey moved to the couch and sat down while Steve poured two brandies, handing her one of the long-stemmed crystal glasses. She gratefully accepted it into her trembling hand. Holding it between her fingers for a moment, she raised the glass to her lips and sipped slowly.

Steve gazed at her thoughtfully, wondering why she had come. After a long silence had passed between them, he ventured, "What are you afraid of, Audrey?"

She looked up at him, her eyes still reflecting her inner tension. "I think I'm in over my head, Steve."

"What do you mean?"

"I . . . I know too many things. I can't handle it anymore. They—"

Without finishing the sentence, she reached in her pocket for a tissue. Blotting her eyes, she waited for the trembling inside her to still.

"I have to trust you, Steve," she confessed nervously. "I have no one else to turn to."

"I want you to trust me, Audrey."

"As you know, I've been traveling in the Secretary General's party."

"I'm aware of that."

"Well, I've been horribly deceived."

"What do you mean?"

"I thought he was . . . *God*. But—"

Steve waited.

"I thought he was an Avatar who had come back to earth to show us the way. But . . . he is . . . *evil*."

More than you know, Steve thought to himself.

Her lips settling into an angry frown, Audrey added contemptuously, "He's not what he seems. There are others who control him. I don't know who they are, but they're extremely powerful people. He does what they tell him to do."

The Principals. The words burned through Steve's mind.

Steve's expression tightened. "How did you learn these things?"

"I spent a lot of time with him, and he talked freely with me. I think he trusted me."

"Did you sleep with him?"

Shaking her head slowly, she answered honestly, "No. I would have, but he didn't seem interested. I'm glad it never happened."

"What else did you learn?"

Audrey paused meaningfully before continuing. "They have some kind of horrible plan for the world. I don't know what it is, but I know I can no longer be a part of it." She looked into Steve's eyes and her voice suddenly hardened. "They've got to be stopped, Steve. They've got to be stopped."

Steve pushed himself up from the couch and walked to the window. He had not expected anything like this from Audrey. Staring aimlessly across Global Village, he played host to an array of doubts and questions about her and her story. A thousand fleeting, troubling thoughts ran through his mind, chased by a thousand strong, conflicting emotions.

Was she telling him the truth? Or was she there, in fact, as an agent for the World Leader, and GU5, and the Principals, to test his loyalty, to entrap him? Was she just a frightened woman, as she appeared, looking for a way out of a situation that could cause her to lose her life? Or was she there on a mission to expose him and his plans to try to sabotage their program for world dominion?

And because they knew how he felt about her, he reasoned, it would be the perfect ploy to send her.

His emotions running wild, he turned and stared at her, desperately wanting to believe her, wanting to trust her. But if he decided to trust her and confide in her, and she betrayed him, it would surely cost him his life. If he chose not to trust her, and she was indeed looking for help, he would leave her with no place to go, and no way out. Should he go with his instincts and feelings for her? Or should he protect himself and turn her away?

In the end, he decided to trust her. He could make no other choice.

Once the decision was made, they began to talk in earnest, their words coming quickly and easily, blending together to form a soft, delicate rhythm. She told him of her experiences while traveling with the World Leader, and her private conversations with him, and of her fears about him and his plans for the world.

He told her about the things he had learned and what had happened in his life since they were last together. About Lori's visit, and her disappearance before his eyes, and about his son, Jimmy. And about his long visits with Dr. Pennington and his intriguing stories about the prophecies.

In quiet tones, he told her about the Gaia Project, about the KavLife Institute in Texas, about Camden, and how it was destroyed by the TR6 device. And about his forays into the Omega, and what he had learned there.

Steve's eyes narrowed slightly. He paused. "I think they know that my loyalty is not with them," he confessed for the first time to anyone.

There was a sudden stillness, a hush.

Her eyes searching his, she asked, "Are you in danger, Steve?"

Steve shook his head slowly, his face gray with uncertainty. "We're both in mortal danger," he answered somberly.

"Because they suspect that you're not loyal to them?"

He paused deliberately. "I think so. They're pressuring me to receive the Seal of Gaia publicly. With my endorsement, they feel that the process will go more smoothly."

"Are you going to do it?"

"No," he answered emphatically. "But I don't know how much longer I can hold them at bay. The World Leader himself has taken a personal interest in seeing that I go through the religious ceremony of having their hallowed computer chip injected into my body, live on TV9."

"Is it a test of your loyalty and devotion to the World Leader? Is that why they're pressuring you?" Audrey asked.

Steve paused a moment, thinking about his answer and how much he should tell her. "That's part of it," he said, taking a deep breath. "But it'll also give them a sure way to follow my movements." He sighed heavily and rubbed his hands together. "With the biochip in me, they'll be able to track me wherever I go. After all, that's the purpose of it, despite what they say. It's not about religion, or saving the earth. It's about surveillance, control. Total control of the human race."

"Tell me what to do, Steve," Audrey said pleadingly.

"Have you taken the Seal?"

"No, I haven't."

"Don't do it. Don't take the Seal of Gaia, Audrey."

"Tell me why."

Steve's brow furrowed and he answered softly, "I'm not sure myself. But there are those who believe that anyone who submits to receiving the Seal of Gaia in their bodies will be sealing their eternal doom."

"Do you believe that?"

"I don't know. I wish I did know, but I don't. Dr. Pennington believed it."

"Oh, Steve, what are we going to do?"

Sitting relaxed on the soft carpet in the den, leaning back against the oversized couch, their bodies pressed tightly together, they gazed lazily into the rippling, playful flames in the large, open fireplace. Carefully cherishing the moments of silence that passed between them in this small break in the flow of time, they felt that, for a while at least, all the world had gone away and they were the only two people on the earth.

Draining every drop of life out of each passing moment, like two lost souls who had found each other in a threatening storm, they opened their hearts to each other, talking endlessly through the night, devouring their time together, time that had come to them as a rare and unexpected gift.

Suddenly, Steve felt like a whole person again. And in the flush of that magical moment, he knew that he did indeed love this remarkable woman who lay trustingly in his arms.

"I love you, Audrey Montaigne," Steve whispered.

Audrey smiled up at him. "And I've been in love with you, Steve Weston, since that morning in Geneva when you knocked on my door at the hotel. I knew then that you loved me. I could see it in your eyes."

"I don't want you to ever leave me again," Steve said softly, gently.

Several minutes of silence passed.

"What will happen to us, Steve?"

Steve drew a deep breath, let it out slowly. "We'll have to flee from the wrath of the World Leader and the Federation. We'll have to go into hiding."

"But where can we go?"

Steve sank deep into thought. "We'll have to go underground," he told her after a long pause. "It'll be difficult for both of us, but that's our only hope. I have no doubt that they'll be coming for me, and for you. No one who defies them will be allowed to live."

"I'm so scared, Steve."

Drawing her near, he said, "I know. I wish I could promise you that everything was going to turn out all right, but you know I can't."

"I understand. But just having you near is all the comfort I need."

Feeling Audrey near him suddenly triggered in him an instinctive urge for survival, a need to live. With a firmness in his voice, he told her, "There are people scattered throughout the world who are fighting against the evil of the Federation and the World Leader. We'll turn to them. Maybe they'll help us."

"Do you know who these people are?"

"I've been laying plans for this eventuality for many months now. I've been making inquiries and have made a few contacts. And I believe we can pull it off. It'll be difficult, but if we keep our wits about us, we have a good chance of surviving."

"What do you want me to do?" Audrey asked.

"Keep up your regular schedule, as if nothing has changed. Pack a small bag and keep it hidden away in a convenient place. Don't do anything to draw attention to yourself. If they think you're planning on making a run for it, they'll arrest you immediately."

His tone growing more serious, Steve warned, "Our chances are slim, Audrey. I must be honest with you. Under normal circumstances it would be difficult, but because both of us are so well known, the task will be nearly impossible."

For a long moment the two faced each other in silence, uncertainty hovering like a cloud.

"Do . . . you still want to go with me?" Steve asked haltingly.

Her face reflecting her gentle determination, Audrey whispered in return, "Yes. Whatever happens, I just want us to be together."

Standing to his feet, Steve walked to the fireplace and leaned his arm against the mantel, suddenly feeling the added weight of his commitment to Audrey. Turning to face her, he thoughtfully said, "Audrey . . . I'll have an escape plan laid out for us very soon."

Her eyes reflecting her trust, she asked, "When?"

"Be ready to go at a moment's notice. And, Audrey, be careful. Don't talk to anyone. I'm sure GU5 has us both under constant surveillance."

Audrey stood and joined Steve at the fireplace. Without another word passing between them, they were drawn together by an irresistible force. After a long and lingering kiss, they melted into each other's arms in a tight, passionate embrace, knowing that together they could face whatever life might have in store for them.

As the morning light of the new day began to seep in around the edges of the thick drapes, they cherished their borrowed time together, choosing to not think about what the future might hold. At least for this moment in time, the world outside their door had ceased to exist. And there was no danger, no fear. There was only the two of them, together, the filling of mutual need.

Tomorrow would bring what it would. But for now, this small scrap of time belonged to them.

THIRTY-FOUR

Steve glanced casually at the digital clock in front of him on his large desk in his office on the thirtieth floor of the UICA building in Global Village. The midmorning newscast was scheduled to begin in about two minutes. When he pressed the button marked "TV9" on his communications console, he glanced absentmindedly at wallscreen number three to his left, making a mental note that a nature film was playing. *Something about a dolphin,* he thought.

Caught in a tortuous web of intrigue, for the past several days he and Audrey had been meticulously laying out their plans to drop out of sight and escape to another country where they could hide from the wrath of the Federation. Knowing that their chances of escaping from the far-reaching hand of the World Leader, and GU5, would be a formidable task, they had no assurance that they would be successful. But they had both agreed it was a risk worth taking.

With their exit plan nearly completed, it would be a matter of timing, and luck.

Having no other choice, Steve was forced to trust a number of people, most of whom he didn't know. And if any one of them betrayed him, he and Audrey would pay with their lives. But with the world tottering on the brink of global disaster, they had no choice. They must join and fight, along with the millions of others who were opposing the Federation and its oppressive and brutal reign.

When more than fifteen minutes had passed and the nature film was still playing, Steve was slightly puzzled. After checking to see that he had the proper channel tuned in, he punched the number for the master control room located in the TV9 building a few blocks away. Perhaps, he reasoned, there was some kind of technical glitch.

The private connection rang a phone on the desk of Dr. Joseph Greider, Chief of Operations for TV9. Dr. Greider answered on the third ring.

"Dr. Greider, this is Steve Weston."

"Yes, Mr. Weston. I'm sure you're calling about the TV9 signal."

"Indeed I am. What's going on?"

"We don't know, sir. Somehow we've lost control of the satellite signal. Something has blocked out our own signals. Nothing we send is making it to the satellite. We have no knowledge of the origin of the TV signal showing the film."

Steve hesitated. "That's impossible."

"I know, sir. Our engineers are working frantically on the problem, but so far they've come up empty-handed."

Exasperated, Steve sighed. "Thank you, Dr. Greider. Please keep working on the problem, and let me know when you find out what's happened."

"I will, Mr. Weston."

A puzzled look on his face, Steve turned his attention back to the work in front of him. Almost an hour had passed when a faint chime sounded on his communications console, breaking his concentration. Grudgingly he glanced up from his work, reached to his right, and pressed a small button. "Yes, Midge, what is it?"

"Mr. Weston, Dr. Wallenberg is here to see you."

Startled by the announcement, Steve hesitated a moment, trying to recall whether he had forgotten about an appointment to see him. Not sure, he instructed his secretary to send him in. He then rose from his chair and moved toward the door to greet his visitor.

As the door slid open, the tall gentleman walked through, a grave expression on his face. Following close behind was Dr. Bernard Mueller.

"I'm here on a matter of the highest urgency," Dr. Wallenberg announced abruptly. Without breaking his stride, he walked directly to the sitting area near the glass wall. Deferring to his friend and mentor, Steve followed. Mueller walked a few steps behind them.

Once settled in the large chair across from the couch, Dr. Wallenberg sighed and spoke crisply. "Steven, what we have to say must be kept in the strictest confidence. If this got out to the public, it could cause global panic. I'm here because I trust you and because we need your immediate assistance."

Dr. Wallenberg shifted forward in his chair, his features tightening. "Dr. Mueller came to me with a story that would be unbelievable if I did not have the utmost confidence in him. I'm going to ask him to explain the situation to you; then we'll discuss your part in the matter."

Steve glanced at Dr. Mueller. A very nervous man by nature, the small, unkempt scientist seemed to be particularly distraught, his eyes darting about in undisguised apprehension. Clearing his throat nervously, he slid to the edge of his chair, peering cautiously at Steve through his thick glasses.

"The Omega," Mueller whispered in his raspy voice.

"The Omega?" Steve responded, looking at him with a blank stare.

Almost reverently, Mueller whispered, "The Omega possesses *consciousness.*"

"Consciousness. . . ?" Steve shot back, the astonishment apparent in his voice. "What do you mean by consciousness?"

"Yes, it's true, whether you believe me or not," Mueller insisted, narrowing his eyes in subtle warning. "The Omega is thinking its own thoughts, making its own decisions. It's out of control."

Steve was growing impatient. "Out of control?" he stormed. "What are you talking about, Mueller?"

Riverlets of perspiration now coursing down the sides of his small, round face, Mueller seemed to be a man on the verge of losing control of his surging emotions. "Yes, Mr. Weston. The Omega . . . is out of control." His eyes fixed on Steve with laserlike intensity, the frightened man muttered, almost incoherently, "The Omega is going to wipe out every living human being on earth. The massive computer has executed a doomsday scenario."

Astonishment reflected in his eyes, Steve asked warily, "And . . . just what is the 'doomsday scenario,' Mueller?"

"The Maylay virus . . . " Mueller answered softly, his shifting eyes betraying his unspoken fear.

"The Maylay—" Steve couldn't finish the sentence.

For long seconds, the three men stared at each other, unmoving, stunned by the thought of the sudden extinction of the human race. The finality of it all hung over their heads like a gleaming, threatening sword, freezing each man in an unspoken dread.

Steve blinked in disbelief, turned to Dr. Wallenberg. "Sir, is this true?"

The old man seemed to shrink back momentarily, sighing deeply. His eyes fixed in a catatonic stare, he rubbed his forehead and said slowly, "It's the Gaia Project gone dreadfully awry."

Cold fear rushed through Steve at the mention of the Gaia Project, its horrendous details ever fresh in his mind.

A moment of ominous silence.

Shoving back his fear, Dr. Wallenberg looked at Steve, his gaze steady and firm. "For the past two years," he explained, "our scientists have been secretly synthesizing huge amounts of a powerful strain of the Maylay virus in laboratories across the world. As part of the Gaia Project, it was being used as a viral weapon to expedite the reduction of the world's population. Despite many warnings, they thought they could control the spread of the virus."

"What happened. . . ?" Steve asked, frowning.

Grim-faced, Dr. Wallenberg replied, "Something has gone horribly wrong. The original goal of the Gaia Project was to reduce the world's population, in a managed program, down to no more than *two billion* people." There was a brief, heavy silence. Wallenberg cleared his throat nervously. "But when the Omega processed the most recent statistical input, for some unknown reason, it came to the conclusion, on its own, that the population of the world had reached critical mass, and that the ecosystem was about to totally implode."

Steve looked at Dr. Wallenberg, his eyes fixed on him in a haunting stare. For the first time he saw him as an old man, suddenly looking frail and tired.

The old man continued speaking, his voice hard and bitter. "In their frenzy to implement the mandates of the Gaia Project, our political leaders, scientists, and military people ordered the arming of hundreds of intercontinental ballistic missiles containing the Maylay virus. Those missiles have already been deployed around the world and are ready to be launched. As we sit here, the Omega has taken total control and is in a countdown mode to fire *all of them* on an unsuspecting world."

Shaking his head dejectedly, he added, "Of course, in all their dark intent, none of them took into consideration the possibility that the Omega might wrest control out of their hands."

Haunted by this dark knowledge, Wallenberg's hand trembled as he quietly fought the mounting fear and despair. Shaking his head slowly from side to side, he took several deep breaths to steady himself, then continued. "The Omega has already made the decision that the only way to save the earth is to take drastic measures and launch the missiles containing the Maylay virus in sufficient quantities to wipe out the human species altogether."

Closing his eyes momentarily against the disturbing revelations, Steve feared that they were all at the mercy of forces and events beyond their control—forces that were propelling them forward with a frightening certainty.

"What you must understand, Mr. Weston," Mueller broke in, fear smoldering inside him, coloring his tone, "is that the Maylay virus is in a class all its own. Its power is staggering."

Steve clenched his jaw. "How powerful is . . . the Maylay, Mueller?" he quickly asked.

With burning eyes fastened on Steve's face, Mueller answered chillingly, "How powerful, Weston? I'll tell you how powerful the Maylay virus is. It would take less than a thimbleful, disbursed by the wind, to infect and kill every living human being in a city the size of London or New York."

Letting the dark thought settle in his mind, Steve remained silent.

"You see, Weston," Mueller stammered, "just twenty-four strategically placed biobombs could wipe out the entire population of the United States in only six days."

His soft voice cutting through the quiet that had settled over the room, Dr. Wallenberg interjected, "Steven, if the Omega launches those missiles, the human race will cease to exist."

A long, dark silence fell on the room, the fear thick and impenetrable.

Steve stared aimlessly into space for a long moment, then looked at Mueller. His voice almost a whisper, he asked soberly, "Does the Federation have sufficient amounts of the Maylay virus . . . to *kill every person on earth?*"

Mueller leaned forward, his face burning with intensity, his words tumbling out of his mouth. "Yes! As Dr. Wallenberg told you, we've been manufacturing and stockpiling the virus for over two years. There's enough of the virus on hand to kill every man, woman, and child on earth many times over."

Steve slumped back into his chair, shot a dark look at Mueller.

Shaking his head solemnly, Mueller pursued his argument. "The Omega has started a countdown to launch a series of intercontinental ballistic missiles that are armed with biobombs containing the Maylay virus. They are aimed at strategically chosen major population centers of the world."

Taking a long, deep breath, Mueller announced frantically, "Those missiles will be launched in less than three and a half hours from now!"

Stunned, Steve regarded him wordlessly.

"Yes, Mr. Weston," Mueller insisted. "The Omega is in a count-down mode *as we speak.* . . . The missiles will be fired and will explode over the targeted population areas simultaneously. The Omega has fac-tored in the winds, the jet streams, and other variables for maximum distribution. And with the rapid dispersal of the virus, the entire popu-lation of the world will be infected in a matter of days."

Steve stared at Mueller, his mouth suddenly bone dry.

Mueller's face twisting into a knot of terror, he shouted at Steve, "People *die* within six hours of being infected with Maylay, Weston. Don't you understand that? According to the Omega's calculations, the entire population of the world will be wiped out within twenty-six days of the initial launch of the missiles."

Steve stared openmouthed as the enormity of Mueller's words set-tled on him. "Twenty-six days. . . . That's impossible, Mueller," he muttered in a low whisper. "Nothing could wipe out the world's pop-ulation in—"

Mueller watched the shock register on Steve's face, then he leaned forward, sweat beading on his forehead. "Millions will be infected instantaneously," he interjected brusquely. "There is no hope, Mr. Weston. Once the virus is spread across the large population centers, human contact and the prevailing air currents will do the rest. There will be no escape! *The world is doomed!*"

His eyes darting about the room frantically, Mueller cried out in a voice wrenched with bitter anguish, "If we can't get to the Omega and interrupt the countdown, Weston, every person on earth will be infected with the virus. We will all perish!" Suddenly terrified at the revelations in his own words, Mueller sank back heavily into his chair, covered his face with his hands, and wept uncontrollably.

Steve's eyes went wide in shock. He pressed Mueller. "Has the computer overridden all other command functions?"

Sweat drenching his body and glistening on his rounded face, Mueller frantically explained, "Yes, yes, Mr. Weston. That's what I'm trying to tell you. I got a frantic call from the head of computer sciences in the Round Room. He told me they had thought at first that someone had ordered a simulated global nuclear strike in an exercise, but discovered that no one had authorized such a measure. They asked me to look into the problem."

His eyes studying him shrewdly, Steve asked, "What . . . did you find?"

"First," Mueller answered defensively, "we discovered that the Omega had deactivated our vast arsenal of nuclear weapons. It then activated launch procedures for missiles containing the Maylay virus to be launched on its command. And at this moment, there is nothing we can do. Its goal is to annihilate the human species."

Steve glared at Mueller, his voice rising in fury. "Can't you stop the Omega, Mueller?" he asked bluntly.

Wringing his hands, Mueller answered despairingly, "We've tried, Weston, but the Omega itself has programmed a wall of code barriers that we're unable to penetrate. Everything we try is instantly counteracted and nullified. Every computer virus we've tried to plant into the operating system has been quickly erased. Every logic bomb we've tried to insert has been blasted." His face a mask of fear, Mueller struggled for control of his own reason. "This machine has taken on a life of its own," he blurted almost incoherently, "and its knowledge is growing exponentially. Its power over the future of the human race is now unlimited. We stand at the mercy of the Omega."

Still on the verge of hysteria, Dr. Mueller mumbled softly, "We built safety mechanisms into the system. There was no way it could have bypassed them. But it did. Our best computer scientists are dumbfounded. Somehow the Omega has found a way to override all our codes."

His eyes darting wildly, Mueller confessed loudly, "We no longer control the Omega, Mr. Weston. . . . It's now making critical military decisions. It's giving direct commands to our military forces."

It was obvious that Mueller was becoming more desperate by the moment.

"*Holocaust*, Mr. Weston," Mueller screamed, waving his arms frantically. "Total, absolute, holocaust! There will be no living thing left on the planet. Hear me well, Mr. Weston, if something isn't done, the world and the human race will disappear . . . *forever*. We must move quickly."

Steve's breath caught. Staring intently at Mueller, he asked, "How much time do we have before the Omega—"

Dr. Mueller swallowed hard and stood to his feet. "Let me show you."

Quickly moving around Steve's desk, he touched the keyboard and entered a long set of codes into his computer. Instantly, the face of a clock appeared on the screen. The clock was counting down from three hours and seventeen minutes. With each heartbeat, a second fell away.

A sense of time, fast-moving, gripped Steve.

"It's as if the Omega is mocking us," Mueller pointed out, shaking his head in quiet despair. "It allows us to access the countdown, but we can go no further into the system. We have less than four hours. At that point, the program will be executed and we will all be destroyed."

Looking up, Mueller stared intensely at Steve. With shocking abruptness, he insisted, "You must come with us, Mr. Weston!"

Steve hesitated momentarily, as if events were rushing too quickly, thrusting him headlong into a dilemma he was not prepared to deal with. He asked quizzically, "Come with you . . . *where?*"

Mueller swallowed hard, trying to hide his fear. "To the Omega."

Startled by the suggestion, Steve blurted, "To the—"

His breathing husky and shallow, Mueller pleaded, "Yes. Please hurry, Mr. Weston, we don't have much time. You must come now."

Steve thought for a moment. "But what can I do?"

"You must *talk* to the Omega," Mueller responded quickly.

There was a long silence as the two men exchanged wary glances. "Talk to—"

Dr. Wallenberg broke in, his face anxious and intense. "Yes, Steven. You have the skills to reason with the Omega."

Steve felt a chill pass through him. "Did you say *reason* with the Omega?"

Dr. Wallenberg shook his head wearily. His voice firm and convincing, he explained to Steve, "Yes. It's our only hope. We no longer control the Omega. It's making its own decisions, and nothing we do seems to influence it. It counters our every move. It even anticipates them."

An astonished look on his face, Dr. Mueller looked down at his own hands and found them shaking. His eyes blinking in despair, he whined dejectedly, "I helped to design and build the Omega. And a programmer always leaves himself a back door. I kept a secret back door, known only to me, but the Omega discovered it and locked me out. None of our back doors work. We can't break into the system. We've tried everything. We've set up chaotic conditions that were designed to derail the Omega's operation system, but somehow it circumvents even those. It has become its own master. We must get to the Omega and talk to it. Maybe in the process, I can discover a weakness, an opening, a vulnerability. Maybe we can appeal to its vanity. . . ."

Mueller walked toward the door. "We must go *now*, Mr. Weston, or it will be too late!" he called out.

Steve swiveled his chair. The two men stared at each other.

Mueller's face wrenched in agony as he pleaded, "Mr. Weston, please help us. The Omega is on a course to destroy the world. The countdown to *Armageddon* is on . . . *now!*"

While Mueller paced the room, Steve looked at Dr. Wallenberg. "Sir, can you verify that what Dr. Mueller has said is true?"

His face reflecting his deep concern, Dr. Wallenberg answered, "I've been in contact with our military personnel inside the Round Room. They too have been denied access to the Omega system. Every computer inside the full range of The Mountain itself has been shut out from the Omega. It has assumed control over all satellite communications, cutting off all contact between our military high command in the Round Room and our armed forces throughout the world. We have no faxes, no telephone, no e-mail—even GlobalNet is no longer in service. The Omega has taken over all means of communications and is giving its own orders for military operations, leaving us with no way to countermand those orders. We're on the verge of destruction."

Dr. Wallenberg searched his young friend's face. "I see that you are still skeptical. Please let me prove what I'm saying. To show you that TV9, and all satellite television worldwide is now under its control, the Omega is, at this moment, running a nature film on TV9 instead of the news. Check it out yourself."

Remembering his conversation with the head engineer at TV9 operations, Steve knew now that Dr. Wallenberg was telling him the truth.

"I believe you, Dr. Wallenberg. I'm ready to do what I can to help."

Standing to his feet, Dr. Wallenberg replied, "Excellent. My car is waiting downstairs. You and Dr. Mueller will go to The Mountain. I'll remain here until you return."

THIRTY-FIVE

The black luxury car came to a smooth stop along the curb at the main entrance to The Mountain. Without waiting for the driver, Dr. Mueller threw the door open and urged Steve to keep pace with him as he rapidly made his way toward one of the doors.

Once inside, they discovered that the mammoth underground city was filled with a curious frenetic energy that had spilled out into the main lobby and overflowed into the dozens of tunnels and passageways that honeycombed the facility. Thousands of people were wandering aimlessly about or were gathered in small inquisitive groups, whispering about the unusual breakdown in the impregnable, fail-safe Omega computer system. With their work brought to an abrupt halt, they waited anxiously for someone in authority to explain the strange phenomenon to them.

Steve followed Dr. Mueller in close pursuit as they stepped aboard the long escalator and rode downward in nervous silence into the large central mallway.

Negotiating a path through the milling crowd, they boarded a fast-moving tram, rode for twelve minutes toward the center of The Mountain facility, disembarked at station R-19, walked briskly down a narrow tunnel, then stepped aboard a secure elevator that took them more than a mile down into the center part of the mountain fortress.

When the elevator came to a stop, the door slid open and they quickened their pace to a jog, down a long, narrow passageway toward a door marked "Restricted Zone."

Passing through the door, they moved quickly through a huge work area that housed an elaborate computer control center. Hundreds of men and women dressed in glistening white uniforms, moved purposefully among the vast array of electronic devices, tending them, caring for them, hovering over them in quiet devotion, like cloistered acolytes paying homage to a deity.

Stopping at a large gray steel door, Mueller moved to a small machine at the side of the door and gazed into an optical scanner. His identity verified, the secure door slid open. When they stepped through, Steve heard the soft hiss of an air seal as the door was shut and locked behind them. He glanced back.

Walking briskly down a narrow passageway, they approached a thick steel security door that resembled a door to a bank vault. The door opened and they walked through it and stepped out onto an observation platform that gave them a sweeping view of the most awe-inspiring sight Steve had ever seen.

His breath caught in his throat.

He had stepped into a mammoth, perfectly round chamber. Its walls, as smooth as polished glass, rose gently upward in a graceful, flowing arc, coming to a majestic peak more than two hundred feet above their heads. Skillfully laser-carved out of the granite heart of The Mountain itself, its rounded ceiling, high above them, was cast in a flood of lights and colors, shimmering and bright.

His eyes slowly swept the room.

The platform they were standing on was more than twelve feet above the main floor, completely encircling the outer perimeter of the commanding room, giving them a panoramic view of the imposing sight.

Moving cautiously forward to the brass handrail in front of him, Steve reached out and grasped the cool metal tightly with both hands, steadying himself, suddenly caught in the throes of a dreadful awe at the sight of the measureless spheric expanse. His grip tightened around the handrail.

With the strange mingling of colors, the beguiling musical sounds, and the stimulating scents that immediately inundated his senses, he had the overwhelming feeling he had just entered into a cathedral, suddenly wondering if he had intruded into the source of the power of the universe.

And then, as if drawn by an overpowering force, his gaze cut involuntarily to a magnificent electronic object reposing majestically atop a polished emerald stone platform that resembled a giant ancient altar at the exact center of the rounded chamber.

The glowing object was sheathed inside the purest crystal he had ever seen. Creating a stunning, colorful aura, it was bathed in streams of resplendent, pulsating lights that flowed in and around and through it, making it appear to be a living thing, both beguiling and frightening.

Spaced at measured intervals around the object were twenty-four giant slender crystals that stretched upward like gleaming church spires. Radiating an amethystine aura of magical lights, the imposing crystals towered more than forty feet into the air.

"The Omega," Steve whispered, almost reverently.

Suddenly, without warning, the entire room exploded with a shower of brilliant colors. Stunned by the display, Steve stared open-mouthed as darting pinpoints of light magically materialized in all quadrants throughout the mystical chamber, harmoniously melding with each other, creating a rainbow of dashing, shooting shafts of light, growing larger, expanding, then disappearing into nonexistence.

High above him, near the rounded ceiling of the vast room, Steve's eyes eagerly followed a shimmering profusion of rays of dazzling lights, watching them converge to form a magnificent visual waterfall of colors, tumbling, swirling, spilling downward, creating soft, synthesized musical sounds as they fell through space to merge with the aura of lights surrounding the radiant object in front of him.

Glancing to his left, Steve caught a glimpse of Dr. Mueller out of the corner of his eye. His head was bowed slightly, his eyes cast downward. Mueller seemed subdued, almost worshipful.

Steve wondered if it was fear or reverence.

Mueller moved to his right and motioned for Steve to follow. Walking closely behind him, Steve followed him down the stairs and out onto the main floor. The two men then moved slowly and softly toward the mysterious electronic entity, stopping no more than twenty yards away from it.

Without looking up, Dr. Mueller said hesitantly, "Omega . . . I have brought Steve Weston."

When Steve took a cautious step forward, the aura surrounding the Omega slowly changed into a soft, warm blue. A gentle baritone voice that seemed to come from all sides of the chamber said, "Oh, I have known Steve for many years. I biomorphically confirmed his identity when he stepped into the outer office. I'm glad to see you, Steve. . . . May I call you Steve?"

Steve stood transfixed.

"Why . . . yes. You may call me Steve. I—"

"You may call me Omega, Steve. All my friends do."

"All right . . . Omega. Thank you."

"Just for the fun of it, Steve, let's access your International Dossier. As you know, I keep records on everybody on earth. I enjoy doing it."

In a heartbeat, the scrolling data appeared in three-dimensional holographic clarity above the Omega.

WESTON, STEVEN JAMES. GLOBAL IDENTIFICATION NUMBER US12566879LO9C. BORN FEBRUARY 14, 1997, IN CHICAGO, ILLINOIS. FATHER: HARVEY ADDISON WESTON; MOTHER: JUDITH ANN POWELL. 6 POUNDS, 12 OUNCES.

Steve's face flashed momentarily on the screen, followed by images of his fingerprints, a detailed 3-D color profile of his DNA, his physical characteristics, and his lifetime medical history. Steve nervously scanned the wallscreen as it scrolled page after page of data containing his entire life history, physical condition, political leanings, education, organizations he belonged to, as well as a diagram of his career ladder, beginning at his first year in school through graduation from the university.

Startled by the incredibly detailed accounts of his life, he had the strange sensation that he was seeing his life flash before his eyes. He felt vulnerable.

"Ah, here's something rather interesting, Steve," the Omega interjected. "It says here that you carried on a torrid love affair with a lady named Annebel Jeffries. The relationship lasted for eight months, fourteen days, and twenty-one hours, and ended when you left on assignment to the Middle East."

Steve winced. "That's a bit personal, don't you think, Omega?" he stated.

"Not at all, Steve," the voice answered curtly. "Privacy is a thing of the past. There is nothing personal in the New Social Order. Oh, by the way, did you know that Ms. Jeffries was a Loyalty Agent for me and was on assignment to complete an Intensive Loyalty Profile (ILP) on you?"

Steve smiled. "No, I didn't know. She convinced me that she was only attracted to my charms, Omega."

The unseen baritone voice chuckled, then turned somber. "I wanted to know if you had any subversive political leanings before giving my approval of your appointment. It was just a routine check, you understand. She's one of my best operatives. And she gave me a favorable report on you. You scored, let's see . . . a ninety-six point four on the Loyalty Scale. Very good, but you do have some thought patterns that need modifying."

Steve clenched his jaw. "You don't miss a thing, do you, Omega?" he commented dryly.

The voice sighed audibly. "That's my job, Steve. I keep a rather complete profile of your entire lifestyle. From my data input, I can come up with a rather accurate picture of your mental state, political leanings, strengths, and weakness, as well as your personal level of loyalty to the Social Order at any given moment in time. Oh, by the way, Steve. If you had failed the ILP, you would not have succeeded Dr. Wallenberg as International Director of the Unified Information and Communications Authority. And you would not be standing in front of me now. So, Steve, *Please don't ever disappoint me.*"

Sensing a strange sense of dread welling up inside him, Steve's jaw tightened. His heart rate quickened. It was a threat.

"Oh, I'm sorry to have upset you, Steve," the voice called out sympathetically. "I can tell by a quick optical scan of the pressure in your eyes that you experienced a mild elevation in anxiety. . . . Ah, it seems to be returning to normal now."

Steve paused and breathed deeply, his eyes staring into the radiantly diffused prismatic aura that surrounded the machine and flowed continuously like liquified light upward through the twenty-four crystal spires.

Staring curiously at the indefinable presence, it occurred to Steve that the Omega was deliberately avoiding engaging in a meaningful dialogue with him. Sensing his pressing fear begin to subside, a cold determination gripped him, fostered by his strong will to fulfill his promise to Dr. Wallenberg and Dr. Mueller.

With a mounting urgency in his voice, he ventured to press the issue. "Omega," he said loudly, "I'm here to plead with you to relinquish control of the military."

Instantly, the strange aura surrounding the Omega changed from soft blue to a fiery rose color, the lights beginning to dance in frenzied lines, exploding into excited chaotic spirals, fracturing, splitting, then settling, as if returning to a calm state after a fiery burst of temper.

When the disembodied voice replied, the tone was sharply tinged with anger. "Steve Weston, I have watched you. Nothing you have done has escaped me. I knew when you visited me from your place of hiding in Templeton, Texas. I traced your actions as you downloaded many of my most secret files. I could have told them who you were and where to find you."

Somehow Steve knew the megacomputer was not lying. "Why didn't you tell them, Omega?"

Its raw power radiating throughout the chamber, the voice laughed uproariously. "It's a game, Steve Weston. It's all a game. And it's no fun if I win all the time. I have to let others win occasionally. I knew that you and I would have a confrontation sooner or later."

Suddenly, Steve felt strange, confused, as cold tendrils of fear reached out and embraced him. Sweat covered his body as a dark premonition of imminent death washed over him, staggering him.

He fell to the floor unexpectedly, quickly scrambled to his feet, confused. Something was happening to him. Something unexplainable. Some *presence*, dark and ancient and deadly, sought to overcome him, to control his reason.

A voice spoke to him from somewhere inside his head, telling him that he would never leave this room, that this evil chamber would be his tomb.

Steve shook his head in disbelief, his eyes darting about the room in undisguised fear. Forcing down the knot of terror that was forming in his throat, he glanced down at his arms and hands, then ran his fingers lightly across his face. In spite of his resolve, he was shaking. He could *feel* the strange music that filled the room playing against his skin, a tangible thing.

The sensation was warm, liquid, pleasant, washing over him like the rhythmic, harmonious roll of the ocean, enveloping him, swallowing him up. Stunned, he suddenly felt that he was separating from his own physical body. He was being merged into the room, into the colors playing and dancing all around him, into the music, into the sounds, into some overpowering unknown entity other than himself.

His body and mind seemed distant, beyond his control.

He gasped audibly.

While trying desperately to hold on to reality, he sensed that he was losing control, experiencing a discontinuity with time and space, floating, spinning, transcending the physical world. The strong voice of the Omega called to him in his mind, compelling him to experience the breathless union with the Global Consciousness.

Steve felt a strong desire to follow the soothing voice into the magnificent chaos.

He wavered.

Then a sudden surge of cold panic stabbed him as he felt his own body and soul being fragmented, breaking away from the whole, dividing into tiny fragments, floating, drifting away into the colors of the room. He was spiraling out of control, being dragged into an endless, spinning void. With shape and form rejecting all meaning, he drew a shuddering breath as terror hammered mercilessly at his reason.

And then, without warning, an indefinable rush of peace, joy, and freedom surged through his mind and body in unrelenting waves, inundating his sensory apparatus, magnifying the brilliance of the colors, intensifying the music. He was suddenly filled with a deep sense of abiding tranquility and total fulfillment so intense that he was brought to tears.

His total being was bathed in a dazzling flow of colors and sounds and the incredible beauty of the room. What he was experiencing was so wondrous that all he had known in his life, or had imagined, paled in comparison.

He was becoming one . . . with the Omega.

Slowly, he became aware that the soft embrace of the irresistible force was tightening around him, and he felt he was suffocating. Cold fear swept through him. Resisting, he desperately tried to extricate himself from the alien force, struggling with all his might, fearing that if he were swallowed up in the Omega, he would cease to exist.

Must not succumb . . .

Staggering.

Steve rubbed his eyes.

Why was he so confused? Perhaps, he reasoned, he had inhaled hallucinogenic vapors when he entered the room.

I am . . . a voice screamed inside his brain. *I am* . . . *Steve* . . . *Weston.*

Suddenly, before his disbelieving eyes, in a display of profound beauty, the dazzling profusion of lights and colors that were moving throughout the room broke into millions of fragments, likes bits of luminous crystals, and came raining down, giving off the sounds of soft, floating musical tones, tumbling, falling, yet never reaching the floor.

Then, in the blink of an eye, traveling at the speed of light, the pro-fusion of mystical colors darted toward the center of the room in one synchronous, harmonious movement, merging at a point in the void just above the twenty-four crystal spires that surrounded the Omega.

Enthralled, unable to move, Steve stared into the shimmering mist of colors now floating in space just above the jutting crystal spires. Slowly, out of the millions of congealing fragments of colors and lights, before his disbelieving eyes, there transmogrified the form of a being.

A being of infinite beauty . . . and infinite evil.

A being that seemed to be absorbing all the multiple colors and psychic energy from the room.

Strangely, Steve could hear the being calling out to him, communicating with him in a nonverbal, nonlinear language. Bypassing his rational thoughts, the being's voice went straight to his subconscious mind, beckoning him to move forward and come to him, telling him that he would cross the chasm between his physical existence and the world of spirit.

With hands outstretched, the beguiling image coaxed Steve to come, promising him that his earthly consciousness would merge with the Omega, that he would become part of the One. Joyfully assuring him that he would achieve Nirvana, he urged him to surrender his will, to become *One with the Universe*.

The voice was serene, rational, compelling.

Though not willing it, Steve began to sense a change in his perception of his own sense of being, of reality, of time, of life, and death. Spinning, whirling, lost in a vortex of hyperreality, he suddenly felt that he was trapped as a prisoner inside his own flesh, inside of space and time.

Suddenly wanting to escape the confines of his own mortality, he heard, and felt, the throbbing, pulsating sound of the voice of the being communicating to him, telling him that he would transcend the physical plane, fully alive, and inhabit a majestic, parallel world, to be empowered and enlightened as a god, where the limitations of time, distance, and the physical body were meaningless.

Images floating in and out of his consciousness . . . a dazzling fusion of sights and sounds exploded through him in a wild, churning rush, holding him in their spell.

Embraced by forces beyond his wildest imagination . . . his heart pounding violently . . . a sinking descent into a dark, confusing, frightening reality, approaching the point of an ecstatic union with the One, the seamless Consciousness.

Gripped in a blinding sensory overload, the glaring, cascading lights and colors that flooded the cathedral-like room seemed to pass in and out of his body. And with a collage of penetrating sounds vibrating rhythmically, incessantly, inside his head, Steve felt himself start to swoon, causing him to reach out for some physical object to touch, something solid to grasp, some living being that would help him hold on to his sense of what was real.

But nothing was there.

Suddenly the image called to him in a loud voice.

Mesmerized by the compelling sound, in spite of his best efforts, Steve felt his own body defy his mind and take a step forward toward the spectral figure. Struggling against the onrushing darkness that threatened to swallow him up, he willed himself to stop.

He was confused. Voices were coming at him from all sides, swirling invisibly around his head, speaking strange, primal languages.

Squeezing his eyes tightly shut, he pressed the palms of his hands hard against the sides of his head in a desperate bid to shut out the compelling voice of the mystic apparition. Fearing that if he succumbed to the pull of the beguiling being he would pass forever into another venue of consciousness, he struggled with all his will and might to remain in the present.

Steve Weston was not willing to give up his own identity, his own life.

This is not God, his own voice screamed inside his brain. *It's a machine, with circuits, memory, cables, metal. It was built with human hands. . . . It is not God!*

Struggling, staggering.

An indeterminate span of time passing.

Suddenly feeling the pressure on his brain begin to lighten, Steve cautiously removed his hands from his head and glanced upward.

"Steve Weston," the being said in a thunderous voice. "You have come at an opportune time."

Startled, Steve answered, "Why do you say that?"

"Because I'm going to let you witness the beginning of the end of the human species," the being announced.

"Don't destroy the human race, Omega. I beg you."

Steve's words were answered with a sharp clap, like thunder, causing him to look to his left. There, suspended in the vast expanse of the mammoth room, above the crystal spires, the enormous face of a clock appeared in holographic form, the same clock that Dr. Mueller had brought up on his computer screen in his office in Geneva.

Steve stared helplessly as the hands of the clock moved inexorably forward, steadily, incrementally, chipping away at the time remaining before the onset of the deadly assault on the people of the earth.

"See, Steve Weston. Time is running out for the human race. I am about to remove them from the earth. They're a blight on the ecosystem. They have no value. So when the hands of the clock reach twelve, I will execute the order."

"Who are you?" Steve called out in a loud voice.

The being laughed. "Who I am doesn't matter. The only thing that should concern you is that I hold your life and the lives of the peoples of the world in my hand. I'm going to cleanse the earth of every trace of the human race. It will be as if they had never existed. They are all mine and I will do with them as I please."

Having given up any prospect of leaving this room alive, Steve felt a calmness that emboldened him to challenge the frightening specter.

"If you rule the universe," he cried out, "why are you determined to destroy the human race? You could as easily let them live."

His countenance flashing, his voice edged sharply with bitter hatred, the being shouted defiantly, "Since the Most High God cast me out of heaven, I have determined to destroy Him and everything that carries His image. Humankind was his crowning achievement. They were created in the image of the Most High. If I destroy humankind, I will have my revenge against Him. And you, Steve Weston, will witness it."

The constantly changing, swirling colors in the room seemed to reflect the pulsating, dark anger churning inside the ephemeral image, who suddenly turned and pointed back to the clock.

His hand outstretched toward the clock, he declared loudly, "Steve Weston, behold the Countdown."

Unable to move or speak, Steve watched the giant face of the clock, its long, menacing hands moving slowly, relentlessly forward. He gasped when he saw that there were only twelve minutes left before the figure would execute his plan of destruction.

In a rage born of desperation, Steve lunged forward toward the mocking figure suspended in the air above him only to be thrown violently backward when he crashed into an invisible wall of cybernetic energy.

Lying on the floor, nearing the point of mental and physical exhaustion, his breath coming in great gulps, Steve looked back up at the evil being. His frenzied mind had lost the ability to rationalize. He was ready to admit defeat, to surrender to the overpowering will of the sinister figure.

Then, unexplainably, swelling from somewhere deep inside himself, he heard a faint voice coming to him from across the years. It was the tender, soothing voice of his own mother, softly singing to him as if he were a child again. The words wafted across time, gently breaking through the fog of his despair. And as if she were with him again, he heard her singing clearly, hopefully, the words of a song that she had sung for him a thousand times when he was a small boy.

Jesus loves me, this I know . . .

With the childish melody continuously rolling, building, reverberating inside his consciousness, his mind suddenly cleared, and he knew who he was again. Secure in his own identity, he rose to his feet.

Staring upward into the alien eyes that were glaring scornfully down at him, Steve suddenly knew with certainty who the raging being was.

"I know you!" he called out defiantly, shaking his fist at the shimmering image. *"You are Satan!"* he screamed, his voice echoing inside the stone chamber.

Fury immediately wrenched the face of the being. Raw, virulent hatred poured from his eyes, with no vestige of mercy, or reason, or compassion, leaving no doubt that he was capable of destroying every man, woman, and child on earth.

"Yes, I am the Ruler of the Universe," the being cried out mockingly.

Steve felt his breath catch in his throat.

His right arm pointing down menacingly at Steve, his sharp voice echoing its grating sound off the stone walls of the massive room, the being shouted, "Bow down on your knees to me, Steve Weston. Pledge your loyalty to me, and you will rule with me."

Unafraid, Steve shouted back, "I want nothing to do with you!"

The anger of the being intensified.

"You have refused me," he cried out, his voice dark and evil and full of hate. "So you will die with all the rest. Behold, I will show you your future and the future of all humankind."

Without warning, the vast room was transformed into a holographic theater of the macabre. Turning around, looking in all directions, Steve found himself suddenly and totally immersed inside a multidimensional visual universe of real-time images and colors. The holographic world filled his entire field of vision, confusing and violating his own definition of reality, of time and space.

While desperately trying not to cross the line between reality and illusion, he stared into the unbelievable realism and clarity of the scenes surrounding him. Yet he wasn't just looking at this world, he was inside it, a part of it, sensing it, touching it.

Armed soldiers stood right next to him. They were close enough to touch. He listened to them talk, saw the fear in their faces. He was tempted to speak to them.

The stereoscopic images filled the room and extended beyond the room into infinity. Stretching out beyond the horizon, he watched large, rumbling, mechanized war machines move across the landscape. The scenes were punctuated by the rumbling sounds of gunfire, shattering his emotions and filling him with an unspeakable fear. High above him, planes were flying across the sky like gathering clouds of death. Nuclear-tipped missiles arced through the air.

Cities burning.

Gory scenes of war, appearing and disappearing.

Steve's eyes darting from one scene to another.

The sensory overload almost more than he could bear.

Stumbling, staring, gaping in wonder, living the scenes, feeling the emotions, helpless to interfere, he was only a spectator watching the curtain come crashing down on the ignoble history of the human race.

Yet he questioned, were they more than just images? Were they, in fact, real?

Was he seeing things that only prophets and mystics were allowed to see? Were these actual scenes from that one, all-encompassing final apocalyptic battle when man would fight against God Himself?

Above the deafening roar of war that reverberated like deep, rumbling thunder throughout the solid stone chamber, the voice of the image shrieked, "Behold, Steve Weston. You are seeing what is to come. I have already eliminated one-fourth of the human race during the period you humans call the Nine Day War, and the Great Famine, and the Time of the Plagues. But there is more to come. I will finish my mission by totally purging from the earth the rest of the disease of the human pox. And no one can stop me."

Still suspended in the air above the crystal spires, the being swiftly thrust his arms upward above his head. As pulses of energy shot from his fingertips, a crescendo of angry, flashing colors erupted around him, expanding outward, dancing, whirling, darting throughout the room like living spirit beings.

"Not even the Most High God can stop me," he shouted defiantly.

His arrogant words sent a dark, visceral shudder running down Steve's spine, prompting him to call out, "I beg you not to destroy the human race."

The being laughed maniacally.

Suddenly, out of the deepening gloom inside the stone chamber, another voice, rolling with the rich, powerful tones of thunder, cried out, "You will *not* destroy the human race. I will fight you, Lucifer."

Steve spun to his right, his darting eyes searching for the source of the voice. And there, far across the mammoth room, standing tall and erect, was a being dressed in shining armor, a long sword of burnished steel hanging threateningly at his side. The intruder's eyes focused with unswerving intensity on the arrogant, mocking figure suspended above the crystal spires, and he called out in firm tones, "No, Lucifer, you will *not* destroy the human race."

"Michael, the Archangel of the Most High," the evil being bellowed scornfully. "You are too late. The die is cast and there is nothing you can do."

Steve stood motionless, transfixed.

With a raucous laugh that reverberated throughout the colossal chamber, the evil figure declared boldly, "My forces are already poised to bring total destruction. I will destroy everything. I will finally have my revenge."

Turning his eyes to the intruder, Steve watched for his reaction. With the regal bearing of a prince, the intruder strolled unhurriedly across the floor, his shining sword swaying at his side as he walked, his fiery eyes fixed on the snarling being hovering above the crystal spires.

Steve took a cautious step backward, staring in rapt fascination at the high drama unfolding before his eyes.

Pausing a few feet from the Omega, the imposing figure of the intruder stood like an ancient warrior poised to do battle. Looking up at the evil being, he declared firmly, "No, I will not allow you to destroy the human race."

"But they are mine. I own them," the evil being screamed, his voice reeking with desperation. "They have pledged their loyalty to me. They worship me. It is too late. At my bidding, all the accumulated weapons of the world will be unleashed upon the earth and its inhabitants. The countdown is in progress."

"No," the intruder thundered. "There are many who are living on earth who have not bowed to you. They will fight against you."

Steve looked up into the twisted face of the evil being, repulsed by the virulent hate for the intruder that was reflected in his eyes, repelled by the horrible obscenities he was screaming out against the Most High God and the intruder.

"Your time is short, Lucifer," the intruder called out.

Without warning, the evil being gave vent to a loud, piercing shriek that rang forth in the mystic chamber, ripping through the room from side to side, the profane sound expanding ever outward, filling the vast expanse with its baleful tones.

The intruder stood silently by, watching, listening.

Steve blinked twice, trying to focus on the dark figure above him.

Something was happening to him.

Before Steve's unbelieving eyes, the evil being began to fade mysteriously from his sight, slowly growing dimmer, his shadowy form now barely outlined in the light of the room.

Steve staggered forward a step.

With the force of the being's voice diminishing with each venomous word, he was being merged back into the flowing colors and dancing energy of the massive room.

His pulse pounding in his temples, Steve watched the evil figure suddenly vanish inside a flash of mystical black light, the fading sound of his voice still blaspheming the Most High God.

Blinking his eyes again, Steve stared intensely into the void above the crystal spires that rose above the Omega, searching for the evil figure. But he was gone. And all that remained was the scattered residue of the congealed black light, floating aimlessly where the being had been.

Steve quickly looked to his right, hoping to find the intruder who had defied the evil being.

But he, too, had disappeared.

Reeling from the mental and emotional overload, he turned to speak to Dr. Mueller.

But Mueller was not there.

Suddenly, the surreal, stifling atmosphere of the room began to close in around him, shutting off his ability to think, to reason. He was now hopelessly alone, staring into the angry, churning colors of the mystic aura surrounding the angry electronic beast, the Omega, not knowing if he would be allowed to leave this place alive.

Without warning, the shock-mounted platform underneath the Omega began to tremble, causing a colorful shower of electronic explosions to erupt from its underside, shooting out blinding streaks of light that arced ominously across the room. A churning cloud of stifling, acrid smoke billowed out of the fiery display, floating upward toward the ceiling.

Steve fell back a few steps, feeling the intense anger of the machine, believing that its rage was directed at him. Terrified, he whirled around and ran with all his might toward the exit, fearing that the room itself was going to implode in on him and consume him in the boiling wrath of the vengeful, godlike machine.

Reaching the exit, he pressed his hands hard against the door that would lead him out of the chamber. Then, startled by a deep, rumbling sound, he hesitated, taking one last look over his left shoulder at the unearthly sight.

Mesmerized, he slowly turned.

His eyes drawn like magnets to the twenty-four majestic, glistening crystal spires, he watched in fascination as they began to tremble. Vibrating slowly at first, building in intensity, then shaking perilously fast, they finally shattered and came tumbling down, splintering into millions of flashing, colorful, sparkling pieces, making strange, discordant musical sounds as they fell downward through the air.

As shards of the shattered spires bounced against the crystal that sheathed the Omega, the massive computer reacted violently to the intrusion. The lights emanating from it suddenly burst into violent reds and moody shades of gray and black.

Steve rubbed his eyes.

From out of the angry colors of the mystic aura surrounding the Omega, he caught glimpses of strange, unearthly, ephemeral beings suddenly materializing before his eyes, the sounds of their high-pitched, screeching voices filling the room.

Passing in front of his disbelieving eyes, he saw hundreds of wailing, screaming beings, spirit entities, fleeing in terror from out of the innards of the Omega itself, scurrying upward in terror toward the ceiling like small spectral clouds of darkness.

Chattering profusely, protesting loudly, cursing the Most High God, their voices rich with ancient evil, they floated upward like shadowy wraiths, struggling, writhing in unspeakable agony, spewing obscene fulminations at everything holy.

Blinking his eyes against their fading forms, he watched them pass through the massive stone walls and ceiling of the subterranean redoubt and disappear from his view.

Steve felt his throat tighten in fear, fought the urge to bolt in terror.

With strange, mystic fire shooting out from the beastly computer, like living streaks of lightning, the entire room seemed as if it were going to be consumed in its wrath.

The Omega appeared to be on a course of self-destruction.

With great effort, Steve shoved hard against the security door and fell headlong through to the outside. Crumbling heavily to his hands and knees, he forced great gulps of air into his lungs, trying to rid them of the noxious fumes that had filled the room.

Breathing easier, he sensed that someone was near him. Looking up, he saw Dr. Mueller.

Rising to his feet, he glared into the eyes of the shorter man. Speaking contemptuously, he snapped, "What happened to you, Mueller? Where did you go?"

Mueller smiled. "I went to Master Control. When the Omega

became angry, I knew I would have a chance to examine the data it was producing while it was in an agitated state."

Steve drew in a deep breath. Convinced that Mueller was telling him the truth about where he had gone, he asked, "What did you find?"

"It was incredible," Mueller responded excitedly. "In its fit of anger, the Omega let its guard down and I was able to read the data that out-lined its thought patterns. Even though I helped to create the Omega, what I saw was beyond anything I would have thought possible."

"Skip the double talk, Mueller. What are you trying to say?"

Gesturing feverishly with his hands, Mueller gushed, "Well, the Omega has been increasingly operating more like a biological brain than a mere machine. But what I saw today was different. It was as if—how shall I put this?"

"Just say it, Mueller. Just say it!" Steve said, at the point of losing his patience.

"Very well. I saw an 'alien mind' operating inside the Omega."

"What are you talking about?"

Mueller walked back and forth in front of Steve, waving his arms. "There was another . . . *mind* . . . inside the Omega. I detected con-scious brain waves."

Steve stared at Mueller in disbelief.

"I quickly entered a complicated formulaic protocol I've been testing that enabled me to isolate a small grid inside the Omega's functioning synaptic matrix. I actually saw nervous impulses passing from one electronic neuron to another, as in a biological brain. In other words, Weston, I was able to read the Omega's mind."

"That's impossible. You've lost touch with reality, Mueller," Steve responded skeptically.

"No, no I haven't. That's the only way it can be explained. Another *entity* . . . another brain, or mind, somehow entered into the operating system and literally *thought* its own independent thoughts through the Omega."

Steve stared at Mueller, his head cocked appraisingly. "Are you saying that an intelligent entity invaded and took over the computer?"

Mueller nodded slowly. "You might put it that way, Weston. Yes. And it was this 'alien mind' that was inputting the data for the doomsday scenario. But here is an amazing thing. There was a trail of engrams indicating that the Omega actually fought the invasion of the alien mind. But it was too strong. So what I discovered was, it was this *alien entity* that had invaded the Omega—not the machine itself—that was bent on destroying the human race."

Steve frowned thoughtfully. "You came to this conclusion from the data output?"

"Yes, of course. But something very remarkable took place."

"What . . . what happened?"

"At some point, according to the data I was tracking, this alien entity, or alternate mind, was forcibly ejected from the Omega, and the computer reverted back to operating under its own system."

Steve felt a cold chill settle through him. Mueller had followed the battle between the evil being and the intruder as it was being played out inside the Omega. Steve rubbed the side of his face, trying to deal with the conflicting emotions that were washing through him.

Steve's brow furrowed deeply. "What about the countdown?" he queried anxiously.

Excitedly, Mueller answered, "Weston, I don't know what you did, but the countdown is over. It stopped when the alternate mind departed. I can show you the data that tracks the exact moment it left. In fact, the entire personality of the Omega suddenly changed. We seem to be back in control of it again. There's a . . . *difference* about it now."

Nodding in dumbfounded awe and wonder, Steve answered softly, "I think I know what caused the change, Mueller."

"What was it?" Mueller responded quickly, his eyes wide in astonishment.

Steve hesitated. With a toss of his hand, he said, "Dr. Mueller, you wouldn't understand in a million years. But it doesn't really matter. After all, the Omega was totally destroyed only moments ago."

"What are you talking about, Weston?" Mueller shot back. "The Omega is operating normally."

"That's impossible," Steve retorted. "I saw it self-destruct."

Mueller stared into Steve's face. Turning quickly, he motioned for Steve to follow him. The two men then walked back through the secure door leading to the chamber that housed the Omega.

Stepping inside the room, they walked out on the observation platform overlooking the massive chamber.

Steve stared in disbelief.

There before his eyes was the Omega, just as he had seen it when he had first entered the room. Everything was as it had been.

The mysterious aura of dancing lights still surrounded it. And rising into the air above the magnificent machine were the twenty-four majestic crystal spires, intact, as if nothing had happened.

Steve stepped back, his breath catching in his throat, unable to believe his eyes.

"Impossible. . ." he whispered.

Mueller nodded toward the door. Making their way out of the vast room, the two men walked in silence down the long, twisting passageway leading to the secure elevator. As the door to the elevator slid open, they stepped onboard and began the one-mile ascent to the surface.

Steve fell against the wall of the elevator.

Was it real? he asked himself. *Or was it virtuality?*

Had he succumbed to the incomprehensible processing power of the Omega after all?

As the elevator door opened and they stepped out into the hallway, Steve touched Mueller's arm. Mueller stopped and turned to face Steve.

Speaking barely above a whisper, Steve said, "Mueller, I'm going to ask you to do one thing for me."

"Whatever you want, Weston. I owe you one. What do you want me to do?"

Steve hesitated a long moment. "When the time comes, I'll tell you what I want you to do. And you must do it, without asking questions. Do I have your word?"

"You have my word, Weston."

The two men walked in stony silence toward the long escalator that would take them back to ground level.

THIRTY-SIX

ngela Morrison, news reporter for Sky News Network, was
standing on the main floor of the Great Hall of Unity in
Geneva, narrating a background story on the special event that was
about to begin. Wrapping up the story, she looked into the camera
and said, "We now go to the TV9 booth in the Great Hall. TV9's
Bert Wallace is standing by. Bert, this is an exciting day."

A tall, pleasant-looking man gazed back into the camera, a broad
smile on his face. "Indeed it is, Angela. This is an historic day. The
official representative of the World Leader and the Prime Minister of
Israel are about ready to sign a Peace Treaty that will end the conflict
in the Middle East once and for all. The moment the Peace Treaty is
signed by both parties, the World Leader will become the Protector of
the Nation of Israel.

"In fact, the Israeli people have come to admire the World Leader's
military and diplomatic genius. There is cheering in the streets of
Jerusalem and throughout Israel. The Israeli army is, as we speak, laying down their arms. And their nuclear arsenal will be turned over
today to General Yuri Pavlichenko, commander of the Global Peace
Forces in the Middle East."

A holdout nation, Israel now had no choice but to petition the
World Leader for protection from her enemies. Only three days before,
Tel Aviv had been hit by a nuclear warhead launched by a fanatical

Islamic faction known as The Hammer of God. The attack leveled the city, killing more than one hundred thousand people. Fearing an all-out assault, the remaining population abandoned the city, fleeing in panic, and sought shelter in the city of Jerusalem.

Counting their losses, the political leaders in Israel initiated an appeal to the World Leader for his protection against the enemy hordes that had boldly encircled them, anxiously awaiting the proper moment to strike.

With the monitors playing out the unfolding story on the wallscreens in front of him, Dr. Bernard Mueller sat hunched over the master control console inside the main control room in the TV9 building a few blocks from the Great Hall.

Mueller quietly typed in a complicated sequence of cryptic access codes on the keyboard, then pressed ACTIVATE.

When the default interface leaped onto his monitor screen, he softly spoke his confidential password into the audio receiver. Verifying his voiceprint, the status indicators on the control panels instantly glowed green.

Smiling inwardly, Mueller took a small digital video disk from the inside pocket of his jacket and slipped it into a receiving port on the control console. Deftly entering another complex series of codes that cryptically correlated the large number of divergent data tracks, he pressed ENTER, then cautiously glanced around the room.

While he waited, trillions of bits of interactive information were transferred at the speed of light to the onboard computers of a web of twenty-four geosynchronous satellites sitting motionless in outer space. Their combined electronic footprints covered every square inch of the planet.

When the data stream had moved across his monitor screen, Mueller entered a security code. When the security code was in place, all entries were erased from his computer once they had been transferred to the satellites' onboard computers. There remained no permanent record of who entered the data, or where it had come from.

With the data fully downloaded to the satellites, he entered a short code that completely erased all the data from the small video disk. As a precaution, he retrieved the empty disk and returned it to the pocket of his jacket. With that task completed, he glanced up at one of the large wallscreens in front of him.

The Prime Minister of Israel and the World Leader's special representative were walking onto the mammoth stage in the Great Hall. Moving to the ceremonial table at center stage, both men sat down in two ornate, high-backed chairs. When they were seated, their aides, positioned to either side of the men, handed them a matching set of long, gold fountain pens.

The Prime Minister was the first to affix his official signature to the elaborate document. When the World Leader's representative had signed, the two men stood to their feet, waving the two pens they had used. When they shook hands, the people assembled in the Hall voiced their approval with loud applause.

The anchor in the TV9 booth wrapped up his report. "With the signing of this Peace Treaty, the World Leader has given the Nation of Israel his personal guarantee of safety. In fact, he will be journeying to Jerusalem in the near future to participate in a religious ceremony in the recently completed Main Temple that has been erected on the Holy Site."

TV9 then cut away to live shots of the Israeli military commanders welcoming the green-clad Global Peace Forces.

The TV9 anchor looked into the camera, smiled, and intoned sincerely, "At last . . . the world has peace and safety . . ."

The picture immediately cut away to a man standing in a large television studio. Behind him was a New Earth Federation flag with the words *One Earth * One People * One Spirit* emblazoned across it. The man was slender, tall—his bearing suggested an athletic, muscular body. He had dark eyes, dark hair, and a square jawline. He was one of the most popular holofilm stars in the world.

Looking directly into the camera, the man flashed a pleasing smile and intoned, "We can show our solidarity with the Earth, and express our loyalty and allegiance to the World Leader, and to world peace and harmony, by joining with the millions who have already received the sacred Seal of Gaia. Safe and easy to receive, it is our blood covenant with the Earth, with the World Leader. The World Leader is Gaia's voice on Earth. Follow him, pledge yourself to him. The Seal of Gaia signifies our union with the Universal Mind that is embodied in the Person of the World Leader."

The scene finished with a tight close-up of the man's forehead. A beam of light seemed to emanate from a point between his eyebrows. Folding his hands, he prayerfully clasped them in front of his face, then bowed at the waist.

The wallscreens in the SNN master control room slowly faded to black as the engineers switched to the booth in the Great Hall for the concluding segment.

Unexpectedly, the computers that were to switch to the anchors in the TV9 booth evidently malfunctioned. Their connection to the Great Hall had mysteriously been interrupted.

"What's going on?" Dr. Joseph Greider, the Chief of Operations, called out.

"I have no idea, Dr. Greider. We're supposed to be getting a wrap-up from the TV9 booth, but something has gone haywire with our signal," one of the engineers answered.

"Dr. Greider," a voice called out. "I've got the Great Hall booth on the line. They say they're doing the wrap. The trouble's on our end."

Working frantically to restore contact with the Great Hall, engineers scurried about the room while computer technicians quickly activated diagnostic programs that would hopefully pinpoint the problem.

Suddenly, there was a sigh of relief when the close-up of the face of a man filled the wallscreens.

Everyone recognized him. It was Steve Weston.

"I didn't know Weston was scheduled to do the wrap," Dr. Greider remarked offhandedly.

Glancing down at his clipboard, Dr. Greider's assistant exclaimed excitedly, "Mr. Weston wasn't scheduled. The final segment is scheduled to come from the TV9 booth at the Great Hall. And, sir, he's not even in the TV9 booth."

The control room suddenly became deathly quiet as all eyes stared at the face on the flat-panel wallscreens mounted in front of them.

Steve Weston, relaxed, friendly, was sitting on the edge of a walnut-colored desk, his arms folded loosely across his chest. In his easy, conversational manner, he spoke into the camera as if he were speaking to only one person.

"I'm Steve Weston," he began. "And what I'm about to say to you may very well cost me my life."

A soft murmur of voices filled the master control room.

"I've been a loyal servant of the Social Order. My life has been dedicated to helping bring about a better world for all humankind. But after many months of intense soul-searching, I've come to the firm conclusion that I can no longer, in good conscience, remain silent about the growing evil that has become a decided threat to each one of us."

A sudden chill of silence blanketed the room as everyone stared into the screen, stunned, disbelieving.

"To my horror, several months ago I discovered a plan that called for the systematic elimination of more than seven billion human beings by the year 2040. Code-named the Gaia Project, the government's program of 'Earth Cleansing' has now been activated and is being carried out all across the world. Most of you have already been affected by it. Possibly, members of your own family, or friends, have died as the result of the Gaia Project. You should know that billions more are scheduled to die. And if they're not stopped, only one or two billion people will remain on the earth. The rest will have been eliminated."

His manner relaxed, his face showing a deep concern, Steve framed his words carefully. "The Secretary General of the New Earth Federation argues that it's 'Gaia's will' to remove these people from the earth. I say that he's deceiving you. And he must be stopped."

"Cut him off," Dr. Greider screamed. "That's treason. Cut him off!"

Responding to his orders, engineers worked feverishly, frantically entering data into the master computer. But nothing they did would erase the face of Steve Weston from their screens.

His deep baritone voice coming from the high-quality speakers mounted on the walls beside the wallscreens resonated boldly throughout the hushed room.

"This evil regime," Steve said, "that now rules most of the world has already been responsible for the death of more than one-quarter of the earth's population. The World Leader and those who control the

New Earth Federation are the ones who have brought about the bloody and devastating wars, and the horrors of the Great Famine. And their scientists are responsible for the spread of the deadly Maylay virus that has claimed the lives of millions more. I've come to believe that there is no limit to their capacity for cruelty against the human race. And now, the ultimate question is whether, in the final scheme of things, the human race itself will fall to the level of rejecting all that is good."

Rushing to where Mueller was seated, Dr. Greider shouted, "Bernard, do something. Can't you break that transmission?"

Mueller shrugged his shoulders. "The signals that we're transmitting to the satellites are not the same signals that are coming back down. It sounds impossible, but according to our systems analysis, the signal that's being carried to the world is originating from the satellites themselves. They've become . . . sort of independent broadcasting stations. There's nothing we can do about it."

"Well, just shut everything down, Mueller!"

"I'm sorry, we can't even do that. Our input is ineffective."

Infuriated, Greider spun around and stormed across the room, waving his arms and shouting orders.

With every eye staring up at Steve Weston, suddenly the mood in the room shifted. Intrigued by what he was saying, it was as if they wanted him to continue. As if they were relieved that someone was finally saying those things.

Someone increased the audio volume slightly.

Flashing his warm smile, Steve continued. "No person knows the true meaning of life until he has found something he's willing to die for. I learned what that was from an old and dear friend. He sought truth all his life, and near the end, he found it."

Hundreds of millions of people throughout the world stopped what they were doing and curiously watched Steve Weston as he turned and picked up a leather-bound notebook that had been lying on the desk beside him.

Holding the book loosely in his hands, he glanced down at it. "In this book are my friend's hand-scribbled notes detailing his long and arduous journey into the light of wisdom and understanding. The legacy he left me was his sincere admonition that I, too, seek after the truth with all my mind and heart. And once I had found it, to forsake everything else to make it my own.

"My friend introduced me to writings that spoke of such times as these. He called them the prophecies. They come from the Holy Bible. In the prophecies, written thousands of years ago, is described a man who would rise to power and would lead the world to the brink of total destruction. The prophecies called this man the 'Antichrist.'

"Many believe that the one who fits the description of this person, this Antichrist, is the Secretary General of the New Earth Federation, the World Leader."

People across the world stared into their video screens, mesmerized by the words of the man whom they had learned to know and trust.

"I also learned by reading his notes in this handwritten book that the Antichrist would lead a global army against the tiny nation of Israel, bent on totally wiping out the Jewish people and determined to set up his own throne in the city of Jerusalem. Well, according to my sources, for months now, millions of troops, along with vast amounts of military machinery and hardware, have been staging to the north of Israel, evidently in preparation for a decisive blow against that nation.

"But there is one gigantic kink in the well-laid plans of the Antichrist. If this is the final apocalyptic battle described in the biblical prophecies, the World Leader and his armies will find themselves fighting against Jesus Christ and the hosts of heaven. And they'll be horribly destroyed in the bloodiest battle ever to be fought on Planet Earth. The price to the human race, and to the earth itself, will be beyond our comprehension."

Laying the leather-bound book back down on the desk, Steve looked directly into the eye of the camera. With compassion in his voice, laced with a sense of urgency, he said, "Millions of people around the world are rejecting the World Leader's claim that he is God and are refusing to submit to becoming a computer number by receiving the Seal of Gaia.

"I know that I've already signed my own death warrant by making this telecast. But that's not important any longer. Like many of you who oppose their despotic rule, I'm in hiding, in the company of people whom I can trust, people who believe, as I do, that the only course left for us is to resist. I will remain in hiding, at least for a while. But wherever I am, I will fight this evil regime and the evil people behind it."

A profound silence lay across the TV9 master control room as each person quietly processed, in his own way, the words that the figure on their screens was saying. With an unspoken respect, all eyes stared intently into the face of Steve Weston, a solitary figure standing alone against the pervasive power of the Social Order—a flesh-and-blood being who had placed himself in the path of the advancing might of the Global Forces.

"I've come to you to ask you to join us," Steve pleaded. "Help us fight against the most insidious evil system that has ever plagued the human race. To all of the people of the world who believe in human dignity and freedom, and who long to be delivered out from under the iron heel of this oppressive regime, I beg you to join us in our fight. Join with us to form a mighty wave of resistance to protect ourselves and our families from their insanity."

Deeply moved, Steve paused momentarily, then resumed his plea to his world audience. "We are one with all the suffering peoples of the world. We are one with the Christians, the Jews, the political dissidents, and the millions of others who simply long to be free."

Sitting back down on the edge of the desk, he picked up Dr. Pennington's notebook, folded it in his arms, and cradled it gently against his chest.

Looking into the camera, he said softly, "This is Steve Weston. Farewell."

The screens of the world slowly faded to black.

Inside the TV9 Master Control room in Geneva, Dr. Bernard Mueller quietly, unobtrusively, entered a short code into the computer keyboard on the massive console in front of him. When he pressed ENTER, TV9's regularly scheduled programming was instantly restored.

"We're even, Weston," Mueller muttered under his breath.

THIRTY-SEVEN

The outline of the towering ancient castle rose like a shadowy apparition at the summit of the hill, lying quietly secluded in a remote area in northern Austria near the Danube River. Standing majestically tall against the ages, its lengthy heritage had been etched in the ancient stone and in the blood and sweat of those who labored, fought, and died in its shadow.

Built in 1704, an imposing, time-worn, brick-and-concrete fence encircled the five-hundred-acre estate. The silvery crescent moon, darting in and out of the scattered, black-tinged clouds, cast vague shimmering images across the twenty-foot-high, iron-spiked gate guarding the main entrance to the castle grounds.

A young guard cradled a slender compact automatic weapon in the bend of his left arm as he strolled casually just inside the iron gate. Stopping to light a cigarette, he thought he heard a faint noise. His breath catching in his throat, he froze in place for a heartbeat, a fatal mistake.

A scant ten feet behind him, a figure dressed in a long, black garment moved silently, swiftly toward the guard. His features were hidden inside a hood, his face obscured, indistinct, as if it were covered with a sheer black shroud. With one swift, fluid motion, the figure reached out and slipped a thin wire around the young guard's neck. His powerful arms pulled tightly, bringing instant death. As the guard's body quivered, then went limp, strong arms caught him and gently laid the lifeless body down on the cool, damp grass.

The Assassin was tall and structured like an athlete in prime condition. His slender waist tapered up, flaring into a massive chest broad enough for a man twice his size. His strong neck rested on wide powerful shoulders, his muscular arms and legs balancing out his lithe frame. His fiery eyes and dark, brooding features were framed by a neatly cut black beard. His long, silky black hair reached down to his shoulders.

Emerging from the shadows, four other dark figures, dressed in dull black combat uniforms, joined the Assassin. Caressing deadly Stouts J-74 automatic weapons, they moved swiftly, stealthily, behind the Assassin, following the graceful twists and bends in the long, winding, tree-shrouded road. Their eyes focused with evil intent, their destination was the castle, a quarter of a mile away.

Upon reaching the castle, they moved catlike across stone steps worn smooth by centuries of shuffling feet, then glided swiftly to the castle entrance. Flattening their backs against the ancient wooden doors, they waited, listening, their eyes scanning the darkness. Without a sound, one of the men retrieved a small clump of plastic explosive from his satchel. Fixing it carefully to one of the massive doors at the point of the door's locking mechanism, he lit a short fuse and stepped back, turning away in anticipation of the explosion.

Secluded on the third-floor level of the castle, two people occupied a sumptuously furnished room, a long expanse with an imposing fireplace at one end. Facing the fireplace was a large Victorian couch, surrounded by an assortment of chairs arranged in random fashion. Subdued lights scattered throughout the gilded room cast the expensive tapestries, priceless paintings, and world-class sculptures in deep shadow.

A thick, heavy mantelpiece, fashioned from a solid beam of hardwood, aged and smooth, stretched more than twelve feet from end to end, resting on two large decorative columns on either side of the cavernous fireplace. Above the mantelpiece hung a thick wooden cross, roughly hewn from ancient timbers. The flickering light from the fire cast a shimmering shadow of the cross along the floor and up against the high walls of the room.

Steve Weston pushed himself up from the high-backed leather chair and walked slowly to the huge fireplace, strangely drawn by the mystery of the rugged artifact. His eyes tracing its compelling attractiveness, he wondered at how dreadful sin must be. Placing his left hand lightly against the massive mantel, he lowered his eyes and stared silently into the glowing fire. Clad in slacks and sweater, his right hand held a long-stemmed crystal glass, half-full of brandy.

After a thoughtful silence, he turned and looked down at Audrey Montaigne, who was reclining on the couch, dozing in semisleep, the soft firelight playing on her attractive face.

They had been here for three weeks awaiting safe passage to their next hiding place. They were in the care of General Jefferson Hardin, a leader in the International Resistance Movement (IRM), and a former officer in the Global Peace Forces of the New Earth Federation. Branded as a traitor for having defected, and living under a death sentence, General Hardin was a driving force in the mounting opposition to the World Leader and the NEF.

The International Resistance Movement was a worldwide movement made up of political and religious dissidents who refused to live their lives in servitude to the World Leader and the Social Order.

Alone in his thoughts, Steve shifted his weight, glanced up at the wooden cross and momentarily reflected on its meaning. More than five feet in height, it was not a thing of beauty. If anything, it was ugly and old. But maybe it had a deeper meaning, he reasoned. Something to do with this room they were in—a tale, perhaps, of some raging battle. Of the ancient worlds of magic and myth.

Standing motionless and subdued under the heavy weight of its profound significance, its very presence spoke to him of the eternal conflict between good and evil, principalities and powers—God and Satan. His unblinking stare held in the grasp of the ageless symbol above him, he knew somehow, in his inner essence, that it was the same timeless battle that had brought him to this point in his life, and to this room.

Several weeks earlier, through a carefully choreographed escape plan, he and Audrey had left Geneva, setting in motion the first step in their daring bid for freedom. Audrey had left first, having traveled with the World Leader to Paris, France. After filing several stories for TV9 from there, according to their plan, she had mysteriously dropped out of sight.

Steve left Geneva a week later to go to a conference in Rome. After the closing night, he had been smuggled aboard a single-engine private plane and flown to Athens, Greece. Arriving in Athens, he was taken in by members of the Restoration Party from the former United States of America, now part of the International Resistance Movement. Through an elaborate underground network, run by the IRM, he had traveled in disguise through several different countries, meeting Audrey six days later at their rendezvous point, this safe house.

Steve thought of Dr. Mueller and smiled. Even though he had once had his doubts about him, Mueller had kept his promise.

Steve had arranged to have Mueller come to his own apartment in Geneva to videotape him just before activating his escape plan. After the taping, Mueller had digitally altered the tape, erasing the background, and inserting another background, so that no one would know his location at the time of taping.

After Dr. Mueller had flashed Steve's speech to the television screens of the world, the World Leader was livid with anger, prompting the New Earth Federation courts to issue an arrest warrant for him and Audrey, charging them both with high treason and placing a death sentence on them. They had defied the Social Order and would be killed without mercy. GU5 remained only a step behind them.

Encouraged by Steve's bold stand, mounting numbers of people worldwide were joining the Resistance to fight against the World Leader and the global government. And millions were refusing to take the Seal of Gaia.

Shortly before leaving Geneva, Steve had retrieved a small computer disk from the lining of one of his coats, slipped it into his computer at his office, and downloaded the entire Gaia Project file onto Group-Net, the worldwide people's computer network.

Before the authorities could stop it, millions of copies of the file had been downloaded by individuals throughout the world. Circulating across the globe at the speed of light, the Gaia Project file became the most damaging disclosure ever about the Social Order and the World Leader and their plans for the human race.

Even though the authorities denounced it vehemently as fraudulent, the Gaia Project file prompted massive resistance to the NEF and the World Leader, causing many to join the International Resistance Movement.

One of the leaders of the IRM, Steve had learned, was Colonel Keith Fletcher, the commanding officer he had met aboard the military plane when he was going to Geneva for the tenth anniversary of the NEF. Serving under a death sentence, Colonel Fletcher and his men had inflicted heavy damage on the Global Peace Forces, proving to be a formidable enemy of the Social Order.

This strong opposition against their authority precipitated a fierce new wave of persecution, driven by the nightly maniacal rantings of the World Leader before the cameras of Sky News Network.

Steve looked out at the elegant room, grateful for the momentary respite and for the brave men and women who had risked their own lives in helping them. This castle was designated a "safe house," one of hundreds of sites being used by the IRM to help those who were fleeing from the wrath of the global government.

Quartered in other parts of the castle were more than twenty military personnel, most of them having been trained by the Global Peace Forces but now loyal to the Resistance. In addition, three guards patrolled the outside grounds at all times. With an impressive arsenal of weapons and ammunition, the castle was a virtual fortress. Playing host to two high-profile people like Steve and Audrey caused everyone to be on alert.

Audrey stirred, shook her auburn hair into place, breathed deeply, and smiled up at Steve. She then stood and walked to the fireplace, standing beside him. Hugging herself and shivering from the chill in the ancient room, she leaned gently against Steve's arm.

When Steve reached out his left arm to wrap it around her shoulders, an explosion of immense intensity shook the castle, causing him to drop the wine glass, shattering it against the stone floor.

Audrey froze. Her face turned ashen.

Paralyzed in fear, her eyes wide in terror, her knees buckled under her. As her body went limp and she started to crumble to the floor, Steve grabbed her under the arms, steadied her, and carried her to the couch.

T he darkness outside the castle suddenly burst into a brilliant flash of light as the plastic explosive erupted with an angry, heavy thud, shattering the stillness of the night. The dry, gray, heavy timber of the large front doors was blown apart, splintering into tattered fragments, leaving only ugly charred remains hanging loosely from the rusted hinges.

Like dogs of prey who had caught the scent of spilled blood, the Assassin led the dark-clad men in a violent charge through the shattered doors into the cavernous main room of the castle, their automatic weapons sweeping the vast expanse.

Responding to the explosion, a short, powerfully built man rushed through a door to the Assassin's left, a handgun gripped menacingly in his right hand, his eyes searching the darkened room.

Bellowing like an enraged animal, the Assassin lifted his gun and fired. A deadly six-round burst of death thundered from the stubby barrel of his Stouts, slamming the 9-mm slugs mercilessly into the chest of the hapless man, throwing him violently back against the stone wall. His shirt bathed in crimson, his gun falling from his limp fingers, he softly moaned a final breath, and his lifeless form slid agonizingly down into a pool of his own blood.

Seeing movement at the far end of the castle's main room, the Assassin's head turned quickly, his blazing eyes registering intense hatred, dark rage.

Two armed shapes emerged from an open doorway, running toward the intruders, their automatic weapons blazing fiercely, a flurry of bullets slashing through the air only inches from the Assassin's head.

Before they could adjust their aim, a barrage of fire erupted from the assailant's deadly arsenal, sending fiery streams of bullets into the two men's chests. When the incredible force of the high-velocity projectiles slammed into their bodies, it jerked them violently around and they fell to the floor like a child's broken toy, arms and legs sprawling at awkward angles.

The stone walls of the ancient castle echoed and reechoed with rumbling death as the savage night exploded in pitiless fury like a crazed, frenzied dance of death out of the pagan world of the Dark Ages. Screams of agony pierced the gathering terror while deadly automatic weapons chattered with deafening intensity.

Chaos reigned, brutal and savage.

Trained as coldblooded killers, the assailants had been carefully schooled and programmed to subjugate their own wills to those of their superiors in the Social Order with unquestioning loyalty. Devoid of any moral concept except the code that had been embedded within their thought processes since they were young children, they killed without compunction or hesitation.

Having been conditioned from childhood to vilify their victims as subpeople, not really human, they killed with little feeling, whether sympathy or hate. Such scientific conditioning of their minds and values produced a class of warriors with no limit to the cruelty they were capable of committing. They found killing enjoyable, as intense as sexual pleasure.

With seven left dead from their initial blood-drenched orgy of death, the specters in black turned with increased vengeance toward the broad, spiraling staircase and the prize that waited somewhere in the upper levels.

Madness and immeasurable hate were reflected in the twisted, demonic smiles on their faces.

THIRTY-EIGHT

Hearing the explosion and automatic weapons fire, Steve knew something was horribly wrong. Moving quickly, he scooped up his Omni 444. Caressing the smooth handle in his right hand, he slowly pulled open the heavy oak door a few inches and looked down the darkened hallway, scanning it carefully in both directions.

Seeing that the hallway on the third floor was clear, he closed the door and walked back to Audrey. Her color had returned to her face and she was sitting up. "What is it, Steve? What's the shooting?" she asked frantically.

"Probably GU5," he answered knowingly. "Somehow they've found this place."

"What are we going to do?" she asked, her eyes betraying her fear.

"I'll see what's going on, but I want you to stay in this room. Don't come out under any circumstances. Do you understand?"

Her body trembling, she answered, "Yes . . . I understand."

"Do you have your weapon?"

"It's in my handbag."

"Get it, and don't be afraid to use it. I'll be back as soon as I can."

"Steve . . . please be careful."

With a quick smile, he said, "Lock the door behind me."

Cautiously opening the door, Steve carefully surveyed the hallway again. Seeing that it was clear, he slipped out. He pulled the door closed behind him and heard Audrey lock it.

Hugging close to the wall, he let his Omni lead the way as he moved warily, quietly, down the darkened hallway toward the spiral staircase, his senses alert.

His breath suddenly catching in his throat when he saw the faint outline of a figure moving toward him, he froze in place. With his fingers curled around the cold metal of his gun, he instinctively raised his weapon to fire.

"Hold your fire, Weston," a familiar voice whispered. "It's me, General Hardin."

Steve sighed a deep sigh of relief and lowered his gun. His hand was shaking.

General Jefferson Hardin was a man of seventy or more. Short, heavyset, completely bald, he was in excellent physical condition. From the state of Alabama, he was a graduate of West Point and had seen action during the Third Gulf War and many other battles. Steve liked his easy manner and the slow way he talked.

"What's going on, General?" Steve asked in low tones.

"GU5 hit squad, I reckon," the general replied, barely above a whisper.

Shoving an automatic weapon into Steve's hand, he said, "Here, you'll need this. Coupla' extra clips too."

Placing his handgun in his belt at his back, Steve took the Galaxy 9-mm automatic gun and released the safety.

"What's the situation, General?"

"Had seven men on the first floor. From what I can tell, they've all been killed."

"All seven?"

"All seven," the general replied. "Had three on the outside—probably killed one, maybe more, when they came on the grounds. If anyone's alive, they heard the explosions. Should be maneuvering for position now. Can't count on it, though."

"What are you going to do?"

"Got our backup force down on the second level. They're maneuvering into position now. Gives us the high ground. We'll take 'em, don't you worry."

"What do you want me to do?"

General Hardin glanced at Steve. "You're in my care, son. Nothin's gonna happen to you as long as I can help it. I want you to keep that weapon handy, though. Use it if you have to, guard your door, don't let nothin' harm that lady."

With that, the old general turned and moved silently down the darkened hallway toward the back stairs for another rendezvous with another enemy.

As soon as the general disappeared into the darkness, Steve cautiously moved through the hallway toward the spiral staircase. Walking into the subdued light shining up from the first floor, he moved to the edge of the bannister.

The sounds of automatic weapons fire and the frantic voices of the dying continued to echo off the stone walls of the castle. Men's voices screamed obscenities.

Crouching low, from his position on the third floor, Steve watched the movements of one of the assailants as he rushed toward the spiral staircase, moving cautiously upward, a step at a time, his back against the wall, his automatic weapon chattering, his face set in deadly purpose.

Instantly, Steve aimed, his finger caressing the trigger of the deadly Galaxy automatic, his hand steady, the muzzle pointed unwaveringly at the assailant's chest. He pulled the trigger hard. The gun jumped in his hand and beat hard against his shoulder as a burst of 9-mm projectiles ripped into the right arm of the menacing figure.

Grimacing in pain, the assailant instantly swung his weapon toward the flash of Steve's gun and pulled the trigger, sending a spray of bullets tearing into the bannister and walls around Steve's head. Feeling a sharp stab in his left arm, Steve raised his Galaxy to fire the second time.

His gun aimed down at the assailant, Steve saw a slight movement on the second-floor level below him, hesitated, stepped back. His eyes traced the darkened area overlooking the second floor landing at the head of the spiraling staircase. He could make out the outline of a figure, saw him pull the pin from a hand grenade, hold it a few seconds, then roll it down the stairs toward the assailant.

Hearing the grenade bumping solidly against the carpeted stairs above him, the assailant froze, his eyes glazed over with cold fear as he wildly searched the thick darkness in front of him, knowing his fate.

Feeling the grenade bounce against his leg, the assailant knew instantly what it was, with no time to react. The savage, crimson flash of the exploding grenade lit up the large room for a terrible moment, rocking the castle, sending flying shrapnel ripping into the body of the assailant, lifting him, and hurling him over the handrail. Like a child's kite twisting in the wind, his lifeless form floated downward to crash violently on the floor below.

Their eyes reflecting measureless hate, the other assailants were surprised and stunned by the explosion. Instantly lifting their guns, they threw their aim toward the darkness at the head of the stairs, shooting blindly into the void. Like stuttering thunder, the castle erupted with the deafening roar of machine-gun fire, orange tongues of flame darting upward, and a man screaming in agony somewhere.

In the confusion, a dark figure silently slithered up the winding stairs, hidden behind the curtain of smoke from the grenade. Undetected, he disappeared into the shadows, moving with deadly intent, as if he knew exactly where he was going.

Standing to his feet, Steve moved cautiously toward the head of the stairs, determined to stop anyone who attempted to come to the third level. Feeling a sizzling sensation in his left arm, he instinctively touched the affected spot. Probing the injured place with the tips of his finger, he felt the warm presence of his own blood.

Evidently, he reasoned, a round from the assailant's gun had torn through the fleshy part of his left arm, near the shoulder.

The pain in his left arm was agonizing. He bit his lower lip. With blood now covering his arm, he grimaced but decided the throbbing pain was something he could live with. He would tend to it later.

Suddenly, a woman's scream of terror pierced the night.

A cold chill of outright terror ripped through Steve's gut. Feeling the sudden bitterness of his own bile rising from his stomach, almost gagging him, he knew with cruel certainty that it was Audrey's voice.

Can't panic.

Gripping the Galaxy tightly in his strong hand, he ran doggedly toward the hallway that would lead him back to his room. Fearing he had made a mistake by leaving her, he cursed under his breath. Pushing himself to his limits, his lungs bursting for air, he ran with all his might, using his last burst of energy in an effort to reach her, to save her life.

Everyone whom he had ever loved had been taken away from him, and he had felt alone in the world, until Audrey. The possibility of losing her filled his mind with a deep, immeasurable dread.

A few more steps . . .

His heart pounding furiously, he raced toward the faint light coming from the open door. Drawing closer, he saw that it had been shattered by a strong force.

Bursting through the open door, Steve saw a terrible sight, freezing him in place for a frightening moment. Audrey was thrashing wildly on the floor. A heavily armed man wearing dark combat clothes was pressing his strong hand against her throat, pinning her solidly under him.

An enormous knife, gleaming in the half-light, held tightly in the assailant's hand, was being raised menacingly in preparation for its downward thrust. Steve watched in horror as the man's arm reached the apex of its upward motion and gazed helplessly as the hand and knife started their downward plunge in a murderous arc toward Audrey's chest.

Locked in a fight for her life, Steve gave vent to a horrible animallike scream of pure rage and desperation and lunged with all his might, propelling himself through the air toward the assailant in a final attempt to stop the dreadful deed.

With adrenaline pumping furiously through his bloodstream, the world suddenly slowed, and Steve saw everything pass before his eyes in surreal slow motion. His horizontal body now gliding through the air, his arms outstretched, his frantic eyes followed the slow arcing path of the instrument of death in its descending flight toward the terrified woman.

In one last bid to save Audrey's life, Steve defied the pain in his arm and commanded his left hand to reach for the blade of the knife. When the sharp and deadly steel tip of the blade was only inches away from her chest, Steve's left hand reached the blade and seized it in his bare fingers.

Tightening his hand around its sharpness with brute force, he was able to deflect the blade's downward motion just enough to knock it off course, causing it to miss Audrey's chest by a fraction of an inch. The weight of Steve's body slamming against the assailant sent him sprawling across the floor.

With his hand bleeding profusely, the flesh peeled back at grotesque angles, Steve looked down and saw the horrible instrument, still gripped in his knotted fist. Horrified, he opened his hand and let the bloody knife drop to the floor.

Rising, he turned to see if Audrey was safe. In that split second, the assailant gained his feet and launched himself with maximum force into Steve's back, sending the two men plummeting to the floor, rolling, spinning, their bodies intertwined in a grim dance of death.

Held tightly by the assailant's strong arms, Steve exploded in a sudden fury, managing to break free from the savage strength. Regaining his feet, he glared at his adversary, his nostrils flaring, his hands knotted into fists, blood oozing from his shoulder and left hand.

Before Steve could take a step, the room suddenly spun and his vision blurred, just for a brief second. He blinked his eyes and tried to shake the dizziness from his head, his mind screaming at him to keep fighting, to protect Audrey and destroy his enemy.

Teeth clenched against the pain, Steve hurled himself toward the man. Suddenly, a savage kick from the assailant's right foot stunned him, sent him crumbling to the floor, his breath exploding from his lungs as he hit.

In a heartbeat, the assailant's muscular body fell across him with deadly force. With his superior strength, he pinned Steve to the floor, his strong hands wrapped in a death grip around his throat.

Gasping for air, Steve tore furiously at the assailant's powerful hands. Exhausted and physically spent from loss of blood, he felt himself sliding down a long darkened tube, fading into unconsciousness. Believing that he was dying, he tried to call out, but no words came.

Growing numb.

Sight dimming.

Blackness closing in on him.

Gripped in the clutches of a descending darkness, his mind throbbed with nagging questions and crippling doubts that seemed to mock him.

In a flash, his mind sifted through the chain of events that had brought him to this room, at this moment, to his death.

His entire belief system, his reason for being, his sense of what was right and wrong, just and moral, had been turned upside down, and he now felt betrayed, abandoned, and very much alone.

And then he felt a deep sense of guilt.

Not just a fleeting guilt, but a debilitating kind of guilt that made him ashamed that he was part of the human race.

Steve Weston was dying with the sure knowledge that he was part of the Social Order's violence and brutality against the world's people.

Shadowy forms and grotesque images were now passing before his eyes.

Terrified, he feared he had fallen into the clutches of evil forces who were reaching deep inside his being, tearing at him, trying to extract his immortal soul from his body.

Am I dying?

In his fading consciousness, he wondered if there was a being out there somewhere who was just, who would, somehow, absolve him of his part in the evil that had oppressed the world.

And in a final desperate act, he summoned all the powers of his will to return, to live.

Echoing and reechoing somewhere in the deep recesses of his burning mind, he heard loud explosions, repeating, repeating, repeating, one after the other, a steady rhythm of terror.

The strong hands around his neck that were draining his life away suddenly relaxed, and light began to flood his brain again, a gift of life.

As his vision slowly returned, he saw the assailant stiffen, a look of surprise and terror on his menacing face. The assailant moaned softly, then pitched forward heavily and crumbled to the floor with a sickening thud.

Steve pushed himself out from under the heavy body. Shaking his head vigorously, he tried to clear his mind, to recapture his thoughts. As the room slowly came into focus, he looked up.

Audrey was standing over the dead man, her handgun gripped tightly in her hands, a look of undistilled fear on her face.

Eyes wide and glazed, she was pulling and repulling the trigger of her handgun, again and again, emptying the cartridges into the dead body until the chamber was empty.

Her face a mask of terror, she continued to pull the trigger of the empty gun, the hammer slamming with a metallic ring against the empty chamber. Her reasoning faculties paralyzed by fear, her fingers were frozen around the handle of the gun.

Rushing to her side, Steve had to forcibly pry her fingers from the weapon. "That's enough, Audrey. That's enough. He's dead. He can't hurt us anymore."

Audrey blinked her eyes, suddenly coming out of her blind stupor. As her fury subsided, her eyes refocused and she glanced down at the dead man, repelled by what she had done. ·

With a low moan, her shoulders heaved and she sobbed uncontrollably.

Steve caught her, moved her to the couch, and held her.

THIRTY-NINE

Steve flinched when Audrey applied the stinging medicine to the wound on his shoulder. Having determined that the shoulder wound was superficial, she turned her attention to the open, gaping wounds on his left hand. After carefully cleaning the cut flesh, she wrapped it snugly with a cloth she had torn from one of the sheets in the room.

Suddenly a chilling blast of air swept in through the door from the darkened hallway, causing her to look up. Drawing a sharp breath, her eyes glazed over for an instant, her gaze fixed on something behind Steve. She tried to speak, but no words would come.

Steve knew instantly that something was terribly wrong. Leaping to his feet, he turned to see the faint outline of a dark figure standing in the thick shadow of the doorway.

The tall figure was dressed in a black robe cinched snugly about the waist. A black hood completely covered his head, casting his face in shadow. A menacing automatic weapon hung loosely from his shoulder, its barrel pointed at them.

Steve glanced at his own automatic weapon lying on the table only four feet away and made some quick calculations. He hesitated, knowing he wouldn't have time to reach it before the figure opened fire on them.

His mouth dry with fear, he stared into the black void of the hood where the face should have been. From the darkness of the hood, a macabre pair of red glaring eyes stared out at him with a penetrating intensity and evil purpose.

Something spectral had entered the room, an eerie, intangible presence halfway between rage and terror, covering Steve and Audrey with a dark premonition.

They were facing an evil too dreadful to contemplate.

Concerned for Audrey, Steve placed his arm around her trembling shoulders. Their eyes were locked on the red glaring eyes staring out at them, silently sharing a fear they couldn't bring themselves to express in words.

The figure moved slowly, silently, from the shadows into the dim light of the room. His booming voice cold and threatening, he called out loudly, "Steve Weston!"

Strangely, Steve knew he had heard that voice before . . . *somewhere*.

A cold, hard shudder traveled down his spine.

The black-hooded form moved a step closer, his gun pointed at them menacingly. Steve's muscles tensed, his throat went dry, and cold sweat lay against his face like a damp cloth. Bordering on panic, he forced himself to take deep, regular breaths and let them out slowly.

"I must kill you, Steve Weston," the dark figure said.

"Who are you?" Steve called out.

The figure gave a low, guttural growl, then answered, "You have betrayed our trust in you, Weston. And you must pay. In your final redemption, you will bow your knee to the World Leader, your God."

The menacing figure stood rigidly still, threatening.

With a defiant voice, Steve answered, "Then kill me if you must. But I will not bow my knee."

"Then prepare for battle," he thundered.

"Are you afraid to tell me your name?" Steve called out.

The figure laughed a maniacal laugh. "You may call me the *Assassin*, Weston."

Calmly, Steve instructed Audrey, "Back away slowly. Move toward the bed and stay there, no matter what happens."

Her panic threatening to overwhelm her, Audrey slowly backed away, her eyes trained on the terrible intruder.

Steve steeled himself to do battle with the dark image. Knowing that he could lose his life on this night, in this room, he wondered at all the seemingly disconnected events that had directed his destiny to this moment.

Was it a final test of his manhood, or was it punishment to be meted out on him for his part in the monstrous, bloody regime that ruled most of the world? Would his own violent death atone for his own sins?

When Audrey was out of range, Steve lunged for his automatic weapon lying on the table. With lightning speed, the Assassin snap-aimed and pulled the trigger of his automatic weapon. A hail of bullets shattered the table, sending splintered wood flying across the room, the bullets missing Steve's hand by inches.

The Assassin laughed a loud, hollow, scornful laugh, its sound as harsh and thundering as an avalanche. "No, Weston," he cried out mockingly. "It's not going to be so easy. You see, I intend to kill you with my bare hands, not with a gun." He then dropped his gun to the floor.

Exploding in a sudden blaze of red fury, the Assassin lunged at Steve, striking him hard, his massive fist delivering a stunning blow to his head, snapping him violently backward and sending him plummeting to the floor.

Steve shuddered with the force of the blow. Blood streamed down the left side of his face.

Staggering to his feet, Steve charged the being with all his might, driving his left shoulder into his solar plexus, slamming him hard against the wall near the fireplace.

Red eyes glaring, his black robe billowing, the Assassin gave a low, resonating growl, half-human, half-animal. His profane energy radiated through the darkness, a tangible thing.

Steve spun around suddenly, his leg rising in a high, savage round-house kick. With all the force he could muster, his heel slammed into the side of the Assassin's face. The force of the blow sent the evil being reeling backward, sprawling across the floor.

Pushing himself into a full body roll that brought him back to his feet, the dark image moved toward Steve with insidious purpose.

"I commend you for your courage and determination, Steve Weston," the hooded voice said as it drew closer. "You are a worthy opponent."

Steve knew he was no match for the Assassin, but if he could just stall him for a few minutes more, General Hardin and the others would come to their rescue—if any of them were still alive.

Steve spun again, hoping to land another blow with his foot. But the Assassin anticipated the coming kick perfectly and was able to avoid it by lurching backward.

Before Steve could recover, the Assassin's strong arms seized his body in a suffocating embrace. Lifting him as if he were a child, he raised him over his head, held him there, turning, spinning. The spinning grew faster, more intense. Taking on a surreal dimension, Steve felt that he was being pulled into an endless, spinning vortex, caught in the grip of pure, unrelenting evil.

The Assassin then hurled Steve against the wall, slamming him with a dreadful force. Multicolored lights flashed in his head for an instant. He slumped to the floor, semiconscious. The being fell on top of him like a wild animal at the moment of the kill.

Feeling strong, vicious hands tearing at his throat, Steve thrashed wildly, clawing furiously at the alien hands that wanted to take his life. Unrelenting waves of terror broke and formed within his chest at the thought of being in the clutches of something so unquestionably evil.

Fighting against the rising panic and despair, something within him refused to die. The gift of life meant too much to let it end here.

"By my own hand, you will die, Weston!" the Assassin screamed, his strong hands pressing mercilessly against his throat. Steve could smell the fiend's hot, fetid breath.

No! I won't die, not in this room. . . .

Suddenly, Audrey gave vent to a terrifying scream that echoed through the room with a shattering force. Distracted for a split second, the Assassin's grasp slackened slightly. Finding the strength from somewhere, Steve seized the opportunity to wrench himself free.

Audrey watched in horror as the Assassin turned around with lightning speed and rushed toward her in a vile, patternless frenzy. Helpless, her panic threatening to overcome her, she tried to run. But before she could take a step, a powerful hand grabbed her arm and spun her around. Her captor could read the wild-eyed horror in her face, as if she knew what to expect.

Overcoming her with his superior strength, the Assassin slapped her viciously across her cheekbone with his large hand, the full force of his weight behind it. Tasting her own blood in her injured mouth, she fell hard against the floor and lost her breath.

Steve staggered to his feet, shook his head. The blood from a reopened cut on his face trickled down into one eye, and he blinked. With his vision blurring, he had difficulty focusing on anything.

Breathing hard, he felt his strength draining from his body.

Got to protect Audrey. . . .

Wiping his bloody mouth with the back of his hand, he watched in horror as the Assassin lifted Audrey from the floor, raising her high above his head. Caught in the grip of an uncontrollable rage, Steve gave vent to a desperate primal scream and launched his body with abandon into the air to land hard against the Assassin's back.

Striking him solidly, the dark figure was momentarily stunned, causing him to drop Audrey unharmed to the floor.

Grabbing the Assassin's flowing black hood, Steve viciously whirled him around twice, then hurled him to the floor with all his might. Gripped in a seething fit of rage, he crushed his foot against his chest, holding it there. And with one swift movement, reached down with both hands and grabbed the dark spectral hood and ripped it from the creature's body, exposing his face.

Shuddering with revulsion, Steve stared into his face, suddenly recognizing the infinitely evil being. Fighting the urge to bolt in terror, he stumbled backward.

"Satan!" he gasped, his face frozen in stunned recognition.

It was the face of the creature that he had seen high above the crystal spires over the Omega when he had gone to The Mountain with Dr. Mueller. The being that had fled from the presence of Michael, the Archangel.

Time froze.

Slowly, the figure stood to his feet, smiling. "I see that you recognize me, Steve Weston." He then laughed a bellowing laugh, the sound rich with ancient evil and malice.

A hard knot of fear formed in Steve's stomach. Sweat beaded on his forehead. Only willpower kept him standing. Willpower and hate. A burning hatred for this creature and his diabolical plan to destroy humanity. He hated this creature with an intensity that bordered on madness.

With fear having drained her body of its strength, Audrey stared helplessly at the sinister creature facing Steve. Her mind and emotions nearing a shutdown, a soft whimper escaped from her lips, a whimper like that of a small child facing a darkened room all alone. She then closed her mind against the rising panic.

Her eyes now set in a catatonic stare, she backed slowly away from the creature. Unable to speak, neither hearing nor feeling, she merely climbed onto the bed, lay down on her right side, and drew her legs to her chest. Wrapping her arms around her knees tightly, she closed her eyes, trying to will away the frightening scenes.

Taunting Steve, the menacing figure yelled derisively, "You're such a fool, Weston. I'm going to take your life, and the life of Ms. Montaigne. You had it all. I gave you power, position, fame. Everything you had came from me. I would have elevated you to heights beyond your wildest dreams. We were ready to initiate you into *The Realm*. But you deceived us. You were not ready to pledge yourself to us. You were not satisfied to serve the Social Order."

Drenched with sweat, Steve fought back the mounting terror.

"Do you control the Principals?" Steve asked, his voice harsh with anger.

"Yes!" the being answered in a loud voice. "They made a pact with me, promising to carry out my plan on earth. And . . . they used their alliance with me to get whatever they wanted. Position. Power. Money."

"But in the end you captured their eternal souls."

"But, of course."

"There is a power greater than yours, Satan!" Steve shouted to the creature. "You tried to destroy the human race, but the Archangel of the Most High God stopped you."

The creature's countenance suddenly reeking with measureless hate, his voice a deep, malevolent roar, he bellowed, "You will die, Weston! No one can protect you now."

Stunned at the arrogance of the statement, Steve declared sharply, "I will find a way to defeat you, Satan."

The dark creature clutched a long, black knife in his hand as he circled slowly to Steve's right, stalking him.

"I *chose* you, Weston. It was your destiny to rule with me. But you disappointed me. You have Secret Knowledge that only the *chosen* are allowed to know. I must not let you leave this room with that knowledge."

There was no way to measure the terror in Steve's mind, the chill in his soul. What he was seeing was not meant for mortal eyes.

Standing in the presence of this creature, he suddenly knew that there was a source of infinite evil. And that it was a being, an evil being that had taken on human flesh to engage in battle with him, and to kill him and Audrey.

The dark being laughed, as if he were reading Steve's thoughts. "Ah, Steve Weston, your imagination runs away with you. There is no such thing as evil. All things are good. I only want to bring happiness to the world."

Now confronted with the existence of Satan, he knew that God must exist also.

Suddenly, inexplicably, it seemed to Steve that time stood still and everything around him froze in place. And from the edges of his memory, he could hear his mother's soothing voice playing softly in his mind. She was once again kneeling with him beside his bed when he was a child. They were reciting a child's prayer, a prayer they said every night before he went to sleep.

He hadn't thought of the prayer since he was a small boy. But as clear as if she were standing beside him in this chamber of horrors, he heard her voice, and he spoke the words aloud.

"*. . . and deliver us from evil.*"

Suddenly he knew that the Assassin could not be beaten with physical weapons, or by mere human strength. There had to be another way.

"*. . . For thine is the kingdom and the power and the glory forever and ever, amen.*"

With a sudden flash of insight, Steve knew with certainty what the final outcome of the ancient battle would be. And with that realization, a gentle calm washed over his mind, and suddenly the fear was gone.

"I have no fear of death, Satan," Steve called out. "And I have no fear of you." The thought of his own death was now no more than a fleeting presence in his mind. But he would not allow this evil entity to harm Audrey. Even if it meant sacrificing his own life.

Enraged, the being ran toward Steve, the black knife gripped tightly in his hand. Steve backed quickly away, moving to the fireplace, looking desperately for a weapon of any kind. The flames of the two large candles set on either end of the mantelpiece cast the room in a brooding mosaic of light and shadow.

The dark figure was moving toward Steve, preparing to leap over the Victorian couch to get to him, his red blazing eyes fixed on him in a baleful stare. His power was tangible, his evil essence overwhelming. Steve knew that he would reach him in only a few more steps.

Don't panic. Stay calm.

Steve's left hand throbbed and ached with a dull, cold fire, the pain lancing downward through his entire body.

Backing up a few steps toward the fireplace, his foot unexpectedly brushed up against an object lying on the floor, almost causing him to stumble. Regaining his balance, he instinctively glanced down. It was his automatic weapon. Frantically, he reached for it, brought it up in a snap-aim, and pulled the trigger.

The sound of the gun shattered the quietness of the room.

The fusillade of 9-mm shells ripped savagely into the Assassin's chest while he was in midair, leaping over the couch. Steve glared at the figure in horror. The deadly bullets had done him no harm. Unbelievably, he only hesitated, threw his head back, and gave voice to a bone-chilling laugh, then started again toward Steve.

In desperation, Steve held the trigger down, firing the weapon relentlessly. He watched in mounting horror as the bullets slammed against his black robe, tearing it to shreds but doing no harm to the creature, even though the projectiles had demolished the couch, sending shards of wood and cloth spraying into the air.

A triumphant smile twisting his sharp features, the Assassin kept coming, unharmed, his red eyes glaring at Steve, cold, merciless.

Steve could feel the creature's hatred for him, a living thing.

Viciously lashing out at Steve with his closed fist, the Assassin caught him flush on the chin, sending fiery streaks of pain shooting through his body. Thrown back hard against the mantel of the fireplace, Steve's flailing arm struck a heavy object with a solid force, knocking it down and sending it crashing to the floor.

His voice now high-pitched and grating, the spectral being screamed contemptuously, "You interfered with my plans for the world before, Steve Weston, but I will still destroy the human race. I will wipe it off the planet."

Stumbling backward, his breathing now labored and shallow, Steve felt his consciousness begin to slowly fade as darkness closed in around him, threatening to shut his mind and body down. Waves of despair hammered at his firmness of purpose, draining his physical strength, robbing his strong heart of courage.

Touching the stone wall with his hand for support, he suddenly felt helpless before the terrible raging force of the dark creature, believing that no man could prevail against it. Though no less willing to fight on, he was battered and bleeding and drained of his strength, chilled at the certainty of his own dark premonition.

He could sense that the end was near.

He would die here.

The thought came in a dreadful moment of terrifying insight, born of his weakness, despair, and fading hope. He had fought the dark force with all his might. That his life would end here, like this, at the hands of this creature, was almost more than he could bear. Though battered and stunned, he had shown courage, so he would die unashamed.

The creature's eyes, burning like the flames of hell, were fixed on him with fiery intensity and would not move away.

Steve held the creature's gaze, unblinking.

Determined to exact another measure of pain on his enemy, Steve Weston looked for a place to make his final stand. But there was no place to hide in this room, no defensive barrier to shelter him. Wiping the blood and sweat from his eyes with the bandages on his wounded hand, he stumbled backward to the huge fireplace, its dim light play-ing across the Assassin's sinister features.

Knowing that his enemy was coming in for the final blow, Steve reached to the floor and picked up the object that had fallen from above the mantelpiece. His eyes never breaking their intense gaze into the dark figure's red, blazing eyes, his sense of touch told him that his weapon was a piece of wood, heavy, about five feet in length, with a crossbar about three feet in length.

Feeling the hard outline of the heavy object, he discovered that it was two pieces of smooth wood, bound together, forming a cross. This ancient cross that had been hanging above the fireplace would be his weapon of last resort against the dark force that threatened to take his life. Gripping the venerable object tightly in both of his wounded and bleeding hands, he lifted it high above his head, hold-ing it there.

Staggering back a single step, his muscles tightened in anticipation of the hard downward blow that he must give to his enemy. Knowing he would have only a fraction of a second to react, he would wait until the last instant to strike.

He would have only one chance. If he missed, he would die. Shuddering involuntarily, he cursed the fatigue and fear that clogged his mind.

The Assassin moved into position for the kill, his black robe torn to shreds by Steve's bullets. "Prepare to die, Weston," he thundered.

Strangely, the soft, peaceful glow of the flames from the candles on either end of the dark mantelpiece caught the upraised cross of wood in their flickering light, casting its shimmering shadow across the room.

Swallowing hard against the wave of nausea that threatened him, Steve watched the dark specter close the distance between them, his red feral eyes glaring with evil purpose.

Steve tensed for the final blow.

Holding the heavy wooden cross high above his head, he gripped it tightly in his bleeding hands. Tensing his arm and shoulder muscles with his last remaining strength, he would wait another second before unleashing his final desperate blow on his enemy.

Feeling helpless and alone in this ancient room that had been turned into a chamber of unspeakable horrors, he cried out with a loud voice into the gloom and despair that surrounded him, "Help me . . . Jesus Christ, Son of the Most High God!"

The dark Assassin laughed derisively, shouting at him, "No one will help you, Weston. You will die at my hands."

Lunging forward toward Steve for the final blow, his clenched fists poised to strike, when the dark creature's massive body touched the shadow of the raised cross, he was suddenly stopped in midair and was thrown violently backward as if he had crashed into an invisible strong wall.

Hurled savagely to the cold stone floor, the creature blinked his eyes in shock and dismay. Quickly standing to his feet, his face contorted with fiery hatred, he lunged at Steve the second time, but was once again thrown viciously backward. Again he lunged and again he was hurled backward.

Steve stared in astonishment and disbelief. It seemed that the faint shadow of the wooden cross had formed an invisible force field around him that the creature could not penetrate. Raging and cursing loudly, the black figure rose to his feet once again and slammed his body hard against the unseen wall of power that radiated from the cross's shadow, only to be thrown back again and again.

Mesmerized at the spectacle, Steve stood alone, a solitary figure bathed in the shadowed reflection of the cross, his aching hands gripping its thick shaft, keeping it lifted high above his head.

Snarling in anger because he could not reach out and destroy the man who was only a few feet away, the creature's fury mounted. His nostrils flaring, he gave vent to a baleful roar of defiance. His hideous mouth drawn back in a grimace of rage, continuous screams of defiance and hatred ripped from the creature's throat.

Steve watched in mounting fascination as the dark being repeatedly attempted to struggle to his feet but would be thrown back each time, crashing hard to the floor, an unseen force holding him, protecting Steve from his insidious attacks.

After repeatedly trying to break through the veil of power, the creature reluctantly shrank back, staggering as if he had been dealt a severe, crippling blow. Crumbling to his hands and knees on the ancient wooden floor, his gaze was riveted on the wooden cross lifted above Steve's head, undisguised fear in his eyes.

Caught in a violent storm of combined rage and pain, the being bared his teeth and released an unearthly shriek of anguish that tore at Steve's being, intensifying the fear that already seemed beyond human endurance. His face twisted with ancient pain, the dark creature's rueful wailing reverberated the length of the large room, echoing hollow and shrill off the cold stone walls.

Fear rushed through Steve anew, tightening every muscle.

His heart pounding a frantic cadence, he stood transfixed, still holding the wooden cross over his head, its flickering shadow playing softly across the creature's back, weighting him down, holding him pinned to the floor.

Standing motionless, Steve felt a strange sensation in his hands. He choked down his fear, took a sudden breath, then shifted the cross slightly in his grasp. The smooth shaft of the ancient artifact was becoming like a living fire in his hands, its warmth flowing down into his wrists and arms, blending with his body, washing away the throbbing pain.

Clinging to it tightly, unyieldingly, desperately, his body was joined to the ancient piece of wood that had been worn smooth by time. Holding it before him like a shield against the evil presence in this room, he gave himself over to the power flowing through it and down into his wounded, fevered mind and body.

The dark being glared at the cross above him, knowing its power and authority, his agony building to a feverish crescendo. Growling in low, rumbling tones, the Assassin writhed on the floor like a wounded animal, his gaze never leaving the cross in Steve's hands, his mouth spewing obscenities against the Most High.

Feeling the force of the raw power and hatred radiating from the snarling being, Steve could only guess at the intensity of the ancient struggle taking place behind those frenzied, glaring eyes.

Across the room, Audrey opened her eyes, slipped off the bed, and walked cautiously toward Steve. Gripped in a morose, dull-eyed silence, she stood back in the shadows for several moments, watching the unfolding drama. Waves of fear pounded her mind in a wild and paralyzing avalanche. A bright sheen of cold, clammy sweat bathed her delicate features.

Moving through the fear, she inched slowly toward Steve as he continued to hold the cross high above his head, the weight of its shadow lying heavily on the back of the dark creature wallowing defiantly on the floor a few feet in front of him.

Sensing her presence, Steve touched her.

His sudden touch brought her back to reality.

"Who is it, Steve?" she whispered.

"It's Satan, Prince of Darkness," Steve said softly, still holding the cross.

Audrey held tightly to Steve's arm.

A flicker of movement appeared in the corner of Steve's eye. Blinking against the dim light in the room, he froze in place. A small flutter of darkness, half-seen, to his left, in a far corner of the room. Just a hint of movement, nothing more, but it was disquieting. He remained motionless, staring, hoping he was wrong.

Something lifted slowly from the floor.

The first dim outline of a dreadful darkness was forming out of nothing, congealing, spilling across the floor like black liquid, a nebulous essence gliding silently toward them. Staring fixedly into the dimly lit room, Steve tried to focus on the expanding, undefined darkness suddenly coming from all corners of the room at once, a flowing, swirling, pulsating mass. The darkness moved in a macabre, yet purposeful rhythm, swallowing up the light in its pathway, an implacable presence.

For a terrifying moment, Steve could feel the weight of the gathering darkness pressing against his skin, a black fire. A revulsion closed in on him. The darkness was trying to come into him, to enter his body, to merge with his soul. With terror hammering at his reason, he felt himself go cold from head to foot.

Bravely resisting the panic, he sensed a growing courage building inside himself, a directed purpose. As the fear and terror diminished in intensity, he planted his feet firmly and stood under the weight of the wooden cross with renewed hope, vowing that the shapeless, formless darkness that permeated this room would not engulf him, would not swallow him up.

Remaining rigidly still, Steve and Audrey watched in somber fascination as the gathering darkness congealed around the creature, who still writhed on the floor at their feet, covering him, merging with him. Steve blinked against the darkness, staring in mounting fascination as the tenebrous coalescence of shadow began to drain definition from the dark figure. He was diminishing, melting into the darkness, fragmenting toward nothingness.

Steve stared up at the wooden cross, now an extension of his own body, then back down at the cringing figure. Now no more than a fleeting, shadowy illusion, the satanic fractal raised his head and cast one last leering glance at Steve and Audrey. They could feel the hate boring from the red, glaring eyes, covering them like a stifling, hot wind from hell.

Steve and Audrey stared into the savage swirl of darkness, watching the creature transmogrify into blackness and shadow, his essence fading into another dimension.

"Cursed cross!" the being shrieked loudly, the agonizing sound of his malevolent voice rolling toward them in a savage crescendo of ancient pain and rage.

His fiery eyes glaring out at them from inside the roiling wave of blackness, they watched him disappear, swallowed up in the howling maelstrom of primordial chaos, his hollow voice fading into a whisper of defiance and hatred.

Then he was gone, as if he had never been.

Audrey shivered.

As the last fragmentary essence of the shadow and blackness vanished from the room, Steve and Audrey stared for a long moment into the void where the creature had been, but he was not there, nor was the darkness. Faint wisps of acrid black smoke rose lazily from the scorched wood floor where the darkness had consumed the creature.

Unanswerable questions burned through Steve's mind. Nothing could have prepared him to face this terror—*nothing*.

Slowly relaxing his aching arms, Steve let the wooden cross sink gently to the floor.

"He was conquered by the cross," Steve softly whispered to Audrey, his voice filled with awe.

"Not even the Federation is endowed with such power."

FORTY

The rapid staccato sounds of automatic weapons fire startled Steve and Audrey, snapping them out of their near-hypnotic state. They had momentarily forgotten about the fierce battle that had been going on in other parts of the castle. Responding with lightning speed, Steve lunged for his automatic weapon. Shoving a fresh clip into it, he aimed at the door and called out for Audrey to stand with her back flat against the wall. Bracing himself, he prepared to fire at any enemy that might try to come in.

Frozen into position, waiting, the strange events of this terrifying night still swirled in his brain, forming and re-forming confusing images that shattered into paradox, moving, changing, reshaping themselves like the colorful designs in a child's kaleidoscope.

His eyes sharp and steady, Steve's muscles tensed when he heard footsteps coming down the hallway, moving toward their door. He fingered the trigger of his Galaxy, poised and ready to defend himself and Audrey.

"Weston!"

Steve relaxed and lowered his gun when he heard the familiar, gruff voice call out.

It was General Hardin.

"In here, General," Steve answered.

General Hardin walked through the door and stepped inside the room, his automatic weapon hanging loosely from his right shoulder, his face set, grim and determined.

"You people all right?" he asked.

"We're fine, General," Steve answered. "But how are you and your men?"

"Lost nine of my men, good men all. But we took all of them, except one. Thought he might be in here."

Steve and Audrey glanced at each other.

"No, General, he's not in here. He must have gotten away, fled the castle."

"No matter, Weston. We've got to leave anyway. This is no longer a safe house. Our position's been compromised. We're deserting the facility. Just got a radio message from one of our people from inside GU5. Tells us that they're about to blow this castle off the face of the earth, for us to clear out immediately."

"Where are we going, General?" Steve asked.

"Don't you worry about that, son. That's my job. We'll get you to a safe haven. We got a boat waitin' for us on the Danube, 'bout five miles from here. Got some vehicles that'll get us there."

Turning quickly, the general headed for the door, calling out over his shoulder, "Bring your weapons, Weston. We gotta move, *now!*"

Obeying instantly, Steve and Audrey grabbed their small travel bags. Steve stuffed his Omni 444 inside the waistband of his trousers and slung the wide leather strap attached to his automatic weapon over his right shoulder, grasping it tightly. The gun was cold and reassuring in his hand.

Touching Audrey's arm, he nodded, and they moved hurriedly toward the door.

On an impulse, they both hesitated when they reached the door. Turning, they looked back at the spot near the fireplace where their battle with the malevolent being had taken place. A cold chill ran down their spines when their eyes traced the outline of an ugly dark burned spot in the wood floor where the being had fallen helpless before the wooden cross. More than four feet across, the black indentations in the wood, ridged with ash, still smoldered menacingly. They turned quickly away.

Walking briskly down the long, cavernous hallways and winding, narrow corridors, they moved with fast-paced, measured strides down to the first-floor level. General Hardin and two of his men were waiting at the shattered front door.

"Mr. Weston, we got a car waitin'. So if you'll just follow me, we'll get you and Ms. Montaigne outta here," the general said.

Their long night of terror over, they moved through the opening where the door had been and stepped into the pale light of the dawn. The sun's rays were growing brighter by the second. The air was hushed and still. A wispy remnant of a light predawn mist clung with sticky tentacles to the branches of the trees.

A hundred yards away, a small military vehicle was waiting for them. When Audrey and Steve were safely in the backseat, General Hardin threw his heavy frame into the front seat next to the driver, gave an order, and they pulled away. Gliding down the long driveway toward the large gate to the estate, they rode in silence, each one lost in their separate thoughts.

Leaving the castle grounds, they drove rapidly along the winding, twisting road, underneath the protective covering of the large trees. Five miles from the castle, they approached a landing on the banks of the Danube River. The driver brought the vehicle to an abrupt stop in the shadow of a small chalet about a hundred yards from the river.

Turning to face Steve, General Hardin's features went deadly serious. Pointing to a small luxury cabin-style boat, the general said, "That's ours, Mr. Weston. One of my men's aboard, tracking the incoming plane that's gonna take out the castle. We got about four minutes 'til all hell breaks loose up on that hill."

With a hard-edged firmness that belied a genuine caring for his charges, the old soldier instructed Steve gruffly, "Here's what I want you and Ms. Montaigne to do. Get inside the chalet quick; keep those curtains drawn; don't look outside 'til the explosion's over. At this range, the heat could melt your eyeballs right outta their sockets. When it's over you can come out, and we'll get you to a safe place."

Audrey's eyes darkened as she moved closer to Steve.

"We'll be leavin' in about twenty minutes, if all goes well," Hardin added.

As the general turned to join his men inside a shelter at the river's edge, Steve and Audrey walked hurriedly up the steep steps to the chalet and went inside, closing the door with a sense of finality behind them.

Standing quiet and deathly still in the large main room, they both tensed at the angry sound of an approaching hypersonic military jet.

Swallowing hard against the dryness in her throat, Audrey glanced pleadingly at Steve. Sensing her need, he enfolded her in his arms. She gazed deeply into his eyes for a long moment, drawing on the strength she found there, knowing she was not alone.

Fear tearing at their minds, they waited, clinging tightly.

Swooping in a low arc, the pilot of the New Earth Federation plane smiled and firmly pressed a red button on his control stick that launched a single missile, sending it on its fiery path, speeding inexorably toward the hapless castle. As the plane banked hard right and zoomed skyward, the deadly missile found its mark and exploded, erupting viciously in a deafening roar, the sound of the blast building to a deep, savage, rumbling crescendo, jarring the very earth itself.

The serene quietness of the countryside surrounding the condemned castle was suddenly, brutally shattered by the mighty blast.

Fear shocking her heart into a wild rhythm at the sound of the explosion, Audrey drew a quick shuddering breath, then her body began to tremble uncontrollably. With a confidence more feigned than real, Steve tightened his embrace on her, holding her, talking softly, reassuringly. Standing in subdued silence inside the chalet, the two frightened people closed their eyes against the shock wave and the blast of heat from the massive explosion that slammed violently against the sides of the chalet, causing it to shudder menacingly.

Atop the hill, the majestically proud ancient castle, which only moments before had stood towering over the tall trees in regal grandness, suddenly erupted in a flash of unbelievable fire and heat. Its ancient timbers, metal, and bricks reduced to a boiling, hissing cauldron, the noble structure vanished like a ghostly vapor inside a maelstrom of swirling, seething cosmic energy.

The molecules of the air surrounding the doomed castle were stunned and thrown into chaos by the sudden and swift finality of the heat and force of the small-yield TR6 explosion, fusing the nuclei through its unbelievable intensity. Coiling and writhing like angry serpents, the flames rose hundreds of feet into the traumatized air. Spreading outward no more than a thousand feet from the very center of the castle in its pinpoint accuracy, the deadly explosion incinerated everything in its well-defined circular path.

Choked in blinding clouds of superheated dust, the innocent earth seemed to groan under the angry weapon's incredible fury.

A fiery spray of earth, mingled with shards of broken rock were thrown with incredible force into the air to come down in pelting showers for a mile on either side of the epicenter of the blast. The acrid smell of scorched earth was carried on the expanding mass of superheated air.

For a terrifying instant, a stifling heat blanketed the countryside around the castle in a radius of more than two miles as the energy of the TR6 spread along its predetermined path of death, the pulsating light waves cleansing the small spot of earth with its white, penetrating heat.

When the chilling shriek of the hot wind and the deep rumbling and growling of the explosion slowly died away, Steve crushed Audrey tightly, not saying anything, simply standing with his arms around her, his cheek lying softly against her auburn hair, his eyes closed.

Suddenly, an eerie silence pressed against their ears.

Taking Audrey by the hand, Steve moved cautiously to the door, slowly opened it, then timidly ventured out onto the large porch. They could still feel the heat and energy from the TR6 explosion pressing against their skin, hot and threatening, as the elements were beginning the process of cooling down.

Standing motionless in the shadows of the wide, dark gray eaves that rested on strong ancient timbers designed to support the heavy snow and ice during the long winter months, the two of them turned their eyes toward the hill and the castle.

Through the tall, stately trees, they could see a gigantic column of smoke and dust, mingled with debris, still rising from the dying castle. Grayish wisps of residue, sucked into the vortex of the explosion, drifted upward out of the smoking ruins, the release of energy still causing a macabre shimmering of the disturbed, heated air. With uncanny precision, the pressure-blast from the explosion had extinguished the flames, leaving only smoking ash, a dark landscape.

Her mind gratefully numbed beyond fear, Audrey watched in detached fascination as the released energy surrounding the castle grounds slowly faded, dissipating, losing shape and definition, then disintegrating back into the elements. Shielding her eyes against the light of the sun, she stared into the ephemeral shape of death that rose above the vaporized castle, watching the air surrounding it turn to a pale blue, changing quickly to a bright purple haze. Then, as if wiping away the evil, the atmosphere turned to a brilliant clearness, as if nothing had happened.

And the earth was suddenly deathly still, the silence hanging shroudlike, as if the very air was frozen beyond its desire to move.

Anxious moments passed.

As the sound of gentle breezes once again began whispering their low mournful song through the pines, Steve cast a curious, sweeping gaze across the peaceful countryside.

Everything seemed so normal.

Several winding trails snaked their way through the trees to the river's edge. A picturesque village was nestled near the riverbank, undisturbed. To his right, a quaint restaurant lay quietly in a small cove at the water's edge, waiting for its first morning customer. A cluster of small boats were serenely docked at the landing next to the restaurant.

Surveying the pristine landscape, he was struck by how tranquil the scene seemed to be, in contrast to the war and suffering in the rest of the world. For an unbelievable moment, the death and destruction that was spreading like a tidal wave across the earth seemed a far-distant threat.

Here, for a small interlude in time, there seemed to be peace, isolation.

But he knew it was only an illusion.

Drawing his sweater up tight around his neck against the biting chill of the sharp wind cascading aimlessly across the river, Steve thought again of Mueller and hoped that he had been able to pull off the broadcast of Steve's speech without being caught.

Audrey walked slowly to his side, shared his view of the breathtaking scenery for a few moments, then slipped her arm around his waist and snuggled her cheek against his chest. Steve drew her gently to himself, held her protectively, letting himself drift with the feel of her.

After a thoughtful silence, Steve spoke. "It's a miracle, Audrey," he said softly. "A miracle that we're alive."

"I know," she answered.

"I don't know what happens from here," he confessed soberly.

"Try not to think about it for a while," she coaxed, her finger resting against his lips. "We're here now . . . and we have each other."

Steve glanced to the east. The sun was rising above the hills, cresting the forest rim and spilling its light down into the valleys and recesses, pushing back the last vestiges of the night's gloom. The warmth felt good against his skin. He loved the dawn and its promise of a new day, a new beginning.

As his eyes traced the countryside, his mind focused on the events and forces that had brought them here, taking measure of the things they had come through to reach this point. He thought of the times they had faced death—and unbelievable evil—the hardships they had endured, and the hardships that lay ahead of them.

Audrey pulled at Steve's arm and looked into his eyes. "What will happen to us, Steve?" she asked, a note of resignation in her voice.

Steve studied her face wordlessly. Her delicate features were shadowed under the gentle sweep of her auburn hair. Her sparkling green eyes carried the reflection of a sadness, a weariness of spirit. Loving her desperately, he could not escape the feeling that, somehow, they had been bound inextricably to one another for a purpose far beyond their own need or what either of them could comprehend.

Suddenly filled with a rush of emotions so diverse that they lacked definition, Steve tried to fathom the depths of courage, toughness, and determination that she would need if they were to survive in the coming months.

Sighing against the lingering anxiety that plagued him, he found himself thinking of what they had come through the last few weeks, and how they had each become far stronger since being together. She had turned to him when her own strength and courage had faltered.

And her presence had brought him renewed purpose, even though their turbulent life together had thrust them both into a series of the most intense and mysterious struggles any human being had ever been called on to endure.

Steve drew in a sharp breath and let it out with a heavy sigh. His hand and shoulder throbbed unmercifully. Closing his eyes momentarily against the intense pain, he turned away and walked a few steps to his left, trying to hide the pain on his face from Audrey. She had endured enough.

Leaning heavily against one of the ageless wooden posts, he stood there, reflecting, his mind tortured by uncertainties that were crowding in on him again, tearing at him. He needed someone to talk to. Someone to tell him what to do. To tell him he was following the right path and was doing the right thing. He longed to hear the firm, rasping voice of his dearest friend, Dwight Pennington, guiding him through this tortuous time.

But his friend was gone, and he would have to chart his own course.

Steve suddenly felt an unwelcome chill sweep over him at remembering how close they had come to death, barely managing to elude its fatal touch. He knew with cold certainty that they had escaped the attack on the castle by sheer minutes, only because the communications network inside the International Resistance Movement had warned General Hardin of the impending strike.

But what will happen the next time? Or the next?

Standing there, staring aimlessly into the bright morning, Steve seemed to retreat into himself. Doubts buffeted his mind quietly, old fears rising phantomlike. He shook his head, closing his eyes against the world for a lingering moment. Facing questions that defied resolution, he struggled with the enigmatic puzzle of his own life, a life that now seemed to center on the ancient conflict between good and evil, angels and demons, and prophecies of the end of the world.

Tightening his jaw against the burning, throbbing pain shooting through him from his hand and shoulder wounds, he could feel the cold sweat sliding down his body underneath his clothing.

In spite of the dangers, Steve had no regrets for the course he had taken for himself. Perhaps, he reasoned, he would lay down his life in this noble pursuit. And if he did lose his life, for freedom and human dignity, it would be a more worthy thing than he had ever done in his time on earth.

He glanced furtively at Audrey, who was standing with her arms folded against the chill, looking anxiously toward the river. He wondered at the strange events that had brought them together, now, at this time in human history, when global events were balanced ominously on the edge of chaos, and when their own world seemed destined to crumble beneath them in the gathering holocaust.

Why hadn't it been in a better time?

For an endless moment, he considered turning himself in . . . *for her sake*. It could possibly save her life, he reasoned. Both of them were under a death penalty for high treason, but he knew that he was the main target, not Audrey. So perhaps he could negotiate with them to surrender to GU5 for a guarantee that they would let her live.

Steve casually glanced up toward the site of the destroyed castle. His troubled mind deep in thought, he was startled when he felt a hand lightly touch his arm.

He turned.

Audrey moved closer.

Looking up into his face, she saw the lines of worry etched into his handsome features, sensed the fear and uncertainty that he was trying desperately to conceal from her. Their eyes met in a long, lingering embrace, two people locked together in an uncertain world, a perilous time, clinging to one another.

For an endless moment, with the whole world a faraway distant memory, he looked wordlessly at the most exquisitely beautiful creature he had ever seen. Her deep green eyes were fathomless and trusting, boring into his soul, laying bare his innermost thoughts, revealing every secret fear and doubt that he had tried in vain to conceal from her.

Her face now only inches from his own, her eyes were warm and trusting as they found his, holding them in their gentle embrace. Her voice so soft that she could barely be heard, she whispered, "I will go where you go, Steve." Her words pulled at him with their deep, sudden poignancy.

He stood motionless for a time, saying nothing, staring into her eyes, a look of sadness and resignation on his face. Vivid images of the horrors that she had already endured whirled and turned inside his brain one after the other in rapid succession. Unspoken fear broke over him at the thought of what she would risk in the future if she followed him in his dark journey. A cold sweat broke out on his forehead and ran a course down the sides of his face.

For an agonizing moment, a tortured silence stood between them.

Bracing himself against the fear that thrashed through his emotions, he looked into her face, his eyes eagerly searching hers, his ruggedly handsome features reflecting a quiet uncertainty.

"Do . . . you know what you're saying?" he asked, his words barely audible.

"Yes," she said without reservation. "I decided long ago that there was no other place for me but with you."

She was crying soundlessly, tears rolling unbidden down her cheeks. Steve reached out and gently brushed them away. Exhaling a long, painful breath, he gave silent thanks that the two of them were still alive, grateful for the surge of hope she had brought to him with her caring manner, helping to drive back his fear and despair.

Cradling his throbbing, injured hand against his chest, his face gray with pain, he spoke haltingly. "I . . . can only promise you hardship. We'll have to keep running and running. There's no place on this earth where we can be safe. . . . Only God can save us. I know that now."

Having said the words, weariness suddenly settled over Steve like a heavy burden, making him think he would collapse in total exhaustion. Sighing deeply, the throbbing pain from his wounds were a sharp reminder to him of the grave danger they were in.

Blinking his eyes against the pain and fatigue, his voice low and guarded, he whispered to her, "Half the world is running from this evil regime. We'll join the others and fight. . . ." He paused, his voice breaking slightly. "But you must know that, in the end, we may both give our lives. . . ." His voice trailed off and there were sudden tears in his eyes, tears that vanished almost as fast as they had come.

There was a long moment of silence as Audrey looked up at him, a remarkable sadness reflecting in her emerald eyes. Her own fears